lost ranch
books

www.lostranchbooks.com

Clean Cut

A Romance of the Western Heart

Laurie Marr Wasmund

Clean Cut is a work of fiction. Names, characters, places, and incidents portrayed in this novel are the products of the author's imagination or are used fictitiously. Any resemblance to actual events or locales or persons, living or dead, is entirely coincidental.

Front cover photograph: Elk in Yellowstone National Park
Back cover photograph: Lion Geyser
Both photographs by Laurie Marr Wasmund

Cover design by Laurie Marr Wasmund

Published in the United States by lost ranch books
www.lostranchbooks.com
ISBN 978-0-9859675-2-9

For my father,

James L. Marr,

who left this world far too young,

and for my mother,

Wilma F. Marr,

who soldiered on

West Pindall

1986

ONE

AUGUST 2

Dying, he saw.

Not the light at the end of the tunnel, or his life flashing before his eyes, or his dead relatives waiting for him on the other side, halos on their sad old reprobate heads. In fact, it wasn't even a true vision, but a memory.

But it wasn't a memory—it was so clear and so intense that he felt he was living it again.

She sat in the shade of the pines, her legs stretched forward, her belly thrust out, watching him as he worked, building their house. One of her hands was behind her for support, and the other was laid on top of the rounded swell of their baby, gently patting. Through the fringed fingers of pine boughs, sunlight flecked her dark hair with red, and lit up the freckles on her nose and cheeks.

Your baby's a wild one, she had called to him. *You should feel him, raising hell in utero.*

He had put down his tools and gone to her. Spreading calloused palms over the bulge, he felt the kick and jab of that new life, the eagerness, the earnestness, the great desire of the unborn to be free. *That's my boy.*

That's my *bladder,* she said.

And he had placed his hands on either side of her face and kissed her.

Why this moment, so simple, so placid? He, who had straddled the slippery rocks of the last untrammeled rivers and willed his way through wilderness so remote that he knew he was the first to see it, who had lived and dreamed under open sky for so long? Why not a panorama of water and trees and boulders, a sky so bright that it burned?

It was never what they had expected, marrying so young, parents before they were properly wed. Never what he expected, anyway, and never what she wanted.

But if he could find her in this new weightlessness that's come to him, this new formlessness that his mind is thinning into, he would say, *But we were, the two of us, together, each other's soul, each other's heart, we were the very life of each other—*

TWO

EULOGY FOR A MARRIAGE

This, then, was my marriage.

I married Brad Brock a week after my high school graduation, fifteen days before my eighteenth birthday, and six and a half months before Jason was born. Oh, it was no shotgun wedding. We had known we would marry from the night he walked into my parents' house, looked at me with his nothing-stands-in-my-way eyes, and said, "You're the girl who sings the national anthem at the school games."

"That's me," I said, all at once aware of the blood in my palms and the fullness of my lips and the heat that flushed under my collarbone and over my breasts. I pulled the sleeves of my sweater over my bare wrists.

Brad had come to see my father because he was building his own house. He needed a mathematician to figure out the angles and areas for him, and my father was the logical choice. Dad taught math and science at Pindall's school, gamely living in a town where everyone believed the theory of relativity had to do with their aunt's sudden marriage. He was kind and popular with his students, which Brad had been years before.

Dad and Brad sat before the fire in the living room, while my mother made cocoa in the kitchen. I sat at the dining table in the corner, pretending to read *Crime and Punishment* for Mrs. Rayhill's sophomore English class. My brother, Lance, and sister, Amy, sat next to me. Whenever I looked up from my book, Amy would bat her eyelashes, and Lance would snicker. I did my best to ignore them, but poor Raskolnikov didn't stand a chance against Brad Brock.

"What kind of house do you want?" my father asked him.

"Big."

Dad laughed. "Well, apart from that."

"I want to build it the way they would have a hundred years ago. I don't want to buy the lumber and logs, I want to fell them and cut them myself. I can use Glenn Wexler's Belgians to drag the logs."

"The horses that pull the stagecoach in the parade every summer?"

"Yeah." Brad looked around him, imagining. "Everything has to be done by hand, you know. Cutting the logs and transporting them, then debarking and peeling them, cutting the saddle notches in them—"

"The what?" Dad asked.

"Saddle notches." He demonstrated by laying one strong, capable hand in the other. "Every other log has a round notch cut in it so it cups the log set on top of it, holding everything together."

"That's quite a vision," Dad conceded. "You're going to be busy."

Brad shrugged. His dreams may have seemed common to him, but we all knew that they weren't. In Pindall, most of the boys who graduate from high school—and nearly all those who don't—go to work in the sawmill. At twenty-one, Brad was already beyond Pindall's or the sawmill's grasp, and he knew it. He knew he could have just about anything he wanted. Including me.

He took me up to his land, five miles north of Pindall, on an abandoned logging road. The parcel had belonged to his father's family for four generations, claimed before the national forest was established around it. Most of the property was still heavily treed, with slash piles here and there, left by long-dead loggers.

We walked through trees that were draped by shadow. Every once in a while, he would swing one-handed around a tree trunk, so we came face to face, and I'd reach for him and kiss him quick, touching his face just long enough to be sure that I was kissing him and not some wild creature.

Coming into a meadow, he stopped. A sizeable square had been mowed in the grass. On the ground inside the square was a paper plate, held down by a piece of granite. Farther along, lay a sleeping bag.

"Are we having a picnic?" I asked, starting toward the plate.

"Wait." He caught my arm. "You have to use the door."

"What door?"

"Right here, up the steps." He held out a hand. "There's three steps up to a wide open porch that wraps all the way around the house."

I played along. We went up the invisible steps—"Look behind you, barn's over there, workshop there, or maybe there," he said—and into the rectangle of house. He showed me the kitchen, where the well-anchored paper plate lay, and paced off the distance between refrigerator and stove.

"And then you come out here," he said. "It's all one big room, really, but the counter separates the kitchen from the living room. Now you're walking on floors of pine, with a twenty-foot ceiling and a big old window that overlooks the meadow and catches the last rays of the sun."

"You've thought of everything," I said.

He knelt down and patted a stadium cushion that the High School Pep Club had once sold to raise money. Gold and purple, it read "Pindall Pioneers have *Pride!*"

"Take a load off and sit here on the couch for a while."

We sat back to back, jockeying for position on the cushion, nudging each other with elbows and hips. I leaned my head so that it rested against his shoulder blade.

A couple of feet away, an elk jawbone rested in the grass. Two brown-ringed molars clung to it. "What's that?" I asked.

"Guess."

With a laugh, I took the challenge. "A hat rack, um, a chandelier, ummm, a sink—"

"A sink? In the living room?" He snorted. "It's a piano. So you can tickle the—"

"Ivories." We said it at the same time.

"—while you're singing," he finished.

I laughed. "So where are the bedrooms?"

We both looked toward the sleeping bag, lying about fifteen feet away. "Two down here—right over there, for the kids. The master's upstairs, a sort of loft over the kids' rooms. There's a bathroom up there, and one down here, too, stacked, you know, so the plumbing runs through."

"Well, we don't want the plumbing to get stuck," I said. "How many steps to get there?"

"Fourteen, I think. I'm not sure—your dad's still working on that. Nine foot ceilings on both levels."

"Where are the stairs?"

"Right there. They're half-logs, flat on top, round on the bottom."

"Hand-felled and hand-cut," I teased, jumping up and running up the stairs, pantomiming holding onto a railing and lifting my knees high, counting all the way. "Debarked and peeled and served sunny side up!"

"Laugh all you want," he called, chasing after me. "I'll be the one laughing when we're living in it!"

We zigged through the "loft," yelling warnings to each other: "Don't fall off the edge!" "That's the closet!" "Oh, man, you stepped on the dog!" "Damn dog! What's it doing in the middle of the floor?"

He caught me and carried me to the sleeping bag. I tipped back his black cowboy hat and covered his face with kisses. He was beautiful, with his dark hair closely clipped and his face clean-shaven, and brown eyes that could blaze a hundred different colors, depending on the light. He lay me down, and then stretched out beside me, the two of us panting to catch our breaths.

"When will the house be done?" I asked.

"Sometime before you graduate, I hope." He put his hands behind his head, and I rolled to my side, my head and hand on his chest. "This room will be under the peak of the roof, you know. The walls will go up about three, four feet and then start to slant."

I reached up into air and felt phantom wood. "So I'll be able to touch the ceiling from our bed."

"Maybe. And every morning, when the sun comes up and it gets warm enough, it'll smell like a forest in here."

I breathed in the cooling night air. "The whole room has a golden glow, doesn't it?"

He drew me against him. "Now you're seeing it."

"And your mom's quilts," I said. "I want your mom to make us a quilt for the bed."

"She will. Now, look at the view out the window. It's no different than what you see now, except you'll be up higher, have a better angle over the trees. Look at that sky."

The Wyoming sky is a marvel, black and deep, complete in itself, with stars from horizon to horizon. I started to point out the constellations—the Big Dipper, the Pleiades, the easy ones—but Brad laid a finger on my lips.

"I don't want to hear about constellations," he said. "That's just made-up crap."

"What's wrong with that?"

"I want what's real. What's right here. The rocks, the flowers, whatever animals are in those trees over there. You can't ever know it all, you can't ever figure out the mysteries that are right under our feet. So why go searching for others?"

I said nothing, my throat tender all of a sudden.

"Sing something," he said.

"You've heard me sing plenty of times."

"Not up here."

I waved toward the jawbone lying in the grass a few feet away. "My 'piano' is downstairs."

"Come on," he coaxed.

The only song that came to mind was "On the Wings of a Dove." I didn't sing loud, but I wasn't timid either. I soared where I should, kept it low when I ended a phrase. It didn't feel unnatural or showy, because the sound just floated through the meadow into the trees.

"Now, see," he said. "That song is part of this place. Our place, our land. It's caught up in the trees, in the rocks, in the grass, even in the stars if you want it to be. It's become a part of what's out here. Part of what's real."

He let the wind carry away his words.

"And someday, it's going to come back to us. When we're real old, maybe. It'll come back in our memories, maybe, or we'll talk about it, and we'll hear it again like an echo. You see what I mean?"

For a moment, I thought I could see that song—or hear it maybe—as it touched on the wildflowers in the meadows and the rough bark of the pines. For a moment, I thought I understood.

But Brad had started to play with a necklace I was wearing, teasing the little pendant back and forth along the chain until I could feel tiny sparks of heat from the friction, and I thought—a memory, an echo, who cares?

"I'm glad you're real," I said, and he leaned over to kiss me. And this is what I knew: the warmth of his fingers on my breast, the weight of his thigh on mine, the way I could open up to him right there on that hard ground, and let him push into me, my palms pressed against his shoulders, his mouth on mine. I remember that wonderful flush of pleasure that made me laugh out loud, my tongue and the roof of my mouth tingling, my fingers fluttery, and my stomach pulsing low and deep.

Brad easily established himself in the guiding business—after all, he had grown up with a rifle in his hands, a horse beneath him, and a million wild acres of land in his sight. By the time we married, he was specializing in long tours, not for the faint of heart, but deep into grizzly country, where the best fishing and hunting could be found. It wasn't long before the world found out, and he entertained sportsmen from the east coast and Canada and even Japan.

He built the house, too, the way he wanted it, felling the trees with the help of his best friend, Dave Phillips, who works as a saw setter at the mill. The logs were still green enough that first winter that wind came through the cracks as the wood dried and warped. We plugged them with newspaper, but it wasn't unusual to find snow drifted on the floor in a miniature winter wonderland. At night, Brad rocked Jason to sleep and laid him in a crib close to the warm interior wall. Then he came to me.

It lasted one season.

It wasn't that we were unhappy—that didn't come until later—but Brad wasn't a man to be kept in tight spaces. After hunting season ended in the fall of our second year of marriage, he left for the winter.

I understood, and yet I didn't. I knew he wouldn't go into the sawmill to work, and I didn't want him to. His father had died at the mill, in what is still known as The Worst Accident in the History of the Sawmills in the State of Wyoming, and Brad wasn't about to repeat history. But he wouldn't take a job at the Wickiup, his mother's grocery store, either. So he disappeared like a migrating animal, to Casper or Cheyenne or some other city, where he worked at whatever he could find until he came home to guide through the spring, summer, and fall. Even then, when he was in the area, he wasn't truly *home.*

Jason kept me living and breathing. Our son, our baby, the reason —or so I thought—for our existence. I pulled him in an old metal saucer sled over the snow, we roasted marshmallows over the fire in the wood stove, and we sang through the long evenings. Jason's hair turned from white-blond to the color of autumn, and his teeth grew in straight enough. He passed through elementary school and junior high and into gangly manhood with one ear cocked to the sounds outside, listening for the approach of his father's truck.

I took a job as a waitress at the Rambler Bar so that I could hurry away the nights. I took up singing, too, and not just at weddings and funerals. I wanted something more, something I hadn't heard or felt before. When Evelyn Drew, the organist for the Methodist Church in Pindall, died, I bought the bin where her daughter, Wanda, had dumped all her music. It cost me five dollars.

I found all sorts of treasures in that load. Italian arias that I couldn't begin to read, sheet music from the forties, a book of American patriotic tunes, a primer of children's songs. I started with an old Cokesbury hymnal, because it was the easiest music to sight-read while pounding out the accompaniment on the piano, and sang about the beauty of the earth and my father's world and a mighty fortress.

My voice is simple, pure, without demands. It asks nothing more of me than safe passage into the world, and that I have always been able to provide. But I asked more of it. I wanted it to soar, and soon enough, I was straggling through Handel and Mendelssohn and Gilbert and Sullivan, singing about a maiden's wish and nightingales and raven hair.

I tested my dynamics on the out of doors. My favorite spot to sing is at the highest point on our property, near a ridge of sandstone rock that is cut through by water, ribbed by wind. The cliff is no more than fifteen feet high, but it cups inward to form a gentle basin at its foot. Pines grow on the crest of the cliff, but at the base, there is only deep sand, shining with quartz and mica, eroded from the volcanic rocks and poured as if through gentle hands into a soft pile. There's not a soul within five miles.

Standing in that amphitheater, I let my voice float free. A grand fortissimo, I found, could shatter the forest into a flight of birds or scatter of squirrels or crash of mule deer through undergrowth. On a day when there was no wind, a pianissimo could do the same.

I asked Brad what drove him away from Pindall, but he didn't have a good answer. "It's not just one thing," he told me.

It became a joke between us, funny at first, bitter later. I offered him a calculator, an abacus that I found in my father's study, and the phone number, 1-800-CAN-HELP, which I'd heard about on television, but which had to do more with arranging bail than with solving marital problems. To me, it was simple. Pindall was home. It was our birthplace, our birthright.

I visited him once in Cheyenne, driving six hours to surprise him in his room at a motel on Highway 85 that rented by the month. The building was tan, with second-story concrete walkways and metal railings that shivered and clanked when I walked across them.

When he opened the door, he said, "Jesus Christ, baby, what are you doing here?"

The room had a single queen-sized bed, a brown bedspread that once had a floral print, and a dresser consumed by a television set. *Three's Company* was airing, but the volume was muted. Spread across the bed, draped over the nightstand, and laid flat on the round vinyl-topped table in the corner were topographical maps. Some of them already had his handwriting on them, marking routes and trails and meadows.

He put his arms around me and kissed me. Not yet, I told myself, working my way out of his embrace. We had to talk first.

"You have new maps," I said.

"Picked them up the other day from the BLM office."

I fingered one of them, studying the squiggling lines.

"Why are you here?" he asked.

"I don't know," I admitted. "Is this what you do at night?"

"Yes," he said with a laugh that told me he couldn't believe I'd asked. "This is it. You think I'd cheat on you?"

I looked at the gray-gummed carpet, the vinyl drapes that pulled with a cracked plastic handle. It was a cheat, shabby and dull. I even resented Suzanne Somers in baby doll pajamas and pigtails, skipping to a silenced laugh track on the television.

"Why in the hell are you here?" I caught fire. "You have a beautiful house, and yet you live here like somebody who doesn't have a home. You leave me and Jason behind for this. What are you doing?"

He didn't say anything for a minute, letting me fume my way into silence. At last, he warned, "We've done this, Shari."

I slapped the table, tumbling a map to the floor. "They were talking about hunting up near Hulett the other night."

"What about it?"

"They talk about you more than I talk to you." I didn't want it to sound like a woman's silly complaint, but it did.

"So what would I talk about if I came back?" he asked. "Myself?"

"Sure. Why not? Why am I always hearing about you from somebody else? Why am I always having to listen to what I've missed out on?"

"You make me come back," he rasped. "You bring me back to where I can't get out, where I can't find anything to do besides work at that damned mill or with my mom, where every night it's listening to somebody tell the same story at the Rambler—"

"What about me? What about Jason?"

"Why do you think I come back? I could live anywhere, I could work out of anywhere. Five thousand miles away—I could do what I'm doing here. But it's you, it's you and Jason and knowing that you're there. It's always been you."

That was it, the best explanation I ever heard from him. But it didn't matter. I stayed the weekend in Cheyenne, I would have stayed the rest of my life. Brad was my greatest weakness, our love was my greatest strength. He was the response to my song, and the echo and the memory, too. I was young then, and what I didn't know about the world didn't bother me. Every conversation I had was with Brad—whether or not he was present—and every feeling I felt was for him.

I always knew when he was coming home. Long before I heard the pickup pull off the Yellowstone Highway onto the dirt that leads to our house, I felt an odd sense of urgency and restlessness, a desire to cry or laugh, and I knew that it was because he was moving closer. I could smell him—strong soap, cotton shirt, the felt of his hat. I could almost see him, traveling over pocked asphalt roads, headed home to me.

On chilly nights, I stood by the window until he pulled in the driveway, turned off the ignition, and came to me. Warmer nights, I would wait for him on the porch. The fights we'd had didn't matter any longer, because he was home. Sometimes we didn't even close the door before we made love. One night, he didn't even turn off the truck, and we came together with the pickup lights shining down on us like heavenly rays.

Every year, the town of Pindall holds Sawmill Days during the first weekend in August. There's a carnival set up in the vacant lot near Asa Pindall Park, a rodeo at the arena south of town, and a reunion for every graduating class from Pindall High School, whether one year or thirty have passed. Pindall's former residents flock home for the celebration, bringing with them new families and old grudges.

Business booms in town, and even the Rambler posts a NO VACANCY sign. The churches hold bazaars, and the school clubs hawk baked goods, candles and flags. The Wickiup doubles its business. All weekend long, bands and entertainers perform on the wooden stage in Asa Pindall Park, everything from the preschool choir to the occasional recording artist from Cheyenne.

Friday night kicks off with a street dance. Townspeople polka in the street until ten, when the volunteer firefighters, dulled by too few fires and too many car accidents, happily ignite fireworks on the ridge east of Pindall.

A parade is held on Saturday. Mountain men sport home-tanned pelts that dangle legs and teeth, cavalry re-enactors parade with sabers slapping their thighs, and the Republican Women crow about the fact that Wyoming women voted two whole decades before women in the East and elected the first female governor in the United States.

The highlight of Sawmill Days is the Derby, a no holds barred, can't-miss, old-fashioned horse race. The contestants—all Pindall boys born and bred—thunder over a treacherous route, leaving the park and pounding up the vertical slope behind Pindall past a wind-pocked rock formation called the Honeycomb. Then they spread out across a wide, level meadow on top the ridge, where the grass grows knee-deep in drought years and waist-high in wet. The first to plunge into the saplings that mark the edge of the national forest wins.

For weeks before the race, the townspeople drink and bet, wondering whether any horses will collapse, or break legs, or drop dead. They debate the guts of the riders. Who will go hellbent-for leather and who's likely to fall and break his dad-burned neck?

Last summer, the answer was Brad.

The Heart of Pindall

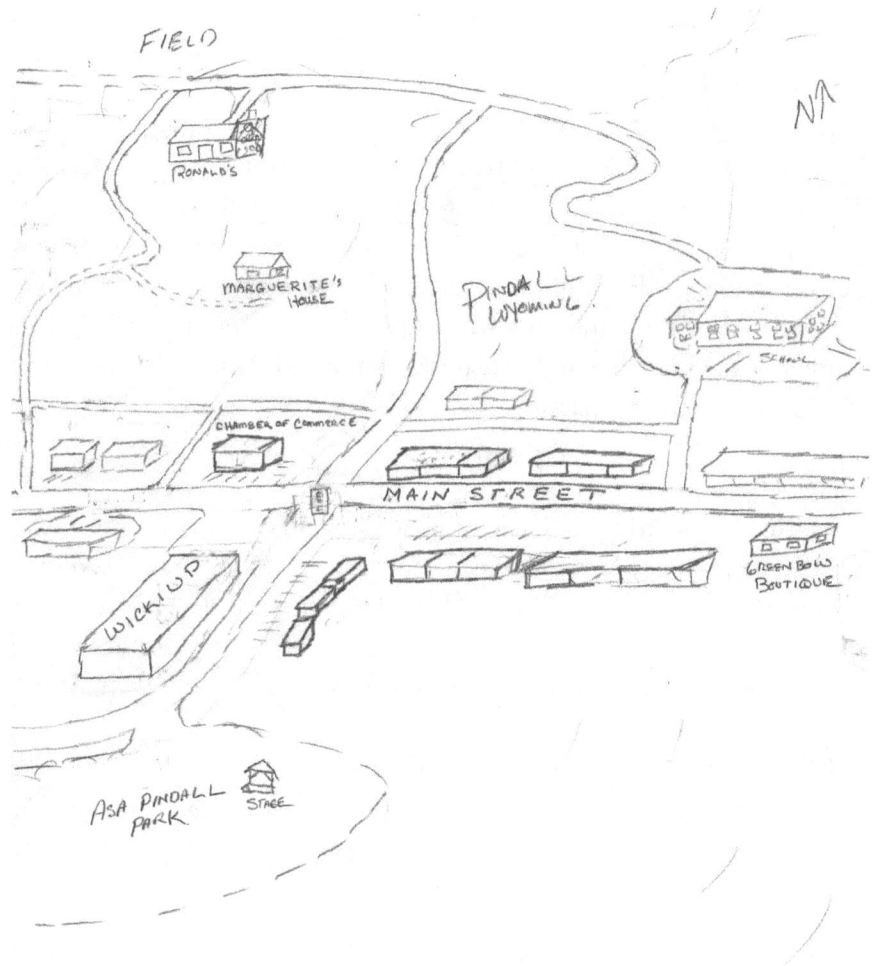

1987

THREE
FLAVOR FIESTA

Tuesday night is Flavor Fiesta at the Rambler Bar. Walt Ruggles mixes ninety-nine cent margaritas, concocting new flavors, which Robyn always calls terrible, although her taste buds were crippled years ago by chain smoking. Her opinion never jars Walt, who came back from World War II with a limp and an absent stare. In the years since, the limp has grown less noticeable and the absence more so. Tonight's Flavor Fiesta features a blueberry margarita.

It's too early in the evening to start drinking, but Walt pours one for me. "Try it out, honey."

There's so little tequila in it that the only drunk we are likely to encounter tonight is the worm in bottle. "It's tasty," I say, running my tongue over my teeth to dislodge bits of blueberries. "Doesn't have much kick."

"It's got ninety-nine cents worth of kick," he says. "After they buy six or seven, they'll feel pretty good."

The Rambler Bar is an oversized steel shed tacked onto the original Rambler Motel, which Walt built of cinder block and then, in a moment of inspiration, painted the color of plastic flamingos. Not many tourists have the nerve to enter here. They go for the Sportsman's or the Silver Spur, which serve German beers and have happy hours and signs that read COME ON IN, Y'ALL. The Morning Glory, the Rambler's most-hated rival, even has planters filled with—you guessed it—morning glories and a wall dedicated to photographs of the thermal pool in Yellowstone that bears the name.

The locals have settled into the Rambler, and we serve mostly mill workers, men who favor a Coors or Bud. So far this afternoon, we have had one customer, Johnny Hart, who tottered in around two and not so much sat as sank onto a stool. He plays Solitaire with a grimy deck that Robyn keeps behind the bar. Johnny once worked as a bounty hunter up in the Park, bringing in wolf and bear and lynx until times changed and he found himself on the endangered species list. He has traded Walt a set of snowshoes, a shotgun, and an elk head to cover his bar tab.

He tips in blessings.

"May we sit at God's right arm, Shari," he wishes as I deliver his Bud. "Just like Brad."

"Sure thing, Johnny," I assure him with a pat on the back.

Johnny twitches another card, his hands swollen with arthritis, onto the spread in front of him. Robyn leans over the bar and straightens the lines, ash falling from her cigarette. She is squat and round, her hair still blond with the help of Clairol. Her bosom rests on the ledge of the bar, and her breath comes in a ratty wheeze. She wears sky blue eye shadow so thick, you'd think it was done with oil paint.

Reading the cards, she growls, "Black six on red seven."

Johnny doesn't see it, though his hands trill enough to spill the deck.

"Black six, there," Robyn says. "Put it there." Finally, she does it for him.

I go to the plate glass window and glance outside. I'm the only one working tonight—Donna Rae has called in sick again—and the hours already feel long.

Outside, the weather is kicking up its heels, and the temperature is dropping. I watch as a truck rolls by on Main Street, its tires dredging up frozen slush. On the creamy white door panel is a silhouette of a pine tree, with "CNM" written beneath. It's a newcomer to town, one of the fleet that is replacing the battered, orange and brown Wyoming Woodmill vehicles.

Only a couple of weeks have passed since it was announced that Cascadia Northern Mills of Portland, Oregon bought the sawmill, but the news has struck a sour note. Pindall's mill has always been locally owned, and now, with America's farms failing, and houses in foreclosure, and small businesses being gobbled up and spit out by corporations, everyone in town is worried.

The sky starts slinging snowflakes, and I turn away from the window and head for the bar. It will be another tough haul up the hill and home tonight after work.

Jason comes in through the hallway that leads to the motel, fresh from his job at the Wickiup. He stands at the end of the bar, as far from the pool table and the hurly-burly of drinking as possible. He wears a baggy flannel shirt, which was once Brad's, over his black t-shirt and jeans. His hair sifts across his ears and eyebrows in long, blondish strands.

"How's Grandma?" I dump the rest of my margarita in the sink.

"Fine," he says.

"How was school?"

He hoists himself onto a bar stool without answering. As easy as it was to lose Brad, it's been easier to lose Jason. The muscles in his neck are tight, and there's a jittery stiffness in his hands. I long to lay a hand on his shoulder, but mothering a sixteen-year-old boy in public isn't wise. It's barely advisable in private.

I rinse my glass and put it in the bus tray. "Did Grandma drive you over?"

"I walked."

"It's too cold for that. You should have asked her to drive you—"

"Jesus, Mom. I made it, didn't I?"

As usual, I've overstepped my bounds. Jason was only fifteen when Brad died, not quite a man, but definitely not a boy. It's a bad age to lose a father.

At a few minutes after six, pickup trucks sled over the ice in the parking lot and the first mill workers arrive, stomping snow and sawdust off their boots. Dwayne Black shoves a quarter in the jukebox, an old-fashioned whirligig that blinks with red and blue lights, and Steve Wariner's "What I Didn't Do" starts to play. I gather up a frothy armful—I know what they all drink—and carry them to the table where they've settled. Most of the guys take Buds, but I set an O'Doul's next to Dave Phillips, who's been trying to quit for years. He nods his head in my direction, but doesn't quite meet my eye.

It's a sticky situation. Brad's horse, Shiloh, pulled up lame on the day of last year's Derby, so he borrowed Rain, Dave's horse. It was Rain who threw Brad on the flats as she galloped across the wide meadow, where the visibility is clear and where the racers pull away from each other and pick up speed, because the meadow is the safest—in fact, the only safe—stretch of the course.

It was Rain who killed Brad.

"How're you doing, Shari?" Dave asks, and I tell him the same as I tell them all. Fine, great, not to worry.

"If there's anything," he says, and the words trail off. He has made this statement so many times that it has come to stand on its own.

Dave and I don't talk about that day, and he never joins in with the others in telling stories about Brad. In fact, each time I see him, he is paler, his blond hair fading, his skin more parched and ashen. One day I'm afraid he's simply going to flicker out, like a burned-out light bulb.

"What have you heard?" I ask.

"Nothing yet," he says. "The big Kahuna is due any day now, I guess. It's gonna take some getting used to, receiving them paychecks from Oregon."

"Heard from Renee?" I ask. Dave's ex-wife, Diane, and their only daughter, Renee, live in Minneapolis, where Renee has fallen in with a wild crowd.

"Nope. Heard from Jason?"

We laugh at our sad, tired joke. Dave glances toward where Jason sits at the bar. Robyn has served him a coke and a bowl of maraschino cherries. He skewers them with a fishing knife his father made for him. Cherry juice drips like weak, watery blood down his fingers.

Dave says again, "If there's anything, Shari."

I squeeze his shoulder before I move on to the next table. Dave means well, but the two of us have taken up posts on opposite sides of a chasm, the soil cracking and crumbling away beneath our feet. It's not that there's any ill will between us, it's simply that we can't bridge the loss of Brad.

The noise is picking up—Dwayne's deposited more quarters and unleashed a storm of Johnny Cash: "Ring of Fire," "Folsom Prison Blues." The girls from the beauty salon drift in with a whiff of chemicals and perfume and take over the corner booth that Robyn and I call the Nookie, because it is the prime negotiation spot for one-night stands. A few wives settle next to their husbands, and a couple of ranchers from south of town take a table near the door. There's even a tourist family— father, mother and two kids—in one of the booths ordering food from the Rambler's limited menu.

They all look beat up. The little girl's face shows the strains of motion sickness, and, poor little tyke, her coat is a mess. She keeps crying, moaning low over and over. The baby, ensconced in the Rambler's one and only booster chair, bangs the table with a spoon.

Neither husband nor wife seems to have the energy to attend to the kids. The husband is obviously aghast at what he sees. Walt has festooned every barstool with Wyoming's famous bucking horse and rider. Photographs of sepia-eyed roughnecks, some of whom Robyn claims are related to her, decorate the walls. The Rambler is a zoo of mounted heads, a few of which have been shot a couple of times after they were stuffed. It's Robyn's contribution to keeping Wyoming wild and free.

As I take their order, the wife asks about Yellowstone. "We're traveling so early in the season," she says, "because he"—she nods toward the husband—"can't get away in summer. We'll enjoy the Park all the same, won't we?"

I'm stuck with the same old quandary: how to answer the unanswerable.

Pindall's location is one of its greatest ironies. Despite squatting on AAA's scenic route only one hour from the gates of Yellowstone National Park, it is usually overlooked by tourists, who rush on, eager to find bison and geysers and pelicans. So we cater to those who just can't stand another hour of carsickness or whose Winnebagos have overheated or who are foolish enough to visit the Park in July without first making reservations. We soothe the fears of the lost, the desperate, and the nauseous: Will we see elk? Will grizzlies pounce on the car like on the National Geographic special? Will 400-speed film in an automatic focus camera with a zoom lens catch the true colors? Will Old Faithful erupt? "Not before I do," Robyn usually answers.

"Where are you from?" I ask. It's standard fare, guaranteed to return an answer.

"New Hampshire," she says.

"You've come a long way."

"It sure feels like it." She gives a tired laugh. "Today, anyway."

"Well, sometimes people come here with what we call the 'This-had-better-be-the-best-time-of-my-life-I-better-see-a-moose' look," I offer. "And most people see one, and it's all right. They go home happy and with plenty of great memories."

"Thanks," she says. "But just in case, bring me a blueberry margarita."

"Shari!" Robyn's voice booms across the floor. "Come over here!"

I wend my way across the dance floor, which is crowded for a Tuesday night. The beauty salon brigade is line-dancing just beyond where the boys from the mill are shooting pool, with a lively repartee going on between them.

"Come on, Dwayne." Kit Griffiths opens her arms wide. "Come and dance."

"I got my work boots on," he says. "Ain't too light on my feet tonight."

"You ain't light on your feet any night, darlin'!"

When I reach the bar, Robyn thrusts a sheet of paper toward me. "Jason's got some lame-ass English paper to write. Read this."

The assignment, given by Mrs. Rayhill, who was my high school English teacher, prompts students to consider how metaphors reflect our personalities. It asks them to choose a highway term that reveals their self-images: "For instance," the assignment reads, "do you see yourself as an intersection in the middle of a city, where bustling roads meet (i.e., an active, social person), or as a highway such as I-80, which travels through lonely stretches such as the Red Desert (i.e., someone who prefers to be alone)? Are you on the northbound, going up, or the southbound, going down, or following a straight path from east to west? Here is some highway terminology that might be useful: toll road, expressway, service road, thruway, causeway, turnpike, etc."

"I think Velma's been sniffing red ink for too long," Robyn huffs.

"Well," I hedge. "It's different. You have to give her credit for that."

Robyn blows a stream of smoke. "It's all this touchy-feely horseshit that everybody's into these days. I.e., what in hell are taxpayers paying for, anyway."

"Hit-and-run," Jason suggests.

"That's not a highway term," Robyn protests. "That's a—"

"Crime," Jason says.

Robyn and I exchange a look over Jason's head. Since Brad's death, Jason has done some stupid things. He and a couple of friends set off fireworks that he'd stolen from the Wickiup on the roof of the school gymnasium last New Year's Eve, and altered the word "fun" on a sign at the fairgrounds that read "4-H is Fun" to a more colorful adjective. Today, the high school counselor called me to report that he has been skipping classes. Wild oats, I'm told by the men from the mill. He'll outgrow it. But I want to know, what will he grow into?

"All right." Robyn gulps a shot of Jack. "I'll bite. I'm a causeway. Don't get in my goddamned way 'cause I've got a cause, and it's me."

"What's Walt?" Jason asks. "Dead end?"

I stifle a smile. Walt pours drinks and cooks, never rushed, never connected. The Rambler could fall at his feet in chunks of peach concrete, and he would hardly vary his motions.

"Pasture lane." Robyn casts a cold eye toward Jason. "What about you, Shari? Pick a highway."

"I'll think on it." I avoid the issue by fixing a margarita for the tourist from New Hampshire. "When's it due?"

"Tomorrow," Jason says.

"How long have you known about it?"

"I don't know. A couple of weeks."

"Well, you better take a detour, son," Robyn advises. Cackling at her joke, she says, "Here, let me take that over to them, so's I can see if they need a room tonight."

Left alone with Jason, I don't bother to scold. "So what do you have so far?"

He rips out a sheet of paper from his notebook and slides it toward me, jagged edges littering the bar.

I read: "One road leads into town, one out. Depending on which way your headed you're going either to Riverton or Yellowston. You might see a grizzly along the way so don't be stupid and feed it Cheetos and lose your arm. In the winter both roads are closed because of the snow so your trapped in town. Roads open in May but then they do construction and a ton of tourists who don't know how to drive so there's traffic jams both ways. So if you live where I do you're pretty much stuck. That's what kind of person I am."

"Come on, Jason, you know how tough Mrs. Rayhill is," I caution. "At least put an 'e' on Yellowstone—"

He scratches a ferocious "e" onto the page just as Robyn comes back to the bar. She snatches it up, smudging it with ash from her cigarette. Holding the paper a good foot away, she squints. "That's a pretty damned accurate description of this place, if you ask me," she says. "Except you need some apostrophes, son."

This from the woman whose mailbox reads "The Ruggle's." When she looks at me for support, I say, "Runaway Truck Ramp. Straight up with a dead end at the top."

"Oh, shoot, honey." She gives the essay back to Jason. "Hand it in. If Velma don't like it, tell her she can come talk to me."

I say nothing. Jason has pointed out a soul-shaking truth: Pindall is too isolated, it is too small. Robyn says that the family tree here has no branches, what with everybody married to everybody else's ex and taking in their drunkard sister or jailbird cousin's kids. My own family tree was cut down right in the midst of flourishing, and I'm afraid I'm nothing more than a stump.

"Turn in it," I concede. "When you're still in eleventh grade English next year, don't come crying to me."

In response, Jason crams his notebook into his backpack.

The door to the Rambler opens and hangs, in a moment of indecision.

"This ain't the goddamned Sahara," Robyn bellows. "I'm paying for that heat."

A woman steps into the bar dressed in a heavy coat and jeans. She's wearing fashion boots, the kind you wear for show, not for trekking through Wyoming snow. The bottom half of her face is shrouded by a colorful knitted scarf, while the top half is hidden under a straw cowboy hat that's too big for her head.

The talk in the bar sputters out. The boys at the pool table leave off, hawk eyes on her. Dave lifts his head, and Robyn stops shouting long enough so that we can all hear the radio that Walt keeps in the kitchen. In a town the size of Pindall, any stranger is guilty until proven innocent.

The door closes behind her, and she comes across the floor to the bar. The way she moves unnerves me—there's a challenge in her walk. She reminds me of something so far back in my memory that I can't pull it up just now; she makes me feel restless and impulsive and on guard all at the same time. Settling on a stool, she pulls off mittens that match the knitted scarf.

"So who's this little thing?" Robyn mutters, gathering up a menu.

She goes over to the woman—she's actually only a girl, I see, as she unwraps the scarf—and gives her usual greeting to strangers: "What can I getcha for?"

The girl smiles. "I saw the sign outside for margaritas."

"That's right," Robyn says. "Ninety-nine cents. Blueberry or regular?"

"I'll try blueberry," she says as she wrangles out of her coat.

"Drinking age is twenty-one now," Robyn announces. "Ever since the feds told us they wouldn't give us no more money for highways if we didn't. I need to see some identification."

Robyn rarely—in fact, never—asks for identification, preferring to break the law and flout it in the federal government's face. I know that she's only checking the girl's driver's license to snoop. She reads loudly, "Erica Wy—"

"Wiegel," the girl says. "With an 'e'."

"From Columbus, Ohio," Robyn continues. "What brings you here in the dead of winter, Erica Wiegel?"

"I wanted to see this part of the world."

"So you're vacationing? All by yourself?"

Robyn's blatant poke for information doesn't seem to rattle the girl. Politely, she answers, "You could say that."

The balls clap again at the pool table, relief spinning through the room. The inevitable—the arrival of Cascadia Northern management from Portland—has been postponed again.

Robyn gives a sour shrug. She is always looking for drama—runaway bride, somebody sleeping with somebody they shouldn't be, money or mother-in-law troubles. This girl is far too normal for her taste.

She's beautiful, too. Her features are all knitted from the same dark hues. She has black-brown hair that waves over her shoulders, black eyebrows and lashes, a mouth the color of a Jonathan apple. Her eyes are nearly black in the dim light of the bar. The tips of her ears peek through her hair, pushed out by the cowboy hat. She looks tender, lovable—which, for some reason, makes my stomach jolt.

The evening shuts down, uneventful, after all. As the snow piles up outside, inside we cling to what we can rely on. I shuffle drinks to the tables and the Nookie, and the guys down them without thirst. The contest at the pool table fizzles into a half-hearted chunking at balls, and the hair salon girls' feet get tired. The jukebox falls silent, but no one plugs in more quarters. Even Walt's radio blurs into static, the station's signal too weak to catch in this weather.

Johnny Hart finishes his last beer. "I'm going." He slides off his stool. "God bless you all, Robyn, Walter, Shari, uh . . ." He falters at Jason's name, but waves it away. "Remember the Lord will protect you."

"Well, you make damned sure you look both ways when you cross Main, Johnny," Robyn shouts. "Just in case the Lord ain't watching."

He staggers to where the girl sits. "Marie?" he says, his neck rising from his coat collar like a turtle's.

"I'm sorry," she answers. "I'm not Marie."

He shrinks back into the washed-up little old man that he's become and edges out the door. He lives directly across the street from the Rambler in a room above the Greenbow Boutique, but it's a perilous journey for someone who hasn't been sober since Ike was in office.

Robyn shakes her head. "Now, there's a traffic hazard you can write about."

"Grub's on," Walt reports from the kitchen.

I gather up the food and take it to the tourist family. The wife's margarita glass has been drained, and both children are crying. She rocks the baby against her. "Deb," the husband says. "Give him to me."

"He's just hungry," she says. "Hungry and miserable, that's all."

She's talking about the baby, but there is an extra punch in her voice when she says "miserable." She hands the baby to her husband, then leans back as far as she can into the shadows of the booth. The husband walks the baby back and forth, offering him spoonfuls of applesauce.

"Everything's okay?" I ask.

"Oh, yes." Deb herself sounds nauseous. "Just fine."

"Did Robyn find you a room?"

"It's all taken care of."

"Do you want another margarita?"

"Blueberry," she says. "I want a blueberry."

The husband warns, "Deb—"

But I've turned away. Before I deliver the drink, I add an extra shot of tequila. Setting the glass before her, I advise, "Take your time. Nights are long here."

"That's what I'm afraid of."

"You know, you're all just tired, you just need a good night's sleep. Tomorrow morning when you wake up, you'll look at your husband and your kids, and you'll think, thank God, I'm not alone."

I've gone too far—for her and for myself. My voice is brimmed over by tears, and she is staring at me. The crazy woman in the dive bar in some godawful town in the middle of nowhere. She asks, "Will I?"

I wipe my hands on my apron and look at the door as if I'm expecting someone, not certain if I should walk away with my dignity or try to explain. You see, on the day that Brad died, I was running late. Every year, I sing on the stage in Asa Pindall Park—the old stuff, the cowboy songs we all know, like "Back in the Saddle Again" or "Yellow Rose of Texas"—with Eddie Fenton on harmonica and Art Canaday on guitar. But that day, our poorly-rehearsed trio got off to a rough start, and we did too many encores to make up for it. As I was hiking up the hill to the meadow, on my way to catch the end of the Derby, a swell of sound reached me. It wasn't a cheer or scream or clamor, and it wasn't wind or heat, but a release, a breath that was exhaled and never redrawn, and I knew. Something had gone wrong, something had gone bad.

Someone caught me by the arm and said, "Stay here, Shari. You don't want to see it."

But I did. I wish now that I had seen Brad, laid out flat, as if he had stretched out in the grass for a nap. Wasn't there anything after he fell? A flick of an eyelid, a tremble of his lips, a twitch of a finger? Anything that would have served as a farewell to this earth? To me?

That is what I would tell Deb: Don't squander it.

But the baby cries louder, and the husband picks up the girl and marches through the door that separates the bar from the motel. Deb takes a couple of desperate gulps of her margarita before unhooking the baby from the booster chair. She aims a "Thanks" in my direction before she flees.

I bus the table, gathering up plates of half-eaten food and the barely touched margarita glass. When I return to the bar, Robyn says, "I sure hope they left a tip."

"I think they left in too much of a hurry."

"Well, hell," she says. "I should have upped the room rate."

"Ssh," Jason says. "Listen."

Dwayne stands with his pool cue propped under an arm, his hands freed up to light a cigarette. "Now, Brad," he says, "he knew how to sweet talk a bull elk. One day when we was up near Flathead, Brad's got his diaphragm in his mouth and is bugling away, a nice squeaky call, 'cause no bull in his right mind is gonna come fight one that might whup him. So Brad bugles, and he gets this prissy ladylike bugle back, somewhere up the hill. It sounds like this"—Dwayne lets out a pitiful warble, like a cat meowing under water—"and he looks at me, a big old shit-eating grin on his face, and I can't help but say, 'Shit, you got yourself a raghorn. Watch out, Brad, you might be the only thing it can attract.' But he says, 'Bet ya it's a five-point or up. Ten dollars a point.'"

Tommy Dole shakes his head. "No way."

I lean against the bar. Beside me, Robyn says, "Take it easy, honey."

I wait for the next line, although the end of the story is clear to me and to every other person in the bar. It sets me on edge, takes me back, takes me forward, makes me so I cannot think, breathe or see. I expect Brad to walk in any minute and say, "Now, Dwayne, you know that ain't the way it happened."

"Well, that's what I said." Dwayne laughs. "But then we hear it. Goddamned fucking six-point tearing up the goddamned brush, stomping down the slope, size of King Kong, piss dripping off him—God, the stink—in full rut. Cost me sixty fucking bucks."

Every eye in the bar falls on me, waiting, watching. Why, I wonder again, have I been left alone? Why couldn't old age have crept up on me and my husband through years of forgotten birthdays and anniversaries, indistinguishable Christmases, and the few flashes of glory that radiate through every life? I look away, watching Jason carve at the edge of the bar counter with his knife until Robyn reaches over and takes it out of his hands. "That ain't no good," she says.

Erica Wiegel spins around on her barstool. "I think you're talking about my dad," she says to Dwayne.

Dwayne is slow on the uptake, and several seconds pass before he says, "No, I'm talking about a friend of mine from around here."

She's moving now, headed toward the pool table. "My father was from around here. He was a hunter and a fishing guide. His name was Brad Brock."

Blueberry margarita rises up in the back of my throat. In the corner, Jason leaps off his bar stool, as if he is going to lunge at Erica. He stops just as suddenly, his arms hanging at his side like broken wings.

Dwayne's eyes flicker, moving from Erica to me. "No," he says. "I don't think—"

"According to my mom, he was famous in this area for his outfitting skills."

Each word she speaks feels like an assault: hunter and fishing guide, outfitting skills, famous, mom.

"Nah," Dwayne says. "He was married. His wife's right—"

Dave stands up. "You must be Lael's girl."

"Yeah, I am."

My heart hurts, the blood in my veins is too heavy to flow. Dave knows her? Knows of her? This newest betrayal hits me as hard as Erica's claim to my husband's name. Now it's confirmed, now it's not a mistake or an impossibility. I've clenched the bar counter so hard that my fingers have turned white.

"Sit down, Shari," Robyn says behind me. Turning around, she hollers, "Walt, get out here and help me!"

"You're Brad's daughter?" Dwayne's voice lifts on the final word.

"Yes," she says. "He met my mom in Casper, and they dated for just a short time. They weren't even together when Mom found out about me."

"So he didn't know about you?"

"He knew. But my mom was before her time, I guess. She decided not to get married."

Dwayne stares, uncomprehending, and no one picks up the slack. The strength has left my legs, and I am sinking. Dated? Married?

"You knew my mom's name," Erica says to Dave. "Did you know my dad, too?"

The abyss yaws wider. Dave glances toward me, then says quietly, "Come over here."

All those winters away from us, was that what he was doing? Leading the classic double life, the sailor's life, a family in every port? I curl forward, trying to escape into myself. The sticky wood of the bar touches my cheek.

"Jesus Christ," Robyn whips. "Walt, call Marguerite and get her down here."

"Don't," Jason says. "I want to go home."

He is out of the bar so quickly that Robyn and I are left to call into empty space. Then I'm running behind him, without coat or hat or gloves, catching him just as he reaches the truck. The bitter wind whirls around me, numbing my lips and burning my lungs.

"Jason, come back inside."

"I'm not going back in there. I'm going home."

I crawl into the passenger's seat, and we are on our way.

§§§§§

It's a long drive home, but it's not the snow.

Jason drives well—he knows how to handle these roads. I glance toward him, but the only light is from the dash, and his face is unreadable. The whole mess replays itself in my head, thrumming through my brain with the rhythm of the truck's engine. Ever since Brad died, people have been stopping me in the aisles of the Wickiup, or the halls of the school, or when I'm filling up at the Conoco, to tell me stories about him. Each one shocks me, as if it couldn't have happened without my knowledge, as if it must have some stamp of authenticity from me in order to be true.

But nothing has hurt like this—

"I don't know anything about this, Jason," I say. "I don't know any more than you do."

He doesn't answer. The truck slips a little as he hits the gas too hard.

"I don't know why your dad didn't tell me—"

I'm not sure if I'm talking to him or to myself, but I'm doing it aloud.

"He evidently didn't love . . . this woman," I rationalize. "And she didn't love him—"

"That doesn't even matter!" Jason explodes. "It doesn't even matter! He was a liar! He was a piece of shit! A fucking piece of—!"

"Stop it!" I shout. "Don't you dare talk about him that way! We can't do this, we can't . . . maybe she's not telling the truth."

"Did you look at her? She looks just like him!"

I bury my hands in my face. I knew it when she walked in, I knew it before she said a word.

Jason turns off the Yellowstone Highway onto our logging road and pulls the emergency brake. It's an old custom we have kept for years. Whenever we have serious questions to ponder, or when we're sharing a tender or funny moment, or when we simply want to stall the return home, we seek out the shoulder of the road. On warm nights, we'll open the windows and let the air wash over us. In the dead of summer, we'll climb into the pickup bed and stretch out full length to look at the stars. Tonight, snow falls thickly in the beams of the headlights.

"You know," Jason says. "One time, I tried to go with him. I went outside to the camper the night before he left, after you two were asleep. I took a sleeping bag and my clothes stuffed in a sack. When I heard him come out in the morning, I crawled into the very back of the camper. I was sure he didn't know I was there. I was way back under some camping gear. He loaded all sorts of stuff right on top of me, and I thought I would get away with it. But right before he left, he said, 'Come on out now.' He'd known I was there all along."

"When was that?"

"I guess I was seven or eight. He picked me up, sleeping bag and all, and carried me into the house and put me in bed. He said, 'You gotta stay here, so I'll know where to come back to.'"

I'm unable to catch my breath. The weighty burden of life without Brad shifts, no lighter, no less.

"You gotta stay here, so I'll know where to come back to," he mimics. "More like, you gotta stay here because I got my damned little daughter to spend the winter with—"

"We don't know that, we don't—"

He slams out of the truck and starts walking up the road, struggling through the heavy snow. "Come back!" I call. I slide across the seat and let go the brake, inching the truck forward, tracking him along the tunnel we've dug through the drifts with the front-end loader. He turns, snowy-shouldered and shivering.

"Dad just didn't want to be here," he shouts into the night. "You know that! You fucking know that! Otherwise, he wouldn't have left every chance he had. He wouldn't have gone—"

I scramble out of the truck, stumbling on ridges of crusted snow. The wind whips my face like the branches of a tree. "Don't you say that!" The words echo from the tunnel walls around us. "You know Dad loved us!"

"Really? That's what you call it? You're as fucked up as he was—!"

"I don't have the answers. I don't know how this happened or why it happened! I just don't know!"

My voice slams against the banks of snow, the words dying. Jason disappears beyond the safe ring of the headlights.

"Jason!" I cry. "Come back!"

He inches into the light to where he is barely visible. We face each other, and I find I can't speak. I can't comfort him. I can't end this. I don't know how. "Come and get back in the truck," I say. "Please."

"You know if they didn't always have to be telling those stories, maybe she would have just gone away. Why do they always have to tell those stupid stories? Why can't they just shut up?"

"They were your Dad's friends." The ache creeps around my heart. "Some of them knew him before I did."

"Yeah, and of everybody, I knew him the least."

The words catch my heart. I want to say: Not the least. But it's true.

He stalks toward the truck. Launching himself into the cab, he lumps into the passenger's seat, his shoulder lodged against the window. I crawl behind the steering wheel and flick up the heat.

"You suppose Dave's going to tell her that his horse killed him?" Jason demands. "Is he going to tell her that it should have been him? That he's the one who should be dead—"

"Don't talk like that—"

"Well, he knew about her, didn't he? He must have written to her about it—"

"No, he wouldn't do that—"

"And you just stand there and smile when they go on about it, like you always do, just nod your head and say, Oh, isn't that nice? You don't ever tell them to shut up and leave us alone—"

"I can't do that—"

He slams the dashboard with the palm of his hand, silencing me. "If you'd just tell them to shut up, she wouldn't have found out! She would have gone away, and left us alone—"

He's right—I don't stop them. He's right—Dave should have been riding Rain. He's right—Erica Wiegel should have stayed in Ohio or wherever the hell she's from. But just because he's right doesn't mean it's right.

"I don't know what we'll do," I say. "I don't know how we'll manage."

He says nothing more, and I release the emergency brake, guiding the truck along the tunnel, fresh snow trenching beneath the tires. As soon as the truck rolls to a halt in the driveway, Jason opens the door and tumbles out. Yet he hangs in the shadow of the door.

"Do you think Grandma knows?" he asks.

I can't imagine that betrayal, either for myself or for Jason. He adores his grandmother, and Marguerite is my rock.

"I don't know."

"Well, everybody else does."

He slams the door so hard that the truck shimmies, its springs screeching in the cold air.

He's right about that, too. The guys in the bar will tell their wives tonight when they go home, and their wives will tell their friends tomorrow. And if there's still a single soul in Pindall who hasn't heard by tomorrow afternoon, Robyn will put an end to that. I lay my head against the steering wheel, feeling too tired, too stunned to go inside. By the time I look up, the snow has knitted a blanket over the windshield.

Jason has left his backpack behind. As I drag it across the seat, his essay for Mrs. Rayhill slips out onto the floor. It is a relic of a more innocent time, an eon ago, a lifetime.

I pick it up and try to smooth it out with the heel of my hand. What a stupid assignment, what a waste of precious time. But when I touch it, I start to do the math. Erica Wiegel is of legal age, which makes her at least twenty-one. Twenty-one years ago, I was fourteen.

And Brad Brock had not yet walked into my life.

I let out a laugh, or maybe a sob. I want to run inside and tell Jason, no, no, he didn't cheat on me. We're all right, it isn't what we thought.

Yet it is what we thought. Erica Wiegel is Brad's flesh and blood. And he did cheat us, out of all that time, all that love.

I zip the essay back in Jason's backpack. What we need here is a continuous lane. One that doesn't merge into a traffic jam or pinch out in a dead end. One that runs as straight as possible, with no hairpin curves or potholes or other surprises. A road you can follow and not get lost.

It's up to me to be just that.

FOUR
WHY SHE WENT WEST

Erica swears there is a vomit stain on the box springs. It's not that the room isn't clean—the towels and sheets have the bleached smell of a school cafeteria. Yet the fixtures have apparently been there since the day that the motel opened in . . . was it 1954, or 1945, or 1905? She can't remember the date on the SERVING THE YELLOWSTONE REGION SINCE sign that hangs in the motel office.

It doesn't matter. The furniture is sticky from too many fingertips, and the corners carry the smell of too-long-in-the-car, too-little-sleep, too-far-from-home tourists. And there's a vomit stain down the side of the box springs.

All the same, she does not move from the bed.

Last night, after Shari and Jason—she learned their names from Dave—left, Erica had become the center of attention. Robyn, Dwayne and most of the others had crowded around the table where she sat with Dave, coaxing her story from her.

"My mother met Brad Brock when she was eighteen. They were both going to the community college in Casper—"

"I remember that," Robyn said. *"He went there for a while."*

"And they fell in love the way teenagers do. Head over heels, sure that it's forever—"

"Damn, I don't remember him ever bringing anybody back here," Dwayne said. *"He never had eyes for nobody but Shari ever since I knew him."*

"That's just it," Erica had said. *"It was over within six months. My mom transferred to Colorado State College in Fort Collins. They wrote a few letters back and forth, but it just didn't work."*

"But she was pregnant?" Robyn asked.

"She was. Pregnant and in her first year of 'real' college, as she said. She didn't want to quit." She took a sip from the fresh margarita that Robyn had

given her. "And my grandparents were way before their time. They didn't disown her or anything. They helped her out with me."

"The Wiegels?"

"No, my mother's name was Lael Sheridan," Erica explained. "So, it was Grandma and Grandpa Sheridan. When I was eight, Mom married Mike Wiegel and he legally adopted me. By then, we were living in Ohio—"

"How'd you come to be there?"

"She got a job teaching sociology—"

"What the hell is that?" Robyn snorted. "Soo-see—"

"The study of society," Erica said. "She got her Ph.D. at OSU, which is where Mike teaches, too."

"What's OSU?"

"Ohio State University. That's where I went to college."

"You been to college?"

"I graduated in December."

"Fuckin' A," Dwayne said. "Brad's kid went to college."

"So your mom teaches at the college?" Robyn asked.

And that was where Erica's mouth had gone dry, and her throat had started to ache. It isn't easy to talk about her mother, about the cancer that sucked the energy and intelligence and wisdom out of a woman who lived her entire life as a model of energy and intelligence and wisdom. Her mother has been gone for three years now, and still Erica cannot breathe when she is mentioned.

And now, Mike Wiegel—who cannot be faulted in any way—is getting married again.

She rolls from bed into the chilly morning air. The electric heat boards along the walls creaked through the night, emitting the odor of smoldering dust bunnies, but the air isn't warm. She turns on the shower, hoping for hot water, at least.

She isn't disappointed. The shower spews a scalding stream, and she twists the cold tap to open. Nothing happens, forcing her to dart away from the powerful stream of water after she rinses.

She dresses in a clean sweater, her blue jeans and boots, zips up her parka, and wraps the knitted scarf around her neck. As she leaves the motel room, she sticks the cowboy hat on her head, and it slides down nearly over her eyes. Impatiently, she pushes it back. It was an impulse purchase, bought somewhere along I-90. Something to make her forget that she is a stranger in a strange land.

Outside, the day is no warmer than the previous evening, and the parking lot of the Rambler is deserted except for her Honda Accord and a minivan with New Hampshire plates. A logging truck blasts by on Main Street, and Erica starts—her heart hasn't beat in the same rhythm since she left home. No one knows that she is here. Not Mike, not Royce, her half-brother who is a freshman in high school this fall, and definitely not Natalie, Royce's twin, who has never been able to keep secrets. She is completely alone.

That realization is enough to jolt her into a purposeful stride along Main Street.

For a few blocks, boutiques line both sides of the wide street. They are closed now, but she gazes through windows at an assortment of tourist junk—leather-headed tom-toms, beaded purses, keychains that billow Old Faithful, shot glasses with the same image. A Victorian-scrolled sign reads, "Have Your Wild West Portrait Done Here!" A sampling of the photographs hangs below—men dressed as outlaws with six-shooters and spurs, and women decked out as floozies in bustiers and fishnet stockings. *WINTER HOURS,* the sign on the door reads, *WHEN WE DAMN WELL FEEL LIKE IT.*

Erica keeps walking, passing a saddle and tack store, a car dealership with fewer than ten cars on its lot, and a laundromat. Almost no one drives along the street, and no one is parked along the curb. At the center of town, she comes to an intersection large enough to sport a traffic signal. The road splits here, with Main Street continuing straight in one direction, while a towering brown sign announces, YELLOWSTONE NATIONAL PARK, 64 MILES. The light shines green, the left arrow permanently giving permission. Only when a battered pickup truck grunts to a stop at the Y of Main Street does the light flicker from green to yellow to red.

Across the street, overlooking the junction of the Yellowstone Highway and Main Street, is the Wickiup. The day's specials are painted in tempura on the luminous plate glass windows, and a permanent sign welcomes all to FREE PARKING IN BACK.

Erica crosses the street and goes inside.

The store is warm, shining, with spotless linoleum and neatly-kept aisles. A buzz of conversation drifts up and over the piped-in Muzak.

Erica greets the people she meets, aware of their looks following her as she passes. She is only halfway down the second aisle when she glances up at the convex mirror anchored in a nook of ceiling and wall above her and realizes that she is being watched by two women at the checkout stand, one of whom talks rapidly. She pushes her hat off her forehead, suddenly nervous. She wishes there was someone in this town who had known Lael Sheridan, who could help her to put the pieces together. Last night, Dave Phillips had been of little help.

"You knew my mother's name," she had prodded. *"Did you know her?"*

"I met her once," he admitted. *"A long time ago, in Casper. Pretty girl— long reddish hair, blue eyes, right?"*

"That's right, she was," she said. *"Tell me about Shari and Jason."*

"What's there to say? It's been a hell of a time for them."

"I wish I'd seen them before they left. I would have liked to talk to them."

He took a long drink from a bottle of Budweiser that Robyn had brought him. "I don't know how she's like to take this," he said. *"Secrets can be a damned hard thing."*

She walks parallel to the back wall of the store and ends up in Produce. Directly ahead of her, through French doors, is a coffee shop called The Daisy. She goes inside, seeking sanctuary.

At first she thinks she is alone in the glass-walled sunroom. No one appears to be behind the counter, and no one sits in the lyre-shaped soda fountain chairs or at the wrought-iron tables. On the interior wall of The Daisy, opposite the broad windows that overlook the Yellowstone Highway, hangs a collage of quilts. They heap over racks or tumble from doweling, all of them made with bright, lavish colors. She's seen Amish quilts, but the fabrics of these quilts aren't the bright cotton calicos of Americana. These quilts are sewn from velvet and satin, the textures of the fabrics adding as much definition to the designs as the patterns themselves. Each one is voluptuous, almost shameless, begging to be caressed with the tip of a finger or tangled around the legs of a lover.

Someone clears a throat. Erica turns to find a woman behind the counter. Her face is weary, and her blond-frosted hair is caught back in a half-hearted ponytail. "Do you want something, hon?" she asks.

"Coffee," Erica says.

"What kind? We got espresso and mocha and—"

Erica smiles. "Just hot and black, thanks."

"You sure? We got all kinds of special brews—"

"I'm sure."

Disappointed, the woman pours into a Styrofoam cup. "That's ninety-seven cents."

Erica is pawing through her change purse when she hears a voice behind her.

"Patti, can you give us a few minutes?"

Behind Erica stands an older woman dressed as if she's just come in off the range. She wears jeans and a Western shirt buttoned to the base of her chin and clamped tight by a silver bolo. Silver and turquoise earrings weigh down her earlobes, and her fingers and wrists are ornamented with matching jewelry. Her eyes are black, her face majestic and richly featured.

But it is her hair that makes Erica's breath stall in her throat. A lush salt and pepper braid is pulled forward over her left shoulder. At the end of the green band that holds the braid is a curl of gray in the shape of an upside-down question mark. Whenever Erica braids her hair, that same question mark appears at the end of the plait. She even pulls it over her shoulder in the same fashion.

This is Marguerite Brock. Her grandmother.

"Yes, Miz Brock." Poor Patti nods furiously, almost running for the exit. Once she's gone, Marguerite closes the French doors that lead into the Wickiup and flips the sign against the window panes to "Closed."

Erica holds out her hand, the payment for the coffee in her palm. "Here's the money."

Marguerite raises her eyebrows dismissively. "Never mind."

"Thank you." Erica shoves the change into her jeans pocket. Stepping forward, she offers her hand. "I'm Erica Wiegel."

Marguerite's handshake is as intimidating as her stare. Erica steels herself to keep from glancing away or saying something stupid. It's all too strange—this stern woman, who she will resemble in another four or five decades, the riot of quilts, the smell of roasting coffee beans.

"You look very much like your father," Marguerite says at last.

Relieved, Erica smiles. "Thank you."

"What are you drinking?"

"Black coffee."

"Nothing in it? No sweetener?"

"Just black."

Marguerite goes behind the counter and pours herself a cup. Bringing the decanter with her, she says, "I put in this coffee shop because I was told that tourists were demanding better coffee. The fancy brews, espresso and such, but it isn't true. Tourists drink Folger's just like the rest of us. And so I am stuck with all these gizmos that brew Italian coffee."

Erica laughs nervously. Her grandmother sets the decanter on a nearby table and sits, motioning for Erica to do the same. The legs of the lyre-backed chair grate against the tile floor as Erica settles into it. Marguerite leans back, one hand on her cup.

"Did you know he was dead when you left Ohio?" she asks.

Her bluntness catches Erica off-guard. She stammers, trying to maintain her poise. "Yes. My mother kept up a subscription to the *Pindall Pioneer*. After she . . . when I . . . I subscribed to it when I was in college."

She finishes badly, and Marguerite offers no help. "So why did you come? You can't meet him, you can't reunite your parents, or some other youthful daydream—"

"I'm a little old for youthful daydreams," Erica reacts. "That was never my intention, anyway. I came for my own satisfaction."

Marguerite's eyes snap, and she takes her time stirring sugar into her coffee. Erica cannot tell if her grandmother is offended or amused by her tart reply, but she suspects the latter.

"I came," Erica begins. "I came because I thought he might have left something behind, like a will or something—"

"There is no inheritance."

"No, no, that's not what I meant." She swallows back the raw feeling in her throat. "I thought there might be a photo or a gift she had given him that he would want me to have or . . . something."

A locket with a curl of hair, a book with an inscription, a ring—

Marguerite's voice is gentle. "I wouldn't know about that. Perhaps Shari will find something. God knows, she's at home today tearing apart her heart."

The words make Erica's chest hurt, but she forges on. "Did he tell you about me? He told his friend, Dave. Dave even met my mom."

Marguerite winces, but says, "No, I didn't know."

"My mother told me all about him." Desperation edges her voice. "She talked of it as if it was the greatest time in her life, and it was, I think. It was one of those innocent times before you find out how hard life really is. I can't believe he didn't see it the same way—"

"Your mother was luckier than most women in her situation, I think," Marguerite says. "There aren't many pregnant teenagers whose parents aren't bent on hiding the baby somehow."

"She was lucky." Erica laughs. "She always said she was the luckiest woman. Until—"

Marguerite waits, her dark eyes meeting Erica's. "Until what?"

"She passed on," Erica says. Then, it is too hard to keep going. She presses her palms together and brings them up in front of her lips.

"She was young."

"So were we. The twins—my brother and sister. And me."

"So you have family in the east?"

"I have a stepfather and the twins."

"You'd be wise to hold on to that much family."

"I have family here, too," she says pointedly.

"Yes, you do." Marguerite rises. "And so, if you need anything, just ask. I'll see to it that you have whatever you need."

"I told you it's not about money," Erica flares again.

"It's only an offer." She eyes the wall of quilts and pulls down one on which amber patches spiral against blue in a conch shell design. "I know how warm Robyn keeps the motel. You'd better have this."

Erica regrets snapping as her grandmother hefts the bulky fabric into her arms. "Thank you," she says.

"Whatever you need," Marguerite says again.

She moves toward the door, reopening The Daisy for business with a flip of the sign, and Erica realizes that she will soon be alone again. Stay here, she wants to plead. Just a while longer, just a little, I'm scared—

Instead, she says, "It was nice to meet you."

She offers her bravest smile to Marguerite, which elicits a surprising frown. "You will have to give us some time to get used to this," her grandmother says gravely. "But, Lord, you do resemble him."

"I think I resemble you," Erica says, tentatively, almost shyly.

Marguerite's stony expression melts at last. "So you do," she concedes. "So you do."

§§§§§

After she eats lunch—alone—in the parking lot of the drive-thru All Nite Grub & Go, Erica coaxes her Honda up the dirt streets toward the apex of the mountain that looms behind Pindall. The streets run up, steep and rutted, with crooked ledges carved into the mountain providing cross streets. Reaching the pinnacle of the town, she finds a number of elegant, expensively-built homes. She parks in front of a handsome brick and clapboard house that sports a "For Rent" sign.

Stepping out of the car, she looks down at the town. Pindall is closed in by its dramatic scenery. On one end, Main Street is swallowed by a red rock canyon with walls that rise straight up for a hundred feet. On the other, the Yellowstone Highway disappears into dense trees and what looks like an engine-challenging climb. Below, most of the houses—either worn-down single-level houses or double-wide trailers—cling to the undulations of the hillside. The lots are cluttered with parked RVs and cars up on blocks and mangy dog runs and rusted skeletons of swing sets. Main Street looks shabby from up here, and the western end of Pindall seems to be overtaken by a junkyard. It isn't a lovely town she's come to, even in its magnificent setting.

She catches in her peripheral vision a movement to her right. Outside a chalet-type house that sits higher on the mountain than the rental house, a man in a ski mask is shoveling snow from the driveway.

"Hi," Erica says.

He nods without speaking.

She turns—her feet are already cold—and strikes up a slick embankment, her heels sticking with every step. Beyond the bank, flat open tundra lies before her, swallowed by snow. It stretches for a half mile or so, with a cluster of sandstone boulders on one end and a fringe of trees on the other. This, she knows from Dave, is the meadow where her father fell from his horse, where his neck broke on impact, killing him instantly.

She hears someone scuffing up the embankment behind her and turns. The man in the ski mask has followed her. She takes a step backward, then scolds herself: this isn't Columbus.

"How are you today?" she asks.

Without a word, he offers a steaming, blue-gray cup to her.

"Oh, thank you." She can feel the heat through her knitted mittens. "My name's Erica Wiegel."

The man bobs his head, his eyes blue and bright even in the overcast day. He turns and slips back down the embankment.

"Thank you," Erica calls, but he does not respond.

His footsteps crunch as he walks down the street and up his driveway. The sound of the chalet door closing reverberates through the cold air and down into the valley.

The cup is heavy and handmade, and it contains caramel-colored tea to which milk or cream has been added. Spices, too—cinnamon and nutmeg, maybe. Looking across the field, sipping the tea, Erica sees that there is nothing to be seen here today.

She finishes the tea and stumbles back down the embankment, her heeled boots even more of a liability now. Walking past her car and the rental house, she hikes up the short drive to the chalet and knocks at the door.

No one comes. Leaning closer to the wood, she hears voices from inside and something that sounds like a flute.

She knocks again.

Nothing.

Carefully, she sets the cup by the door. "Here's your cup," she calls, feeling somewhat foolish. "Thanks again. It was nice to meet you."

The words ricochet off the wooden door and into the valley below.

At the Rambler again, Erica sits on the bed, the blue and amber quilt on her lap. She is worn out—by the cold, by the blur of the three-day drive, by the sun that rises too late in this town so far from Eastern Standard Time. She awoke this morning hours before dawn.

She fingers the fabric. She does not want the quilt to touch the vomit-stained bed, and yet, she wants to sleep beneath it, to feel its loft over her, its warmth around her. She wants to breathe in its scent of coffee and starch. After all, it has come from her grandmother.

More importantly, it has come from her father's mother.

She slips out of her boots and strips off her jeans and sweater. In bra, panties and socks, she wraps the quilt around her, the satin backing chilly against her skin. She strokes the velvet spiral on the quilt top. Something scratches, and she finds on one corner a handwritten price tag that reads "$650" safety-pinned to the quilt.

She removes the tag and lies on the bed, the satin warming now with her body heat, the heaviness of the velvet reassuring over her thighs and shoulders.

Wrapped in her grandmother's creation, she sleeps.

The sun has nearly set when she wakes. Carefully, she folds the quilt into a rich mound and leaves it at the foot of the bed. She pulls on her clothes, drapes the knitted scarf around her neck, and goes through the door that separates the Rambler Motel from the bar.

There, she finds herself alone, save for the old man who called her Marie last night. He slumps on a stool, mumbling and snorting, caught up in conversation with himself. He doesn't raise his head when she takes a stool down the way. The only eyes she catches in the semi-darkness are the shiny marbles of the animal heads mounted on the walls.

Shari comes into the bar from the kitchen, swinging through the saloon-style doors with a load of glasses steaming from the dishwasher. She checks on the old man. "You okay, Johnny?"

He makes no answer. Shari clears away the empty glass in front of him and wipes up the damp ring from the wood.

"God bless you," Johnny offers.

"And you, too," Shari says. "You too."

Her voice carries a wistfulness that makes Erica feel as if she is eavesdropping on something intimate. As Shari turns, she spots Erica sitting near the other end of the bar. "Oh, hi, I didn't see you there," she says. "Would you like something?"

"I'll have what he's having," Erica says bravely.

Shari's lips curl in a way that makes Erica think she has a quick, ready smile. Scooping up a glass, Shari goes to the Budweiser tap and holds it under at an angle. Setting it down, she fills another glass and carries both over to where Erica sits, the beer clear and with just the right amount of head.

"You're good at that," Erica says.

"Practice," Shari says. "So what did you do today?"

"I drove around town some. Walked along Main Street."

"What did you do with the other twenty-three and a half hours?"

"I met my grandmother."

Shari looks down at her beer. When she lifts her gaze to Erica's, her eyes are watery. "What did you think of Marguerite?"

"She's very straightforward. She says what she thinks."

"That's not a bad description." She fiddles with her drink. "How old are you?"

"Twenty-two. Almost twenty-three. My mom was nineteen when she had me, a year older than my dad."

"When Brad was eighteen, I was thirteen," Shari says. "There was a full five years between us. We didn't fall in love until he was twenty-one. You would have been almost three."

The cost of confiding is on her face, which is etched with pain, and in her shoulders, which curve inward. She crosses her arms over her breasts, her hands hooked on her elbows. Erica wants to reach out and place her hand on Shari's or offer some word of advice. Yet she senses a reserve of something—orneriness, perseverance, self-preservation. What her mother would have called prairie gumption.

Shari speaks again. "Tell me . . . you know, tell me everything, I guess."

Erica tells Shari the story she told the folks in the bar last night. Once she is finished, silence falls. Shari seems to realize, as Erica does, that there are no witnesses now, no one to set the record straight, to shore up memory and fill in the gaps.

"I wish I would have known," Shari says at last. "It would have made this a whole hell of a lot easier."

Erica starts to speak, but the saloon doors bang open. Jason stops when he sees Erica with his mother, then turns and walks out, shoving the doors so brutally that a splinter of wood flies from a louver as it hits the wall.

Shari hurries after him, leaving Erica alone with Johnny.

On Friday evening, Robyn comes to Erica's room. Erica has taken to leaving the door open through the evening, "holding court," as she refers to it. There's always someone who wants to check in on her or drop by to see her—Dwayne Black with his vulgar tongue, or Ben Markum, who brings her cellophane-wrapped, peanut butter and cheese crackers and Junior Mints from the vending machine. Tommy Dole has offered her a pistol to protect herself against the "wild characters" who stay at the Rambler, and Marty Sholes wants her to join a cattle drive at his ranch. He has described how to brand, castrate, and dehorn a calf to her in clinical detail.

"You use anesthetic, don't you?" she had asked, appalled.

"Sure do." Marty laughed. "A fifth of Jim Beam for each of us."

Today, Robyn sits on the bed, not far from the vomit stain. The bed is neatly made by Erica in the mornings, because Robyn doesn't hire housekeeping until summer, but Robyn eyes Marguerite Brock's quilt as if it's putrid and rank. Erica stands in front of the dresser, the edge of the wood pressed against the backs of her thighs.

"Well, see, here's the deal." Robyn fidgets, and Erica knows she would be far more comfortable if she had a cigarette in her hand. "Some of the guys don't think it's right for you to be living here. Not that I care one way or the other"—she holds up her hand—"but you probably know that Jason don't come in the bar anymore, now that you're here."

"No, I didn't—"

"Well, to make it easier on them, I've talked with Merrilee at the Morning Glory and she's agreed to give you a room for the same price as I'm charging. It's usually five bucks more."

Erica hooks her fingers around the ledge of the dresser top.

"We do this a lot for each other," Robyn continues. "She sends her problem guests over here, and I send mine there. Sometimes a different room will settle them down. Unless they're from Colorado. They're asses no matter what."

Erica opens her mouth to defend herself against the accusation of being a problem guest, but Robyn gives her no chance.

"Jason's had a hard time accepting Brad's death. Shari's worried if he ain't being watched, he'll start acting stupid. Here in the bar, we can keep an eye on him."

Erica sees the inevitable. To stand her ground—as she is accustomed to doing—will bring down an avalanche on her head. Still, it stings. She feels as if she's taking a step backward from finding her father, as if she's being banished from his world.

Robyn continues. "What I figure is it's too cold for Jason to be wandering around out there in the dark. If you go, Shari can pick him up when he's off work and bring him down here."

"You want me to leave tonight?" Erica asks.

"I like you just fine." Robyn shrugs. "Remind me of your dad, You got his grin. Pure angel with enough devil in it to make it right. Lordy, he was special."

Erica looks at the floor. "It will take me a few minutes to pack."

But after Robyn leaves, she sits on the bed, kneading the precious fabric of the quilt. Why is she here? Why didn't she just stay in Ohio, cozying up to Mike and his new wife, and spending Saturdays at the country club pool with Royce and Nat, and holding on to her family, just as her grandmother suggested?

She pulls her suitcase out of the closet and jimmies open the drawers of the dresser. She didn't bring that much with her, but for some reason it no longer fits in the suitcase. Dumping everything out again, she starts over.

Someone knocks at her door.

She opens it to find Dave Phillips. He's leaning a little against the jamb, but when he sees her, he straightens.

"Are you all right?" she asks.

"Sure," he says. "Sure. Always."

But his eyes, never quite focused, are red-rimmed, and his skin is pallid. His blond hair and mustache frost to gray in the glare of the light from the ceiling fixture.

"What's going on?" he asks. "Robyn said you were leaving."

"I've been evicted."

"What for?"

Erica flips a hand toward the bar.

"Was it Shari's idea?" he asks.

"I don't know."

He watches her wedge a sweater inside the suitcase.

"Listen," he says. "Why don't you come stay out with me? I got an extra bunk in my trailer. Nothing special, but I ain't charging rent for it."

She sits on the bed, trying to figure the pros and cons of agreeing, but she's too upset to think. "You wouldn't mind?"

"I'd welcome the company. It's kinda lonely out where I am."

"I need to pay Robyn first."

"Oh, hell, let her wait. She's the one told you to leave."

Erica closes the clasps on the suitcase. Dave picks it up, and she pulls the quilt from the bed. Together they trail out into the snow-smothered night.

At the door of his pickup truck, he gives a lurch and wobble.

Erica's heart sinks. "Do you want me to drive?"

He looks into the distance. "Sure," he says. "I wasn't planning on having anybody with me tonight. Drank one more than I should have."

Erica ignores the obvious arguments to that confession and goes to the driver's side. Climbing in, she discovers that the truck is a manual. "I don't know how to work a stick shift," she admits.

"You have a car, don't you?"

The Honda Accord feels as if it's rolling through wet cement as they leave the parking lot for Main Street. The snow drags at the tires, pulling the car off course, and Erica tries to remember—steer into the skid, steer against the skid, which one is it? As the Honda slides around the first curve of the canyon, she finds herself following the tracks of another vehicle that has passed through too long ago to be wholly reliable, and her resolve fails.

"Do you think we should keep going?" she asks.

"It's up to you," Dave says. "I can see if Shari can take me."

"No, that's okay."

For some reason, she does not want Shari to think she is afraid or incompetent. She repositions her hands on the steering wheel. The snow drives so hard against the headlights that she feels disoriented, carsick. It is Hollywood snow, the snow from the *Nutcracker Suite*—the flakes too large, the volume too thick to be falling for anything but dramatic effect.

"Have you lived here a long time?" she asks Dave.

"All my life."

"And you've always made it home?"

"Most nights," he says. "Just take it slow. You've got just over eight miles to go."

"Eight?" The number seems far too great.

"I'm right at the end of the canyon. Don't worry, you're doing all right."

She glues her eyes to the road. In a few minutes, the snow will be too deep to travel through. She needs to hurry, but she can't. The road through the canyon twists, unforgiving rock wall to her left and stream to her right. She remembers that the curves are sharp, but because she is going so slowly, she has no sense of the shifts in the road. Only the reflective-tipped posts along the side of the road guide her.

When Dave speaks, he startles her. Her attention has been focused so intently on driving that she nearly forgot he was in the car with her.

"I don't know whose bright idea it was to kick you outta the Rambler," he says. "It don't sound like Shari's."

"Don't you think she'd do it for Jason?"

"More like she'd invite you home with her than throw you out in a snowstorm."

"Maybe it was Mrs. Brock," she says, ashamed that she calls her grandmother by the name that she hears Patti and the other Wickiup employees use.

He laughs. "Don't let Marguerite fool you. Half this town has her to thank for still being alive. Nah, she wouldn't do that."

Erica squints to see the road, glad that she has an excuse not to answer. If the Brocks are so beneficent, why haven't they tried to contact her again?

It can't be much farther—they have been in the car for hours, haven't they? On this road for miles, right? At least for so long that she has to turn down the heat and pull at the scarf on her neck to fight the wooziness.

"You okay?" Dave asks.

"Yeah," she says half-heartedly. "I think so."

When they finally arrive at the ranch, Erica's hands are sweating, and her palms ache from gripping the steering wheel too tightly. Her fingers have lost feeling. Dave directs her to pull the car up next to a mobile home. A bluish yard light shines from the top of an electrical pole, a pallid sentry in the storm.

"It's a trailer," she says.

"Yeah," Dave says. "Nothing fancy."

She catches the embarrassment in his voice and foolishly offers, "No, it's nice."

He laughs sadly. "Come on in, you'll be okay."

The blue and amber quilt in her arms, Erica follows him up the cinder block steps into the trailer. On the last step, she is nearly knocked off her feet by a gray-blue Australian shepherd. The dog scratches at the door before Dave has a chance to open it. "Ah, quit," Dave growls.

"It's probably cold."

"He's a knucklehead, that's what he is." The dog wags its bobbed tail furiously, looking up at Dave. "Just a fuzzy-haired, no-good knucklehead. Ain't you, Ratso? Ain't you?"

Ratso barks, eliciting an echoing "woof, woof" from across the barnyard and a yowl from a yellow cat that huddles at the edge of the porch.

"Hey, shut up!" Opening the door, Dave commands, "Get in there."

The dog skitters into the kitchen, but Dave blocks the cat with a boot in its face. Closing the door, he clicks on the lights, and Erica takes in what she can in the yellowish haze: motel-lobby shag carpeting, couch stained by age, harvest-gold appliances, patchy beige linoleum in the kitchen. The trailer smells of tobacco and sawdust and farm animals.

"Take off your coat," Dave says. "As I said, it ain't much, but it's home, sweet home."

She hangs her coat next to his on a peg, and he leads her down the narrow hallway, Ratso at his heels. When he turns on the light in the second bedroom, Erica takes in another deep breath. Posters of kittens and round-eyed gentle girls grace the walls, and a trashcan with smiley faces covets the corner. On a bookshelf opposite the bed is a row of dolls—Barbies, Cabbage Patches, some delicate Madame Alexander dolls in lavish costumes with flesh-colored plastic faces meant to look like china, more. All of their eyes focus on Erica, asking where their loving little girl might be.

"You have a daughter?" she asks.

"Yeah, Renee. This was her room."

"Where is she now?"

"She lives with her mom in Minneapolis."

"How old is she?"

"Sixteen. But she left when she was nine."

"And she didn't take her dolls?" Erica strokes a finger down the rosy, plump cheek of a Beth March doll. "Nine years old, and she left her dolls?"

"I don't know." He sits on the end of the bed, as if he's too tired to stand any longer. "Diane left in a hurry."

Suddenly, Erica is in tears. She misses Natalie, she misses Royce, and Mike, who has always been a father to her. She misses the house swaddled in oak trees near the college where she has spent so much of her life. And, oh, God, she misses her mother.

"Hey," Dave says. "Hey now, come on, it's all right."

"Oh, I'm sorry." She starts to sob. "I just don't know—"

"What's wrong?"

"What am I doing here? Why did I think I could come here? Why did I think they'd accept me?" Words tumble from her mouth, too rushed for sense. "I thought I was taking control of my life by coming here, but now it just seems like such a stupid mistake, such a stupid act!"

Dave rubs her shoulders. "Hey, you're young. You're brave—hell, I don't think many girls your age would drive cross-country like you did. And not many would do as good as you did in the snow."

"But nobody will have anything to do with me!"

"Hey, hey, don't do this." Dave leaves the room, returning with a skein of toilet paper. Handing it to her, he says, "Come on, now. You let yourself get too low, it's hard to get up again."

She blows her nose, trying to regain control. The toilet paper is immediately saturated, and she has to wipe under her nose with the back of her hand.

"I'm sorry," she says. "It's not your problem."

He opens his mouth to speak, then decides against it. "You need to get some sleep," he says. "Hell, we both do."

He helps her to make the bed and fusses over the heat—"It ain't been used for a long time"—trying to uncover the electric boards behind the headboard of the bed. Erica takes her pajamas into the box-like bathroom next door and washes up. Flicking out her contact lenses, she puts on black-framed glasses with lenses that stretch from eyebrow to cheekbone.

Dave is still waiting in the bedroom. "You okay?" he asks nervously.

"I'm just tired."

"Yeah, okay." He lingers, poking at stuff, moving it out of her way. It reminds her of how Mike acted just after her mother's death, always searching for some way to fix what couldn't be fixed.

"I'll see you tomorrow," she says, releasing him. "Thank you for everything."

"Sure," he says. "Goodnight."

Once she's alone, she shivers, already cold. The sheets smell of years in a closet, and the quilt that Marguerite gave her mounds on the twin bed and falls onto the floor.

In one corner of the bedroom sits an ungainly child-sized rag doll in striped knee socks and mini skirt. Her hands are just cloth nubs, her feet stubs. She smiles goofily from beneath a mop of black hair, freckles and lips and eyes painted on the beige fabric. Erica picks her up and strokes the yarn hair. When she lies down in bed, she cuddles the doll against her and weeps.

§§§§§

When she wakes in the morning, she cannot see outside. The windows are cloudy, sightless. She puts on her glasses and pulls on her jeans and stumbles out of the room, tracing the viewless view through a succession of windows. Are they snowed in, is she trapped here? Coming into the living room, she reaches the end of the trailer.

Dave is in the kitchen, making coffee and frying bacon. He seems recovered from last night, no baggy eyes or stiff movements or other signs of hangover. "You sleep okay?" he asks.

"Fine, thank you. How much did it snow? I can't see out the windows—"

"There's plastic on the bedroom windows. Keeps it warmer."

Erica looks out the living room window, which has no plastic. The snow drifts to the grill of her Honda Accord. She pulls on her boots, but as she straightens to go outside, a montage of photographs on the wall opposite the door catches her attention.

The photos chronicle Dave's life—his graduation from high school, a snapshot of him in fatigues in a tangle of vines that must be Vietnam, his wedding, the appearance of a baby that he holds proudly in his arms. At a rodeo, he rides a horse, lariat whipped around his head. In wilderness, he squats with rifle in hand next to a dead buck. In many of the pictures, he's joined by a man who is handsome and dark, grinning as he stands, in waders, thigh-deep in a wild river, fishing rod in hand, or cooks over a fire in a wilderness camp, or straddles a horse.

Erica reaches for the picture frame before she asks, "That's my dad, isn't it?"

"Yeah. We did a lot together."

Sitting on the recliner, she studies each photo. It's easy to see why her father mesmerized her mother with his Hollywood looks and clean-cut cowboy sleekness. He poses for the camera with his arms loose, his legs slightly spread in a promise of strength and virility. He is David in denim.

"He was a pretty good looking guy, huh?" Dave calls from the kitchen.

He comes into the living room and hands Erica a cup of coffee. With a gnawed finger, he indicates a photo of Brad lofting a reel over a tumultuous, white-capped stream, "Look at that. When he was out in the wild, I tell you, he would wade out and just stand in a stream, and you'd hold your breath, waiting for him to cast, but he wouldn't. He'd just stand, watching—no, seeing—and listening—"

"Hearing," Erica supplies.

"Yeah," Dave agrees. "All those guys know how to fish—we all do—but Brad was different. He was"—he shies away from the tender words—"I guess you'd say it was all about living and breathing and being a part of the earth to him."

Dave's eyes water. When the phone rings, he says with relief, "I got to get that. Help yourself to breakfast."

In the kitchen, he picks up the cordless phone. "Hey, sweetheart," he says, going toward the back of the trailer. "How's it going?"

Erica tilts the montage toward the light, painfully aware of what she has missed in never knowing her father. Now that she has seen his smile, his eyes, his face—so much like hers—she wants to know everything about him. She wants to know *him*.

From the back of the trailer, she hears Dave say, "Yeah, what happened? . . . Christ, Renee, why'd you go and do that? "

She looks around, but the trailer offers no refuge from the conversation. Grabbing her parka, she steps outside. The wind catches her full in the face, chafing her cheeks and lips. She claps her hands over her ears. Squinting against the sting in her eyes, she walks around the corner of the trailer, hoping for some shelter.

Before her, the land opens up into an endlessness of color and shape. Sandstone formations of red and ocher and white rise skyward, their slopes carved into rounded gentle whirls or craggy blocks. Rocks perch atop other rocks, climbing into towers that are not always evenly balanced, so that it looks as if the whole load might topple. Even in the snow, every color in the palette seems to emanate from the stacks and the buttes beyond—reds, whites, grays, browns, purples, blues and greens.

She breathes in air that paralyzes her lungs. Where has she come to?

Dave steps up behind her. "What are you doing? Come back inside."

Erica does not take her eyes from the sight. "What is this? Where are we?"

"This is the Badlands."

"The what?"

"The Badlands. They stretch from here south to Lander."

"It looks like the Grand Canyon!"

Dave laughs. "There's some mighty deep canyons a couple of miles back in there, but nobody's ever called it grand."

"This is your ranch?"

"Yeah. My mom and dad's, really."

"How far does it go? How much land is there?"

"It's about thirty-five hundred acres, give or take."

"More than three thousand acres!" She laughs, delighted by the surfeit of it all. "How do you know where it ends? How long does it take you to drive from one end to the other?"

"It ain't that impressive. There's a lot bigger places around here."

Across the snow-scarred field, near the closest red rock behemoth, Erica sees a shimmer of light. It moves closer and closer, but she cannot name it. Spirit, life, knowledge. Only when it reaches the barbed wire fence does she recognize it as an animal.

"Is that your horse?" she asks.

Dave's voice drops. "Yeah, that's Rain." Then, "Why do you ask?"

"She's beautiful. It's a female, isn't it?"

"Yeah, a mare."

"Why did you name her Rain?"

His words sound forced, tight. "When I first got her, I thought she looked like rain. You know, when the sun is behind it, all silver-gold and shiny. She's darkened down now into a real palomino."

Erica watches the horse as she passes into the corral near the barn. Coming to the fence, Rain tosses her head and whinnies at Dave. Snow cyclones around her legs.

Erica laughs. "She knows her master."

"Come on," he says. "It's too cold out here."

He heads toward the trailer, but Erica does not move.

Rain whinnies again and then tracks along the fence in a trajectory that is parallel to Dave's. He disappears around the corner of the trailer, and Erica hears his boots on the cinder block porch.

The horse tosses her head, neighing again for Dave, something urgent now in her call.

For the third time that morning, Erica falls in love.

FIVE
ADVENT

Ronald Dailey arrives in Pindall on the first day of March. He comes from the west, breezing into town on the Yellowstone Highway and passing by the Morning Glory Motel, Mona's Kitchen, and the sign that reads PINDALL, WYOMING, POPULATION 658, ELEVATION 7,325. Further on, he travels past a Mexican restaurant built of pink adobe, the columned First Bank of Pindall, and two bars called the Sportsman's and the Silver Spur—which cause him to crane his neck.

The town's single traffic light shines red at the intersection of Yellowstone Highway and Main Street. To his left stands the Wickiup, its glimmering steel and plate glass far too modern for this sleepy place. Straight ahead, he can see ramshackle houses built on a slope so steep the whole mess looks as if it could tumble down at any instant.

The signal turns, and Ronald accelerates as he turns right. The tires of his BMW slip, and he lightens up on the gas. He's in the heart of town now, where a string of Western boutiques vie for customers. On one corner, a painted wooden Indian guards the entrance to a hair salon. A logging chain wraps around the Indian's ankles, anchoring him to the spot.

Ronald drives on, seeking more hospitable ground. A Conoco station beckons him to refill, and the sorry-looking Rambler Motel and Bar promotes itself in garish orange cinder block. Before he realizes it, he finds himself in a canyon of towering red rock. Mounds of plowed snow squeeze the highway into a trail. He checks his rearview mirror—that's it? That's Pindall, Wyoming? Surely he missed something. Surely there's more ahead. But the canyon stretches on, six or seven miles in length, and once he's free of that, he's in a lunar landscape of red and white knolls that rise eerily from the valley.

He turns the car around and heads back toward town. The fender rides only inches from the wall of the canyon, and sharp turns obstruct his view of the road ahead. As he comes out of the canyon, he spots the sawmill, located just where the canyon's walls fall back into flat land.

He slows down for a look—there's no shoulder on the highway—and takes in the long, narrow steel shed with corrugated roof and decks at either end. The administrative trailers crouch to one side, and a massive garage looms on the other, its bays gaping. The yard is just beyond. Most of the forklifts and trucks still carry the orange and brown WW logo of Wyoming Woodmill. He makes a left into the entrance, where a newly painted sign reads: WELCOME TO CASCADIA NORTHERN MILLS PINDALL WYO INSTALLATION, A DIVISION OF CASCADIA WORLDWIDE ENTERPRISES.

A movement to his right catches his eye, and he glances up to see a woman standing almost directly in front of his car. My God, why didn't he see her? It isn't just her proximity—she's no more than ten feet away—but the fact that her hair is so red his heart stops at the sight of it. She lifts a handwritten sign that reads, SAVE THE EARTH! STOP LOGGING!

Ronald stares, unmoving. He is no stranger to the environmental movement. Threats of sabotage and arson and bombs permeate this business, but mostly they translate into tree-sits by nutrient-starved vegetarians at which tie-dye and pot are plentiful. But last year, as Ronald was escorting a gang of Cascadia Northern bigwigs through a logging site, a logger plunged his chainsaw into a tree and hit a metal spike that some freak had buried deep in the heart of the wood. The chainsaw went mad, and the logger could not handle the kickback. He died in a pool of blood, sawdust and flayed flesh. Ronald puked on the spot.

He climbs out and approaches the woman with a casual smile that hides the jitter in his chest. Holding out a hand amply warmed by the car's heater, he says, "Hello. My name is Ronald Dailey."

She slips her hand from a knit glove, but her flesh is cold enough to send a chill right up his arm. "I'm Elise," she says simply. Her face, mottled by bluish veins, is beautiful. Stunning, in fact, despite the drippy nose and cold-chapped lips.

"It's awfully cold," Ronald remarks. "Are you waiting for someone? Is there some kind of rally?"

"I'm alone."

"Do you need a lift into town? I'm just going—"

"I leave after the day shift ends."

Good God, that's more than three hours from now. "Are you sure?" he asks in disbelief. "That's a long time—"

"If you'd like to join me," she manages through audibly chattering teeth, "we could talk about the adverse effects that logging has on—"

Ronald laughs, then quickly sobers. No sense in wrecking the good will between them—he's going to need it. "No, thank you," he says politely. "I need to be going. But I'd be interested in talking with you another day."

He walks back to the BMW, intending to leave, but something stops him. He's not quite able to believe what he's just seen, and he's tempted to try one more time, to see if he can't talk some sense into her, bring her in—literally—out of the cold. Leaning against the open door of the car, he offers, "Would you like to sit in here for a few minutes and warm up?"

She glances at the highway, then back to him. "I really shouldn't. I might miss someone."

"I'm afraid you'll catch pneumonia or something."

"All right." She has almost reached the car when she stops. "You have Oregon plates."

"That's right," Ronald says. "I'm the new General Manager at the mill. But, please, get in the car. It's warm."

She doesn't seem able to resist. When they're both seated in the BMW, Ronald boosts the heater fan up another notch. He can feel the cold radiate from her, but he also notices a fine smell, of perfume or soap, maybe.

"Can you feel the heat?" he asks.

"Yes, thank you."

"How long have you been protesting this mill?"

"Almost a year."

"Every day?"

"Every day that I can." She tips her head to look at him. "Were you hoping for less?"

Ronald tries to smile it away. "Not at all. But I think you'll find Cascadia Northern is an environmentally conscientious company. Perhaps you won't need to protest at all."

"All logging is an assault against nature."

It's a textbook response, but he pretends to consider. "As I understand it, the folks who work here are all locals, including our fellers. Some of them have worked at this mill for two or three generations—"

"What about you?" she asks.

"What?"

"You're not local."

He laughs. "Not yet."

As the car has grown warmer, her scent has blossomed. He thinks of lilacs, of something delicate and rich, something you would breathe in again and again. He studies her as much as he can without staring. Her eyes are green, and on her nose is a fine line of freckles.

She looks toward the mill, which is about a quarter of a mile up a sloped driveway. "The people here are honest and hardworking. It would be terrible if an unscrupulous corporation came here and exploited them."

Ronald hears the warning, but forges ahead. "Cascadia Northern does a good job of striking a balance between what it takes and what it leaves behind. Our reseeding program in Washington state—"

"Do you ever say anything that isn't company-sponsored?" she asks.

"I'm only passing on information that I think might be useful to you," he says tightly.

A car flashes by on the highway, and she says, "I shouldn't be sitting in here. Allowing this car to idle is a waste of fossil fuels."

She steps out of the BMW, shutting the door before he can speak. He jumps out his side, calling, "Wait! Can we talk again?"

She reaches her post and turns. "Of course," she replies evenly. "When you have moved beyond the corporate lies you've been told to spread and can speak honestly from your heart and your soul."

She lifts her sign toward a semi that screams south toward the canyon. Ronald retreats to his car, feeling bludgeoned. No one in Oregon warned him about her. Finally, he pulls his car onto the highway, northbound for Pindall. As he passes Elise, she plants the sign in front of her breasts like a shield.

In town, the blinking neon BUDWEISER sign at the Rambler Bar catches his eye. Just what he needs.

It's as dingy inside the Rambler as it is dismal outside. Cigarette smoke dirties the air, and an aroma of vomit, cherry liqueur, and decades-stale chewing tobacco rises from the wooden planking. A few scuffed tables huddle near a billiard table, while dark-wood booths line one wall. A scratchy country radio station whines from somewhere in the back, indicating, at least, some sort of life. Ronald takes a seat on a stool at the bar. There's an eerie vibe in here, as if this place has been hollowed out, the life and heart stripped from it.

His eyes adjust, and he catches movement near the sink. A waitress dumps melted Cheez Whiz over tortilla chips that lie in square cardboard sundae boats, jimmying the jar while wearing bulky oven mitts. "Be with you in a second," she sings.

She's nearly as pretty as Elise. Hazel eyes, chestnut hair cut short and sassy, pleasant curves under her sweater, but there's something about her that separates her from Elise. Hometown girl, he thinks.

When she comes his way, Ronald teases, "Hard job."

"It keeps crusting before I can pour it, it's so cold in here." Pushing a boat of nachos toward him, she asks, "What can I get you?"

"Hello, Shari." He reads her name from the embroidered apron she wears. "I'm Ronald Dailey, the new General Manager at the Cascadia Northern mill."

"Oh, so you're the man with the answers." One of her eyeteeth crowds pleasantly forward, making her smile sweet and sexy. "The boys have been wondering who would take over out there."

"So you know some of them?"

She laughs. "I know all of them. Where'd you come from?"

"Portland."

"Well, you've arrived just as winter is hitting its stride."

"It's nearly spring."

"Which is usually worse than winter."

"Is that so?" He's been driving all day on roads that confirm how long and cold the season must be. "Can I get a double Scotch, and another in fifteen minutes?" He reconsiders. "Never mind, just bring them both now."

Her eyes travel over him, taking in his sunglasses hanging on a cord around his neck, his gold watch, his argyle sweater. In the voice of a mother, she says, "You should eat first. You've driven a long way today."

"Hey, I have these." Ronald gestures toward the nachos. "That's plenty for me."

She turns away. As she pours in the shadows behind the bar, he gazes out the window at the street through Xeroxed ads for scrap metal dealers,

AA meetings, the Mormon food bank, and guns for sale that are Scotch-taped to the glass. He should have made a better go of it with Elise. He should have been more confident, more forceful. Even now, he thinks of her scent, of the color of her hair, of how slender her body must be beneath that heavy coat—

When Shari sets the glasses in front of him, he asks, "Say, do you know Elise? The woman at the mill?"

"I've never met her, if that's what you mean," Shari says. "I know of her. She's been down at the mill every day for quite a while now, unless the weather gets the better of her."

"Is she always by herself?"

"She's the only one I've ever seen out there."

"Do you know where she came from? Who she is?"

"She lives with Darnell Hillyard. Up near the Park. He's sort of, well, some folks say he's loco. I don't know—I think he's just like the rest of us. He's lived here too long. Doesn't come in to town too often, but he drops Elise off every morning."

"Really? And she lives with him?" Sweat tickles Ronald's armpits. Plots of eco-terrorism, of a full-scale assault on the mill, rush through his mind. Christ, why didn't the on-site transition team tell him this? Bastards.

Shari seems to sense his panic. "Did you look over Pindall before you moved here?" Flipping a hand toward his raincoat, she adds, "You won't need that here. We don't get much rain. You have snow tires?"

He looks ruefully at the coat, a camel-colored London Fog that drapes over the stool beside him, its plaid lining peeping out as if scared to show itself in such an unrefined place.

"Snow tires, eh?" he asks.

"Take your car to Vern Stacy's in the morning. You'll regret it if you don't."

He regrets it now.

The Rambler is slowly filling. Most of the arrivals are men, dressed in heavy coats and boots, and Ronald catches the telltale scent of sawdust. He switches drinks, ordering Bud now instead of Scotch, then stands and walks over to the table where they've landed. His beer conspicuously in hand, he asks, "Are you folks from the mill?"

"Sure," one says.

He introduces himself. The men shake hands, then pull away, eyes on their beers, their mouths an unyielding line.

"You think you can make the mill better?" The Head Sawyer, Jerry Whistledorn, challenges.

"I'm sure we can." Ronald summons his confidence. After all, he isn't a novice or a local hire. He's from corporate, from a mill three times the size of Pindall's. "We need new ideas, new ways of doing things, more efficient procedures. We have everything to make it work. We just need to make it happen."

"New ideas, huh? Like Wyoming Woodmill selling us out to Cascadia Northern?"

"You haven't been sold out," Ronald assures him. "Cascadia Northern takes care of its employees. Whatever you need, come to me, and I'll see what we can do." Yet when he returns to the bar, he says to Shari, "Another Scotch and a chaser."

"Don't you think you'd better eat? Walt's heating up the grill. He can put something on—"

"Just the Scotch, thanks."

She flashes away without answering, tray in hand, a city of bottles and mugs clinking together. She has her hands full now. About fifteen men and a few women have come into the bar. Most sit at tables, but a few shoot pool, and one party claims a booth. A tourist family wanders in, husband, wife and two kids who look like they've been thrown into hell. Shari seems to be the only help in the place. The proprietor, Robyn, does nothing but stand behind the counter and shout at the mangy old bartender, Walt, who appears to have permanently turned off his hearing aid.

After Ronald downs his third Scotch, he makes his way to the hallway that leads from the bar to the motel proper. He is about to push open the door of the Men's when he glimpses a shadowy figure loitering in the hallway.

A teenager leans against the wall beneath a NO SMOKING sign. He's a ratty kid—hair too stringy, legs too long, hand-me-down clothes from a more robust male. He puffs on a cigarette with the kind of hair-trigger calm a cat has before it pounces on its prey.

"Hello, there," Ronald offers in his most authoritative and confident tone.

"Howdy," the kid says.

Ronald keeps a sharp eye on the door as he uses the urinal. The kid's not about to catch him with his fly unzipped. When he leaves the restroom, the hallway is empty, the boy gone.

In the bar, Friday night is in full swing. Women eye him, trying to figure out who he might be. Let them look. He knows he's attractive, even as he approaches his mid-forties. His hair is thinning a bit on top, but it is a tawny blond, and his eyes are greenish-gray and nicely set. He carries with him the air of a man who has made it somewhere and is still going places.

He tries to catch the attention of Robyn, who is behind the bar yelling, "So I shot him in the ass. And you know what he did? He sat down!" Finally, he signs to Walt that he wants another Scotch. The old man delivers it with a snail's energy.

At the end of the bar, Shari is talking to the teenager, who slumps sullenly against the counter, eating a sandwich. When she drifts by Ronald again, he asks, "Who's the boy?"

"My son." She casts a tender glance in the hoodlum's direction, and Ronald sees the resemblance: the kid has the same clear eyes, high cheekbones, and diminutive build. "What about you?" she asks. "Is your family joining you here?"

"No," he laughs. "No, but I have a son in Portland. He's five."

"And yet you're here. That's pretty far away."

"Yeah, I'm here."

He busies himself with the Scotch. No need to tell her about his messy divorce. Last year, Becky had sought to deny Ronald custody, and Ronald hadn't fought it. He couldn't. After the eco-tage in the forest, he'd missed a week of work, then a month, then longer. Cascadia Northern demoted him, sent him down like a losing pitcher to the minors. In the end, it was easier to hope that God will strike Becky dead in the near future than to argue with her.

But, Christ, he loves Craig with a fierceness that burns in his empty stomach far more than the Scotch. That little boy—white blond hair soft as cotton, lively blue eyes, a smile that can set off fireworks—runs rampant through his heart. The kid's a whirlwind, always moving from one thing to another, only skin and bones that poke out of his clothes and grow overnight. Ronald cups his hand and wonders if it would still sit gracefully on Craig's head, nearly swallowing it. Even if it does, how long before Craig becomes someone else?

Smoothing out a clean napkin, he sketches a circle filled with rectangles and squares. "Know what this is?" he asks Shari.

She considers. "Some kind of medicine wheel?"

"I'm not sure what that is," he says. "No, this is a logging pattern."

"I'm not sure what *that* is."

He laughs. "In the big mills, they have laser scanners—log x-rays, if you will—that spot all the knots and imperfections. Then the computer generates the best possible pattern for sawing the log, the one that saves the most money and utilizes the most wood. Like this." He explains that the circle is a log end, the rectangles and squares boards to be sawn. "When the log is cut, the laser guides the saw. It makes for a clean cut."

"What do you know?" she muses. "You plan to do that here?"

"Not here." He rotates the napkin, looking at the sketch from all angles. He could tell her so much more. He knows so much more. "You don't have sophisticated equipment here."

"Oh," she says, as if truly disappointed. "I just thought—"

That Cascadia Northern would come into this community and revive the mill? That it would improve the equipment, and the pay, and the hours, and the men's lives? That it would take an interest in the location, instead of simply exploiting the few resources left in this part of the world for its own profit and then stripping down and dismantling the mill in the end? He remembers Elise's words: *When you have moved beyond the corporate lies you've been told to spread.* He wads the napkin and tosses it onto the bar.

"You sure do have a fine life here," he says brightly. "You know, Shari, I'm going to be a stronger, saner man here. Yellowstone National Park for my back yard. All that wildlife, all that beauty."

"I hope you find what you want," she offers.

He chooses to ignore the ring of sadness in her voice and charges ahead. "I've taken a house on Ute Street. But I haven't seen it yet. It was all arranged between Cascadia and a realtor in this area. They sent me the key. I hope it's nice."

"Oh, you don't need to worry about that." She wipes up water rings from the counter. "Pindall's a true mountain town—more vertical than horizontal. The farther up the mountain you go, the better the view, so it stands to reason that the houses get nicer. Up where you are, it's all dream homes that some rich vacationer built before he lost interest. The house you're renting's one of the nicest."

"How do you know which house I'm renting?"

"It's a small town." She laughs. "Give it a month, and you'll know where everybody lives, too."

"I won't get lost, will I?" he asks. "Everything seems kind of wild around here."

"Oh, no," she soothes. "Really, it's all pretty easy—in fact, embarrassingly easy. I think they thought that everyone who lives here would be dumb as a post. The main street through town is Main Street, and the highway to Yellowstone is the Yellowstone Highway. And if you're worried about finding the mill come Monday morning, it's on Sawmill Road."

He laughs, then says, "If it's that easy, one more Scotch."

"Are you sure—?"

"No, I don't want anything to eat." He grins, a smile that he knows charms. "But as soon as I have my kitchen set up, I'll cook you the best meal you've ever had. How about it? Something French, maybe?"

"Around here, we don't eat or drink anything we can't spell." She waves toward the kitchen. "Which makes for a mighty short menu."

Ronald laughs again. "Say, come with me now and show me my house," he says. "I promise I won't keep you away from here too long. I just don't want to get lost my first night here."

Shari wavers, a whole gamut of emotions running over her face— the most noticeable of which looks like fear. Surprised, Ronald starts to retreat, but Robyn has overheard. "Go on ahead, Shari," she shouts. "Donna Rae's just sitting over there on her butt." To Ronald, she says, "What kind of car you driving?"

"A BMW 735i."

"Well, now," Robyn says. "You be awful careful driving that kind of car, Mr. Ronald. Especially since it's got out-of-state plates. Macky's sure to think you're a tourist with a wad of dough in your pocket. Once he knows who you are, he'll leave you alone."

"Thanks for telling me. Who's Macky?"

"Our deputy." She drags on a cigarette and blows the smoke more or less in his face. "You see, our town's got both a chief of police and a fire chief, but just one deputy. And that's Macky, whose mother is Shoshone. So, around here, we say we got two"—she vees her fingers to illustrate— "many chiefs and half an Indian."

Shit, Ronald thinks.

He smiles obligingly as Robyn hoots with laughter. After he pays his tab, he goes over to the men at the tables for one last round of handshakes and assurances, feeling decidedly less confident than he had earlier.

Outside, Shari whistles at his BMW. "I hope you don't mind following my broken-down old pickup," she says. "It's more rust than metal anymore."

"Lead the way."

He navigates the hill behind her, shutting the heat vents against the smell of truck exhaust. At the house, he unlocks the door and switches on the entryway lights. "Wow," Shari says as she walks inside, and Ronald agrees. The house is a wonder of glass and wood, with a peaked ceiling above a spectacular great room. A massive moss rock fireplace angles across one corner, and a sliding glass door leads to a spacious balcony.

Yet it is so cold that ice has formed on the inside of the windows.

"Did you call ahead and have someone light your pilot?" Shari shivers.

"I didn't think of it." Shit, it must be thirty degrees.

"Well, you'll need to light it, then. And you'll probably need to turn on the water. Did anybody tell you where that is?"

"No. My furniture arrives tomorrow. Maybe somebody will show up then."

She gives him a look as if she finds him pathetic. "You better spend the night at the Rambler. At least you'll have Robyn's idea of heat."

"No, no, I'll be all right."

"Well, you can always build a fire."

He eyes the fireplace balefully, a memory of dark mornings in a plywood shack in British Columbia, his father lighting the woodstove for the boys before he left for work. Bare feet on plank flooring, earaches, green-goop-oatmeal for breakfast.

Fortunately, Shari takes pity on him. Kneeling, she pushes up the sleeves of her sweater and expertly stacks newspapers, kindling and wood. She looks good, Ronald notices, crouched on the floor, reared back on cowboy boots that have seen better days, the seams of her jeans strained.

"Thanks," he says. "I never was a Boy Scout. I'm Canadian."

She laughs, wipes her hands on her thighs, and drifts toward the sliding glass door. Pindall's lights twinkle beyond.

Ronald joins her. "I'm going to love it here, I know. It's just a lot smaller than I thought it would be." He tells her of driving through earlier that afternoon.

"Well, you missed most of Main Street," she says. "You know, where the traffic light is. It breaks off from the Yellowstone Highway and goes on for three more blocks west of the Wickiup."

"The grocery store? I see. And what all is on Main Street?"

"There's the All-Nite Grub & Go—which actually closes at ten—and TruValue hardware store, and LadyBug Western Wear." She recites it as if she's doing a walking tour. "There's David's Variety, too—you can rent VCR tapes there—and a few small businesses. Insurance and real estate and the like. Across the street, there's the Chamber of Commerce and the youth rec center, which shares the parking lot with the liquor store."

"Good planning, that."

"And then there's the Fixin' Block."

"What's that?"

"Well, the police are on the second floor of the library, and the fire station is right next door. Next is the Methodist Church. And just before the forest, the street ends at Vern Stacy's Autobody and Garage. So, you have the cops and the EMTs, and the library ladies, and God, and your mechanic all on the same block. There aren't many problems that can't be fixed by visiting one or the other of them."

They laugh together. She's a sweet one, she is. Warmth seeps from the fire. It will never be enough to fill the cavernous space of the living room, but he'll make do with his sleeping bag and a bottle of whiskey—and Shari, if she'll have him.

"Let's go see the Park this weekend, Shari," he says.

"The interior roads don't open for another couple of months."

"You don't say? Well, then, save me a date in, let's see, um . . .?"

"May," she says wistfully. "It would be May."

"Say, do you know where there's a good running path? I'm a runner. Forty miles a week."

"Forty miles a week," she says, "and you always end up back at the spot where you started."

He laughs, and she motions toward the front of the house. "Up beyond," she says, "there's a meadow, up on the ridge, more or less just out your door. It's a really beautiful meadow, especially in summer when the wildflowers bloom." She falters, drawing in an audible breath. "There's a path that runs the length of the meadow and then goes into the forest for a stretch, and actually comes out next to the highway pretty close to the sawmill. Cross the highway, and you can run parallel to the mill property and over the bluff and down into the west side of town. Cross the bridge in Asa Pindall Park—down by the creek—and you can follow it by the Methodist Church and the garage and back here. When the snow melts, it should be an easy run."

"Something to look forward to, then." Looking helplessly around at the empty spaces, he says, "I'd offer you coffee, but—"

"I need to get back to work."

"Why don't you come back when your shift's over? I'd like to talk more."

"I have to take Jason home," she says flatly.

Ah, yes, the raggedy son. Ronald wonders how many times Jason has been rounded up by the part Indian, part whatever deputy. The kid simply looks the part.

Once Shari has gone, Ronald wanders onto the balcony, where it's as warm outside as it is inside. He can see the full town now, even the part he missed this afternoon. He traces the rackety roar of Shari's truck down the slippery hill to the Rambler, and hears a wedge of music from the jukebox when she opens the Rambler's door. Sounds echo sharply in this valley—the slam of a car door, voices, the barking of dogs, a horse's neigh from somewhere surprisingly nearby.

Suddenly, a weird drone drifts through the air, some kind of Gregorian chant, coming from higher up the mountain. It triggers a memory of Elise's parting words: *When you can speak honestly from your heart and your soul.* It's no use wondering when that will be—both his heart and soul have been shut down for a good, long time. It is then that he realizes that the night is so dark in this corner of the world that only the hard glitter of stars distinguishes the sky from the black, unyielding earth below.

SIX

MY HEART FLIES FREE

Jason ditches school at least once a week by hiding out in the Boys' Locker Room. At 8:15, half an hour after the bell has sounded at Pindall Consolidated School, where all thirteen grades gather daily, he slips out through the door at the back of the gym. He casts one furtive look around the teachers' parking lot, then sets off up the slope on which all of Pindall teeters. He doesn't want to see or talk to anyone. As if it's not bad enough to be the only son of the only man to die in the Derby and the only grandson of the only man to die in the sawmill, now there's that bitch from Ohio.

He's breathing heavily by the time he reaches the ridge, so he pauses to urinate into the leafless lilac on one side of Ronald Dailey's garage, right beside where Ronald parks his BMW. Jason hates the way Ronald and his mother play around. She drinks with him, something she rarely does with the Rambler's other customers. She shoots pool with him, and Jason notices what he is always reminded of by the eyes of the men in the bar: the blouses she wears are too skimpy and her jeans too tight.

He comes to the highest house on the hill, which belongs to a couple of former monks who've retired in Pindall. The house, built like a cathedral, tinkles as he passes. Along the wrap-around porch hang wind chimes of crystal that splatter prisms across the wooden planks. Heavy copper pipes bang out a doorbell chime in the breeze. A clay-colored statue of a priest holds a bowl of water for the birds.

Those two have to be gay. Who else would decorate with little deer and rabbit sculptures when there's a whole forest full of deer and rabbits just a stone's throw from the front door? Of course, no one knows for sure, because the monks maintain a vow of silence, some carryover of monastery mania. They smile and nod and use fluttery hand gestures to communicate, thinking that's enough. Once when he was sacking their groceries at the Wickiup, Jason grew annoyed by their fuck-the-rest-of-the-world attitude.

"What's with you two?" he had demanded. "God got your tongue?"

One of the monks, an old guy with white hair and blue eyes, had smiled, calm and unruffled. The younger one, who looks like a weather-beaten scarecrow, just stared. Big surprise, neither answered.

Jason has climbed nearly to the crest of the hill, on his way to the meadow where his father lost his life, when something behind him attracts his attention. He doesn't know what it is—a motor revving, a logging truck burping its jake brake, the sound of someone *going somewhere*—and he decides to walk past the sawmill and down the canyon. He scrambles down the hill, giving wide berth to the school. Assistant Principal Hamilton has been known to troll Pindall's streets and round up truants in the bed of his pickup truck.

He passes Rob Grenville's Outfitters, where his father used to sell the knives he made. In a case in the back, the last few unsold knives lay on a bed of white felt, near a lined index card that reads, "Knives by Brad Brock, local legend." Jason owns only a skinner created by his father. The handle is a chunk of antler, and his father' signature, BB, appears on the blade. He carries the knife with him everywhere, even to school, hidden in a sheath beneath his shirttails.

Right next to Rob's is the Greenbow Boutique. As Jason peers into Rob's shop, a second story window in the Greenbow creaks open with the sound of ripped sheet metal. The odor of piss and cranberries wafts over Jason in a downward gust of wind. He steps back and looks up.

It's Johnny Hart, that worthless old alky. An orange tabby cat lounges on the windowsill, looking sourly at Jason.

"Hey, kid," Johnny heaves in a voice that sounds as rusted as the window. "Do you have a quarter? For . . . just a dollar? I need a dollar or two. My cat needs food."

"Oh, come on, Johnny," Jason calls. "You'll just spend it on booze. Everybody knows that."

"The cat, his name's Tiger. Needs food."

"Tiger, huh? That's original. Here, kitty, kitty." The cat flicks back its ears. "Listen, Johnny, come down to the store this afternoon and I'll give you some food for him."

"Just a dollar," Johnny whines. "My cat . . . needs . . ."

"Come down to the Wickiup," Jason says patiently. "You know where it is. Find me and I'll get you some cat food."

"It ain't no fair," Johnny mutters. "Marie used to, but now it's too hard to . . ."

Johnny shuts the window, and Jason calls, "Well, God bless you, then, Johnny." Johnny won't come to the Wickiup. He'll be back in the Rambler by noon, downing whatever Walt is generous enough to donate. The cat'll go hungry again.

Jason rounds the curve leading from town, so that Pindall is behind him, out of sight. The sawmill is directly ahead of him, to his right, tucked away on the last flat space before the canyon walls heave up and squeeze out the land. A plume of smoke snakes from its stack, smelling of scorched rubbery pine. Jason moves past the fortress of the mill, past the yards where the finished lumber is stacked, toward the gates. He stops just short of them when he sees Elise stretched out on her lawn chair, her head back, bathed by sun, her mouth slightly open as she sleeps. Oh, man, she should be on a magazine cover. Preferably *Playboy*. Today, she cradles one of her signs in crossed arms: TREES ARE LIFE. LOGGING IS MURDER.

He stops and searches inside his insulated vest for a match. Elise's skirt is dotted with round, feminine faces wrapped in bright scarves, each one outlined by heavy black. She wears a heavy, cabled ivory sweater that rises and collapses as she breathes. She keeps a Navajo blanket around her shoulders to ward off the blustery March chill. In the sun, her hair is the color of a new penny.

He smokes and waits for her to notice him, tugging at his jeans to relieve the pressure. She wakes when a rickety old Cadillac speeds around the corner, heading for Pindall. Jumping to her feet, she pans her sign for the driver to read. As she turns, she sees Jason. The sign falters for a moment, then she lifts it toward him, as if thwarting an enemy ambush. He drops the butt of his cigarette and smashes it into the earth. Elise glances toward it. Jason hurriedly picks it up, puts it in his pocket.

"Howdy," he says.

"Come join me." She sits on the chair, leaning forward, her sign resting against her shins.

"I don't think you missed anybody, while you were sleeping."

"I don't know what's wrong with me today." She lifts her arms and arches her back, stretching, and Jason sees the roundness of her breasts beneath her sweater. "I must not be drinking enough water or something. I don't usually sleep on the job."

"Somebody pays you to do this?" The surprise in his voice echoes in the quiet morning.

"No." She laughs. "It's a higher calling."

Jason has nothing to say. All he wants to do is to ask her if Darnell Hillyard really has an arsenal big enough to blow up Colorado, which most people agree wouldn't be much of a loss. Or did she blow her brain on drugs in the seventies, when Angel Dust and mushrooms were as easy to buy as candy? Or is she really an heiress from Jackson who protests at the sawmill to humiliate her father, a lumber mogul? Jason has heard all the rumors. To him, each one offers as many erotic possibilities as the next.

"Are you here to apply for a job?" she asks.

"I wouldn't work here," Jason says. "My grandfather died here in the Worst Accident in the History of Wyoming's Sawmills. My father wouldn't set foot inside it, either."

At the mention of his father, he starts to sweat. Jesus, why did he bring him up, the last person in the world he wants to talk about? And even though it's true about his grandfather, he doesn't know the details. His grandmother never talks about it, and his mother seems to know no more about it than he does. All Jason has is a vague certainty that his grandfather ended up looking like sausage and that his father used it as an excuse to escape from Pindall and fuck his family.

"It's a dangerous place." Elise digs through a canvas bag at her feet. On the bag is a drawing of a kooky-looking dog scratching its neck with sharp-pointed toes. The name under the cartoon reads BOOTH. She pulls out a book and opens it.

"'We plant the seeds of our death from our first moment of waking,'" she reads, "'when we cry out to our parents to give us what we demand. But what they give us, in almost all instances, will not sustain our spirits or make them grow healthy or strong. So we live the lives of the stunted plant. We want, we thirst, we crave sun and light, only to know rootlessness, cold, drought, and the darkness of the misunderstood. And so we commit spiritual suicide through our dimwitted dedication to routine, through corporate work that skins our spirits from us like the tanner strips the mink, through the ritual debasement of capitalist and Judeo-Christian traditions.'"

"Cool," Jason says. "Did you write it?"

"No, a professor of mine did. Brilliant man."

Elise waves her sign at a purplish Volkswagen bus, which toots in response. Two longhaired men flip the bird toward the mill. One blows a kiss to Elise. "That's the way!" Elise shouts. "Yes!"

Jason knows them—of course, he knows them, since he knows everybody in town. They paint houses by morning and deal pot pipelined in from Colorado to the high school kids in the afternoons. He wonders if weird old Darnell will show up. Darnell lives up on the Park boundary where, Robyn has told Jason, only God can find him. He has seen Darnell plenty of times in the Wickiup. He's a frowning, furry man who glides noiselessly along the aisles. Sometimes Grandma and Darnell go into her office and close the door.

"What college did you go to?" Jason asks Elise.

"It was a correspondence course. I wrote to a Ph.D. in Maine who served as my spiritual guide and mentor. He ran a one-man university, you know, a one-on-one experience at the time when the big universities were enrolling four hundred students in a class. It was a novel idea. Absolutely brilliant. We wrote to each other for two years and then"—she laughs, as if she is about to reveal a marvelous secret—"we realized we had fallen in love."

"Through letters?"

"A beautifully written passage is a powerful aphrodisiac. We actually agreed not to meet, or to send each other pictures, because we didn't want to fall prey to judging each other by our looks. You know, get hung up on physical appearance. Is he handsome? Is she pretty? Are his feet too big? We were on a metaphysical plane."

"Yeah?" Jason says, envisioning an actual aircraft.

"The first time I saw him was at Town Hall in his little town of Rockport. We met there, in front of the judge who was to marry us. It was an act of faith for both of us."

"So what happened?" he asks eagerly. He wants the professor to be hideous, a mass of acne scars, with no chest hair, scrawny arms, and enormous feet. He wants Elise to run, screaming in horror, rather than allow the dweeb to touch her.

"We moved to his cabin on a lake, and I saw loons for the first time in my life. Autumn was amazing, with so many deciduous trees. Truly glorious." She laughs again, and he wishes he could see what she does. "Oh, that first winter was wonderful. We were off the grid, you know— no electricity, no telephone, total isolation. We just talked through it all, the ocean crashing against the cliffs below, the snow beating against the windows."

He thinks of the rare occasions when his dad was home during the winter. His mother would curl up next to him on the couch, as close as she could be, always touching him, like she would die if she didn't keep some contact. "So you're married?" he asks.

"Not any longer." She flashes her sign at a green Oldsmobile. "Our realities didn't coalesce. And his children visited holidays and summers. They weren't at the same point in the universe as their father or me."

He nods, as if he knows something about it. Then, he says, "Wait a minute, aren't we all at the same point in the universe? I mean, like sitting here. You're here, on planet earth, and so am I. We're at the same point in the universe, right?"

She tilts her head. "But we grow, we change, we're always evolving. Spiritually, that is, and intellectually and psychically. And we do that in different ways, at different times. We move independently of others within the universe of the mind."

"I wish I was about a million light years away."

"Really? There aren't many places left in the world like this."

He doesn't know. He's never been farther away than Denver. "Did you get divorced by mail, too?" he asks. "Or was it in another universe?"

She laughs. "No, it was through the courts. I'd already met my third husband by then."

Jason starts in surprise. "So the professor was number two?" He wonders if his mother will marry that many times. "Boy, you must have trouble keeping track of all your last names."

"I never changed my name. That's an outdated concept, a patriarchal holdover. Women are no longer chattels."

He doesn't know what a chattel is, but he's glad his mother is still outdated. "My last name's Brock."

"You're Marguerite's grandson, aren't you?"

"Yeah. I'm Jason. How do you know Grandma?"

"She and I are old friends," Elise says. "Jason. That's strong. Are you named after your father?"

He starts sweating again. "No," he says. "After . . . well, I guess, nobody."

"Jason was a great adventurer in Greek mythology. A warrior and a king, and actually a bit of a cad. It's a powerful name."

She stretches out in her lawn chair, drawing her shoulder-length hair up on her head and letting it slip away. Jason breathes a sigh of relief that she didn't pursue his family history. Maybe she is the one person in Pindall who doesn't know about Erica Wiegel.

"Why do you protest here?" he asks. "I mean, there are bigger mills somewhere else. You could be flashing your signs to hundreds of people."

"It doesn't matter how big the mill is," Elise says. "All logging is an assault on nature."

Jason mulls this over as he watches new studs jerk along the green chain. It takes guts to hate the mill, and his father is the only one he's ever known to get away with it. Jason's friends's fathers work there; his teachers's husbands work there; the customers at the Wickiup work there. It's sacred ground in Pindall.

"What sort of degree did you get?" he asks Elise.

"What?"

"What sort of degree did the college professor give you?"

"Oh," she says. "That never worked out, either, although we're still good friends."

Jason stays with Elise through lunch, sitting on the cold ground beyond the jagged asphalt of the road. He bends one knee and then the other up to his chin, trying to find a way to stay warm. Elise offers him a portion of her lunch—crusty French bread and cheese and grapes, hardly what Jason would call a meal, and something from a thermos that is greener than anything Jason would voluntarily swallow.

"No thanks," he says.

"Don't let yourself get dehydrated," she warns. "It's easy enough to do."

They lapse into silence, which is mirrored by the road, where not a single car passes. The quiet makes Jason twitchy. At last, above his head, he spies a white contrail in the sky. "Look," he says. "An airplane."

"We don't see those too often, do we?"

"My second grade teacher used to let us go outside whenever she heard an airplane. For some of the kids, those airplanes were the only ones they'd ever seen."

"For you, too?"

He shrugs, embarrassed by his backwardness. "Yeah."

"You're so lucky to have been raised without the distractions of technology and commercialism. I grew up in California. There was no innocence there."

"California," Jason breathes, and all the possibilities of that rapturous state come to him. Women and beaches and movies and highways jam-packed with cars. He feels so hick, so redneck. Finally, inspiration strikes. "There's a couple of guys who live in town who never talk. They took a vow of silence or something."

"They don't speak?"

"No, they use hand signals that nobody understands."

"Can you imagine a connection so pure as to be free of language?" She abandons her sign. "What sort of energy must arise from the visceral power of non-verbal communication! I'm envious of such harmony. It's so rare. Almost unheard of, in this world."

"It's bullshit," Jason argues. "I mean, how do you tell each other, we're out of milk or the cat threw up?"

Elise places a finger on his mouth to hush him. She takes his face in both her hands and looks straight into his eyes. Without warning, the ground beneath him shifts, and he thinks of spilling his guts, literally, of his intestines and stomach falling to the pavement, although his heart lobs upward, into his throat. She releases him.

"What did you feel?" she asks.

"What did you say?" No message had telegraphed itself into his brain. Flustered, he pulls at his pant legs. His arms and legs feel undone. His boots slip along the loose gravel.

"I didn't say anything, Jason. I just felt. Openness, trust, affection. What did you feel?"

"Weird."

She laughs, not at all disappointed by his reply.

A car approaches from the south, and Jason senses an opportunity. Heart pounding, he stands and thrusts the sign over his head. He hopes it is not someone he knows. The news would be around Pindall, and into his mother's ears, in a matter of minutes. She has told him to go to school, threatening to attend classes with him if he doesn't wise up. Then, again, he hopes he knows the driver. Maybe then everyone would realize that Pindall is such a piss hole that anyone with any brains would be out protesting it.

The car whizzes past, without reaction. Jason lowers the sign and places it at Elise's feet.

"Good job," she says.

"You told me to do that, silently, right? Through ESP?"

"You told yourself to do that," she says quietly. "Without any help from me. You're reaching beyond yourself."

"Yeah." He kicks the ground a couple of times. "I guess."

It's getting on toward two. At two-thirty, the school buses will start to load, and within minutes, number 7 will pass this way, carrying the kids who live on ranches in the Badlands. At three, his grandma will expect him at the Wickiup. He needs to leave, but he doesn't want Elise to think he is pressured by the ritual debasements of capitalist America, the most frightening of which is his grandmother's wrath.

Amazingly, though, Elise understands. She smiles up at him and says, "It's been a pleasure spending today with you."

"You, too," he says.

"Maybe we'll talk again another day?"

"Yeah," he says, pleased. "That'd be good."

As he walks, he feels stuck in a heartless rut of gravity that pulls him back to town. He stops and lights a cigarette, watching the forklift at the sawmill laboriously rearranging the lumber. That's all some of the men at the mill do, hour after hour. Rearrange this stack, shift that stack.

Jesus, what a lousy place to be stuck in the universe.

That evening, as he's sweeping Aisle 3 of the Wickiup, Jason hears the back door near his grandmother's office open and close. The front doors of the store are locked at this hour, and once Jason finishes cleaning, he will lock up the back and hike down to the Rambler to meet his mother. Glancing up at one of the convex mirrors that his grandmother had installed to keep the tourists from shoplifting, he spies Erica Wiegel in the back hallway.

His hands clench around the broom, grinding its splinters into his palms. He keeps sweeping, letting her come to him.

Her boots click on the linoleum as she walks up the aisle behind him. Without turning, he says, "Store's closed."

"That's okay," she says easily. "I'm not here to buy."

"Then you need to leave."

She steps around in front of him, blocking the broom. He turns and starts to sweep where he has just swept.

"I wonder if we could talk," she says.

"I don't have anything to say." It's a lie—he wants to scream at her, he wants to shove the broom into her face, he wants to rip apart the store, pull out his hair, beat his own chest until it is bruised and bloody.

"Then I'll talk." Still behind him, she says, "I don't want to hurt you, Jason. I never wanted to hurt you or your mom."

He says nothing, focusing on the rhythmic movement of the broom.

"I came here because I wanted to know," she says. "What he was like, how he talked or acted, even what he looked like—"

"What, don't you remember? Wasn't he with you every winter?"

"I never met him. He was never a part of my life."

Jason swings around toward her. She's wearing that stupid cowboy hat that covers half her face, and a down-filled coat, and her little-girl knitted scarf and mittens. She looks young, even younger than he is, but she's almost as tall as he is, close to six feet. "You didn't know him?"

"Didn't anybody tell you that?" she says. "I didn't even know what he looked like until Dave showed me a picture of him."

He looks toward the shelves of cookies to his right. Every time his mother has tried to talk to him, he's run to his room and slammed the door, or gone outside to the barn, or just ignored her. At the store, he avoids his grandmother by hiding out and smoking near the dumpster.

Erica speaks again. "Your mom and our grandmother"—Jason winces—"have been so nice to me. Grandmother gave me a quilt. I like her, Jason. I like your mom, too, but I really like Grandmother."

"That's not what she's called," he growls. "If you knew her, you'd know that."

Erica gives a shivery laugh. "I don't feel right calling her Grandma yet. I'll get there."

"I wish you'd get out of here instead."

"Well, I'm not going to." She speaks in the voice of a teacher who is explaining something to a slow student. "So you had better get used to me."

Her arrogance irritates him. "Why are you here?" he demands. "Did you think he had money? Or do you want Grandma's fortune? Well, let me tell you, we've never had more than next week's gas money, and Grandma's too smart to be swindled out of her money."

Erica's mouth opens, but Jason doesn't let her speak. "I suppose you thought we would just lie down and say, oh, she's so smart. She's from Ohio, from the big city. She's gone to college. Isn't she special?"

"That's just stupid."

"Yep," Jason says. "Well, we's jes' stupid as logs o' shit in ol' Wy-O-min'."

"I wasn't aware of that until just now," Erica sparks. "Listen, he was our father. I've always known that. Since I was a baby. It was never a surprise to me, and I'm sorry it was a surprise for you. But that's not my doing."

"Are you calling him a liar?"

"I don't know," she shoots back. "Maybe he was, if he didn't tell your mom about me—"

"What do you know about it? You said you never met him."

"I'm not the one jumping to all sorts of conclusions."

Jason feels a rush of fury. "So what do you want me to do? Jump up and down because I have a"—he fills the word with venom—"*sister?*"

She pushes the hat back, and he sees what he hates about her: the dark eyes, the black eyebrows, the image of Brad Brock in her face. Why isn't there a trace of his father in his own?

"Let me tell you something," she says. "I already have a brother and a sister. Their names are Royce and Natalie, and they're twins. They're nine years younger than me because my mom didn't marry until I was eight. I love them both, they're the best brother and sister I could want. But I've always wondered about that nine-year gap. Most people have kids every two or three years, and I always thought"—she swallows—"I've always felt that there was somebody else. Somebody closer to my age who would bridge that gap. I always knew it. And there is. It's you."

Jason has no idea what to say. The disappointment on her face is too familiar—it's how his grandmother looks when she scolds him—and the hope too evident.

"Well," he says at last. "At least your mother had the sense to get married before she got knocked up again."

Erica's face freezes. She turns on the heels of her too-new cowboy boots and walks down Aisle 3. A few seconds later, he hears the back door slam.

He leans against the broom handle, his chest folding in on itself. He pants like a dog a few times, and tears sting his eyes. One rolls down his cheek, and he runs his hand under his nose so hard that it feels as if he's jammed his nostrils into his brain. Straightening up, he swipes at the packages of cookies on the shelves, scattering an armload of Chips Ahoy! and Oreos that he'll have to spend the next half-hour restacking.

Who in the fuck does she think she is, anyway?

On Friday evening, Jason, Terry Holt and Russ Whistledorn cruise Main Street in Terry's Dodge Colt, driving the eleven blocks again and again. At the south end of town, they swing around in the parking lot of the Rambler, where Jason's mother's truck is parked. She won't leave until early morning—she waits tables until two nearly every Friday and Saturday—which gives Jason plenty of time before he has to report to the Rambler. When he was younger, his mother used to sleep until noon on Sundays, leaving him to his own devices. He learned to fry grasshoppers, blow eggs, and control small fires. Now that his father is dead, his mother doesn't sleep in. She joins Jason in bathrobe and moccasins to watch television on Sunday mornings, drinking tea and working crossword puzzles in pen, no turning back if she's wrong. She sticks her feet under him for warmth and wiggles her toes, trying to get a reaction from him. Jason knows she wants him to talk to her about that day, but he just can't. Not yet.

Oh, God, that day. His mother was off singing, as she always does, but he was with his father, who was saddling Rain and talking with Dave Phillips, who hobbled along on his crutches. Entrusted with the reins, Jason had paid little attention. He's never loved horses the way his father did, and he had no interest in Sawmill Days or the Derby. He could have said anything—I love you, don't leave this winter, Mom is so sad when you go—but he didn't. He doesn't even remember what he said.

After the accident, his father's body was laid out on a gurney in the police station. His mother sat beside him, clutching his limp hand. At the door, Jason stood with his grandmother, who kept a hand on his shoulder to support him. Other faces—a couple of volunteer firefighters, the

Methodist minister, Macky Bain, Dave—swirled around them, shadowy and half-drawn. But it is the memory of the sound that unhinges him, even now.

His mother was weeping—violent, harsh sobs that he has never heard before or since. His grandmother went over to cradle his mother's head against her breast. It was then that Jason heard a second voice calling out in despair.

His own.

His mother is a mess, now. All those years when his father worked away from home during the winter, his mother was capable, in control. For years, she stuck her head under the hood of the pickup and popped hoses off without hesitation, put animals out of their misery with a single shot, and cleared dead trees with a chainsaw. She made breakfast, signed his report cards, drove him to the hospital in Riverton when his appendix ruptured. Now, she burns bacon, leaves her wet socks stuffed in her boots beside the door, breaks things. She keeps the door to her bedroom open— something she has never done before—as if she's waiting for someone to come home, but she never hears Jason come in, even on the nights she hasn't worked at the Rambler. It's not him she's waiting for.

On the east end of town, Terry turns the car around in the dirt lot between the Methodist Church and Vern Stacy's Autobody and Garage. They drive down Main Street again.

"It's dead," Russ says, chewing on a hamburger from the All Nite Grub & Go.

"No shit," says Terry.

Jason sits in the back seat by himself, eating fries. He doesn't really like Terry and Russ, but they usually have something to drink or smoke. Their fathers both work at the sawmill, and they tell the tales of their fathers's scars with pride. Terry's father once laid his thigh open with a peavey. Russ's father spent two years in a back brace after a pile of green lumber fell on him and crushed three vertebrae.

Terry turns the car around at the Rambler, and they head down Main Street again. "We could find Buddy Houser, see if he'd get us something," he says. "What you got, Russ?"

"Nothin'," Russ says, still eating.

"You got any money, Jason?" Terry calls over his shoulder.

"Five," Jason says.

"Shit," Terry says. "What'll five buy us? Where's all your money from your bag boy job?"

They both laugh. His job is a great source of amusement for them, destined as they are for manly undertakings at the mill.

"Hey," Russ calls into the back seat. "Does your hot tamale of a new sister have money?"

"Shut up," Jason growls.

"My mom told my dad she'd take a shotgun to him if any extra kids show up at our door," Terry says. "You think she's the only one, Jason? Maybe there's a whole bunch of others somewhere."

"Fuck you," Jason says as Terry and Russ laugh. He's so sick of thinking of Erica. If she doesn't leave town soon, he will.

This week, Jason has missed two days of school. He spent both of them with Elise, sitting on the ground beside her lawn chair and book bag, watching the curves of her body when she lifted the signs over her head. She always keeps the book by her ex-professor ex-husband in her bag. Jason has tried to determine the professor's name from brief glimpses of it. To ask to see it seems too bold, and besides, he's afraid she'd expect him to read it and talk about it. He has discovered that one or the other of the names was Malcolm. No wonder the marriage didn't work.

"Who's that?" Russ asks, motioning toward Vern Stacy's garage.

"Who do you think, asshole?" Terry says. "It's Juliana I-fuck-anybody Stacy."

"Do you think her brother'd buy us some booze?" Russ wishes. "He's a hippie."

"Let's pick her up. Maybe she's got something."

"No, don't," Jason says.

Terry brakes the car next to the garage. Juliana stands at the door, amply filling out a Montana State University sweatshirt and licking a red Popsicle. Hers is one of those long, complicated stories that people rack up around here. Her parents were killed in a car accident up on the pass, and she has had to live with her uncle Vern and his wife out south of town since she was a baby.

Russ rolls down the window. "Want to go?" he asks. Juliana shouts something into the interior of the garage and comes to the car. She climbs into the backseat with Jason. "Hi," she says, sliding across the seat until she's nearly sitting in his lap. Her lips are unnaturally red, stained by

Popsicle juice. She smooths stray hairs away from her eyes, chasing them back toward her thick, straw-colored braids.

Juliana reminds Jason of a tub of butter, velvety smooth and sweet, with all sorts of swells and curves. Recently, she has taken an after-school job at The Daisy. She waves at him from behind the counter, where she tends the espresso machine, and brings him cups of hot chocolate on her breaks.

"Where are we going?" Juliana asks Terry.

"Where we end up."

"You have anything on you to smoke or drink?" Russ asks her.

"I don't do that," she says primly.

Terry leaves Main Street, headed south, toward Riverton. He speeds up once he is free of the Pindall city limits and charges toward the sawmill. Jason leans against the window, craning to see, and Juliana presses herself against him. "What is it?" she whispers.

"Oh, nothing."

But he can see Elise, standing just north of the gate, her sign above her head. Russ rolls down his window and uncaps a strawberry milkshake from the Grub & Go. "Watch," he says.

"No!" Jason calls, but it's too late. As the car passes Elise, Russ lets go of the shake. "Bullseye, bitch!" he shouts.

Jason and Juliana turn to look back at her. She has dropped the sign and lifted her hands to protect herself. It couldn't have hurt her, Jason knows, it couldn't have. A Styrofoam cup, a clot of cold milk, a straw and lid. But, Christ, what if she saw him? What if she thinks he had something to do with it?

"That was really stupid, Russ," Juliana lashes.

"Stupid bitch gets what she deserves," Russ says. "Why can't she just go back to where she came from and leave us alone?"

"Because she's screwin' Darnell Hillyard," Terry answers. "He puts his rifle up her ass. It's a blast when she comes."

"Oh, God." Russ laughs. "That's good."

"You guys are sick!" Juliana says. "Have you ever thought she's just doing what she believes in? That maybe you ought to listen to her?"

"Where you'd get that?" Terry taunts. "From your pot-smoking brother?"

"No, Terry, I think for myself," Juliana snips. "And I don't think logging is very good for the earth, either. I don't think we should cut down all those trees just so we can have toothpicks and toilet paper."

"I don't use toilet paper," Russ says. "Want to smell my hand?" He licks the heel of his hand, dragging his tongue in slow motion. "Mmm, good."

Terry laughs so hard that he twists the steering wheel, causing the car to zig back and forth. Juliana makes a gagging sound.

"Jesus, Terry," Jason says. "Watch the road."

"My dad says someday somebody is gonna take a potshot at her, if she don't leave them the hell alone." Terry eyes Juliana in the rearview mirror. "Better watch out."

"I'm not scared," she says steadfastly.

"I wonder if she's really a redhead." Russ casts a lurid glance toward Juliana. "You know, there's one way to tell—" He points to his crotch, his elbows pumping up and down, his index fingers driving downward.

Terry convulses with laughter. "Holy shit, Russ!"

"So is she a redhead, Jason?" Russ asks. "You see enough of her."

"What?" Juliana turns toward him. "You know Elise?"

"Sits out there all day long talkin' to her, don't you?" Russ squints over the seat at him. "Dad says he seen you. That's why you're never in school."

Jason feels like he's just walked into quick-dry cement. Russ's question skewers him against the back seat, and Terry sights him in the rearview, while the car steers itself down the canyon. Worse is Juliana, who has puffed up into a fruity-smelling ball of feminine pique that is about to burst.

"You know her?" she demands.

Jason panics. "Jesus Christ," he says. "Let me out. Now!"

"All right." Terry brakes suddenly, hard. The car skids down the highway, a seventy-mile-an-hour sidewinder. "Now what?" he asks. "Going back to see your girlfriend?"

They have stopped on a blind curve. Jason opens the door and says, "You guys are fucking idiots." He hops out on the highway, glancing for the lights of oncoming traffic. From inside the car, he hears the sound of struggle. "Let go of me! I'm not staying in here with you! You're gross, you're—!"

Juliana spills out onto the asphalt, clutching Jason's arm to keep from falling. The car spins away, spewing gravel and hot exhaust over them.

"You better not bother Elise!" She screams at the taillights. Pulling at the neck of her sweatshirt, which is stretched and loose, she fires off, "He scratched me! He wrecked my shirt! Lex gave me this shirt!"

A ragged reddish nick, probably from a hangnail, runs along Juliana's collarbone. Jason's knees buckle beneath him, and he feels gut-punched. Why is he always left with the mess that things become? And now, here he is, stuck with Juliana Stacy, whose eyes—darker than he'd expect— bore into him.

"How can you be friends with those guys?" she demands.

Jason ignores her. "We'll have to walk back to town."

Without budging, she turns to the south, looking in the direction that Terry's car disappeared, then pivots to the north, toward Pindall. She looks just like a sun-bleached Indian princess, scouting the terrain.

"What are you doing?" Jason asks.

"I'm trying to decide which is closer—town or Uncle Vern's ranch. He's just at the end of the canyon, you know."

Proximity be damned, Jason is not about to be stuck in a houseful of bossy Stacys. He strikes out at a quick pace toward town. Without waiting for Juliana, he crosses the highway. The narrow shoulders, shaded by the canyon, are still buried beneath crusty, exhaust-blackened snow, and he is forced to walk in the traffic lane.

"I see you've decided for us!" Juliana wings after him. He can hear her scuffing along, trying to keep up with his long-legged stride. "I was just trying to help."

"Sorry," he says, sarcasm boiling over in his voice.

"I like you, Jason. You're not like Terry or Russ. You're not immature and gross like the boys in my class. And you'll be a senior next year."

He ponders her remarks. Does she like him simply because he'll be a senior, which he sincerely doubts, considering the number of truancies he's racked up in the past two months? Or are the two comments unrelated?

"I'm going to be living with Lex this summer, instead of out at Uncle Vern's and Aunt Sandy's," she informs him. "We'll be living right next to the garage, in our parents' old house. You should come see me sometime."

Lex is Juliana's brother, who has, wisely, lived away from Pindall for years. "Why is he coming back?" he asks.

"He said he missed me." She laughs. "But, really, he'll be working up in the Park." She takes a couple of hopping steps to catch up to him. "You know, I was really sorry about your dad. Your parents were the Romeo and Juliet of Pindall."

Jason remembers the play from Mrs. Rayhill's freshman English class. The old bat, she made him read the part of Mercutio aloud in class. "How's that? They both ended up dead."

"Yeah, but they were so in love, and it was so special and beautiful, and then—"

"They both ended up dead."

"Okay, so it was a tragedy," she concedes. "I just meant that they loved each other a lot, and that's what matters. Everybody in town talks about how perfect your parents were for each other. My parents were the same way, but they died when I was a baby."

"So they really were like Romeo and Juliet." Jason stops to light a cigarette, shielding the match from the wind that constantly whips down the canyon. "How do you know they were in love?"

"Lex told me," she says, as if that forever closes the question. "He says that Dad called my mom his 'Miracle Mama.'"

The name strikes Jason as less than romantic, but he is not required to comment, since Juliana keeps talking. "You know, I don't remember my parents," she confides. "Like what color their eyes were or the sounds of their voices. I was so young when they died. But Lex has told me about them, and I think, well, it's just important to remember, that's all." She glances up at him. "That's the way I see it."

Jason balks. Juliana's confessions embarrass him, make him feel capable of saying something untrue or cruel or kind and stupid. Does he remember his father right?

He dreams of him, the same dream, over and over. They stand in the kitchen. Jason faces the window, looking out. His dad stands behind him, unseen and yet felt, and Jason says, "If I turn and look at you, you'll leave." That's it, the whole damned dream, just that bland statement, that dopey resignation. There is never a response, and Dream Jason never even attempts to whirl around and catch his father's ghost on the run. He simply lets him go.

"And it's so cool about your sister," Juliana blathers. "I wish my sisters would move back to Pindall. They live all over the U.S."

"She's not my sister."

"Well, step-sister, half-sister, or whatever you want to call her. She's nice. You're lucky."

"How do you know her?"

"She comes into The Daisy sometimes when I'm working."

Jason walks faster, wishing that Juliana would take up non-verbal communication.

"So what do you and Elise talk about?" she asks. "I want to meet her. She must be really cool."

He wants to snarl at her—cool, what a shitty word—but he feels like he might cry if he opens his mouth. "Nothing," he mutters.

"Oh, come on," Juliana insists. "She must have told you something. Lex says she's probably a women's-libber, too, and for peace, too. I want to meet her. I like people who really think about things. So many people just talk and talk—"

"Like you—"

"And don't really say anything important." Evidently Juliana doesn't hear him. "But Elise, I bet she knows everything there is to know about how much logging hurts the earth. I bet she's done a bunch of research and read a lot of books. Lex says if you're going to take up a cause as unpopular as hers, you better know your stuff. I bet she knows it all, doesn't she?"

Jason flinches at how close to the truth Juliana has come. "Ask Lex. He seems to have something to say about everything."

"That's because he's smart," Juliana spits. "You don't think Terry and Russ'll really do anything to her, do you?"

Jason kicks a slice of rubber tire into the center of the highway, fresh panic biting at him. They talk big, but they are basically cowards. Unless they find something to drink. Then they'll be brave and tough.

"Do you think we ought to try to get there first and warn her?" Juliana asks.

"If we can." Jason looks ahead, straining to see the mill. He wants to avoid it. Even to pass the place seems an admission of guilt. "I mean, if they rip past us, there's not much we can do, unless you can outrun a car."

"Come on!" She runs, ridiculously fast, considering the melting contours of her body. "Hurry!"

Jason takes a couple of loping strides, but it's hard to run in cowboy boots, and even harder to avoid smashing into the canyon wall. Veering out into the middle of the lane, he tries to match Juliana's pace, but she easily outdistances him. The wind whips against his jacket, and his breath becomes a gasp. He listens for the roar of a logging truck coming around the corner behind him, sensing that he is courting death. He isn't afraid, although Juliana keeps casting quick looks over her shoulder. He wonders if this is what his father felt as he flew off the horse.

Not fear, but a slow dawning of change. Darkness has fallen, the only light a dim glow that rests on top of the canyon walls, like a lid. If he dies now, his last thought will be of leaping toward the light above him. He breathes deeply, and the blood in his veins crescendos into a roar in his head. His heart, too large for his chest, springs against the cavity of his ribs and flies up and into the sky, a lark and an eagle.

As he nears Juliana, she steps out from the rocky wall and holds out her arms. For an instant, he thinks she'll give him a shove, right into the Path of Death, but her arms open and he runs right in between them.

"You know, Jason, we have a lot in common. We're both orphans."

"My mom's still alive."

"Oh, yeah."

Her face is flushed and bright in the dying light, and her bangs have broken free of her braids to hang in long, straight cords on either side of her eyes. She's amazingly pretty, and she looks ready either to cry or to laugh. When she puts her arms around his neck, he kisses her sticky lips. Her tongue tastes of pink bubblegum, and her hands around his neck are so hot that for a moment he believes he has caught on fire.

SEVEN
FEAST

Erica asks Dave if there is a library or bookstore in town that might be hiring.

"Oh, honey," he replies. "There ain't jobs like that here, unless somebody dies. And believe me, those library ladies live to be a hundred. What's your college degree in?"

"I majored in American Studies, with a minor in English."

"Well," he reasons. "As long as you can speak it, you should be able to find something."

Erica finds work waiting tables at Mona's Kitchen at the Morning Glory Motel. The restaurant has red booths that have seen better days—duct tape snakes along one cushion—but the vinyl is clean and the floors scrubbed. There's an old-fashioned pie display case that Merrilee—Mona's daughter, who now runs the restaurant and motel—fills with cakes and pastries that she bakes herself. On the walls are pictures of chickens—roosters in barnyards, mother hen and chicks, cartoon chickens, even a black silhouette of a chicken framed by pink construction paper.

If the Rambler is a gathering place in the evenings, Mona's Kitchen is the morning hot spot. Over cups of dark, steaming coffee, ranchers talk about rising hay prices and falling livestock sales. Pindall's chief of police, Dennis Farrell, and the town's lone deputy, Macky Bain, hold what Dennis calls a "powwow" every morning. The county road crews stop by around nine, already hours into their shifts. The employees from City Hall take a coffee break at ten. Throughout the rest of the morning, Mona's attracts a smattering of county officials, insurance agents and PTA members.

The main topic of conversation at Mona's seems to be Erica herself. As she serves pieces of Merrilee's apple pie crowned by a squirt of Reddi-Wip, she answers questions about how she knew who her father was, how she learned of his death, why she came to Pindall, even how she came to Pindall.

"So you drove all the way out here," Donny Pike, a county snow plow driver, ventures. He smells of black mechanics grease and snow-sopped coveralls that have air-dried one too many times. "You hit snow anywhere?"

"I was pretty lucky." Erica serves him coffee and a bear paw. "There was an ice storm in Milwaukee, but I waited it out at a Denny's."

"Milwaukee," he repeats, crows' feet anxiously crinkling around eyes that have stared into whiteness for too long. She suspects he considers Milwaukee an exotic place, far beyond his reach.

The men from the feedstore come in around 11:30 for lunch. Glenn Wexler, who owns the store, refers to Erica as a "little gal," and tells her she better put some meat on her bones or she'll never survive the winter. He orders the chili cheeseburger every day, even though he pounds on his chest with a fist as Erica delivers the bill and says, "Those things ain't so good for my heart."

One day, she hears his friend, Art, say, "Damn horse had a couple of whorls." He glances up at Erica. "You can always tell a horse by its whorls, ain't that so, honey?"

"Its what?" Erica has never heard the word before.

"She don't know nothing about horses," Glenn says. "Little gal from Ohio."

"I took riding lessons," Erica says, a spurt of defensiveness in her tone.

"Hell," Art says. "You don't need no lessons. The way to ride a horse is to get on him and ride him."

"What's a whorl?" she asks.

Art answers. "You got a horse with what you girls call a cowlick—where the hair parts a different way—they say it's got a whorl. The Arabs have used whorls for years to tell whether a horse is good or bad. One whorl, just between the eyes, it's a good ride. Above the eyes, it's not so easy. Below, that nag can be downright mean."

Glenn winks at her, and she thinks he will call Art's bluff, but he says, "I had me a gelding with three whorls, and by God, that son-of-a-buckaroo like to killt me. One summer we was bringin' in cattle, he decided to run me into a fence. I had bruises up and down all the way from my ankle to my as—excuse me, miss—my hip."

"Now your dad," Art says to Erica. "He could judge horseflesh in the blink of an eye. I never seen nobody with such a good head for horses. Give him a green-broke and he'd have it going through the paces in a week."

Glenn nods in agreement.

"Never thought he'd be the one to get bucked off," Art adds.

"Hey, Art, that's enough," Glenn cautions. "You don't need to talk about that in front of this little gal."

Art shrugs, and Erica moves on, but she feels shaken. It's a new feeling for her, being so visible, so exposed.

Around noon, Rob Grenville oozes in from his outfitting store on the other end of Main, across from the Rambler. He dresses in camouflage and hides his straggly hair under a cap that reads "Vietnam Veteran." His arm creeps around Erica's waist as he orders Salisbury steak, mashed potatoes, extra gravy.

"Your dad used to bring me lots of business," he tells her. "Most of his clients, you know, they was from the east and had the sense of a half-dead cat. They'd come out here thinkin' it's an amusement park or somethin'. Like a twelve-point bull is just gonna walk in front of them, and they're gonna shoot it, bang, that's the end of it. Your dad used to laugh at them, all dolled up in their brand-new polyester gear that ain't never been worn before, rattlin' around like Snap, Crackle and Pop. He said the only elk that couldn't hear 'em comin' was already hangin' over the mantel."

Erica steps sideways, and his hand slips from her waist.

"Your dad knew that to get a trophy buck, you have to work at it—climb straight up hills and over rocks and through streams and whatever else shit Mother Nature throws at you—and you have to be smart, because them old bulls ain't lived so long by actin' stupid. You see, huntin's a mind game, like chess or somethin', only the other side don't know the rules. They only know they don't want to lose."

"It still seems pretty unfair," Erica protests. "An animal can't shoot back."

"They got instinct on their side." His expression darkens. "Only place I ever seen anything like instinct was in 'Nam. Fought like animals there, just tryin' to stay alive long enough to get home."

He is interrupted by Rhonda Helms, who shows a family of four to a booth, hissing at Erica, "Your table."

"Be right there," Erica replies.

"Well, the thing is," Rob says, "if it's a trophy you want, you pass up herds of elk or deer or whatever it is you're after. His clients would complain—why don't I just shoot that one? What's wrong with it? And Brad'd say, It ain't what you've paid for. And the client'd say, Looks big enough, can't be many bigger than that, this is all too hard." He shakes his head. "There's a whole lot of folks out there that can't understand nothin' that ain't already done for them."

"I have to scoot," Erica says, but Rob, lost in his memories or torment or whatever it might be, doesn't reply.

Through some unspoken agreement, the semi-circular corner booth in Mona's is reserved for a half-dozen men who come in every Thursday, carrying with them a smug detachment from the truck stop and Pindall and even the snow-slick streets outside. Their chest pockets and jackets are embroidered with an array of colorful insignia: USGS, National Park Service, Fish and Game, University of Wyoming.

They are a changeable group, but one face almost always appears among them. Lex Stacy seems to be well-known in Pindall—customers stop by the booth to exchange a few words with him now and then—but his shirt bears a Montana State University logo. His dark hair is pulled straight back from his forehead and clasped in a ponytail that reaches just beyond his shirt collar, and a beard covers his cheeks and chin. His eyes are barely brown behind wire-framed glasses, and his lips curve as if he finds amusement in everything.

The men take turns paying for coffee and pastries. When Lex picks up the tab, he tips Erica well, saying, "Thanks for keeping them fed and watered."

"What are you all doing here?" she asks.

"We're a consortium of researchers, all of us with ties to the National Park."

She has not heard this kind of language since she left Ohio. "And you're with Montana State?"

He makes a show of consulting the chest pocket of his shirt. "Looks that way."

"My mother taught at OSU—"

"Oklahoma, Ohio or Oregon?"

"Ohio. I went to college there."

"Did you graduate?"

"Magna cum laude."

"Well done." He holds up a hand to high-five her, and she slaps his palm. "We have to stick together around here, you know."

The book club meets every Wednesday at one, ordering strawberry shortcake that Merrilee makes especially for them. These women are different from Robyn Ruggles and Shari and Merrilee. They are stay-at-home moms in a town where every penny counts. Their husbands run dude ranches or have auto dealerships in Jackson and Riverton, and their children go to Miss Mildred's Three Bears Preschool at the Methodist Church. Most have attended the university in Laramie before coming home to marry their high school sweethearts. The time away from Pindall—even if it was only a semester or two—gives them an edge, like serrated knives in a drawer of dull stainless steel.

"What are you reading?" Erica asks.

"Jackie Collins's *Hollywood Husbands*," Jenny tells her with a smirk.

"Except that we aren't really reading it," Darcy says. "Just the juicy parts."

"That's every other page in this one," Jenny points out.

"No wonder it's taking me so long."

As they laugh, Anita says to Erica, "You're doing so good here. After all you've been through, too."

"You know," Jenny offers. "That horse race is just too dangerous. My mother told Todd—he's my brother—"

"And the star receiver for the Pindall Pioneers," Darcy interrupts.

"—that he's not doing it this summer. Not when he has a football scholarship waiting for him at U-Dub next fall."

"Landon was just heartbroken by what happened last year," Darcy says in a low voice. "He couldn't understand it. One minute we're all yelling, Go, horsey, go, and the next everybody is trying to keep their kids from looking." Suddenly self-conscious, she looks at Erica. "Oh, I'm sorry, I shouldn't have said that—"

"What do you think?" Anita asks Erica. "Surely you don't want to see the Derby run again."

"I don't know anything about it." Erica answers honestly. "In the east, we run 5K races."

Erica ends her shift at two, when Mona's closes. It's then that her day becomes something treasured, beautiful. It's then that she goes home to Rain.

When she pulls into the barnyard at the Phillips's ranch, Rain is waiting for her. She'll be pacing parallel to the fence, tracing a groove in the icy mud of the bare-soil corral, or she will run in from the pasture, bucking and kicking, like a child awaiting a present.

"I'll be right there," Erica calls as she dashes inside the trailer to change from her work smock and black pants. She layers on warm clothing—a t-shirt, a pullover with long sleeves, an Ohio State sweatshirt, long underwear beneath her jeans, two pairs of socks. She pulls on a pair of Dave's cow-manure-caked boots and tough, leather mittens.

Outside, she lets herself into the corral. Ratso follows, always eager for adventure. Rain ambles toward her, and Erica runs a hand down the horse's neck, solid and warm against her palm. She pats her a couple of times, enjoying the dull clap of flesh against flesh. She laughs when Rain swings her head, poking her nose toward her pockets in search of treats. Catching Rain's head between her hands, she looks into those liquid brown eyes. "You old silly," she says. "You think everything's for you, don't you?"

She starts buying carrots at the Wickiup. She feeds them to Rain one at a time, letting the horse nuzzle her hand. Rain's nose is like velvet, so lightly haired that Erica can see the pinkish skin beneath. When the horse chews, her heavy molars grind together with the sound of a bass drum.

"So what's your story, Rain?" Erica asks. "You don't look like you have any whorls. Why doesn't anyone like you?"

The horse tosses her head, as if to protest the last comment, and Erica laughs. "Well, I'd tell you mine, but you've probably already heard it, just like everybody else in this town is."

She doesn't understand why Dave spends so little time with his horse. When he feeds Rain, he throws the alfalfa hay into an old tire laid flat on the ground, so that the wind doesn't snatch it and blow it away, but he doesn't wait for her to eat. He doesn't look at her. He doesn't pet her.

Erica has meant to ask Dave about Rain—how could he not love such a beautiful creature?—but there is something dark in his face. Something bitter.

On cold days, Erica takes refuge from the wind in the wooden barn. Rain can come into one of the two stalls built from two-by-fours and plywood inside the barn. Erica finds an old crate to sit on, so that she can be inside the stall with the horse. Ratso, always her companion, lies on the ground at her feet, and a couple of skinny barn cats skulk around, not tame, but not entirely feral, either.

Together, they watch the winter blow past outside the barn.

Hours pass, whole afternoons, even entire days. Sometimes Erica reads or writes letters to Nat or Royce as she sits with Rain, but mostly she just stays with the horse, peaceful, even happy. It's so easy to love someone who asks nothing of you, who only wants to be with you, who does not care if you are in fine form or feeling lousy. It's so easy to love a great, deep soul whose eyes are tender and liquid, who walks in sure-footed strides, whose body is thick and solid and lovely. You can attribute every virtue to your beloved—honesty, loyalty, faithfulness, patience—and never be disappointed. You can love and never be hurt.

On a Saturday morning, the phone rings as Dave and Erica are eating breakfast. Dave answers it and says, "Oh, sure, hang on."

He offers the receiver to Erica. "It's for you."

"Me?" she asks. "Is it Mike?"

If Mike is calling this early, something must be wrong at home. Nat, Royce—she grabs the phone and says, "Hello?"

"This is Marguerite Brock," a voice answers. "I was wondering if you would come to lunch tomorrow at my house."

Erica laughs airily in relief. "Yes," she says. "I'd love to."

Marguerite lives almost in the dead center of Pindall, in a ranch house that is remarkable only because the lot doesn't overflow with junk. Erica arrives at noon, parking her Honda on the slippery slope of the street and pulling the emergency brake as a precaution. She carries a pan of brownies to the door, an offering that is still warm even through the bulk of her mittens. Marguerite answers, her salt-and-pepper hair drawn back in a stern bun. She wears a western shirt and jeans, and her feet are clad in moccasins.

Erica beams, unaware until just now how excited she is to see her grandmother. "Hi. I brought brownies."

"Come in." Marguerite closes the door behind them. Two German Shepherd dogs race at Erica, tails wagging. "This is Dane," Marguerite points to the smaller of the two. "And Amory."

"Hi, there, you old sillies." Erica rubs behind their ears and pats their rumps.

"I hope you're talking to them," Marguerite says. "I believe I could fall into that category."

"Oh—" Erica stammers, but when she looks up, her grandmother is wearing a closed-lip smile. She laughs, her nerves making it a spasm.

"Let me take that." Marguerite reaches for the pan of brownies. "And take off your coat."

As Erica sheds mittens, scarf and coat, she sees that the room she has stepped into is meticulously decorated. On the windows are 1950's wooden shutters painted the colors of the earth; on the floor lies a richly-hued rag rug of reds and browns over hardwood floors stained the color of mahogany. The furnishings are old and carefully kept—heirlooms, perhaps, from a larger and grander home.

Yet the true beauty of the room rests on an oak table in the corner where fabric is piled more than two feet deep—gold, orange, blue, purple, all exotic and lush. A half-finished quilt of scorching pink and lavender beckons from a quilt rack in the corner, and other quilts-in-progress bunch on ottomans or are casually tossed over the backs of chairs.

"Oh," Erica says. "It's like a bazaar in here—like what James Joyce wrote about in that story, what was it? Arabia—?"

"It's beyond me—"

"Araby. That's what it was. Where do you get all this?"

"Buying trips to Salt Lake City or Denver, mostly," Marguerite replies. "Some things I can order in."

Erica gravitates toward the table, mesmerized by the wealth of fabric. This is not the grandmother's house she has always dreamed of. No cookies in the oven, no craft projects using Popsicle sticks and macaroni laid out on the table, no old-time radio playing songs from a bygone time that has never heard of rock and roll. Energy snaps here, from the bursting palette of the cloth, and the partially-conceived quilts, and the spools stacked here and there, the tender threads pierced by silver needles.

"I love the quilt you gave me," Erica says. "It's so warm."

"I can imagine it comes in handy at Dave's."

"It does. Sometimes the trailer rocks in the wind. Even if it isn't cold, it makes me think it is."

Marguerite laughs. "Why did you leave the Rambler?"

"Robyn asked me to."

"Robyn Ruggles is a busybody who isn't happy unless she's in charge," Marguerite scoffs. "You should have come to me. I'd offered."

"I . . . it happened so fast, and Dave was right there. Going home with him was the easiest thing to do."

"Do you like it out there?"

"I do," Erica replies, surprised at how fervently she feels.

"Well, I guess it's worked out well enough, then," Marguerite says. "Let's go into the kitchen. Lunch is almost ready."

The kitchen is as quaint as the living room, with metal cabinets painted beige and checkerboard squares of linoleum on the floor. A window hangs over the sink, looking down the slope at the half of the town that falls below.

"You can see your store from here," Erica remarks. "That's convenient."

"Some days," Marguerite agrees. "Other days, it's a pain in the patootie."

Erica laughs. "How can I help?"

Marguerite puts Erica to work setting the vinyl-topped, silver-rimmed table. Dane and Amory sniff around her ankles, undoubtedly smelling Ratso. She waltzes around them, carefully kneeing them out of the way when she needs to. When she pulls out a chair, an ancient calico cat snuffles at her from the cushion. "Oh," she says in surprise.

"That's Purdy," Marguerite says.

She comes to rescue the poor old thing, lifting it gently from the chair and setting it on the floor. "Her name hasn't fit her in years. But when Jason first saw her, when she was just a kitten, he said, 'Oh, isn't she purdy?' He couldn't have been more than three or four at the time." The cat sneezes. "Do you have pets at home?"

"We had a dog," Erica says. "Ragamuffin. He was mine—my mom got him for me when I was, well, when I was probably about the same age as Jason was when you got Purdy. We had him put to sleep when I was a junior in high school."

"Ragamuffin," Marguerite says. "What a name for a dog."

"He was kind of like your Purdy. He actually won an ugly dog contest once."

Marguerite chuckles as she sets an elegant pottery bowl filled with mashed potatoes on the table. "Sit down. Help yourself."

As they eat, Erica answers the questions that Marguerite asks—about growing up in Ohio, about how the college campus always seemed like a playground for her, about Natalie and Royce.

"What about your mother's parents?" Marguerite asks. "You said she was from Cheyenne."

"She went to high school there. Granddad was in the military, though, so they lived all over the world. They're in Florida now, and he's retired." She pauses. "I'd like to hear some stories about my father."

Marguerite falters for an instant, her fork wavering. "Between the Rambler and Mona's, you've probably heard more stories about him than I can deliver."

"But there must be one that you know that no one else does."

"Well," Marguerite considers. "You probably know that when he decided to build his own house, he thought he'd do it alone, without using wood from the mill or any power tools."

"I've heard that."

"Shari's dad helped with the blueprint—that's how he met her, did she tell you that?—and he and Dave did most of the tree felling and sawing. But when the walls went up, there was only so much the two of them could do. They'd rigged up some sort of block and tackle system, but they were trying to stack twenty-two foot logs, sometimes more than once if the logs had to be planed down for a better fit."

"Why didn't he want to use lumber from the mill?"

"His father died there when he was nine."

The piece of family history, so casually dropped, surprises Erica. "Oh, I'm so sorry—"

"It was long ago." Marguerite seals the conversation. "Eventually, though, Brad ran out of time. Jason was already on the way when he and Shari married, and they needed a place to live. So one Saturday in late summer, he decided to hold a 'house-raising,' although that wasn't exactly what he was doing. It was a beautiful day—one of those perfect days when it isn't too hot and it doesn't storm in the afternoon.

"Everyone came. The mill workers, some of the ranchers from outside of town, Bill Johnson and the other school teachers, and a whole slew of Mormons boys, who worked their fingers to the bone. Glenn Wexler brought in a couple of teams of Belgians to drag the logs—"

"Oh, I know him."

"And right in the middle of all this ruckus, all this sawdust and noise, we started to see these blue, fluttering ribbons in the air. They were everywhere—around our heads, and in and out of the trees, and in the meadow. It took us all a minute to realize that they were bluebirds, probably fifty of them."

"How beautiful."

"Well, some of the men saw them right away and stopped what they were doing. Brad was way up on the frame—he and Dave were doing the most treacherous job, catching those logs while they were swinging to and fro—and it took him a minute to catch on to what was happening."

She pauses, overcome by memory. When she speaks again, her voice is patchy and rough. "Well, he took off his hat and called down to Marty Huttman, the Methodist minister, asking for a blessing. Most everyone bowed their heads, but I didn't. I watched Brad. There he was, eighteen feet above the ground, his feet splayed one on this support, one on that, one wrong step away from falling and—"

She falters. Erica starts to reach across the table, but Marguerite recovers. "Still he had the nerve to close his eyes and bow his head during the prayer, while those bluebirds flew right around him."

The only sounds are the clock ticking above the oven, and the dogs snoring beneath the kitchen table. Marguerite's face is soft, its harshness melted away, and Erica knows that she is seeing it all again: the summer day and the bluebirds and her son at the peak of his strength and confidence.

"That's quite a story," Erica says, her throat tight.

Marguerite regains her composure. "That's the kind of man your father was. He believed in everything he did."

Erica says nothing, afraid that she might break down and sob like she did the first night she stayed at Dave's trailer.

"What about you?" Marguerite asks.

She swallows. "What?"

"Do you believe in what you're doing?"

She stalls, trying to find her voice. "When I left Ohio," she says at last, "I sort of did it in the middle of the night. I didn't tell anyone goodbye or pack very much"—she laughs—"which I regret now. I just got in my car and started driving. I've always had this sense that half of me is missing or something. I know it sounds stupid, but"—she stops to sort out her thoughts—"I have always known the part of me that is like my mother. She was there, I heard myself—I can still hear myself—saying the same kinds of things she said. But the other half, the half that is my father, has always been like a, a, a picture postcard that says 'Wish you were here.' Wish I was where? Wish I was who? I needed to find out."

"What have you found so far?"

She laughs nervously. "I like what I've heard about him, and I think I like the parts of me that seem to be from him. But—"

She stops, and Marguerite waits for an uncomfortable moment before she says, "Yes?"

"I've been wondering—" Erica's voice wobbles. "My mom felt so much for him. But if he never talked about her . . ."

"I'm not sure we'll ever get to the bottom of that," Marguerite says. "I hear you've been venturing into planning the Sawmill Days Derby."

"What?"

"You suggested turning the Derby into a footrace of some kind."

Erica shakes her head. "I don't—"

"There's a group of women who are sending a petition around. They want to see the Derby become a 5K race."

"Oh." At last, Erica remembers the conversation with the women's book group. "I guess I . . . I just said that in the east, we run 5K races. I didn't know anything would come of it."

"Well, it has."

"I'm sorry, I didn't mean—"

"Don't worry about it." Her grandmother interrupts. "That isn't why I invited you here. I want you to know—and I am speaking only for myself and not for Shari or Jason—I don't approve of what my son did. I find it cowardly that he abandoned a child—"

"Oh, he didn't abandon me. It was a mutual decision between them—"

"Perhaps it was," Marguerite acknowledges. "But whatever was agreed upon between the two of them, it was unfair to the rest of us—including you."

"My mom was never unfair," Erica reacts. "She always did the right thing."

Marguerite lets a tick of silence pass. "I can't speak to that, but I want you to know that I intend to rectify things as much as I can."

Erica's throat closes, and she feels on the verge of tears again. "Thank you. I'm so glad you asked me here today—"

Marguerite waves her aside, as if she, too, is fighting back emotion. "I think it's time for dessert, don't you? What about those brownies you brought with you?"

Erica springs to her feet, her blood rushing, her fingers tingling. What a relief it is to be welcome in this house. Taking the knife that Marguerite hands her, she starts to cut the brownies. Rather than coming out of the pan in neat squares, the chocolate sticks to the knife in clumps. Her elation wanes.

"I don't think I have the hang of high altitude cooking yet," she admits, trying to coax a brownie lump from the knife onto a plate without poking it with her finger.

Marguerite peers over her shoulder at the mess. "Wait a minute." From the drawer, she takes two forks and hands one to Erica. "I don't mind if you don't."

"I don't mind."

Standing at the counter, they both plunge their forks into the brownies.

"They taste all right." Marguerite's words are muddled. "But I'm not sure my dentures can take much of this."

Erica covers her mouth to keep from spitting brownie on the floor. "I'm sorry," she says, but she doesn't stop laughing. In fact, her hilarity grows, turning to great gasps of laughter.

Beside her, her grandmother—Grandma—laughs, too.

EIGHT
BLUE WIDOW

It's a bitter Friday night at the Rambler, and I'm the only one working again. Tonight, it's all talk about the sawmill. Cascadia Northern's takeover doesn't seem to have solved many of the problems. There's still too little productivity, too many equipment failures, and too much butting of heads between management and worker. Now it's been announced that there will be no wage increases, but there will be mandatory overtime.

"What the fuck," Dwayne Black says. "Why don't they just keep us there day and night like fucking slaves?"

Jerry Whistledorn weighs in. "You know what mandatory overtime means, don't you? Layoffs. Why do you need to force overtime if everybody's there and doing their job? Overtime's only mandatory when you're short-staffed."

Anxiety wafts through the cigarette smoke around the table.

"You haven't heard nothing like that, have you?" Eddie Fenton asks.

"Not yet," Jerry growls.

"I'm already doing sixty-five hours just to put food on the table," Tommy Dole says. "When the hell am I supposed to work overtime?"

"Maybe with mandatory overtime, I can buy me a Bee-Em-Double-Yoo," Dwayne jokes.

Jerry turns to me. "I wouldn't get too friendly with Ronald Dailey, if I were you, Shari. He won't last long here."

"Shari ain't that stupid," Dwayne assures us all.

I laugh it away, but something twinges through me. I look forward to Ronald's visits to the Rambler. His conversation comes without demands. He's taken no sides and he hasn't asked anything of me. Best of all, he has no past in this town and no memories of my husband.

The evening grinds on, growing staler and older. It isn't even eleven o'clock when Robyn announces that she's closing up. "Let's pack it in," she says, with a roll of her eyes that indicates she's tired of the self-pity and despair.

But after I've cleaned up and fought my way through the wind to my pickup, it won't start. Dwayne and Jerry open the hood and poke around, but that doesn't last long. After a couple of frostbitten minutes, Dwayne says, "I'll take you home. It's colder than a witch's tit out here."

That's when Walt—who probably doesn't trust Dwayne any more than I do—steps in. He tows my pickup behind his backfiring '58 Ford to Vern Stacy's Autobody and Garage. The garage is closed up tight at this hour of the night, but it doesn't matter. Vern will know why it's there. I leave the keys in the ignition and crawl into the passenger's seat of Walt's truck.

"You let me know if Vern tries to soak you," he growls. "I'll set him right."

"I'll be okay," I say sourly, aggravated by the whole mess.

Next day, I drive Robyn's Cavalier, which she lends me, into town to talk to Vern myself.

His lot spills over with parts cars, oil barrels, hoists, pulleys and dismantled engines. Given that the property abuts that of the one-hundred-year-old log cabin Methodist Church—one of Pindall's main tourist attractions—the Town Council, on which Marguerite sits, has been after Vern to clean up his messy trade for years. Vern's not the most cooperative resident of Pindall, though. He once told the Council to shove a tailpipe up their ass.

Inside the garage, it's a vehicular jungle of fenders, tires and parts. Sunshine streams through high, narrow windows into the shell of the building. At the west end, a flight of wooden stairs leads to an open platform built atop the office and hemmed in by a two-by-four railing. Opera music echoes against the rafters, played by a radio or stereo, a chorus in full pursuit of justice.

I knock on the door of the office, but there is no answer. A calendar hangs nearby, counting off January, although we are halfway through March. I start to fix it, but I'm struck by the illustrations. Staircases, drawn in black ink, lead round-headed figures onto crazy angles and dimensions. Tables pop out of walls, doors unfold horizontally, no one seems to see each other. I flip through the pages to October, and come across a sketch of a three-dimensional hand, which emerges from a two-dimensional sheet of paper to draw a shirt cuff for a second three-dimensional hand. The second hand reciprocates, creating a cuff for its partner.

Pulling the calendar off the nail that pins it to the wall, I study the hands. They are graceful, strong, capable. Everything that hands should be. Glancing behind me, I rip off the drawing, fold it and stick it in my coat, then replace the calendar, still set on January. Without remorse, I call, "Vern?"

No one responds, but the operatic chorus above swells anxiously, either accusing or encouraging. I head to the back door, which opens onto an ice-laden field. Every junker ever owned in this town has ended up here, in Vern Stacy's auto graveyard. Yet in the midst of the wasteland sits a pristine white Honda Civic and a flame-coated Camaro, both idling. I peer through the passenger's window of the Camaro, gloved hands against the glass to shade the glare of sunlight.

"You ever see anything as pretty?"

The voice startles me, and I twist around, nearly losing my balance on the ice. Lex Stacy emerges from the shadows, looking directly at me.

I haven't seen Lex in . . . well, I haven't seen Lex at any time in recent memory. Although he is a Pindall boy born and raised, he's four or five years younger than I am, too young for me to have known in school. His father was a town administrator—accountant, lawyer, city judge or something— until he and his wife were killed in a car accident up on the pass.

"It's a good looking ride," I agree.

He shifts his gaze to the car. "Better than that. This Camaro uses more gas in a mile than the Civic does in a month, but look at the lines in that engine. It's art. Japanese engines should come shrink-wrapped."

He's right—there's a spacious elegance to the curves of the Camaro's engine. Valves and tubes and hoses bend and join back into themselves. So much complexity, so much intricacy. The engine reminds me of the calendar, and I put my hand in my coat to see if the page is still there.

"You've been looking at this a while," I remark.

"Since I was a kid." His breath swirls around his head. "I've always loved American built cars." He steps around me and drops the hood of the Civic, the sound cracking the frigid air into crystalline shards. As he opens the door to cut the ignition, he says, "But, everything is getting smaller these days, our whole world shrinking before us. Not enough resources, too many people, so we're having to embrace smallness. I worry that, eventually, we'll end up thinking that way, too. We'll become a race of Honda Civics."

"It's pretty early in the morning for that kind of philosophizin'."

He laughs as he pockets the key to the Civic. "It's good to see you, Shari."

There's something sweet in his voice that unnerves me—it doesn't sound like the pity I hear at almost every turn. I'm suddenly awake, not in the top-o'-the-mornin' way, but in a Rip Van Winkle way, sloughing off twenty years of hangover. Lex wears a down-filled jacket with a furred hood that sets off his dark eyebrows and wind-reddened lips. His beard clings heavily on his cheeks, and his eyes are greenish-brown in the morning light.

"Your truck needs a new transmission," he says.

"So you've already looked at it?"

"I didn't. Vern did. He's the expert here. He says he can find you a rebuilt transmission. It'll cost less, and he'll work it out with you." He closes the hood of the Camaro, far more reverently than he banged the hood of the Civic. "He says he'll give you a loaner car until it's fixed."

I nod toward the Camaro. "This one?"

"Not a chance." He laughs as he cuts the power to it. "See that Chevy Malibu right over there? I started it this morning. Battery's new, and it has good enough tires to get you up the hill and home."

"That's all right. I can borrow Robyn's car."

"Okay." He sounds as if he is disappointed, and for some reason, I feel the same way. The silence of the morning settles in the air.

"I'm sorry about your husband," he says. "It was a tragedy for the entire town."

His words fall at my feet, lumped around my boots along with the snow and my heart. Every one of my memories of the day that Brad died flashes through my mind. The heat, the wind, the smell of grease-grilled hamburgers, the tinkle of music from the carnival. In the frozen shadow of Vern Stacy's garage, I'm struck by the fact that summer will come again, and the meadow will be vibrant green, shot through with fireweed and larkspur and Indian paintbrush. The flawlessly blue sky will fill with immense, flat-bottomed thunderheads. How could such betrayal happen?

"Hey," Lex says. "Let's go inside and have a cup of coffee. Your teeth are chattering."

He touches my arm, just below the elbow. Nearly a year has passed since a man has touched me, and even through the thickness of my coat and sweater and thermal underwear, I swear I can feel the warmth of his hand. But it can't be warm—not when the whole world around us is in the grip of a minor Ice Age.

He sends me up to the platform, while he goes to Vern's office below for coffee. "Don't mind the mess," he says. "It's a work in progress up there."

I climb toward the opera, my hands grasping the two-by-fours that serve as a banister. On the platform, I find an office where nothing is finished. The rough-hewn floor is hidden beneath a ragged-edged carpet of blue shag, and the empty bookcases are built of cinder blocks and planks. A space heater sits near a heavy oak desk, its grill bright orange, but its heat barely denting the cold. The opera comes from a turntable and speakers in one corner.

I gravitate toward the bookcases, rubbing my elbow, still able to feel the electricity of Lex's touch coursing through my hand and wrist. Moving boxes stack near the bookcases, and a pile of hardcover tomes rests horizontally on the desk—textbooks on biology, ecology, and a full complement of publications about Yellowstone National Park. A heavy, black microscope perches squarely in the middle of the desk. For an instant, I consider turning it on and taking a peek into Lex's private life.

Something else catches my eye, though—a riot of colorful photographs that leans against the back wall. Swirls of ocher and salt white, pools of orange amidst moss gray, a purple deeper than that of the most exotic violet or orchid. I kneel down to get a better look. I've seen these before, I know them by heart. Anyone who has ever lived in this area has tried to capture the splendor of the thermal pools in Yellowstone with a camera at one time or another. But film never reveals the true beauty of the Paint Pots or the Morning Glory. And there's usually the slip-up of thumb, guardrail, or meandering tourist in the mix.

Yet Lex has done something more. He's gone to some trouble to capture trash floating in the pools—Kleenex mired in yellow mud, a pamphlet about Yellowstone National Park afloat on murky gray water, blue beads across a green mat of slime. One after another, the pictures are ruined by junk.

"Ah," he says behind me. "I see you've found my passion."

"There are so many choices here," I say, still on my knees. "The Park? Opera? Trash?"

"None and all of the above." He sets two steaming cups of coffee on the desk. "It's far smaller and grander than that."

He extends a hand to help me to my feet, then gives me a cup of coffee. Freed of his jacket, he wears a solidly-packed flannel shirt and insulated vest. His dark hair is pulled straight off his forehead and secured by a rubber band at the nape of his neck.

"Microbes," he says.

"Microbes?"

"Microbes," he reaffirms. "Most of the pools are colored by microbes. Living organisms. In water and muck that reaches beyond boiling point. It's a mystery, a puzzle. How do they survive under such extreme conditions? Look at this." He points to a pool of brilliant yellow. "Isn't it exquisite?"

I step away so quickly that the coffee sloshes in the cup, nearly breaching the rim. No man I know in Pindall uses the word "exquisite." Lex doesn't notice my skittishness, but folds his arms over his chest and strokes his beard with his right hand, lost in thought.

"And we're killing it," he continues. "If that trash sinks, it knocks off the balance. Lowers the water temperature, clogs the underground vents, destroys the habitat for the bacteria. In fact"—his voice assumes the tone of a lecturer—"when the Park first opened, tourists bathed and washed their clothes in the thermal pools. It was a hot springs, more or less. Thankfully the Park Service stopped it. It's one of the few good decisions they've made."

"I hope they remove the trash, too."

"They do—if they can." He sips his coffee. "Starting this summer, I've got a grant to study the thermal ecosystem up in Yellowstone. When the roads re-open, I'll be up there most of the time." He motions toward an overstuffed recliner, then plops down in a clanking, rolling chair behind the desk. "Sit down."

I find myself swallowed up by the recliner. "Who gave you a grant?"

"Montana State University." He dumps sweetener into his coffee and stirs with a pen. "Sorry," he says sheepishly, handing it to me. "I forgot a spoon."

I wave my hand toward the microscope and books. "So you study—?"

"Microbiology. The underworld of biology. Germs and parasites and viruses and such. What you can't see. What most people don't want to think about."

"Why not?"

"I know what's on the library banister that every kid in town has touched, licked, or snotted on. It makes people queasy to be around me sometimes."

I laugh. "I can see why. But I like the idea that there are all sorts of lives around us that don't even register. It's comforting, in a way."

"Yeah, I think so, too." Noticing that I haven't stirred my coffee, he adds, "What's on that pen won't kill you. But if the coffee's too strong, you've been warned."

With a laugh, I plunge the ballpoint into my coffee. "So they pay you to—?"

"Fiddle around with a microscope, mostly," he says. "Of course, I have to finish teaching this semester in Bozeman, but I wanted to put everything in place while I'm home on spring break. I'll be living here full-time next year."

One of the framed photos is accompanied by a grainy, drab-colored photograph, which is stuck in the corner of the frame, outside the glass. I squint at it, then wrestle my way out of the recliner for a closer look. The photograph is of the Stacy family—the parents, whose names I have forgotten, and Lex, who looks adolescently grumpy. In front of them, three younger sisters, all blond and close in age, mug for the camera. Mrs. Stacy holds a bundle in her arms, and the photographer has caught her glancing down at the baby, cooing to it. The family stands in front of the same thermal pool that Lex has captured with a pamphlet in it.

"That's one of the last pictures of our family all together," Lex says. "But look at the pool. Look at the difference in color."

He comes to stand behind me, and we study the photos in silence. Even given the difference in film quality, the pool has faded from a brilliant green to a mud-colored olive. Yet my eyes keep slipping from the water back to the faces of the family, so happy, so complete.

"How long was this taken before—?" I'm struck by the tactlessness of the question, and stumble to a stop.

"They died a year later. My baby sister, Juliana, was just two."

"I'm sorry."

"It's okay, Shari, we've both been there." He leans against the wall. "You know, there's talk of canceling this year's Derby. Or of making it into something less dangerous—a 5K race or something."

"Where did you hear that?"

"At the Town Council meeting on Thursday evening."

Dismay runs through me. "Marguerite hasn't said a word—"

"They're only thinking of you, I'm sure—"

It's then that the word creeps up on me: widow. That's what I am now. We must think of the widow. The widow's feelings must be taken into account. Widows, I realize, become honored and powerful—for all the wrong reasons.

Lex glances at the photograph of his family. "The thing is this. There isn't a person in town who wouldn't turn back time if they could. You, me, Mrs. Brock, too, I'm sure. I'd like to have Mom and Dad back so Juli could know them. But we can't go back. We just have to change."

"I have changed," I admit, my throat feeling raw and sore. "All I want to, I think."

"Maybe, but you can't choose to stop." He gestures at the photos on the wall. "Look at where we live. Every day something changes. There are as many earthquakes in the Park as there are hours in a day—things reshuffling beneath our feet. Another geyser spouts, or one that always has doesn't. Animals migrate, and canyons erode, grain by grain. It's constant flux. The very idea wakes me every day in a state of sheer, unabated wonder."

An image comes to me of Lex, alone in the night, mulling over microbes and migrations, while I'm lying in my bed, big enough for two, wondering if I'll ever feel right again. Who does he talk to about heat and earthquakes and geysers?

"I should be going," I say, banging the coffee cup against the side of the desk as I set it down. "Sorry—"

"Did I say something—?"

"I need to talk to Marguerite."

He scrutinizes me, and for a moment, I'm afraid he'll call my bluff. "I'm glad you stopped by," he says. "Vern will call you in a few days, I'm sure."

For the moment, I've forgotten why I'm here. "Okay," I agree. "Thanks."

I navigate down the stairs, but at the bottom, my conscience gets the better of me. "Lex," I call.

He appears at the railing above, haloed by a corona of sun through the window behind him. I can't see his features, just the black outline of his body. "I'm sorry," I say. "I took one of the calendar pages. When I came in this morning. Before we talked . . ."

"You did what?"

Humiliated by my own confession, I stammer, "I ripped off a calendar page, off this calendar here, the one with the weird drawings—"

"The M.C. Escher calendar?"

"Maybe." I squint at the illustration. "I think that's the name."

Only the music responds, the chorus swelling. In the middle of a long, growing cadence, he asks, "Which drawing?"

"It has hands." My face feels seared. "Drawing . . . each other."

"Good choice. Take the whole calendar if you want. It's a couple of years old, at least."

Stupidly, I read the date: 1982. "Why do you keep it?"

Above the singing chorus, I hear his chuckle. "It's such a collector's item."

The Wickiup is jammed. On Saturdays, the grocery serves as a community center, and today is no exception. The polished floors squeal beneath the roll of dozens of carts, and the Produce section is abuzz with teachers, cattlemen comparing calving rates, and housewives out for a break.

I'm still feeling the fool over the calendar page—as bad as it was to steal it, it was worse to admit it—when I hear my name being called. Looking over my shoulder, I see Jan Whistledorn pushing a half-filled cart toward me.

"Shari, honey!" she says. "How are you?"

I've grown accustomed to this—the gushing greeting, the question flecked with the set-in-stone-knowledge that I can't possibly be all right, the smile half of encouragement and half of regret. I give a pat response.

"I wouldn't bother you," Jan continues. "But I just wanted you to know. Jason's been missing classes—Kristie Willitts called you, didn't she?—and Jerry says he's been down at the mill talking to that environmentalist who sits outside the gates."

It's another piece to my already jumbled puzzle. What would Jason be doing with Elise?

"She's just trouble, that woman is," Jan is saying. "I don't know what we did to the good Lord to make Him send her here." She lays a hand on my arm. "But you know we love Jason"—her voice clogs—"and I'm telling you, that girl who's come here saying she's Brad's daughter—well, I told Jerry, Brad would never cheat on Shari."

For one morning, Erica had slipped my mind. One morning in the six weeks since she came to Pindall. But here she is again, staring me in the face. A heavy door shuts in my mind, and thoughts of muscle cars and microbes and M.C. whosit drain from it.

"We miss Brad so much," Jan says. "Just last night, Jerry was saying he can't face that stretch of the Gallatin where he and Brad used to go all the time—"

A tear slips from her eyes, and I reach out to comfort her. It's funny how many times I've done this in the past eight months, how often I'm the one offering condolences. By the time I reach Marguerite's office in the back hallway of the store, I'm worn out.

I find she's not alone. Huddled near the filing cabinet, his back pressed against the wall, is Darnell Hillyard. It has been ages since I've seen him, and his hair has turned a muddy gray. His beard is shot through with white, and his great bushy brows nearly obscure his eyes. His right hand curls tensely around a Styrofoam coffee cup from The Daisy, and for a moment, I'm afraid he'll crush it. "Hey, Darnell," I say softly. "How are you doing?"

He doesn't answer, and Marguerite takes over. "Darnell, you remember Brad's wife, Shari?"

He stares at me, unknowing. I glance at her, looking for a clue.

"You won't get me to talk," he says.

In a morning of shocks, this one undoes me. I let out a surprised snicker.

Marguerite sighs. "Shari came to see me, Darnell," she says gently. To me, she says, "Sit down."

As I sit in the spare chair, I feel the swish and clip of movement. The click of the back exit echoes back to us. Darnell is gone. "I'm sorry," I say to Marguerite, although I still can't help but laugh. "Did I insult him?"

"Who knows?" She rises and closes the door, then settles back into her chair. "Why are you up so early?"

"I heard a rumor that the Sawmill Days Derby may become a three-legged race or something."

She twirls a scrawny nosegay of wildflowers between her fingers. Prairie smoke and a couple of pasque flowers—the first flowers of the season. I suspect that Darnell brought them to her. "A petition was submitted to the Council the other night," she says at last. "It proposed making the Derby into a 5K race."

"Who would want to do that?"

"Darcy Merrick, Anita Crane—some of the other young mothers. They say their kids were traumatized by what happened last year."

"Traumatized? I'll show them traumatized—"

"Who told you?"

"Lex Stacy."

"Alex, Jr.," she snorts. "He was at the meeting, all right. I suspect Vern has enlisted him to make sure that the Council doesn't take a bulldozer to that property. Lex—what a silly name. I'm sure Alex and LaVonne never called him that."

"He seems to be the type who does what he wants." I feel raw, untethered, like a pile of burning cinders that could combust at any moment.

"Why were you talking with him?"

"My truck broke down. Transmission."

She lets out a hmpf. "It wasn't meant to be a surprise."

"I suppose not, since it was discussed at a public meeting."

"We've been reviewing the release from liability for the Derby, anyway." She fingers the fuzzy petals of a pasque flower. "The town attorney thinks it's time to rewrite it. It's full of holes."

I stand up and pace, and find myself beside the filing cabinet, wedged into the corner, just as Darnell was. I never gave the release that Brad must have signed a second thought. I never thought of legalities. "Do they think I'd sue them?" I ask. "For what? A share in the sewer system?"

"Don't be upset," Marguerite says. "I'm the one who suggested it. Think about it, Shari. Talk to Jason. The Council wants our input."

"How do you feel?"

For a moment, her true age shows. Her bejeweled hands look too thin and weathered to carry such a weight of treasure. The wrinkles around her mouth and eyes crease, and her shoulders droop a little.

She sighs. "It's up to you. But I may as well tell you. Anita Crane got the idea of the 5K race from Erica."

"Erica!" The word comes out as an explosion. "What's she trying to pull?"

"I don't think she's trying to pull anything." Marguerite's lips tighten. "As I understand it, she had a perfectly normal upbringing back in Ohio. She's not running from anything, she's not trying to hide out here from anyone. She's come here because she wants to know her family."

I hold up my hands. "You and Jason, maybe, but not me—"

"No, Shari," she says. "All of us. If we start slicing it this way and that, we will all end up alone."

"She's the daughter of the 'other woman,'" I protest. "Or the—I don't know—not-other, other woman. Jesus, I wish I'd never found out about her."

"She's the daughter of my son. She's my granddaughter."

Her words carry a flinty edge that I know well. I lean an elbow on the filing cabinet and bring a hand across my mouth.

"You have to remember," Marguerite says, "that Erica was born before you came into Brad's life. It was an episode you weren't even in."

"That doesn't give her any claim to our lives."

"Maybe it does. Maybe she's here to claim what should have been hers all along."

"Are you saying that Brad should have married her mother? That I'm the mistake?"

"I'm saying he shouldn't have pretended he didn't have a daughter," she says evenly. "But there's no sense in discussing that. It's a done deal, and Erica has no firmer footing in this than the rest of us."

There's affection in her voice. "You like her, don't you?" I ask.

Marguerite's gaze flickers, then galvanizes. "She comes to lunch at my house every Sunday."

"Oh," I say, fielding another shock. "I didn't know that. You didn't—"

"What would we gain by ignoring her? I won't give them"—she gestures toward the door and the store beyond—"fodder for gossip. If we just accept her and move on, we'll all be better off. Besides, you three are all the family I have left."

I'm hamstrung again by her counting Erica among us. Marguerite and I have always been close, and the thought of sharing her with someone else daunts me. Is it betrayal? Is it common sense? All I know is it hurts.

"You can't expect us to—"

"I'm requesting, not expecting," she says. "It hasn't been easy for me either."

I could argue—what about those Sunday lunches?—but I don't.

"I'll let you know," I say coolly.

"You do that." She rises. "And let me know what Jason wants, too."

At home, I find Jason outside the barn, shooting arrows into a stack of hay with Brad's elk bow. It's a monstrous thing, with a draw weight of seventy or eighty pounds. The arrows fly through the air with a sharp, clear swish. On the bale, Jason has tacked hand-drawn targets, and one arrow juts outward from nearly the center of the target. The dogs, who I've let out of the house, rush toward him, tails wagging, pink tongues eager to lick.

"What are you practicing for?" I ask.

He lays the bow aside and rubs Katie's luxurious Border collie coat. She leans lovingly against his leg. "So what's wrong with the truck?"

"Needs a new transmission."

"How much is that?"

"We'll manage." Taking a breath, I say, "I ran into Jan Whistledorn. She says you're at the mill during school. What are you doing down there?"

His face sets, his shoulders tighten, and he picks up the bow again, as if to protect himself. "What business is it of hers?"

"She is the school secretary."

"She's an old witch."

"You haven't answered me."

"Why does everybody think they know what's best for me?" he fumes. "Why does everybody think they can just butt into my life—?"

"There's talk of canceling the Derby this year."

The words come out of my mouth without forethought. Maybe it's because the contentment I felt with Lex this morning has evaporated, or maybe because I'm aware, again, of how long this winter has been without the prospect of Brad's return in the spring. The old despair that rises up in me seems barbed with something new.

"What?" Jason says, bewildered. "Why?"

"Because of your dad."

He bends down into a face full of dog—stodgy Nick, the surly blue heeler mix; wiry Dutch, who seems to be some breed of coal-colored terrier; and beautiful purebred Katie, who we found half-starved on the Yellowstone Highway. I hear the horses neighing inside the barn and climb over the wooden rails of the corral fence to open the stall doors. Shiloh comes out first, tossing his gorgeous sorrel head. LilyBelle, my own little black beauty, and Old Adam, an ancient gelding on whose back Jason learned to ride, join him. I rub their noses, let them nuzzle my palm in a futile search for treats. "Old hoss," I breathe, my hand against Shiloh's warm neck. "Good old hoss."

"What do you think?" I ask.

"I'd do what Dad would want," he says.

"What do you think that is?"

He looks up from the dogs. "He'd say it's their lollapalooza now."

I laugh, even though tears prickle my eyes. Brad loved that word—lollapalooza. It meant something big and bold, something that could end up either brilliant or disastrous: toddler Jason in July with a triple-scoop ice cream cone; the Poker Run in January, which involves snowmobiles and liquor and gambling; our marriage. He'd definitely call Erica Wiegel's arrival in Pindall a lollapalooza. I turn back to Shiloh and breathe in horseflesh until I'm strong enough to face life again.

"I'm going out," I say.

"It's too cold."

"I won't be long."

"Be careful."

"I will."

I strike out down the field, heading toward the trees at the far end, while the dogs feather the powdery snow in search of scent. In the brilliant, midday sun, the snow sparkles with the jeweled hues of a sunlit stained glass window. Only the elk path near the stream breaks the glittering evenness.

Following the stream, I move out of the clearing where our house stands and into the dim light of the forest beyond. Here, the snow lies softly in the branches, as if cupped in open palms. The wind rocks them gently. Nothing moves, no harsh sounds invade the silence, no sign of humans mars the earth. It is as untouched as it was thousands of years ago.

Deep in the trees is a sudden, jarring clearing. It's just dirt, everything scorched away for a good twenty or so feet in each direction. In the middle of the clearing lies a small steaming pool no bigger than a bathtub. The pool's water is deep green. Its rim is trimmed in a lace of ice, where the ebb and flow have undercut the snow, then receded. In the years I've lived here, I've seen the ice both pocked and pitted by the water and sculpted so delicately that it looks like the finest spun glass. I've seen it glow emerald in the sun or turn murky in the winter gloom.

I kneel to watch the steaming water caress the ice.

Why is it all such a struggle? Why isn't it simple, clean cut, easy?

And why in the hell is Erica Wiegel in our lives?

I look again at the water, and Lex's words come back to me. This pool is alive, with hundreds of microbes. Hundreds of lives that flourish and multiply without witness, that can never be judged a waste or sorrow. Lives that will never arrive somewhere alone, that will never feel unsuited to the task, or drenched in misgivings.

Exquisite, I think, and then I whisper it. "Exquisite."

The word touches the trees and blends into the sentient world around me. And suddenly, I feel a quickening of every physical and mental function within me. My heart beats stronger, my blood courses, my thoughts bloom with intuition and clarity. My losses drift away, on the wind, on the gentle ebb of the thermal pool, in the deepness of the snow. I'm at peace, calmed by the silent companionship of the earth. We'll be all right, I think. Whatever happens.

Yet I can't stay for long. Yellowstone may be one of the hottest places on earth, but the heat lies beneath. My eyes are nearly cemented shut from the steam freezing in jewels on my eyelashes. The ice has already slicked the back of my coat and the wool of my cap with a brittle shell, and my cheeks feel as if they are hardening into marble. I need shelter.

Back at the house, I shed my coat and boots and seek out the woodstove until the feeling starts to come back to the tips of my fingers. The dogs shake away the cold, then gnaw at chunks of ice between the pads of their paws. Jason stands next to the stove, fixing soup from a can. It's yellow and watery, with some lethargic noodles clumped in the bottom. I put a hand on his shoulder. "I'll see what we can find to go with that."

As I scrounge through the refrigerator, Jason says, "Why would they take away the Derby? I mean, everybody in town loves it."

"Evidently that's not so." I tell him about the young mothers who have petitioned the Council as I paste meat and bread and cheese together with mayonnaise. Once we're seated at the kitchen table, I add, "I guess it was Erica's idea."

"What was?"

"That the Derby become a runners's race."

He doesn't explode as I expect him to. Instead he leans back in his chair, chews a couple of times and announces, "I want to ride Shiloh in the Derby."

"What?"

"I want to ride Shiloh this year."

"I just told you, it might not even happen." My voice rises. "I don't want you doing that, anyway. Not after last—"

"Dad wasn't riding Shiloh."

His words clip my anger. "What?"

"If he had been riding Shiloh last year, he'd still be alive," Jason says. "Shiloh wouldn't have thrown him. And she wouldn't be here."

"What makes you think that?"

"She wouldn't dare try to weasel her way into our family if he was here. He'd tell her to get the hell out."

Would Brad have been that callous, that indifferent, toward his own daughter? Then again, he was—at least, according to Marguerite's version of it.

"What's that got to do with riding Shiloh?" I ask.

"It'd show everybody that we aren't scared of her"—he swallows—"or anything."

My words stick in my throat. Jason is hardly the horseman that Brad was, hardly the daredevil, and Shiloh is a spirited, wicked ride. "You have to be eighteen," I remind him.

Mashing noodles into the side of his bowl, he says, "I could lie."

"Not in this town," I say bitterly. "Everybody knows everything in this town."

He fiddles with his spoon, his jaw tightening. I find I cannot stomach the pale soup or the flimsy sandwich. Pushing my chair back from the table, I say, "It's not going to bring him back, Jason, and it won't chase her away."

He leaps up, sandwich crusts, soup bowl and dogs scattering. Tromping across the floor, he slams the door of his room as hard as he can.

Back at the Rambler on Saturday night, I'm dealing with a full house for such a cold night—the regulars, of course, and four snowmobilers down from Cody. The Do-Si-Dos, the town's square dance club, stop in for a round, and a tourist family from Alabama—parents and two sullen teenagers—comes in around eight. The kids grouse at each other over the foosball table while the parents guzzle Wild Turkey. Around nine, a spur-of-the-moment bachelorette party oozes out of the Nookie. The bride is one of Donna Rae's daughters, snowed in and with no place to go but the place where she'll likely spend a lifetime of Saturday nights.

In the midst of all this, Lex arrives. Coming directly to the bar, he hoists a heavy book onto the wood in front of me. "Hey, sweetheart," he says. "Come over to my place and see my Eschers."

Before I can move, Robyn shouts, "Well, hell's bells. Alexander, Jr. You ain't graced my establishment since you and Vern used to haul firewood to town to sell. Why the hell not?"

She and Lex settle at a table with a bottle of whiskey, shot glasses, beer chasers, and a few packs of cigarettes, and I'm back out on the floor, waiting tables. After a few minutes, Robyn starts to announce to anyone who is in earshot, "Hey, look at this boy. He's the very first 'fud' that Pindall has ever produced."

"What's a 'fud'?" Tommy Dole asks.

"A Doctor of Philosophy," Robyn proclaims. "P-H-D, fud. Ain't that so, Lex?"

"Doc checked my fud last spring," Dwayne Black chimes, jimmying his pants. "Ain't nothin' wrong with it."

Robyn cackles, and Lex tosses a rogue's grin in my direction. I want to cry out: It's all been done, it's all been said—and that joke is *so old*. There's nothing more for any of us here. Just the same thing, over and over and over again.

The hours that pass seem to prove me right. By midnight, the contest at the pool table quiets down, and Robyn seems to have run out of vocal steam. Now she's just smoking and consuming the lion's share of the whiskey. The Alabamans sink into an alcohol-induced stupor, and the kids have abandoned foosball, the girl with her head on her arms, dozing at the table, and the boy systematically tearing off the telephone number tabs on the home-made sales sheets posted on the Rambler's window.

All at once, Dwayne breaks the doldrums. "Hello, foxy lady! Where have you been?"

Erica stands in the door of the Rambler, wearing her scarf and mittens. She wipes her new-looking cowboy books on the mat a couple of times before she crosses the bar to where Dave sits. Instantly, Dwayne and the guys flock toward her, full of questions and flirtation.

And it seems that the lights are a little brighter and the smoke not so noxious. In fact, it feels almost like it did when Brad used to come in, unannounced, home from an expedition to some wild place, full of stories and dreams come true.

When Erica finally heads for the bar, I feel every eye flicker in my direction. Conversations wane—even Lex and Robyn have stopped talking—and the girls from the Nookie poke their heads out, evidently hoping for a showdown or a shouting match.

"Hi, there," Erica says.

"What can I get you?" I ask her.

"Can I just have tea? Or even hot water." She shivers, as if to punctuate her sentence. "Usually I wait for Dave in the car, but it's just too cold tonight."

I scrounge around for tea bags. Serving her a tin of hot water, a cup, and a couple of tattered Earl Greys, I ask, "How's your job at Mona's?"

She glances behind her at the snowmobilers, whose talk has grown big and loud, on the verge of ugly. "Probably less exciting than yours," she says. "Not many brawls break out when someone's had too many waffles with a whipped cream smiley face on them."

I laugh, which evidently disappoints our audience. The pool balls click again, and the Nookie girls start singing "Addicted to Love."

"Listen," I say. "I'm sorry Robyn asked you to leave the Rambler. She sometimes has her own ideas about what's right and wrong."

"I don't mind." Erica drops the tea bag in the water. "I like staying with Dave. It's beautiful out there, and I sort of like saying to people, 'Yeah, I'm from the Badlands.'"

She says it with gum-chewing, tough-guy bravado, and I can't help but laugh again.

"I came in because I wanted to talk to you about Sawmill Days," she says. "Grandma said you were upset—"

"Not as upset as flabbergasted."

"I thought it was just idle conversation." She jiggles the string of her tea bag. "I didn't know they'd really do it."

"There's no such thing as idle conversation in a small town," I warn. "Why didn't you tell them it wasn't your place to make suggestions?"

"All I said was that where I come from, we run 5K races." She flares with a stubbornness that reminds me of Marguerite. "I didn't make a suggestion."

I digest the information. "Before you came here, did you wonder how your . . . dad's family would feel about it?"

She pours tea from the tin pitcher into her cup. "I didn't even think about it," she confesses. "I don't want to sound like a narcissist or something—because I'm not—but it didn't even cross my mind. I'd always known about him, so I figured his family would know about me."

I don't reply. More than anything, I want to be somewhere else right now, far from this.

"What does . . . I mean, how does Jason feel about this?" she asks. "The 5K, I mean."

"He feels about like I do, I think."

"Oh." She breathes out. "But can I ask you something? Why is this horse race so important? Of anybody, you should be the one saying never again."

I glance toward Lex, still sitting at the table with Robyn. His words about change echo in my head—*you can't choose to stop.* "Regardless of what happened to us," I say, "we can't dictate things for the entire town. That isn't the way it's done here."

"I think Anita and the others were thinking of their own families, not ours."

I open my mouth to tell her that she isn't part of my family, that Jason and I aren't inviting her into our lives, that we can never forgive her for breaching our memories of Brad, for taking him away from us.

But I can't.

Because she has my husband's heart-stopping grin, and her eyes are the color of a golden eagle when the sun strikes its feathers, just as his were. When she walks, I remember how he moved. When she argues, her chin juts forward, and I think of his bullheadedness. Just as she's taken Brad away from us, she's also brought him back.

"I have to get back to work." I gather my tray and head toward the floor. Before I reach it, she calls, "Shari."

When I turn, she says, "I wanted to ask you . . . I wanted to know if he . . . if my dad left anything that might be . . . well, something that might be connected with my mom."

My shoulders tense. "What do you mean?"

"Like a photo, maybe, or letter or something."

"No," I say. "I don't know."

"That's okay." She smiles weakly. "I just wondered."

I make my rounds of the tables, trying to keep my eyes and thoughts from traveling back to her. After a few minutes, Dave comes to the bar to pay his tab. "Hey," he says. "You okay?"

"Sure," I say, as always. "Just fine."

"If there's anything," he says, as always, but this time it falls flat.

Dave and Erica make their way to the door, letting in a gust of cold wind when they leave. It has barely reached the bar when Lex comes up to me.

"Want to step outside?" he asks. "Escape Carcinogen City for a minute?"

"You're a welcome sight," I say. "Let's go."

Outside, it is bitter—Erica's right, it is too cold to wait in the car—even with coats, hats and gloves. I wrap my arms around my chest as we stand near the pallets piled behind the motel.

Lex shifts closer to me, so close that I can sense the warmth of his body. "Do you remember the Talent Day at the school when you were a senior?" he asks.

"I . . . yeah, I think so."

"You sang 'Crazy,' Patsy Cline, you know, in front of all twelve grades."

"I remember that."

"I was in eighth grade that year, and I tell you—the entire male population of my class spent the rest of the school year talking about that performance. We'd all fallen in love with Old Man Johnson's daughter."

I laugh, relieved by the distraction. "You called my father Old Man Johnson?"

"We called all our teachers Old Man or Old Lady," he says. "Yep, seven thirteen-year-old boys who were sure they'd never see a prettier, sexier girl."

"Wow, I never realized that."

"Didn't you? You must have known you sizzled on that stage." He eyes me. "And apparently not much has changed in the past few years, either."

"But you've changed," I tease. "You're Pindall's very first—"

"'Fud.'" We say the word together, then laugh.

"I doubt there's anyone in town who doesn't know that by now," he says.

"Except Walt."

He laughs. "But I haven't really changed much. I can still be smitten by a woman who sings the blues."

I look up at the stars, buoyed by his golly-gee attentions. I don't want to go inside, I never want to see Erica or Pindall or my life here again. I want to drive somewhere, to put everything behind me, and start again. I want to wake up to sky that I've never seen before and breathe air I've never breathed before. We could slip into that Camaro and be out of Pindall in a single roar of its V-8. And tomorrow, we'd wake up and say, what the hell did we just do? And we'd laugh and laugh.

But Lex moves on without me.

"You know that Jason and Juli are seeing each other, don't you?"

Jason's relationship with the Stacys comes as a surprise—for one thing, I didn't realize any of Lex's sisters were so young. Then I remember the bundle that Mrs. Stacy held in the photo: the last precious baby.

"He stops by quite a bit," Lex continues.

"I didn't know that. Well, good for him, I guess."

"You don't sound convinced."

"It's not that," I say. "Everything I do right now is wrong, no matter what it is. So it's fallen to everybody else in town to tell me what he's doing."

"That's the way it is with most teenagers," he soothes. "I was like that with my parents and with Vern and Sandy, too. What did Erica have to say?"

The familiarity in his voice surprises me. "You know her?"

"I see her at Mona's now and then. She seems to be a sweet kid."

"I'm sure she is, but we never get that far. She wanted to talk about the Derby."

"So, what are you going to do about it?" he asks. "Have you made up your mind?"

"Nothing." Suddenly, I know my answer. "It's not mine—it's not ours—to stop or change or whatever they want to do. It's the town's. If the Council wants to turn it into a sack race, they can."

"That's a brave call. Will you sing?"

I wince, as if he's struck me. I haven't even thought about whether or not I'll perform on the stage at Asa Pindall Park. "I don't know if I can," I say. "I'm afraid I'd just croak."

He doesn't answer, and I realize what I've said.

"Sorry," I say. "Bad choice of words."

"Shari!" Robyn hails me from the door. "You still here?"

"My master summons," I say.

"Hold on a minute." He touches my shoulder in a shock of heat. "I came down here with one purpose in mind. Why do you like that Escher picture so much?"

"You came to ask me that?" I laugh. "I barely remember it now."

"Sure you do." He calls me on the ruse. "Tell me why."

"I like it, well, I guess it's the sense of the hands creating a safe place for each other," I say, feeling as if I'm walking on a creaking bridge suspended over the deepest of pits. All the while, I'm thinking, it's a shirt cuff, for heaven's sake. How safe is a shirt cuff?

"It's the sense of connection, isn't it?"

"Maybe, I don't know." I hedge. "You don't find that ridiculous?"

He laughs. "That's not what I'm thinking. Of course, this late at night, I'm never quite sure what I'm thinking. But I know that's not it." Offering a gloved hand to me, he says, "Come on, let's go inside."

In the bar, the Nookie girls are dancing in front of the juke box with some of the boys, who spin them out and pull them back in with true cowboy flare. They're joined by the Do-Si-Dos, whose moves are much smoother. The snowmobilers have evidently struck a truce and returned peacefully to downing their drinks, and the Alabamans have disappeared, probably retreating to their room in the motel.

Lex brings the Escher book up to the bar. "Keep it for as long as you want."

"Thanks."

"You're making a good decision about the Derby," he tells me, then gives a scamp's wink. "Just like you did when you kyped the Escher drawing."

I laugh, and he wishes me farewell with a kiss on the cheek.

It's another hour before the evening finally winds down. At home, I check to make sure that Jason is in his room. He's sleeping soundly, but I'm restless. I don't want to sleep. I don't even want to sit down, though it's been one of the most tiring evenings I've put in in a while. I wish I could saddle LilyBelle and ride up to the ridge where the golden eagles nest, but it is three in the morning and seventeen below zero outside. So I stand beside the dresser in my bedroom, where I can reach up and touch the smooth pine of the ceiling, just as Brad promised. On top of the dresser is the book of M.C. Escher's illustrations.

I leaf through it. Most of the drawings annoy me—maybe it's the hour or that my eyes burn from exhaustion—so I come back to the picture of the hands. Both draw energetically, hopefully, giving each other life, space, existence.

After Brad made knives, his hands smelled of fresh oil, the hot motor of the grinder, and the tang of new coins. I would cup them in mine and hold them near my face to breathe in the richness. He'd laugh.

"Oil as an aphrodisiac," he once teased. "What the world doesn't know."

I keep one of the knives Brad made in a drawer beside the bed. It was his favorite. The blade is virgin, smooth except for where he stamped his signature, "BB." The handle of polished elk antler is scrimshawed with a single aspen leaf.

When I hold it, the metal grows warm. When I look at it, it reflects my face by halves—first my lips and nose, then my eyes—rippling in lover's kisses over my features. I feel the familiar burn of want and need in my palms, the rawness in my legs, the tenderness in my throat. I remember Brad's mouth, his eyes black in the dim light, his bold knuckles and long fingers. I can picture him astride Shiloh, or stretched out in a hammock between two towering Ponderosa pines, or in my bed, sleeping with the quilt tangled around his waist. When I close my eyes, I can smell river water, and well-soaped saddle leather, and freshly fallen leaves under autumn sun.

I miss my husband.

I miss a man.

NINE

THE FIRST CUT

Marguerite built the Wickiup on a property where a run-down gas station stood. She herself oversaw the razing of the rotted, clapboard building, rats scurrying around her feet, and she drew the plans for the grocery herself. Everything in the Wickiup is state-of-the-art, hauled into Pindall at great expense. The store carries vegetable seed in spring, lawn sprinklers in summer, and windshield scrapers in winter. Residents of Pindall can buy darned near everything they need from the Wickiup.

She knows who in this town needs help and who only thinks they do. She has delivered groceries to Mary Flying Eagles, whose only crime was to marry a good-for-nothing Pindall boy, and Donna Rae Griffiths, whose inability to grasp the simple concept of birth control has led her to have a flock of kids by different—and usually married— fathers. And she had always taken care of Darnell.

Darnell lives just inside the Park, in a compound resurrected from an abandoned dude ranch. He claims he acquired the property from the government for services rendered in the days of Fidel and Khruschev and Mao. The U.S. government wanted him to disappear, needed him to, and found a place for him to do it. Marguerite senses a kernel of credibility in his tales, but sometimes Darnell has trouble distinguishing between fact and fiction. Still, she doesn't challenge him. She learned long ago that we all construct our own realities.

Fiction never entered her husband, Howard's, life. Neither did romance or sentiment. Marguerite, who was already old enough to be called a spinster, met him at a USO show in Chicago, right before he shipped out for the South Pacific. He had already spent a year in Pindall's mill and knew he would return. Howard offered no surprises.

At the mill, he split virgin logs in two. In lumbering, the first cut determines everything—the number of boards, their shapes and sizes, the amount of waste. A good sawyer has to have keen instincts. At the time Howard worked the mill, sawyers made their judgments by running their hands along the surface of the log, which had been stripped of bark and laid soft and slick before them. By feeling the swells and dips in the log's surface, they translated its lifetime into product, and Howard was good at it. But one day he misread a log. The saw caught a knot, and Howard just followed that blade right around, died as the saw bit gouged its way through that hard spot.

Alpine living has never been to Marguerite's liking. She feels tied up in the mountains, as if she cannot see far enough ahead. When she travels, it is to flat places. She once spent a full afternoon sitting in a field of grass up near the Montana state line. She had left Howard that day for the first time, thinking it was for good.

But it wasn't, and so Marguerite did what any un-god-fearing woman does when she is stuck in an unhappy town and a dead-end marriage. She took lovers.

They were never local—Lord, she wasn't that stupid. There was a rancher who ran Santa Gertrudis cattle up near Cody, and a state legislator who kept a house in Riverton furnished only with a bed. There was a banker from Jackson, and an Idaho well driller who was sterile after spending his youth riding bulls.

For all that trying, there had to be at least one great love in her life. Marguerite has had two.

Mateo was the first. She met him the second time she left Howard, when she drove north to the place where the mountains lapsed into hills and bluffs and, finally, wide, open meadows. Sometime in the afternoon, Brad, who was three or four at the time, needed to pee. Marguerite pulled the car over and, while Brad wet on the shoulder of the road, stared to the west across the empty plain. Something moved, far in the distance. Something else moved—white boulders, unleashed from a gentle rise beyond the meadow—and suddenly the field began washing toward her, a rolling sea. "Look," she said to Brad. "What are those?"

"Lammies," he replied assuredly.

"Lambs?"

She stared into the sunlight, and indeed, saw sheep flooding the meadow. There seemed to be no reason for their migration, no path for their travels. They simply flowed forward, undulating across the grass. "What's making them go?" she asked, speaking more to herself than to Brad.

"The horse," he responded, his hands in fists, clutching imaginary reins. "And there's dogs."

She glanced at Brad, wary of his clear-sighted certainty and her own faulty perception, then at the sheep. Slowly, she picked out, beyond the stream of animals, a lone figure on a brown horse. Several black collies pranced near the horse, then shot away, disappearing into the flock.

The sheep swept onto the highway, closing in around her Buick, blanketing the blacktop. Their hooves clicked on the pavement, and their bleating grew to a raucous orchestra. She waited, trapped in the car. The smell of the hot wool, sweet as the scent of thyme, oily with lanolin, came through the open windows. Sweat poured from her, and her throat grew dry and itchy. Brad fussed in the seat beside her, alternately excited and bored. Finally, the flock began to thin. The last animals clattered past her, sprinting to catch up. She was still watching them when the brown horse appeared beside the car. She could see only the leg, boot and stirrup of the rider.

She climbed from the car and shaded her eyes to look up. The shepherd was a small, broad-shouldered man, draped in a heavy Mexican poncho. His black beard had not been trimmed in a long time, and his hair flowed from beneath his hat. His eyes were black slivers in his dark face.

"You should of moved," he said. "Too late now."

She didn't immediately understand what he meant. But the road was blocked, the sheep so tightly packed in the corridor between the barbed wire fences that there would be no traveling through.

"It's a ten-mile stretch," the man reported. "To the next break. It'll take hours."

"Why are they on the road?"

"Can't take 'em through the wheat. They'd trample it."

She looked at the green fields. For as far as she could see, the hills swelled and rolled with tender, newly-sprouted wheat. In the fall, the land would gleam with gold. "Then I should turn around and go back?"

"Go back. Or follow."

He rode on, and Marguerite sat motionless. Brad attempted a headstand on the front seat. "Look at me, Mommy," he said. "See?"

"I do," she said, without turning her head from the sight of the sheep and the shepherd's back. She started the car and crept forward.

Brad righted himself. "Are we following, Mommy?" he asked.

"Yes," she said. "We're following."

The shepherd had not underestimated the amount of time the passing would take. Marguerite stayed behind, barely moving, frequently stopping the car to allow the engine to cool. As she stood at the side of the road, she felt joyous. Around her, everything swayed—the wind-ravaged grass, the drifting clouds, the singing electrical wires above her head, Brad, the sheep. The motion was intoxicating, lulling, a dance of energy and light.

Near nightfall, the dogs chased the sheep toward the west, into unplowed pasture. Marguerite pulled her car to the side of the road. The shepherd barely glanced up as she and Brad approached. He was already unsaddling his horse, pulling away a sleeping roll and saddlebags.

"Where are you taking them?" she asked.

"Bartlett Ranch."

Marguerite nodded, although she had no idea where Bartlett Ranch lay.

The shepherd produced a small cook stove from the bundle of blankets. He lit it while Marguerite waited, Brad's hand in hers.

"Would you cook?" the shepherd asked. "I don't much get other people's cooking."

"What do you have to cook?"

"Coffee, corn, potatoes, and dried beef."

"What can I do with that?"

He rose from his crouched position. "Same as I do. It just tastes different when somebody else done it."

She laughed. "What's your name?"

"Mateo," he said. "Mateo Echeverria."

"I'm Marguerite Brock. This is Brad."

"Daisy." A grin spread across his weather-blasted face. "That's what *margarita* means. In Spanish, at least. So have at it, Daisy. Cook all you want."

And so she cooked for the three of them, mixing potatoes with canned corn, making the coffee so strong and black that it left a bitter pall over her tongue. Mateo drew a mound of bread from a tin and showed her the cross he had etched in the top of the dough before it was cooked.

"The first piece goes to the dogs," he said, and tossed the golden brown crust into their eager mouths. "Shepherd's blessing."

Brad slept that night in the front seat of the Buick, one of her quilts covering him. She slept in the back, her feet extended out the open door, under a borrowed blanket. The blanket smelled of wood smoke and dust, of fallen grass, where Mateo's body had crushed it against damp, fertile ground. At times, she sat up and watched him as he lay amid his sheep, oblivious to the proximity of hooves to his head. A rifle and a shotgun lay beside him, his fingers stretched in readiness over the stocks. His horse was hobbled out beyond the flock where it had fresh grass to graze; the dogs skulked, ever alert, through the night. He had seemingly enjoyed her meal, such as it was. As they had eaten, huddled around the stove, the evening air rapidly cooling, Marguerite had asked him where he lived when he was not driving sheep. She imagined a wide valley, a shack of some kind on open prairie.

"I have a pickup and trailer," he replied. "With an indoor crapper. First one I ever had."

"Why don't you bring it along?"

"Why should I, when I got the sky?" He laughed. "That's what you people with houses don't understand. The *sky*."

She woke the next morning to the sound of the sheep bleating anxiously. She quickly sat up, wondering if some predator stalked nearby. She slid across the seat to the open door and stepped out into the chaos.

It took her several minutes to find Mateo. He moved slowly, occasionally disappearing as he sifted through the animals. Marguerite threaded her way through the flock toward him, kneeing sturdy ewes and nursing lambs. She came across him at last, as he looped his arm around the neck of a lamb. With his free hand, he flipped it to the ground, on its back. Holding its legs in one hand and lifting its hindquarters in the other, he bent so close to it that his face touched its stomach. After a minute or so, his head bounced back with a violent jerk. Released, the animal rose, staggered forward, fell on its hind flanks, then struggled upward and blended into the flock.

Mateo spat. A wad of raw, pinkish flesh landed on the ground.

Marguerite's stomach turned. "What are you doing?"

"Some of them rams is getting too big." He swiped at the blood on his lips with his sleeve. "They start riding the ewes if they ain't fixed."

"Castration?"

"It's the only way when you're alone," he said. "You need both hands to hold 'em, so you use your teeth."

He took a drink from a canteen, spat again, then grinned. "Only thing is, better be right the first bite."

Marguerite watched the limping lamb until it disappeared amid the flock. "Is that why you're taking them in?"

"That, dip, shearing, culling, breeding. Do it every year, right before I take 'em up to summer range." He made a grab for another lamb. "You want to try?"

Marguerite took a step backward. "No," she said. "No."

He laughed and let the lamb run. "Just thought I'd ask."

She followed him for another day, until the gauge on her car flashed red with heat, until she herself drove with a pool of sweat beneath her legs, until poor, cranky Brad curled up beneath the dash, next to the fresh air vent and cried himself into a nap. Occasionally, she reached from the window of her car to sink her fingers into the dense clot of a straggler's wool, then sniffed the oily residue beneath her nails. It was sweet and rancid all at once, oily and musky. The smell of Mateo's skin.

That night, after they had camped beside a clear stream, and she had cooked the same menu of corn, potatoes, coffee and bread, and after she had put Brad to bed in the front seat of the Buick, she and Mateo rolled into a blanket against the hard ground. It wasn't love making, she remembers, it was sex. Nothing gentle or sweet, nothing romantic or clingy, just two people out to take what each wanted from the other and call it good. Afterward, they lay side by side, looking up at stars so thick that Marguerite imagined she could reach up and clutch a fistful.

"This is what you meant," she said.

"What?"

"The sky."

He chuckled, but didn't answer. Marguerite kept her eyes open as long as she could, basking in starlight.

The afternoon of the third day, they reached Bartlett Ranch. The flock scampered through the barnyard toward a pasture separated from the road by a deep ditch that Marguerite's car could not ford. Mateo rode ahead to speak with the ranch hands. One man glanced up toward Marguerite, who leaned on the hood of her car, stranded on the road. Mateo pivoted off his horse and came over to her.

"Be back next year?" he asked.

"Will you be in the same place?"

"I take 'em into the mountains every summer." He winked. "Come at the right time of year and I'll escort you to the Sheepherder's Ball."

"When's that?"

"I'll let you find out for yourself."

Tourists consider Marguerite's quilts to be American folk art. One woman even goes so far as to call Marguerite the "O'Keeffe of quilters." She travels to Pindall from Las Vegas once a year to buy quilts.

The quilts often feature fanciful, blossoming flowers, with solid centers and hundreds of delicate diamonds flowing into petals. Through the years, Marguerite has learned how to shape the pieces so that they look as if the petals are folding inward, the edges curling, as if the flower is just blooming. She once sewed quilts from scraps, painstakingly collected, but now she orders yards of sumptuous velvet or satin into the Wickiup. She unfolds the fabric first, spreading it fully across the table, and determining her pattern. She has discovered that she cannot simply gnaw away at the sides, taking a scrap here and there, without sensing that she has done something wrong, something contrary to the nature of the quilt, which grows from the heart outward. When she cuts the fabric, the first cut runs right into the depth of it.

Howard took up quilting, once, not long before his death. She had thought—again—that she would leave him, but that time, she made it only as far as Pindall's cemetery, where she sat in the car with her patchwork, stitching as the sun set.

It took Howard two hours to find her. He parked his red Chevy truck behind her car and climbed from it, calling to Brad, who was riding a headstone for a horse, "Hello, son." Then he settled into the passenger's seat of Marguerite's car. "You planning to stay here?" he asked.

"I'll be here someday anyway."

"No sense rushing things."

They said no more—they never talked about their troubles. The sun started to set, and the motor of Marguerite's car clicked as the night air cooled the metal. Time drifted past them, slipping away and leaving them without any recourse but to return to the way they'd been. Finally Howard spoke of his day at the mill, of the raw timber arriving in the yards. "These trees are only about a foot," he complained. "The old growth's gone. What can you do with a trunk the size of a dinner plate?"

Marguerite had leaned back against the car seat and closed her eyes. She imagined whole forests laid to waste, reduced to a table setting of pine—trunks compacted into dinner plates, saucers and coasters, branches folding into knives and forks.

When she opened her eyes, she saw that Howard had started to sew along the open seam. He gathered the partly attached diamond against the bulk of quilt, and he worked with a steady hand, making stitches as fine and disciplined as her own. He tucked the needle through the fabric, then drew up the thread until it pulled tight and brought the two pieces together smoothly. "Thought I'd help," he said. She stared at his hands, so sure and strong, so much like her own when they handled needle and thread, yet so different with their knotty scars and swollen knuckles, and she understood how much it hurt him to lose the feeling of the thick trunks, the big trees beneath his palms.

"That's damask," she offered. "From an old tablecloth."

"Feels good." He caressed the fabric with his thumb, the delicate weave catching against his calluses with the sound of sandpaper on wood.

"You did a nice job," she said.

He handed her the needle and thread quickly, as if he had no claim to it. "I can't do much more than strap it together, though," he said. "I used to watch Ma sew, but I wouldn't know what comes next."

But Marguerite knew. Quilting is an act of fortitude. Every stitch counts. Nothing can be haphazard or half-hearted. It cannot be sloppy. It has to be even, taut, the way love should be. Quilting demands choices, and if those choices become puckered or lax, you repair them, make them whole again. Once she saw Howard with a needle in his hand, she made her choice. She forgave him everything—his dullness, his simplicity, his affection for Pindall. They had a home, they had a son.

She stayed the course.

But the sins of the mother were visited upon the son, it seemed. Year after year, Marguerite witnessed the jagged swath Brad cut through Shari's and Jason's lives when he escaped from Pindall for the winter. Why did he never see it? Why did he never realize that he was creating a trap for himself every time he wandered, that what he had wasn't freedom, but desperation?

She worries about Jason, so sure that he hates this place. She watches him work his petty crimes and rebellions against school, his mother, the town, even against herself. It's his father's blood come to roost within him. Hers, too—what was she thinking, taking Brad on sheep drives and hiding out in cemeteries? Teaching him that running relieves heartache?

It has nothing to do with Erica Wiegel—the fuss over the Derby and the newly-anointed 5K Derby Run aside—although it seems to have everything to do with her. Marguerite and Erica have grown comfortable together, sharing lunch on Sundays. Every week, Erica brings some dessert that she's baked in Dave Phillips's trailer-house oven. The desserts are such failures that it's become a joke between them.

"Cooking has never been my strong suit, either," she told Erica.

"But I buy all these ingredients at the Wickiup," the girl responded. "If anyone saw this, they'd think you sell rat poison."

"I do."

"Then maybe I was in the wrong aisle."

And they had laughed as Erica tossed her rock-hard butterscotch bars—which even Dane and Amory refused to eat—into the trash.

Erica has started taking photos with a Polaroid camera that she bought at David's Variety. The first Sunday she brought it to Marguerite's, she took pictures of everything—of the bolts of fabric in the living room, of the kitchen, the meal, the dogs, even of mange-coated Purdy.

While a nauseatingly acrid row of undeveloped photos lay on the coffee table, Marguerite had asked Erica what she would do with them.

"I want to send them to Mike and the twins," Erica said.

"What does your family think of your being here?" Marguerite asked.

"They don't completely understand it." She had shrugged. "Mike says it's just like something my mom would do. She was pretty good at being hard-headed and determined to get her way."

"So was your father."

"Then I'm doubly blessed." She lifted the camera to her eye. "Ready? Say cheese!"

Erica snapped the photo. When Marguerite saw it a few minutes later, she noticed that the framing of the photo was a little off-center. She appeared to the right, with the vacant couch, and the closed door, and a blank space of wall behind her. The photo made her look smaller, less sure of herself. It made her look like what she has never felt before: a woman alone.

Marguerite is not handy with love. She's never quite known how to act around it, never known how to offer it with grace and dignity. Certainly she loves Shari and Jason—she has always been there for them—but God knows she didn't love Brad the way she should have; there was always the sour scum of disagreement on their relationship. Yet Erica has made her believe in second chances.

"The Brock family has a long history in Wyoming," Marguerite has told her. "Read just about any book on local history, and you'll find a Brock or two."

"I'll do that," Erica promised. "What about your family?"

"I grew up in Illinois, right outside Chicago."

Erica's eyes had sparked. "So you're a Midwestern girl like me?"

It seemed silly to agree—she has lived in Pindall for nearly four decades—but Marguerite had, feeling not quite young again, but vital in a way she hasn't in years.

Marguerite sought out Mateo again after Howard died, when she was finally free to do so. Leaving Brad at the Phillips house, she had driven north alone. She found him at virtually the same place on the same date. When he came across her car mired in the flock, he had grinned at her through the open window and said, "You missed the Sheepherder's Ball again, Daisy. It's the sixth time, you know."

"My husband died," she said.

"That's too bad," he said. "It's tough on a woman."

And then, he let it go. Just as simple as that. No misplaced sentiment, no insincere pity. It had made Marguerite want to jump up and dance.

She had followed Mateo's flock, cooked for him, slept with him. They sheltered in utter darkness, where only the stars looked upon them, and only the wind shared the space. By then, they were old lovers, comfortable with each other's flesh, no longer needy and hurried.

"You know," Mateo told her. "I don't see no more than fifty people in a year, and ninety-nine percent of them is men. You ought to come calling more often, Daisy."

But the following year, when she went to meet him, a young fellow was shepherding the flock. He was not Basque, and when he rode by Marguerite's car, he did not even tip his hat to her.

She learned later that Mateo had died, alone, at a sheep camp in the Absaroka Mountains. And so she moved on. She purchased the lots where the Wickiup now stands with the settlement money from the mill; she became a sought-after customer of bankers and lawyers in Jackson and Lander. She aimed for the Town Council seat, and she bought the Grand Champion steer at the 4-H Livestock Auction, a luxury afforded only to the wealthy. She would never attend a Sheepherders's Ball, held in December, just before lambing season begins.

She rests her needle. She has completed the center of the flower and must now cut velvet for the soft underpetals. It is eleven o'clock, and her eyes are tired, but she spreads the cloth across the dining room table and envisions the shapes. She straightens her glasses on her nose—magnifying lenses, for God's sake, she's growing old—picks up her scissors, slips the blades around the fabric, and makes the first bold cut into the heart of the velvet.

TEN
PERSPECTIVES OF YELLOWSTONE NATIONAL PARK
PART I
45.45N 110.83W

In the four months he has been in Pindall, Ronald has mastered the Cotton Eyed Joe, seen a moose with someone's wash hanging from one antler, and bought a pair of cowboy boots. He has taken up running again, and plans to tour the Park this summer. Western humor, however, still eludes him—it seems to consist of one person ridiculing another. Shortly after he arrived, Robyn pointed at an eyeless, stuffed trophy head that hangs on the Rambler's wall and said, "See that? I shot that mule's eyes out. Once when it was alive, and again the other night."

"That's a mule?" Ronald had asked, confused.

"You are a city boy!" Robyn laughed. "It's a deer. A *mule* deer. You ever see a jackalope?"

For guidance, Ronald had turned to Shari, who had pursed her lips and shaken her head. Sometimes he thinks she wants out as badly as he does.

She has become his guide and salvation. He has learned that she is a widow, which makes her much more attractive than she would be if she were simply single or divorced. Even more intriguing is that she seems untouchable. Ronald has seen Donna Rae, the other waitress, collect a flock of half-plastered admirers around her, each one vying to see who goes home—or to the parking lot or even right outside the door—with her. But never Shari. She orbits the men in the bar like the moon.

The stories about her husband are glorious, triumphant, and inescapable. The Rambler teems with elegy, recited with a passion so intense that Ronald sometimes believes it might be possible to resurrect the dead.

"Everything that kid did turned to gold," Robyn has told him. "So, here he is, not more than twenty-five and working steady enough, doing local trips and whatever makes him a buck or two for Shari and the baby.

Then, some guide from Riverton calls him out of the blue. He can't take his client—had an appendix attack—and he's heard that Brad's doing all right for hisself. So Brad takes this one New Yorker out, and two weeks later, seven Wall Street honchos hear about it and want his exclusive services for their yearly drunk. Two-thousand bucks a day, and they're supplying the booze. And I said to him, I says, 'What's gonna happen when they fly the hell out here from New York and see you ain't nothing but a fresh-face, cocky kid?' He just smiles at me and says, 'Wait and see.' And, by damn, if those New York dudes didn't catch the biggest damned fish you ever seen."

"He was that good, huh?" Ronald had asked, certain that he was hearing a fish story.

"That good and then some."

Now, Ronald watches Shari as she sashays around the Rambler, traveling through the tables, talking to the sullen tourist families in the booths. Tonight she wears one of those sleeveless, plaid cowboy shirts with ivory snaps that just beg to be popped and her remarkable have-to-lie-down-to-zip-'em-up jeans.

When she comes back to the bar, he says, "Do you know why the beer chases the whiskey?"

She tosses a saucy "Why?" over her shoulder.

"Because it's hopping mad."

"But it can barley catch up, you know."

She drops the line without self-consciousness or self-congratulation or even a wink to show she's bent on making time. Well, if she isn't, he is. Between leering at Elise at the mill and ogling Shari at the bar, he's built up a mighty need for a woman.

When Shari returns with fresh drinks, he says, "Let's go up to the Park this weekend."

She takes one wild look around before she says, "Sure. How about Saturday?"

"Saturday, it is, then," he agrees, suddenly energized. Finally, he'll get laid in this town.

He picks Shari up at her house, five miles of highway west of Pindall, and at least one god-awful mile of dirt that dips with washboards and potholes and isn't so much a road as a rut. When, at last, he reaches the barnyard, he swerves to avoid a welcoming committee of barking dogs. Shari is waiting for him on the front verandah, seated in a porch swing that catches patchy sunshine that has broken through the trees.

Ronald waves as he climbs from his car. He's wearing a button-down western-cut shirt, Levi's, and his cowboy boots. From the backseat of the car, he pulls out a straw cowboy hat and plunks it on his head. "Ready to go, angel?" he calls.

"Wow!" Shari replies with a low whistle. For a moment, he entertains the hope that she'll act like the women at the Rambler, who lean toward him with unlit cigarettes pursed in their lips, one hand on his shoulder. "I bet you didn't buy those in Pindall."

Well, not what he hoped. "You're right. I had to go to Cody."

"So the Wild, Wild West is alive and well in Cody. That's good."

"Do I look okay?" he asks, fingering his shirt buttons. The dogs sniff around his new cowboy boots, and he scuffles a couple of times. A Border collie jumps up on him, leaving a dust print.

"Katie, down!" Shari orders. The dog unrepentantly retreats, its tail wagging. "You sure do," she says. "Just about any man looks good in a cowboy hat and boots."

"I'll take that as a compliment." He surveys the yard. "This is pretty."

Shari looks around, as if weighing his observation. A log home settles easily in a clearing just beyond the lodgepole pines. It's traditional in style—prospector's-cabin-cum-hunting-lodge—with the wide verandah and protective overhang. The logs jutting from the walls are massive and consistent, and Ronald finds himself mentally calculating DBI.

"Did all that lumber come off of your own land?" he asks. "How many acres?"

"A hundred and twenty. And yes, it's all from our land."

He laughs at the edge in her voice. "I'm sure the BLM wouldn't miss a tree or two. And you're nowhere near our leases."

"You have every tree tagged and inventoried, I bet."

"You better believe it, darlin'," he agrees smoothly. "Do you have a furnace in the house?"

"Woodstove only. We're pretty far off the pipeline up here, and electric's too pricey."

Jesus, he remembers those days. "What's the coldest you've seen inside?"

"It's never gotten below forty."

"Above or below?"

She laughs in that bouncy way she has when she forgets to remember how unhappy she is. To Ronald's left, three horses watch from the corral next to the water tank, nickering as if they expect to be included in the day's adventure. A traditional, lofted barn rises behind them, roofed, as all Wyoming barns seem to be, in red shingle.

Ronald glances behind him, gauging the distance back to town. "It's a little remote out here."

"That depends on where you want to be." Hands on her hips, she surveys the buildings. "Brad always said that we took a 'piece' of property and created a 'peace' of property. Different spellings, you see."

"I'm sorry about your husband, Shari."

"Not as sorry as I am." She laughs weakly, then reinforces her husky voice with steel. "Don't let me get weepy on you, Ronald. You'll regret it. I'll regret it even more."

Ronald reaches for her, brushing his hand down her arm. He means to comfort her, but he can't help but notice that she smells of freshly washed sheets that are ready for good, hard sex. He tips the brim of his hat. "Let's go see this Park of yours."

Out on the highway, Ronald no longer babies his car. He accelerates rapidly, swinging around curves with zest. Shari grips the armrest on the door. "Relax," he tells her. "I'm a good driver."

"As long as there isn't a buffalo around the next curve."

He lets up on the gas.

"You'll be glad to know that Pindall has fulfilled all my expectations," he tells her.

"Is that good or bad?"

He laughs. "I can't imagine a more pleasing place to live. It's full of people who want to live the right life, not the good life."

"Well, it wouldn't hurt if it was the good life, too. Times can get pretty rough. A bad timber yield or tourist drought makes for a long winter."

"I'll see what I can do to make sure the trees don't pine away."

"Just don't needle them too much."

They laugh together. The sun streams through the back window of the car, and the miles between Shari's house and the Park lapse into streams of conversation. First, Shari tutors Ronald on Pindall's history, then the Park's, then Wyoming's. Then she comes to what Ronald has already learned is every Wyomingite's favorite subject: highway stories. There must be fewer than six degrees of separation on Wyoming's roads. If it has not happened to you, you know someone who knows someone who has driven off the highway in a blizzard; been stuck in mud in the Red Desert after a downpour; struck an animal in spectacularly gory vehicular fauna-cide; come through foot-deep hail near Elk Mountain; or endured hours-long highway closures for accidents on the Summit between Cheyenne and Laramie.

"My truck's starting to look like a Rent-a-Wreck," Shari says. "And now, with Jason driving it, too, I don't know how much longer it can last. Just about everything's broken on it."

Ronald seizes his chance. "You should know, your son comes down to the mill during the day. He talks with Elise."

"So I've heard."

"Do you know what they talk about?"

"No idea. I'm not privy to much of what goes on in his life."

"Shouldn't he be in school?"

"He's supposed to be. The past year has been tough for both of us." She pauses, then offers, "Our lives are like a train that got off track and started chugging down one of the side switches. We're heading in the same direction, but on a different route than we were before. A bumpier route. Not as well maintained."

Ronald says nothing. Whenever he sees the kid at the Rambler, Jason is tinkering with an outlandishly bright, menacing knife. He glowers at Ronald, as if waiting to harvest Ronald's organs in a moldy room at the motel. Ronald cannot imagine breeding a son like that. He recently sent Craig a Wonderful Wyoming T-shirt and cowboy pistols with plastic mother-of-pearl butts and vinyl holsters.

"What about the girl who says she's your husband's daughter?" he asks.

"Who is his daughter," Shari corrects. "There's no doubt about it."

"So, what's that like?"

"Oh," she says airily. "When we aren't talking about her—which is never—we don't think about her—which is—"

"Never," Ronald chimes in with her. "I'm sorry. I can't imagine that kind of betrayal—"

"He didn't cheat on me, if that's what you mean." She laughs sourly. "You know, I really don't want to talk about this today."

"Okay." He searches for another topic. "I hear there's going to be a 5K race in a few weeks at Sawmill Days. I thought I might enter."

Shari doesn't answer immediately. At last, she says, "That goes back to my husband's daughter. It was her idea."

"Sorry," Ronald says quickly.

"That's okay. There's no reason you should know that."

The conversation wanes as the gates to the Park appear. Suddenly, Ronald feels as if he is in the midst of a major city. Traffic snails along the roads, and once inside the gates, it's worse. Ronald curses each time a tourist slams on his brakes when an elk or deer wanders into view. Most of the time, people don't even bother to pull onto the shoulder of the road, but stop where they are, as if everyone wants a snapshot.

As he waits for the roadway to clear yet again, Shari asks, "You want to jump out and snap a picture?"

"What is it this time?" Ronald asks.

"Umm"—she cranes her neck—"something big and hairy."

"At least that's better than a . . . what did you call it?"

"A pika."

"It was a rodent," Ronald complains. "A hundred cars stopped to take a picture of a rodent."

He pulls his Olympus OM 10 from the back seat. At first, he rolls down the window and tries to focus on the animal—an impossibility given the throng of vehicles and gawkers. In front, four college-age boys clamor atop a VW bus. Behind them, a family leaps from its car and trails through his line of vision. Annoyed, Ronald swivels in his seat and snaps a picture of Shari instead.

"Oh, I wasn't expecting that," she says.

Coyly, he advances the film. "You're the prettiest thing I've seen so far today."

"At least you didn't call me big and hairy. Or a rodent."

He laughs. "Far from it."

She squirms. "Are you sure you don't want to see the wildlife? It's what most people come for. Everybody loves the animals, even the pikas."

"That's all right."

He isn't sure why he feels so blasé about Yellowstone. Maybe it is because he is too hot in his new clothes, or because his plan to woo Shari today has turned out to be more work than he expected, or maybe because he hates being thought of as a sightseer. By the time they arrive at Old Faithful, though, Ronald snatches a parking space, cheating a rival minivan, with the aggressiveness of a true tourist. He and Shari chuckle about it as they cross the asphalt to the sidewalk leading to the geyser. Although the geyser is not scheduled to erupt again for ten minutes, the benches are already packed with Japanese tourists whose cameras are trained on the cone; an Indian family in saris and jewels; German backpackers guzzling water from enormous plastic bottles; and noisy American families. Anticipation rises with the heat from the benches.

Ronald squeezes onto a bench next to an orangish-skinned, raven-haired woman in a tank top cut so low and shorts cut so high that staring is irresistible. Shari drops onto the edge beside him, her feet turned out into the aisle between seating areas. He smiles helplessly at her. He should find another place—maybe next to the Mennonites in the rear—but they are only two rows back and he wants a good view. He wiggles a little to try to give Shari more space, and feels himself firmly and pleasantly wedged between steamy female buttocks and thighs.

Not an unpleasant sensation.

The woman beside him turns goggle sunglasses toward him and fingers the Instamatic camera in her lap. "Nice camera," she remarks as he unwraps a telephoto lens from his bag and clicks it into his Olympus. "Long lens. You got a zoom on that?"

"See for yourself."

Ronald allows her to look through the lens, then scoots closer to Shari. The woman follows suit, shuffling closer to him. "Where y'all from?" she asks.

"Right here," Ronald replies, waving a hand expansively.

"Right here?" She eyes Old Faithful as if he has just crawled out of the geyser and she's curious who else might be inside.

"Nearby," Ronald corrects himself. "One of the small towns near the Park."

"My name's Clarice. I'm from Florida," she says. "Tail-lahassee."

Her pronunciation causes Ronald to pause. He swears that if he were not so obviously in Shari's company, Clarice would invite him back to her car for a quick one. She certainly is interested in his long lens.

Old Faithful is late. The ranger assures them that, even though Old Faithful earns its name by being the most reliable of the geysers, it hasn't quite found its footing since the recent earthquakes in Idaho, and the times between eruptions have lengthened. Be patient, he advises, and the reward will eventually come.

"Sounds like my last husband," Clarice comments, lazily fanning herself with the brochure.

Ronald laughs, but stops, afraid of offending Shari. His camera strap is chafing the skin around his neck. To amuse her, he takes it off and hands it to Shari.

"Do you know how to use one of these?" he asks.

"No," she says.

"Just turn the lens until the two halves line up."

"I'm not very good at this kind of stuff," she murmurs, wildly twisting the telephoto lens.

"Real gentle," Ronald coaches her. "It takes an easy touch."

"I betchy'all have that in buckets," Clarice purrs in his ear, then addresses Shari as if she is a slower, uglier sister. "What y'all should do, honey, is go into the gift shop and take a picture of one of those placemats they got in there—ya know, the plastic ones with the scenic views. Works like a dream."

Both Ronald and Shari look at her, the camera lens now pointed at the rounded bottom of the tourist ahead of them, the view undoubtedly lopsided to boot.

"Do you do that?" Ronald asks.

"Sure. Ya take the pictures home, show 'em around once or twice, and they go in a drawer. So I say, don't fix what ain't broke."

"And no one notices?"

"Ya think anybody really looks at those pictures?"

"Well, maybe we'll try it." He reaches over and takes Shari's hand, squeezing it lightly. Her body is shaking with laughter.

At that moment, steam hisses from the cone of Old Faithful and spews over the sinter flats. The crowd oohs and aahs, not entirely sure that this is what they drove hundreds of miles to witness. The geyser gradually gains momentum and pressure, spitting forward, then rushing in a smooth, even cloud. It billows to a lofty peak, a pillar of white glory. People applaud and children shriek. Cameras click in wild succession. Shari photographs the occasion for Ronald, while Clarice yee-haws to show her appreciation. She makes no effort to snap a picture with her Instamatic.

A breeze catches the geyser's mushrooming cloud and begins to wend it toward them. With horror, the visitors realize that the one hundred and twenty foot colossus is coming after them. A murmur ripples through the crowd, and parents gather up little hands and make a mad dash for refuge. The intrepid Japanese surge forward with cameras unswervingly pointed skyward, undeterred by a little scalding water. The German backpackers hurdle the benches like Olympic athletes.

Caught in the middle of the panic, Ronald asks Shari, "We won't be burned, will we?"

"I don't know."

For an instant, they wait breathlessly. Ronald hugs Shari against him. On the other side, Clarice latches onto his arm and presses into him, making them all wobble like round-bottomed dolls, Ronald lofting from side to side.

Moisture dapples the walkway before them as Old Faithful bends their way. The sun disappears behind the cloud. Yet when the mist arrives, the droplets fall harmlessly, rapidly cooled during the descent from the heavens. The spray's touch isn't even as harsh as a bathroom shower's. It's like dew.

"Looks like Mother Nature just flipped us the bird," Clarice comments just as Shari whispers in his ear, "Baptism by Old Faithful. Welcome to Wyoming."

Ronald has packed a gourmet lunch, complete with cheeses, crusty bread and wine. By the time they eat, though, an afternoon thunderstorm has wafted in and brought a downpour. They lunch in the car, looking out across magnificent, wind-pitched Yellowstone Lake through swaths cleared by the wipers on the BMW. Crowns of lacy foam drive toward the shore. Ducks ride out the swells, and gulls skim and swoop, diving for insects.

"So, you've lived near here your whole life," Ronald says.

"My whole life," she repeats, a wondering note in her voice.

"Have you ever thought of living anywhere else?"

"Brad and I went up to Alaska once. We thought we might move up there to get away from the crowds"—she waits for his laugh—"but that's about as far as it went. I'm a bit of a homebody."

After they eat, they venture a walk around the metal-gray lake's edge. Still sloshed by the wind, the water laps at their feet and sprays into their faces. The afternoon has turned cold, as so many summer afternoons do—a vacationer's nightmare of damp and disappointment. Shari is wrapped in a jean jacket to ward off the wind's chill, but Ronald has no jacket at all. He takes pictures of her—beside a pine, near the lake with waves lapping at her ankles, on the pebbly beach. Mosquitoes, lured out by the soggy conditions, swarm around their heads.

He swats at his ears. "Nature's fine as long as it doesn't bite."

When they leave the Park, Ronald turns the heat in the BMW to high, blasting their wet feet. In Pindall, he toys with taking her straight to his house, but decides on dinner. Passing Mona's Kitchen and another restaurant that seems to adopt a new specialty—Chinese, American, pizza—every few months, he parks at the pink adobe La Cocina Mexican restaurant on the opposite side of town from the Rambler, as far from the bar as he can get within Pindall's limited city limits.

"Hungry?" he asks.

"Starved."

The décor inside the restaurant is simple—cactus, river-bottom pottery, a sombrero tacked to the wall. They drink gigantic margaritas while they wait for their food.

"Here's to Old Faithful," he toasts. "May I never see it again."

Their glasses touch, and salt from the rims drops to the table. "But you met Clarice there," Shari says.

"Ah, Shari, honey," he drawls. "Y'all don't think I had palpitations of my li'l ol' heart over her, do ya?"

"I'm jist thinkin' y'all enjoyed her attention in buckets."

He laughs. "Why not? Don't tell me you don't know how to flirt. I've seen you at the Rambler. You play a mean game."

"Most of the guys there think catch-and-release applies to women."

He laughs and brushes a hand through his hair. "My hair feels crusty," he says in disbelief.

Shari runs a quick, sexy hand through her chestnut hair. "I can feel it, too. It's from the geyser."

She laughs breathily as if she knows a secret that Ronald doesn't.

"What's so funny?" he asks.

"There're all sorts of elements in the water. That's what gives the pools their color, their beauty. Microbial bacteria." Inexplicably, she flushes, as if she has said too much, then quenches her embarrassment with a sip from the margarita. "It's a whole world that we can't see and don't even know about. It just fascinates me."

He frowns at her giddy science lesson. "There's nothing toxic, is there?"

With a laugh, she taps her margarita glass. "This is more toxic. It has about four times the tequila that Walt puts in his—"

"The stronger the better."

She straightens up. "It's a mighty sorrow that makes a man as good-looking as you drink so much."

"Mighty sorrows are easy to come by."

"You told me that you're happy here."

"Most of the time." He shrugs. "So, cheer me up, Shari."

She rubs her finger across the lip of her glass, then licks away the salt. "Tell me about your son," she says.

Ronald's gut churns, all his longing for Craig pouring into his heart. "He's one of the mighty sorrows."

"Sorry."

"No, no, not your fault." He smiles, recovers. "Craig's a go-getter. He's five now and bright and quick and amazing."

"You must miss him."

"I do. That's the one regret I have at leaving Portland. And God, do I regret it."

"You should bring him out here for a couple of weeks," she suggests. "Sons grow up so fast. Pretty soon, he'll be clomping around in boots twice the size of yours."

He sips from his margarita. "I'd do that, in a heartbeat, if I could. But my ex-wife, Becky, has made it all very unpleasant for me. It's a long story. One that I'm not willing to tell right now."

She swirls her glass, sending the lime green liquid into a whorl. "It's hard, isn't it? Your ex-wife, my husband's daughter. Sometimes I'm just floored by all the effort it takes to get through the day." She breathes out a woeful laugh. "Or the night."

"That's what this is for, honey," Ronald says, lifting his glass. "Let's have another."

The food comes, a lumpy ocher mess, no matter what it is supposed to be—rice, refried beans, enchilada, chimichanga. The only saving grace is the margaritas. The more he and Shari drink, the more he thinks this will be the night she stays with him. By the end of the meal, he's so convinced of it that he says: "Let's go to my place."

Shari stops dead in his driveway after she steps from his car. A low, wandering chant floats through the still night, followed by unmistakable laughter.

"It's the two men who live up on the hill," Ronald explains. "Every night is like this."

She laughs. "Well, well."

"What?"

"Those two. They never speak in public. Some vow of silence or something. They're former monks, you know, from . . . well, I don't know where, since they've never told anyone." Another smirk. "Not Wyoming, that's for sure."

"It sounds like a party up there until about eleven every night."

She sobers. "When my husband died, they came to the funeral with armloads of flowers—gladiolus and stuff that doesn't even grow well here—from their own garden. It seems like they're always doing something nice like that."

Ronald doesn't want to hear about the monks or—even less—about Shari's husband. "Come on," he says. "Let's go inside."

In the house, the night air has chilled the great, high-ceilinged room. "Shed your boots," he suggests as he sets about building a fire.

Shari pads off in stocking feet to the kitchen to make coffee. When she returns, she sits easily on the couch. From the coffee table, she picks up a notebook of sawing patterns and flips through the hand-drawn diagrams of circles parsed into rectangles and squares. "I remember these," she says. "You drew one on a napkin the night we met."

Ronald glances up from his task, a little unnerved. "A sawing pattern? Did I really? You must have thought, holy shit, this guy needs help."

"So this is your hobby?" She pages through the notebook, squinting at his minute, neatly-scrolled calculations on each page.

"Not a hobby, exactly. I'm always looking for ways to improve productivity at the mill. You see, some patterns yield more finished product and less waste than others."

"So, how are things going at the mill?"

"We're doing okay, I think." Ronald slips into his Cascadia Northern facade. "Even though timber stands in this area are pretty depleted and the government keeps heaping on more environmental regulations. Lately we've been hearing something about a spotted owl." He pries the notebook from her hands. "Hey, I don't want to talk shop."

But, after that, the conversation dies, although the fire blazes and the room quickly heats. Ronald wonders why, so suddenly, Shari has drawn within herself. She has been perfectly talkative all day long. She goes to the window to look down on Pindall. As if it is a fateful sign, the flashing lights of Macky Bain's cruiser outline Main Street.

"Looks like trouble," Ronald says.

"I just hope this doesn't involve Jason," Shari frets.

"Are you worried? We could drive down—"

"They'll find me if they need me."

Ronald nearly groans aloud. Small town life—everyone in everyone else's pocket. Best take advantage of what time they have. He wraps his arms around her. She's warm, and he quickly discovers she is as pleasantly firm as a woman who drives trucks, hunts, chops wood, rides horses, and hefts trays laden with beer bottles should be. But when he dares a couple of kisses into her hair, she stiffens and lays her hands on his, as if she's reining him in.

"What are you thinking?" Ronald breaks the silence. "You're shaking."

"I'm cold."

"Your hands are hot. Are you scared?"

"I don't know," she whispers. "It's been less than a year since . . . I'm not sure how to handle myself anymore."

"Then we'll just take it one step at a time," he soothes. "In fact, you don't need to take any steps at all. I'm right here."

He touches his lips to her temple, then retreats with gentlemanly grace. They stand together, mesmerized by the flashing lights on Main Street, which allow them to ignore their own reflection in the glass panes of the windows. Shari looks as if she is watching her own demise, while he just looks horny. Worse, she is slowly turning into a board in his arms. If she tenses any tighter, she will outstrip the hardness that has arisen in his trousers.

The phone in the kitchen rings. Ronald releases Shari with an "Excuse me." Before he rounds the corner, he sees her step closer to the window, and an image of her leaping from the balcony and escaping flashes through his head.

"Hello?" he snaps impatiently into the mouthpiece.

It's Becky. Oh, shit, of all the horrible timing, Becky the bitch has to call right now.

"Craig has the chickenpox," she says. "He insisted that you'd want to know."

Ronald's heart pivots in his chest. "Chicken pox? Have you taken him to the doctor?"

"Oh, for heaven's sake, it's chicken pox. Every kid gets them."

He bites back the words that threaten to spill out. "Is he still up? It's a little late, isn't it?"

"Well, every time I put him to bed, he can't sleep for itching. So he's right back up again. Neither of us has slept for three days."

"Put him on."

Craig is sniveling. He sounds as exhausted as Becky. "Hey, cowboy," Ronald says. "What's this I hear about chickenpox?"

"They're all over, Daddy, and they itch. I even got them up my nose."

"Don't scratch them, okay? They'll go away in a few days."

"They itch," Craig whines. "I can't sleep."

"Just close your eyes and think about how much I love you"—he falters, his throat burning with emotion—"and send the itches to me."

"How?"

"Just by thinking: Daddy's got the itches now, and I don't. He's jumping all over his house and doing somersaults and dancing the shimmy so I can sleep."

Craig giggles, then sighs, "Why can't you come home?"

The loss knifes through Ronald's heart. "I wish I could. But do what your mom tells you, okay?" He would be there if Becky wasn't such a—"Let me talk to Mom, okay?"

"Okay," Craig squeaks.

"Goodnight, cowboy. Try to get some sleep, okay?"

After a pause, Becky returns, no more amenable than she was before.

"Take some pictures for me," Ronald says.

"Good God!" She explodes. "You know, I have enough to do just trying to keep him from—"

"Hey, I'm not asking much." God, why did he stay with her as long as he did? He should have snatched Craig and run the moment the boy was born.

"You aren't here," Becky is saying. "And you have no idea how hard it is—"

"No, I'm not there," Ronald returns. "But you might ask yourself why. You wanted me gone. You wanted me out of your life. So I am. Listen, Becky—"

The line goes dead with a resounding crack in his ear.

Ronald glares at the handset, then replaces it on the wall. She makes him so fucking mad, she always has. Their marriage was one bloody sparring match. The coffee is burbling in the glass pot—how long has it been ready? Then he remembers Shari—woman turned to stone—in the other room. She must have heard the exchange. His end, anyway. She must think him a horse's ass. Ah, but if she only knew Becky.

He splashes Crown Royal into his coffee cup, filling it halfway. Shari's cup holds nothing but coffee.

He carries it out to her. "Sorry about that. My ex-wife. My son has chickenpox."

She graciously takes the coffee with only one suspicious sniff aimed toward his cup. "That's miserable. Poor little boy. Has she tried Calamine lotion and soda baths or oatmeal poultices? My grandmother sewed me a pair of cheesecloth mittens to keep me from scratching myself."

Ronald has no idea. Civil conversation with Becky never crosses his mind. "I'm sure she's tried everything," he mutters.

"Jason had chickenpox in the middle of winter. We were snowed in for days, just me and this very unhappy little boy. Brad called every night just to tell us he loved us." She exhales, visibly moved by the memory. "That was good, telling your son you're dancing the shimmy so he doesn't itch. He'll remember that forever."

Ronald wilts. The whiskey does nothing to alleviate his misery, the police lights are still flashing at the bottom of the hill, and, now, Shari has invoked the name of her dead husband, which gives her carnal immunity. Oh, shit, he'll never get laid.

He takes her home. When he kisses her goodnight on the front porch of her house, it's a determined-to-be-friends-forever-no-matter-what kiss. He suspects they both sense the omega in the alpha.

"I hate to leave you here alone," he says. "Will you be all right?"

"I'm so sorry," she says suddenly, the words coming in a rush. "I thought when we went to your place . . . I felt good, those margaritas made me feel—"

"It's okay," he says, unsure where she is going. Is she regretting her decision? Will she invite him inside now? His interest re-ignites.

She dives into it. "And I thought, would it be so bad to be in a man's arms? To be kissed by him? Would it be so wrong?" She stops, her face pale in the wash of the porch light. "I feel lodged in mud, Ronald, unable to move one way or the other without feeling that I am forgetting someone, or betraying someone. Brad, I guess. I think, I don't know. I met him when I was sixteen, and had Jason by the time I was eighteen. I never dated anyone else, I never played around—"

"It's all right, Shari," he soothes.

"But he did. I wasn't his first love, even though I always thought I was. He had a whole *life* with this other woman, he had a child with her, and he didn't even tell me. It . . . half the time I can't believe it, half the time I think, if he was still alive, I'd kill him myself. So why should I feel guilty?"

He bypasses the question. "You'll heal in time."

"I don't know," she says. "I don't know what I want or what I can ask for or who to ask. I don't know who I am, or who he was, or—"

Her confessions touch him. Imagine amiable, carefree Shari—who smiles and mugs and flirts at the bar—holding on to all this pain. "It's okay," he murmurs. "It will be all right."

"But all day long"—oh, shit, she is nearly in tears—"I've been imagining myself sitting next to Clarice at Old Faithful. Two old broads, trying to get lucky in the National Park."

Ronald can't help it. He laughs. Shari covers her eyes with her hands, and Ronald thinks that he has done it now. He has driven her to tears. But when she looks up, she emits a wet, irregular hiccup that he assumes is a laugh.

"I don't think there's much fear you'll turn into Clarice," he assures her. "You're so young and pretty."

That does bring her to tears. Toughness hisses from her. He gathers her up and says what every man dreads having to say: "I'm here for you. Whenever you need me."

On the drive home, headlights appear in Ronald's rearview mirror. At first, he pays them little mind. After all, this two-lane blacktop connects Riverton and the Park, a throughway to both. But the oncoming vehicle is traveling faster than Ronald, a true leadfoot, is.

The vehicle streaks up behind him—Christ, the asshole is sitting on his bumper—and the road before Ronald vanishes in the high beams reflected in his mirrors. He roughly flips the rearview to night position, but light floods the interior of the car. Desperately, he twists the side mirror, so that it points downward, but he still cannot see the road ahead.

He slows down and squints to locate the white line. Sweat breaks out on every inch of him—between his thighs, on his back, under his hair at the nape of his neck. What if Shari's buffalo is meandering across the road just now? Even something as small as a deer would take out a BMW.

Suddenly, his car begins to ratchet. He's hit the rumble strips on the shoulder. He veers toward the center of the highway. The driver behind him straddles the broken white line and edges closer, and Ronald waits for the two vehicles to bump. God, why is there no help in these parts? A state trooper? A Podunk County sheriff's deputy? That ridiculous Indian from Pindall? He thinks of slamming on his brakes, of forcing a collision, but the vehicle is large enough to cream his car.

He'll have to take his chances in the ditches. Just shoot straight off the highway, pray to God to miss the steel posts of the barbed wire fences, and not to roll. He blinks, trying to distinguish from the blackness a clearing where there isn't a tree or boulder or pond. Then, to his right, he sees the light-colored stone columns of the cemetery gate, which is a replica of Yellowstone's famous entrance. The road into the cemetery must be wide enough to accommodate hearses; surely it can handle a BMW.

Without braking, he twists the wheel. The BMW careens onto cemetery road, and he slams his foot onto the brake, fishtailing in the gravel, stopping inches from the solid column. He jumps out of his car as the vehicle roars by.

His vision is washed out and splotched, but he glimpses a dark pickup truck with a broken taillight. Shari's truck. He is sure of it.

Jason is out to kill him.

ELEVEN
DISNEY LAND

Jason slouches in the only chair in Johnny Hart's room on the second floor of the Greenbow Boutique. It's Tuesday afternoon, and Johnny's place is the last place that Jason figures his mother or the authorities will check for him. Every once in a while, he glances out the rain-rusted window to make sure that there isn't a posse waiting for him below.

Shit, he's been jumpy since Saturday night. It was such a wild ride, chasing that BMW down the highway. Who would have thought that fate would have played so easily into his hands? He'd been pretty close to home when he'd seen the BMW cruising toward town, and he had felt a black bile of rage boil up within him. Who was this dick anyway? What gave him the right? More than that, what gave *her* the right to think that she could just forget about his father, just go on without him?

By daylight, he knows it was a stupid ass thing to do. He knows he's in for it.

He looks around Johnny's room. Now that he's gagged his way through the smell, this place isn't so bad. The sun has finally come around the building and brought some light to the room. The orange cat, Tiger, stretches out on the grimy windowsill, looking down on Main Street, his ears flicked back in perpetual irritation. Jason scratches Tiger just above where his tail should be. He's a Manx—stub of a tail and clubby paws.

Johnny sits on his bed, digging into a package of lunch meat and a bag of chips and washing it all down with Coke. Johnny has no refrigerator and the coils of the hot plate that sits on the scarred counter are crusted black. He has no forks or spoons either. The first time Jason brought Johnny food that he'd stolen from the Wickiup, Johnny ate the pork and beans directly from the can, using a rust-laden pocket knife. It wasn't that different from the way Tiger eats his can of Friskies.

The room is like a cell. There's nothing in it, save an old camp cot with one, once-upon-a-time-blue blanket, the folding chair in which Jason now sits, and a nightstand with one drawer missing. A zigzag afghan and a couple of pillows bunch on the end of the bed. Johnny's clothes are crammed into a Cragmont box. On the nightstand lies a Bible that looks like it's been dropped in the john more than once. The pages are wrinkled and wavy, and the leather jacket swoops upward at the corners.

Down the hall is the bathroom—toilet, sink, wedge of a shower that Johnny must not know about—and another room that serves as storage for the Greenbow. Bare bulbs light the entire upstairs, swaying in ominous, unfelt breezes, just like in a horror film. The metal radiator in Johnny's room clanks and hisses every once in a while, but Jason has yet to feel heat.

"How much rent do they charge you for this dump?" he asks Johnny.

"Rent?" Johnny wonders, picking chip crumbs from his old man's paunch.

Johnny can talk for hours about his years as a government bounty hunter up in the Park, and if you give him an opening, it's hard to find a closing. Every story Johnny tells is about hunting, rattling off a litany of animals that have met their deaths at his hands. Lynx, bear, bobcat, bison. Moose, cougar, elk, deer. Heaps of animals, scores of them, a veritable Noah's Ark of dead animals.

"What's the hardest animal you ever killed?" Jason strokes Tiger a couple of times. The tomcat's back is covered with mats, and he growls when Jason's fingers probe too deeply.

"Wooverines." Johnny folds a paper-thin slice of turkey and pops it in his mouth. As he talks, turkey rises and ebbs over his teeth. "Them little buggers. Harder than wooves, even, because they're so small, so quick. They can hide just about any place. You got to track 'em long and hard before you get a single shot." He folds another slice of turkey. "Some of 'em thought it easier to live-trap 'em, but we didn't do that much. We was hired to do a job, we did it the way we knowed how."

Jason jerks his hand away just as Tiger whips around to bite him. "Just blew 'em away, huh?"

Johnny wipes his turkey hands on his pants and fumbles near the Bible, pulling out an old black-and-white photo. "Look at this," he says. "Look."

Jason expects a portrait of carnage, but the photo is of a very sexy woman. She leans back against an old-time car with her elbows crooked back onto the top and one dainty leg bent, so that her foot presses against the car door. A shapely knee peeks out from under her polka-dot dress. Her dark hair is caught up under an enormous bow, and her teeth are too bucky, but that doesn't hurt the overall package any.

"Who's this?" Jason asks.

"Marie," Johnny says, his cataract-blurred eyes even dimmer than usual. "My wife."

"She's pretty."

"She was a city gal," Johnny said. "But she got all het up over living out here in the wild. The wild—that's what she called it. She wrote letters home about it, and I think they thought we was living on another planet. Once her aunt, one of them prim and proper schoolmarm types, come out here from Boston, and after we showed her around, she asked, 'Where do you keep the Indians?' She talked like we stored 'em in the basement or something."

Jason laughs and flips over the photo. The date 1939 is penciled on the back. "What happened to her?"

"She went back east," Johnny says, then stops, leaving the room silent and empty. Cars swish by on Main Street below, the playground bell at the school up the hill announces the end of recess, and cheery, feminine conversation tinkles up from the Greenbow.

Jason looks up from the photo, waiting.

At last, Johnny speaks. "I ain't a good man. I used to slap her sometimes. You know, when she'd . . . when I'd had too much to drink. She took the kids and left."

Jason lays the photo aside, as if it is tainted. "How many kids did you have?"

"Two. Ellen and Troy, our son. He don't speak to me no more. Not for years." Johnny puts his hand on the Bible, his fingers rubbing the crazed leather. "But the Good Lord saved me. I ain't a good man, but now I read the Bible every day and I go to that Methodist church every Sunday. God has taught me to be a good man. He taught me patience. He taught me to wait for Him to show me His way."

"So have you written to your wife and told her that? Maybe she'd come back."

"Marie's dead," Johnny says. "Ellen, too. Car accident about twenty years ago."

So what's the patience for? Jason wonders. What good is patience when you've lost everything? When he was a kid, he used to pester his mother to tell him where his father was, to point it out to him on maps, to estimate how many hours it would take to get there, and then home again. He made charts, graphs, his own maps, following his father's journeys. He always wanted to know where his father was. Now, the problem is, he knows where his father is.

Johnny's voice brings him back. Rummaging through a bag of Pecan Sandies, he remembers, "She never liked it. All the killing. She never wanted a coat made of mink or gray fox, although I could have given her one, hell, two or three. Like some rich dame back in Massachusetts, like all those aunts and sisters who thought they was better than her. But no, she hated what we was doing up in the Park."

Jason pets Tiger. "Is that why you drink so much?"

Johnny considers, mid-Pecan Sandie. "Never thought of it that way."

He slowly munches the rest of the cookie. Lunch finished, he lies back on the bed, not bothering to brush away the turkey bits or cookie crumbs. He curls up on the narrow cot, lying on his right side, facing Jason, his legs drawn up. Like a child, he puts his hands between his knees.

Jason waits until Johnny starts to snore. He scratches Tiger one last time with a whispered, "Here, kitty, kitty." Before he leaves, he covers Johnny with the once-upon-a-time-blue blanket.

Three days later, Jason skips school again when his mother oversleeps. Dispensing with the usual routine of taking the bus, hiding at the Wickiup, then sneaking away, he saddles Shiloh and heads toward Pindall. By the time his mom wakes up and goes out to feed the horses, he'll be miles away.

Elise is facing his direction as he rides toward the mill, and for a moment, he fancies that she is waiting for him, her heart beating as fast as his. She wears another flowing skirt and her dark glasses. He reins in Shiloh and walks the horse closer to her. A smile spreads over her face, and his heart lifts at the welcome.

"Jason! How good to see you! What a beautiful horse."

"He was my father's. This is Shiloh. Shiloh, Elise. Elise, Shiloh."

"Hello, Shiloh." She rises, but keeps her distance. "May I pet you?"

"Go ahead." Jason responds for Shiloh.

She strokes Shiloh's nose, and his head bobbles, as if nodding. "His is an old soul."

Jason shrugs. "He's only nine or ten."

She steps back. "You yourself must have an old soul, Jason, to be able to sustain a relationship with such a beautiful creature. A wise old soul that's been through many incarnations."

"Yeah, maybe." Jason looks down the canyon, wondering why if his soul is so old and so wise, the fly of his jeans always feels as if it's about to burst when Elise talks to him. Shiloh tosses his head, trying to shake loose the reins. Obviously his old soul wants to munch the new grass along the edge of the highway. Jason relaxes the reins.

"I've never ridden a horse," Elise says. "It seems like such a misuse of another's life."

"Shiloh doesn't mind. He likes the adventure."

"That's beautiful. Your oneness with your horse."

But even as she speaks, her attention wanders to a car that streaks down the road from town. "Shit," Jason whispers when he recognizes Ronald's BMW.

Elise dutifully raises her sign, but there's something different in her posture. She straightens her spine and holds the sign defensively in front of her breasts, swiveling so that the message follows the car along the highway. The BMW slows and swerves off the pavement just before the turn-off to the mill. Ronald climbs from his car.

"Good morning, Elise," he says. "Jason."

"Good morning," Elise says.

Ronald eyes Jason. "Isn't there school today? I thought I saw buses—"

Panicking, Jason pulls upward on the reins and forces Shiloh to surrender his meal. The horse's indignant snort sends Ronald back a step or two. Ronald wears mirrored aviator glasses, but when he glances at Elise, Jason sees the know-it-all frown of the grownup.

"I'm in a special program," he says. "I don't go to school every day."

Ronald looks as if he's considering a challenge, but lets it go. "Say," he says. "Does your mother's pickup truck have a broken taillight?"

Jason's mouth goes dry. "I don't know," he lies. "I've never looked."

"Well, she should get it fixed if it does," Ronald says smoothly. "It's dangerous to drive at night without it. I'll mention it to her next time I see her."

His stomach curdles, and he thinks he might puke.

With a self-satisfied smirk, Ronald turns his attention to Elise. "Please be careful sitting down here," he says. "The logging trucks make wide turns into the yard—"

"I think most of the drivers are aware of me," Elise says coolly. "I'm not in any danger."

He glances toward Jason. "I'm afraid a horse might buck or rear—"

He stops, and Jason sees that Ronald knows everything. His mother must have told him about that day, the awful nights after, the crying and hurt. Damn her, oh, damn her.

Elise breaks the silence. "You need to prepare for the eventuality of a group of protesters here," she says. "The more educated people become, the more they will begin to mass against the gross exploitation of nature and humankind."

"Right."

Ronald's Adam's apple bobs with relief, and Jason's rage starts to bubble. What is it about him? His mother lavishes attention on him at the Rambler, yet he's such a dipshit of a man. The guy wears these fucking ugly polyester pants, for one thing, and polo shirts. And the car. Like anybody in Pindall has the money to drive a BMW, like anybody would have the balls to buy an import in a town that has no Democrats and about two hundred NRA members.

He should have killed him when he had the chance.

"By the way," Ronald says, "do you have any connections with the Greater Yellowstone Coalition?"

"No," Elise says. "Why?"

"I've been invited to one of their meetings. I just thought you might be going." His voice is gentle and smarmy now, as if he's planning on selling her a car. Jason tugs at Shiloh's reins, at a distinct disadvantage. "If you decide to go, I'd be glad to offer you a ride."

"Thank you," Elise says. "But I'm not going."

"All right, then." Ronald turns and walks back to his car. He ducks his head and climbs into it, his movements as hokey and staged as Elise's. As he shifts gears, he waves one hand in parting.

Jason's rage erupts. "What a shithead."

"He's always been kind to me." Elise's lips compress. "But he is misguided."

"He thinks he's so much better than everybody else. He's always messing around with my mom at the bar—"

"Messing around? What do you mean?"

"They flirt," he says. "They . . . he took her to Yellowstone."

Elise glances toward the mill, where Ronald has parked the BMW and is just climbing out. "He is an embodiment of capitalist greed," she says. "But he's a product of his culture. He only exploits nature because he's been made to believe that it's the right thing to do. But he's right." Her voice grows gentle, careful. "What are you doing here today? Why aren't you in school?"

Not another adult telling him what he should be doing. Ronald could phone his mother, Jason realizes, or Macky Bain, or Assistant Principal Hamilton and his pickup truck. He considers giving Shiloh a sharp jab with his heels and taking off down the highway, never to return. As if reading his thoughts, Shiloh prances to the left, eager to be moving, and Jason deftly evades Elise's question. "Want to go for a ride?"

Elise studies him, then studies Shiloh, then says, "I really shouldn't leave my post."

They both look up and down the deserted highway. No more than five cars a day pass here this early in the season, all of them local. "We don't have to go far," Jason says.

She stands and lays down her sign, which reads, HEED THE CRIES OF MOTHER NATURE. STOP LOGGING! Uncertainly, she asks, "How do I mount him?"

Jason looks around for help. In the drainage ditch behind Elise is a corrugated tin culvert that runs beneath the turn-in to the mill.

"Can you stand on that?" he asks.

"All right."

Once she is balanced on the culvert, he rides Shiloh down into the ditch. He shows Elise how to place her foot in the stirrup of the saddle, then offers his hand to her and pulls her up behind him, so she sits on the flank of the saddle. Her skirt wads up between her legs, and a long strip of creamy thigh stretches out behind him, in his peripheral vision. "You can put your arms around my waist," he says. "Ready?"

Jason clicks his tongue and sends Shiloh into a climb up the bank. Elise's hands lock just above his belt buckle, and his spine goes rigid. Her hands are warm, even in the early morning air, and his fingers press just below his ribs.

She laughs, and he can feel the warmth of her breath. "I never had any interest in horses when I was younger," she says. "Look what I've missed."

Jason drops his right hand to his side, proud of his form. He's a good rider, handling horses with skill and easy command—something he inherited from his father. "I've been riding since I was old enough to walk," he says. "My mom or dad used to let me sit in front of them on the saddle and hold the reins."

Her hands tighten around him. "What a powerful bonding experience. Treasure those memories."

He brings Shiloh to a smooth steady gait along the edge of the highway, thinking about how close she is to him, how her hair blows now and then against his neck, tickling. The stream runs to his right, sunlight strafing the water. He could stay like this forever, he thinks, with Elise's body against his, her lips near his ears. When they reach a trail that cuts a sharp angle upward into the trees, he asks, "Do you like it? Do you want to go farther?"

"Let's go."

"Hold on." Jason clucks his tongue at Shiloh, who responds by eagerly picking his way up the steep sand wash. Soon they have moved into the forest, out of sight of the highway, and beyond the prying eyes of Ronald and Pindall.

"This is so beautiful," Elise whispers. "So perfect."

Jason urges Shiloh past signs warning trespassers.

"Are you sure we're to be here?" she asks.

"It's okay. Nobody really lives here."

He knows where he is going, to a lake hidden back among the trees. It is a half-hour ride—thirty minutes to feel her against him, to hear her breathing, to think about the possibilities. He imagines telling her that she is the most beautiful woman he's ever seen, and that he thinks of her at night. He wants her to know that he would give anything, do anything, just to be with her.

The forest breaks, and the lake stretches deep blue before them. Steam rises from it into the air, obscuring the far shore and wafting one way and another with the changeable breeze.

"It's warm, you see," Jason tells Elise. "A lake with a hot spring."

"This is extraordinary."

Jason guides Shiloh down the slope, reining him in at a stand of pine near a sandy point. "Welcome to Disney Land."

"What?" Elise asks.

"This land is owned by one of Disney's executives or something."

"Really?" Elise says. "Oh, think what they could do with this. A nature preserve with opportunities for education. They could dedicate it as wilderness for eternity and set an example for the world."

"Or build an amusement park. We have enough land around here as it is."

"There's never enough that hasn't been tainted by man." She draws in a deep breath. "Can we get down?"

"Sure." He helps her slide from the saddle, holding her hands until her feet touch the ground.

She stoops and drags her hand through the water. Jason watches from horseback as her hands caress wider and wider circles, as if she is stroking the back of the earth. He half-expects her to summon a spirit from the lake. The sun shines down on her hair, which fans over her shoulders in a golden-red flame. His heart beats a fast double-time.

"How warm is it?" he calls to her.

"Come join me."

She pulls her boots from her feet and traces a path along the edge of the water, the hem of her bright skirt floating on the tiny waves that wash around her. She bends and dips the tips of her fingers into the water, then lifts her palms toward the sun.

He dismounts, turning just in time to see Elise pulling her sweater over her head. Her breasts swing free, her nipples delicate and pink. She slips her skirt from her waist and stands naked before him, her thighs the color of piano keys, her pubic hair golden in the sun.

"Come on," she urges.

But, unlike Elise's professor husband, Jason can't find a seat on the metaphysical plane and can only gape, hung up on physical appearance. She doesn't wear underwear, he thinks, stupidly, before his instincts kick in, and his body reacts in a burning, brilliant arc that shoots from his fingertips to his knees.

She comes toward him and unzips his jacket. She slips it from his arms and then draws his T-shirt over his head. When she starts to fiddle with his belt buckle, he backs away. "Go on," he says. "I'll be there in a minute."

She moves through the water, walking steadily, deeper and deeper, until the water is at her waist. Cupping handfuls onto her shoulders, she closes her eyes, as if in prayer.

Once she's not looking, Jason strips as quickly as he can. He pulls off his boots with such force that his socks peel away inside them and undoes his belt with a clank of buckle against zipper. Ruthlessly, he jimmies his boxers off—man, he's big—and runs, carving into the water until he is submerged from the waist down. Elise opens her eyes and points to the muddy trail he has left behind. "Move slowly. Don't disturb the earth any more than you must."

She arches into the water and strikes out toward the center of the lake. The water is slightly cooler than a comfortable bath, and Jason's shoulders—still in open air—prickle. The scent of sulfur rises with the steam. "Let's swim," she calls.

"I can't swim," Jason admits, embarrassed. "I never learned how."

"Oh," she says. "All right."

She rolls onto her back to float, her breasts bobbing in the water, and Jason slogs along behind her, breathless for more reasons than one.

"What joy. What absolute joy," she whispers. "Give me your hands."

She pulls on his hands, taking him out to a point where his toes struggle to grip the sandy bottom. He feels her body bumping lightly against his and his own swollen response, nearly periscoping right out of the water. Elise keeps moving, and Jason realizes this is some kind of dance, some kind of celebration of nature and beauty. She stops often, noting every variation in the lake's temperature. "It's warmer here," she will say, or "Can you feel how cold the current is around your feet?"

All he can feel is her nearness. How is it that he has been granted this wish? He could pull her against him, kiss her hair, her face, her lips. He could reach out and touch her breasts, let his hands run arcs down her body. He wills himself to do it—what man wouldn't take advantage of this opportunity?—but for some reason, he recalls Johnny Hart and his lost Marie.

"What's wrong?" Elise floats near him, her wet hair a rusty brown.

"Nothing."

"Something went across your face. A flicker. Something sad."

He shrugs, and she tenderly cups his face in her hands. "Don't be sad, Jason. Let the beauty of the earth heal you."

He could kiss her now—

Instead, he says, "I think the beauty of the earth is trying to swallow me."

She drops her hands. "We can go back."

She moves through the water ahead of him, leading him to shore. When she rises from the water, the spring air marbles her skin with purple, pinches her nipples into sweet, pink raisins. She laughs at him, shivering in the shallows, unwilling to leave the warmth of the lake and expose himself to her. "Did you bring a blanket?" she calls.

He rushes from the lake. Reaching under Shiloh's stomach, he uncinches the saddle and pulls it away. He takes the scratchy wool blanket from Shiloh's back and offers it to Elise, then realizes that when she takes it, he will be uncovered. He holds it in front of him as he walks into the sunlight along the shore. Squatting, he smooths it over the ground, then sits, bringing his knees up to his chest. "It's kind of hairy," he says.

"It doesn't matter. We can rinse off later."

She stretches out on her back, leaning back on her elbows, her hair dripping into the blanket. "Lie down beside me."

Jason obeys, flopping down on his stomach as quickly as he can. He leans on his elbows, his head lifted. His stomach itches against the coarse fibers and his backside tingles, speckled with goosebumps, but his eyes are level with Elise's breasts.

"Did you like that?" he asks.

"It was a spiritual cleansing." She rolls to her side, one arm straight and cushioning her head. "Tell me about your father, Jason."

Everything crashes back on him. For a few minutes, he had been free, he had forgotten, he was something—no, someone—more than he has been for the past few months. But here it is again, the whole, ugly mess. He says, "You wouldn't have liked him."

"How do you know what I'd feel?"

"He worked as a fishing and hunting guide most of the time. During the winters, he worked in the refineries."

"It doesn't mean I wouldn't have liked him. I just wouldn't have agreed with his way of living."

"I'm sorry. I guess he was just as bad as the mill guys."

Elise slicks back the hair that strings over his eyebrows. "The men at the mill aren't bad. They're just out of touch with their souls."

"My dad wasn't out of touch with his soul, though," Jason says. "He loved the land, and he always woke us up whenever a mountain lion was around or when the elk crossed through the meadow just below our house. He wanted my mom and me to hear it or see it. When we went for walks, he'd make me stop and listen to chipmunks digging in the pine needles or to the hawks. He didn't hurt the earth, like you talk about. He was a real hunter, and he made the people who paid him be real hunters, too. He didn't use salt licks or anything to lure the animals in—"

"Those are illegal, aren't they?"

"Yeah, but most of the outfitters use them because it's a whole lot easier. He thought so much was wrong, like the way the Park Service just kills animals if they bug the tourists or the firing line."

"What is the firing line?"

"Opening day in Montana," Jason says. "When the hunters line up shoulder to shoulder and massacre any elk that crosses the Park boundary. Sometimes an elk will get hit by twenty bullets all at once."

Elise shudders, and Jason looks at the lake. There's something more he wants to tell her. To him, all hunting is slaughter. He's never liked it—that casual extinction of a creature's life, the mess and ruin afterwards.

Instead, he says, "Dad didn't like the lumber companies either. Sometimes he'd go back to a camp in the forest, and there'd be nothing left but stumps. They'd have clear-cut it. So it's wrong of you to hate somebody like him, who knows what he's doing when he's in the wilderness."

"You misunderstand me, Jason. I don't hate anyone."

"But you hate the mill—"

"I oppose Cascadia Northern. Do you think it gives a single thought to any of the things you've just named? The land or the people who live here, or the wildlife, or how to care for and preserve this special place? No, it wants profit, and if that means fifty men, or a hundred, or four hundred, have to give their souls to get it, then that's fine with them. And if one hundred or one thousand acres of trees fall, well, that's all right, too. It's not just the earth that's ruined by capitalism. It's the individual soul. The whole fabric of humanity." She adds, "You know that, Jason. You know what it did to your grandfather and your father."

He wants to agree, but siding with Elise feels like betrayal. His throat is rocky and sore, as if he might cry, as if all the yearning and excitement he has felt this morning will pour from him in tears. Trying to keep from humiliating himself, he asks, "What about your father? Were you really close to him?"

"I didn't know him," she says. "He lived abroad most of my life."

"Abroad?"

"Overseas, in foreign countries."

"Wow, did you ever go visit him?"

"His work didn't allow it."

She says no more, and Jason doesn't press. "When I was six, I found out that most fathers come home at night," he confesses. "I mean, I knew that the guys from the mill went home, but I didn't want my dad to be one of them. I guess I just thought that if someone's dad didn't work at the mill, he was somewhere else."

"How did you feel when you realized that?"

"I just thought I was stupid."

"But now you know you aren't," she says. "So why do you spend so much time at the mill? Why don't you go to school?"

"I hate school."

She lays a hand on his arm. "But not learning, right? The only true power we have is knowledge."

"I guess. But they just teach crap at school. Read the book, do the assignment. It blows."

"You need to remember that you are an individual, not an automaton, when you're at school," Elise says. "Think about it. You ride that magnificent horse, you see the beauty of places such as this, you think with deep conviction about this earth and your place in it. High school can't take any of that from you. You're a free soul." She takes his hand. "You would never have brought me here today if you didn't have a deep, intuitive understanding of the earth. Just like your father's, I suspect."

Her words wash over him, a balm of comfort. He has not spoken much about his father to anyone else. Not to his mother or grandmother, and certainly not to Juliana, who loves discussing her dead parents. "There's this girl," he says.

"At school?"

"No," he says. "No, she's older, out of college even. She came here a couple of months ago. She's my half-sister, my dad's daughter. We didn't know about her, my mom and me."

Elise sits up, her gorgeous body in profile. Jason tries not to ogle.

"So, the universe has handed you a cosmic surprise, something you never dreamed of before," she says. "Those can be the best events of our lives, you know. Those sudden happenings, those whimsies that lift us up and out of ourselves. How wonderful to find out that there's another facet of your father's being on this earth. Have you talked to her about him?"

"No. I don't . . . no."

"Some cosmologists believe that we live each of our lifetimes with the same set of souls. We may have different roles, different genders even— my mother might have been my uncle in another lifetime, or I might have been my mother's husband. Our lovers, our friends, the people who come into our lives—we have all been players in the pageant before. And we will keep reappearing in each other's lives until we have worked out whatever it is the universe requires us to solve."

"I hope not. I hate her."

"That's strong language," Elise cautions. "Is it true?"

"Why shouldn't I?" Forgetting that he's naked, he sits up, eye to eye with her. "She came here and just took over, and everybody likes her and says she's so much like him. Even Grandma—"

He had seen Erica leaving his grandmother's office in the Wickiup a few days ago, swinging out of the back door of the store with her chip-on-the-shoulder, chin-forward swagger. Had Grandma given her money? Has she signed over the grocery to her?

"I mean," he continues. "She knew he was dead. She just came here to stir up trouble."

"What has she done? Has she threatened you or your family? Has she spread vicious rumors?"

He thinks about the night that he had encountered Erica in Aisle 3. He wishes he had that night back—he would have been smart and snide, saying things so hurtful that she would have left town. "No, she's just . . . It's just stupid."

His complaint sounds weak in his own head, but Elise reaches out and strokes his hair out of his eyes. "What happens to us—even the dark moments—is a gift from the universe," she says. "They help us to grow and become who we should be. What would happen if you just sat down and talked to her? Tell her that you're conflicted and that you need time to assess the situation and understand it all."

He wants to tell her that's bullshit—he's not about to "assess" anything with Erica—but at her touch, his dick has taken on a life of its own again. Quickly, he pulls up his knees.

"Let's ride around the lake," she suggests. "Let's take in as much of the beauty as we can. It will help you to think about what you need to do."

With a jerk, Jason jumps up and goes to Shiloh, who has wandered into the clearing beyond. "Shiloh!" Jason calls. "Shiloh!" The horse raises his head, flicks his ears. Jason rushes over to catch him. Shiloh takes a couple of quick steps, as if he'll run, then swings his head back toward Jason. Jason grabs the reins without effort.

He leads Shiloh back to where the saddle lies. Along the way, he scoops up his shirt—another shield to hold in front of him. "Bring me the blanket," he says to her. "I'll saddle him."

"Let's ride without the saddle. Let's ride this way."

At first he thinks she is suggesting a direction, but then he realizes that she wants to ride barebacked—all three of them. He feels no surprise. It doesn't feel dirty or weird, but like a perfectly natural point to be in the universe. Dropping the shirt and the saddle, he wriggles his way up onto Shiloh's back.

"Stand on that boulder," he says to Elise. He urges Shiloh toward her and offers her his hand. She climbs up easily.

She sits close behind him, her arms wrapped around him, the skin of their thighs brushing, melding together with sweat and the crust left behind by the lake water and the oils of their skin. Jason nudges Shiloh into a slow walk with his bare heels against the horse's ribs. He can feel the warmth of Elise's breasts against his ribs.

"Go faster," she whispers.

He clicks his tongue at Shiloh, and the horse picks up the pace, following a steady path along the edge of the water, kicking up the lapping waves, leaving a trail of foam behind him. He feels the friction of skin against skin—horse, woman, man—and he feels himself growing hard again, but he doesn't care. Let her see it—she has to know that he loves her.

Her arms tighten around his waist. Her hands open, her fingers spread, and she massages his belly. She dips an index finger into his navel, rolls her hands up over his ribs to find his chest. Her fingernails flick at his nipples, and he twists involuntarily.

"Shh," she says. "Don't be afraid. It's not wrong. It's beautiful."

Her hands glide down again, curving over his hipbones, veering over his thighs, and closing across the gap of his abdomen. At last, she finds what she wants. She begins to caress him, bringing the tension in his groin to a steady burn. He groans, but no sound comes from his mouth, it's so deep within him. As they ride, Elise's grip tightens, pulses, lifts him up, rubs him down, makes him come in one gleaming streamer that whips past them to fall on Disney's land.

TWELVE
BROKEN MAN'S DREAMS

Dave wakes in the morning with dry mouth and dim head. He doesn't remember drinking, he never does. He just starts in, and next thing he knows, he's home, delivered by somebody. Sitting on the edge of the bed, he blinks out the bedroom window at the first sun of the morning, rose colored on the twin spires of pinkish white sandstone across the creek, behind the trailer. Rain stands on the far side of the creek, grazing on May grass that has just started to green.

As he moves through the trailer, he can see her—from the square window no bigger than a sheet of paper above the toilet, from the window above the sink in the kitchen.

Outside, Ratso barks, and Dave lets him in. He tosses him a potato chip from a bag that lies open and stale on the kitchen counter, and the dog scrabbles across the carpet to fetch it. "You're a knucklehead," he says, scratching him behind the ears.

Erica has already left for Mona's, and Dave is alone in the trailer. He plugs in the coffee maker, pulls a box of cereal from the cabinet, and sits at the kitchen table. Saturday, day off from the mill. Used to be, he'd be on the road, horse trailer hitched behind the pickup.

The phone rings, and when he answers, Renee beams at him from Edina. "Hi, Daddy!"

"Hey," he says. "How are you, kiddo?"

"Fine," she says, her voice still that of an eight-year-old. His eyes go to the photo montage on the wall that Erica loves to study. Renee in Diane's arms, on the day she came home from the hospital. Renee clapping a sparkly bow into her wispy, white blond hair, her first Christmas. Seven-year old Renee on horseback, barrel-racing around cones, her first blue ribbon. Or biking in the gravel drive, straddling a lamb with arms around its neck, or reaching out to stroke a calf's nose. Always moving.

In her last school photo, taken in Minnesota, her sunshine-colored hair is raven black and she has used so much black gunk around her eyes that you can't even see the iris or pupil.

"But I wrecked my car," she says.

"What?"

"It wasn't my fault or anything. I was backing up, and there was this cement thing behind me—you know, those things that hold up the parking lot lights—and I barely scraped it. It kind of bashed in the side and the hubcap's bent a little."

"Jesus Christ, Renee." Dave reaches for his cigarettes. "Are you okay?"

"Sure."

"When'd this happen?"

"Thursday night. I was at Walgreen's."

"Can you drive it?"

"Not with a bent wheel. Randy's going to have a friend tow it to a garage or something, but Mom said she won't pay for it. She says I should of been more careful."

"Yeah, well, she's right."

"I didn't mean to do it!" Her voice has tears. "I went to Walgreen's to buy some soda—"

Jesus, he hates that. Soda.

"Because I'd had a really crappy day at school, and I just wanted—"

"What happened at school?"

"I hate the people here. They're such snots."

"You could come here."

As he says it, his heart gives a couple of extra thumps, even though he's heard her answer before. Her voice twists from whine to sneer. "No way! What would I do there? There's not even a movie theatre or a mall."

He hears the echo of Diane's voice now. Diane, who started messing around in real estate, and then with Randy Banks, who sold it in Jackson. "I can't stand it here," she had said. "Nothing ever changes. It's like we're all dead." That was after Dave had bought her a house on Sioux Street because she didn't like living out at the ranch. A modular with a carport to one side. His mother had made curtains for it. It was a nice place, better than most.

"You'd be happy enough," he says to Renee. "There's plenty to do."

"And where are you going to put me? In the barn?" Renee snaps. "Now that you have that girl living with you."

That girl. Diane, again, filtered through Renee's words. It's not jealousy, but something dirty, something ugly.

"Hey, now," he says tightly. "I told you, she's just here until she figures out where she's going. She's an old friend's daughter, and I ain't about to kick her out, but if you came back, we'd work it out."

"I'm not coming back."

"Okay," he says. "Let me know how much Randy's friend is going to take me for."

After he says his goodbyes and hangs up, his eyes go back to the photos on the wall. For years, he hadn't looked at them. Not until Erica came to stay. It was then that he realized there are more photos of Brad on the wall than there are of Diane or Renee or even himself. There's Brad with a six-by-six he brought down in the Gallatin. Brad and a gap-toothed Jason, eating marshmallows around a campfire. Brad and Shari on their wedding day, when he was best man. Marguerite, Jason, Brad and Shari at Sawmill Days. When was that taken? Two years ago, three?

They seem, now, like a pointing finger, an accusation.

He pulls back a slat on the blind. Rain has moved. He can't see her.

A couple of weeks ago, he went through his closets, rooting through boxes full of bank statements and tax returns to find the rest of his pictures for Erica. Crammed under the lids of a couple of Tony Lama boxes were black and white photos, negatives wrapped in waxed paper, and color photos that had faded to yellow, some of them curled and warped, some stuck together with the chemicals that are used in development. Handing the boxes to Erica, he had said, "Sort through this mess. Whatever you find of your dad is yours."

She has been doing just that in the evenings, sitting on the couch in her t-shirt and sweat pants, her back against the armrest, her knees tepeed and her feet in woolen socks on the cushion. She wears the heavy-framed glasses that she dons after she takes out her contacts. Usually, her hair is pulled high up on her head in a Pebbles Flintstone ponytail.

"What's this?" she will ask him, and he'll answer, "Looks like Montana. Up around Flathead."

"How can you tell?" she challenges. "There are hundreds of photos here of trees and rivers and deer and elk."

"I can tell. Whole different feel to it."

"How many trips did you take with him?"

"I don't remember, honey," he will say. "Quite a few."

She wants so much to have a clear trajectory, a timeline of Brad's life. Dave can't supply it, and it hurts him to disappoint her.

He goes outside and stumbles down the cinder block steps. His pick-up is parked at an angle near the light pole—Jesus, he didn't drive himself home, did he? Beyond, his parents's house stands in a thicket of brown-needled juniper and a few spindly-trunked plums. A hodgepodge of sheds—the coal shed, the slaughtering shed, the granary, the machine shop—litters the yard beyond, their uses forgotten in this day and age. As he passes the chicken coop, the hens start to gabble, and the rooster crows. The fifty-five-gallon barrel that the family uses to burn trash tilts sideways a few yards away. Flutes of charred paper whip around in the drum, snatched by the wind. A robin's-breast-orange Case tractor rusts nearby, its paint rubbed bare in spots, a stain of black oil crusted on the ground beneath it.

He stops at the corral fence. My God, he and Brad were nearly brothers. They had been loners—Brad left to do as he pleased while Marguerite wheeled-and-dealed and Dave from a home so poor they didn't have indoor plumbing until he came back from 'Nam. At one time, they had shared everything—pocketknives, lunches, tents, girls. They'd skinned their first rabbits together, caught their first fish, gone out alone to hunt when they were just fifteen.

Oh, fuck, if only he hadn't gotten his foot twisted up at the mill two weeks before the Derby last year. If only he hadn't agreed when Brad called to ask if he could ride Rain in the Derby.

Rain is coming back now, her hooves a soft clop on the sand. She had never failed him, never proven skitterish or shy. She'd been on expedition after expedition, she'd logged as many miles as Shiloh, she'd been just as steady as he was. Dave had broken her himself twelve years ago, when she was a two-year-old, just a baby.

He knows what she wants—a checker, a carrot, a flake or two of alfalfa. She'll come in with her head slightly down, toss it a couple of times, neigh in greeting. She'll expect a pat, a rub of the neck. He'll thread his fingers through her mane, taking out the tangles and burrs. He'll run his hands down her neck, over her shoulders, along her flanks.

He turns away. He has already left the barnyard and passed the chicken coop before she reaches the corral gate.

Dave doesn't sleep well.

His insomnia comes from the years he's spent rising at one in the morning to check on cows that are calving. It's a ritual of the winter months. On the bitterest nights, he pulls on jeans and boots and his heaviest coat and goes out in the darkness, driving the truck the half-mile or so to the calving sheds. With the headlights shining, he looks over the cows he's quarantined, the ones who are nearest to calving, their tails lifted awkwardly, the birth canals already distended.

In darkness, in the dead of night, he has pulled calves, reaching inside the fluid wombs of the cows to turn a breech calf. In the dead of night, he's shot a couple of cows who've had their entrails pulled out by coyotes that grab onto the afterbirth and tug. He's brought home orphans, rubbing them down with towels warmed in the oven and bottle-feeding them Calf Manna in the kitchen.

Yet it isn't this habit of anticipating trouble that keeps him awake now. It is his dreams.

They are torments that awaken him to a cold sweat and a heart that feels strained by its frenzied beat. Brad features in every dream—always, he asks for something that Dave cannot give. In one dream, the two of them sat in a sports car that neither of them would ever have had any interest in during their lives. The car idled in the Phillips's barnyard, and Dave was behind the wheel. "Do you want to come with me?" Brad asked him. "If you do, you can't come back."

The sound of his alarm clock had jarred him before he decided, but he couldn't reckon with the morning. The dream seemed far more real. If he had said yes, would he have died? Is it possible to will yourself to death?

In the past year, the dreams have morphed so much that they no longer connect to reality. He and Brad will be driving through pastures, but they are flat and open, or rocky and tight, not the fields of Wyoming. There is a stagecoach paralleling them. Or they will be in a city or at the sawmill. Even Brad will not be Brad. He will be younger, older, a man Dave would not recognize in daylight.

§§§§§

As June bears down on the Badlands, the trailer grows hot and stuffy. Halfway through the night, Dave crawls from bed and pulls on his jeans. As he walks down the hall, Ratso trails after him, panting. Knucklehead dog—Ratso has become attached to Erica and now sleeps outside her door, rather than at the foot of Dave's bed.

He sits outside on the steps. There's a scuffed clock radio on the step, and he clicks it on, immediately turning down the volume. The radio station plays old country standards, the reception lapsing every so often. To the west, a thunderstorm batters the sky. Lightning fingers through the darkness, backlighting the monstrous billowing clouds, but here, the night air is heavy with the smell of currant and sweet grasses from the banks of the creek. In the bottomlands, the coyotes yip up a frantic chorus.

Eddie Arnold's "Make the World Go Away" comes on the radio. Dave lights a cigarette.

Behind him, the screen door opens, and Erica comes from inside. Half-turning, he asks, "Did I wake you up?"

"You didn't." She sits beside him. "It's too hot."

"There ain't many nights like this. Most of the time, it cools off."

"In Ohio, it's humid in summer." She looks upward at the sky. "We run air conditioning night and day."

"All that packaged air. Take a deep breath. If it ain't fresh enough for you, just wait and the wind'll give you something else to breathe."

"And yet you smoke."

"Since I was twelve." He looks at the cigarette in his hand. "Ain't gonna stop now."

"I like it here," she announces. "It's so big, and the sky's so high, and the night is so dark. And, you're right—the air is so pure. It's all so . . . poetic."

He jostles her shoulder with his. "You sure do talk purdy."

She elbows him hard in return. "Knucklehead."

He laughs. "This part of the world's in your blood. The half of you that's Brad."

"My mom was from Cheyenne."

"That part of the world's not in anybody's blood. Ain't nothing down there but windy and flat."

"That's sort of how she felt."

He laughs again. The storm has blown in now, the cool air stirring in him a restlessness, a longing. He wishes he were young again, his whole life ahead of him. He remembers driving to nowhere when he was a teenager, spending hours doing nothing, late nights in the back seat of a car or on a sleeping bag on the ground with a girl as eager and curious as he was.

"Did my dad take Jason hunting with him?" Erica asks.

The question doesn't surprise him—he's used to her out-of-the-blue curiosity by now. "Not usually," he says. "Jason's always been an oddball. I don't know what his problem is, but he never took much interest in what Brad did."

"Maybe he doesn't believe in hunting either. Maybe he's like me."

"You think so, huh?"

"I do," she says firmly. "What about Shari? Does she hunt?"

"She's a fair shot, but she ain't a good hunter. She thinks too much."

"I can see that, too."

"Why do you say that?"

"Because when I've seen her—well, the few times I've seen her—it's like she's spent a lifetime practicing being left behind, but now that she's living it, she can't really believe it."

Who can? But he knows Erica is right. If Shari does not stop mourning, her face will come to resemble Donna Rae's and Robyn's and the faces of most of Pindall's women: crabbed by what never was, mean-mouthed and dry-fleshed.

He listens to the coyotes. At Brad's funeral, Shari's father, Bill Johnson, had pulled Dave aside. "Have you shot that horse yet?" Bill asked with a bitter fury that Dave had never witnessed from the mild-mannered science teacher at Pindall High. "If you don't, I'll come out and do it myself."

It was the right thing to do. He knew it then, he knows it now. But he couldn't do it. Since then, he has felt himself winched apart with every passing day—the man who could make it right growing more and more distant from the coward he's become.

"Were Shari and my dad happy together?" Erica asks.

"Depended on the day." He feels another roll of pain in his chest. "Those two were like fire and fire. They couldn't breathe normally around each other. Nobody could. They just swallowed up the air, and all the rest of us could do was watch and wish it was us. They fought like crazy, but you knew it was just so they could make up later."

"Talk about poetic."

"What?"

"Fire and fire. That's quite an image." She sobers. "If my dad had realized . . . if he'd known that he wasn't going to live to be an old man, I wonder if he would have done it all differently. Maybe he would have stayed in town and made sure Shari and Jason were happy. He might have done things differently with me, too. Do you think he would have gotten in touch with me?"

"I don't know, honey. It's all too far lost."

A coyote chorus rips the air. "It sounds like there are a million of those things out there." She pulls up her knees, wrapping her arms around them, and decides, "I think he would have. I think that at some point, he would have wondered about how it all fit together. His life, my life, the choices he made, and those I've made. I think he would have wanted to put it all together for his own satisfaction."

Dave takes a draw from his cigarette. "There were times when he'd go out on his own just to track. You have to understand elk, you have to understand deer—or any animal. How it thinks, how it moves, what it does in daylight and at night. Brad really researched all that—oh, he never went to college or nothing, like you did—he just learned from doing it."

"He had natural talent."

"Yeah." He breathes out a mouthful of smoke. "It's hard to track in winter. If the snow's a little melted, or the tracks are too old, it's hard to judge which direction the animal's headed. Brad could do it. He moved so quiet, and Shari moves just about as quiet, and we'd find them."

"So all three of you went?"

"Sometimes. One day, we'd been tracking all day, and hadn't seen nothing. And finally, when we'd all just about run out of patience, we got way up on a ridge, where we could look down across a big valley. And Brad says, 'Look down there.' And there was—I don't know how to describe it—it was just . . . a sea of elk. Must have been thousands of them. Bulls, cows, calves—everything was there in that monster herd."

"Had he found them or was it just coincidence?"

"Who the hell knows? Shari just laughed it off, saying something like, 'You always go big.' It didn't matter, though. I ain't never seen nothing like that again, and I doubt I ever will."

She considers. "Why didn't you go into business with him?"

"Couldn't afford it. Brad used to have to lay out some mighty big money to set up those trips. Leasing private land for hunting and getting the licenses, buying all the equipment and trailers to haul it, putting together a string of horses that wouldn't buck off riders who had no idea how to ride, getting all the logistics figured up so's they wouldn't run out of food or fuel on the junket. He had to hold his breath that he'd make back what he put into it. Anyway, I never had his knack for guiding."

"Couldn't you learn?"

"Maybe." He flips the butt into the sand at the foot of the steps. "But I think it's more something that you're born with—what you call natural talent. Anyways, I got Mom and Dad and this place to think about. Gotta work at the mill to keep the ranch going."

"Tell me about meeting my mom," Erica coaxes.

He digs back into his memory. "I was on my way to Cheyenne for some reason," he says at last. "Frontier Days, probably. I stopped through Casper to see if Brad wanted to go with me. Your mom was there, in his room. We went out, had something to eat and some beers. There's not much more to it."

"But you remembered her name."

"Not then, I don't think," he admits. "Not until Brad told me about you, years later."

"What do you remember about that?"

"Not a whole lot."

It's a lie. He does remember. And not just because the trip they were on had turned into a rout—the weather had gone bad, and the topo maps were out of date—but because his own life was in shambles. He'd just found out about Diane and Randy. He doesn't know why Brad decided to tell his secret. But he had told Dave that Lael Sheridan had kept the baby, without expecting or wanting anything from him, not even money.

"Jesus Christ, Brad," Dave had said. "Why didn't you marry her?'

"She didn't want it." Brad had shrugged. "She was going places, and she wasn't going to let anything stop her. She's one of those women who thinks she's better off without a man."

But the baby, Dave thought. The child. Even before he lost Renee, he couldn't fathom giving up a child. Even before, he had felt the loss.

Erica squirms, impatient. "Well, tell me what you know."

"I think he would have made it right with her." He is lying again, but why not? What good is truth? "But he was just too damned young. Just too . . . wild back then."

"That's what my mom said," she says. "But she said she was the wild one."

Thunder ratchets over the trailer.

"We better get inside," he says, holding out his hand to help her stand. Together, they run up the steps just before the sky breaks loose with a summer downpour.

On a warm evening, Dave asks Erica to go with him to check cows.

"Check cows?" she asks. "For what?"

"Just to see that there's nothing wrong," he replies. "Come on, you'll have fun."

They pile into Dave's pickup, Dave at the wheel, Erica as passenger, and Ratso in the middle, where he gets tangled up with Dave's hand every time Dave has to shift. Luckily, it's not often. The truck stays in first most of the trip.

They strike out through a barbed wire gate that Dave opens and shuts behind him, driving along a road that has two parallel ruts where the tires of the truck have ground the vegetation to nothing. Between the tire tracks, a few straggling plants still flourish.

It's not an easy ride. The truck bounces through dried-up mudholes and swales. Sometimes the ruts have been carved so deeply that Dave has to drive up and around them to keep from high-centering. There are even places where the makeshift track, bounded by gully, has been eaten away so much that the truck can barely pass. The roads through the ranch have been there for a century now, used by Dave's father and grandfather and great-grandfather, too, as trails for horses or wagons.

"Either Dad or I do this about every other night," Dave tells Erica. "Now that they're out of the calving pasture, we gotta keep an eye on 'em."

"Why don't you manage the ranch all the time? Why do you work at the mill?"

He snorts. "You can't make a living off ranching, especially with beef prices like they are now. Most of the guys at the mill have a ranch somewhere that they're trying to keep going for the family. It's the way of the modern world—nobody gives a shit about where our food comes from or the people who make it happen. They think that anybody who lives on the land is stupid, a bunch of hicks. Some day, people'll wake up and realize it, but by then, we'll all be broke and the land'll be gone, turned into houses that all look alike."

"I can't imagine that here."

"Drive south to Colorado, and you'll see it happening all over."

Erica grabs the dashboard as the truck bucks over rocks embedded in the road. Ratso—from long practice—presses himself against the seat, his front feet braced to keep himself upright.

Dave laughs at Erica's put-out expression. "Don't try this with your Honda."

"Why don't you ride Rain when you do this?"

He winces—something she can't see in the rollicking of the truck. "You don't have to saddle and unsaddle a pickup. Turn off the key, you're done."

"What happened to the great cowboys of the west? The Marlborough Man?"

"Died of lung cancer."

She laughs. "If you've let the cows out, how do you know where they'll be? You said you have more than three-thousand acres."

"Let the cows out," he teases. "They ain't dogs."

"Well, let them go free, let them go wild—what would you say?"

He thinks about it. "Out here, we say we run cattle."

"Okay, so how do you know where they've run to?"

He laughs. "I know where they'll be. Out here, it's all about water. What's pumped up out of the ground, or what's dammed up during thaw. Downpours like the other night don't happen very often."

Dave drives on, past sand washes and rocks that have been sculpted by wind and water. The pasture lands that flow beyond the canyons are green just now, spiced by mounds of paprika-colored dirt and sage.

They reach a flat spot at the mouth of a deep, narrow canyon that looks as if it goes on for miles—both vertically and horizontally. About a quarter of a mile away, about fifteen pairs—cow and calf—graze. Before them, a windmill squawks rhythmically as its rotor wheels in the wind. Water gushes in time into one of two round, metal tanks from a heavy pipe. The tank overflows, spilling water onto the ground.

Dave turns off the truck engine. "Pipe's plugged again. Come on."

He slides out of the truck, and Ratso leaps out behind him, nose to the ground. Dave goes over to the overflowing stock tank. Erica follows, picking her way through cow-hoof pockmarks filled with water and the churned-up tar of manure.

"Nice smell," she remarks.

"Smell of money."

Erica shades her eyes and looks upward at the noisy rotor. "You need some WD-40."

"You want to shimmy up there and do it?"

"No thanks."

There's a thick layer of green scum near the connecting pipe that allows the water from the first stock tank to flow into the second. Dave reaches into the tank and scoops up a handful. It is slippery and without substance. "Here you go," he says to Erica. "A souvenir." The slime has no staying power. It doesn't pool in his hand, but slips through his fingers and falls to the ground.

"What's that?" She takes a step backwards.

"Good, clean algae," Dave says. "Want to help?"

She hesitates before saying bravely, "Sure. What do I do?"

"Just keep pulling it out of the water. We gotta unplug the pipe."

She reaches in, but immediately pulls her hand out again. "That water's cold."

"About forty degrees fresh out of the ground." Dave flips another handful of algae behind him. "Taste it."

Her face curdles in distaste. "What?"

"Taste it. Not that, but what's coming out of the pump. You've never tasted water so good. Best water in the world."

She goes to where the water comes from the windmill pipe. Cupping her hands, she waits until the pumping rod lifts and water fills her hands. "It has a taste like blood," she says.

"That's iron. What do you think makes all this rock around us red?"

"Iron." She mulls it over. "So the water has minerals in it?"

"Probably more minerals than you could ever take in a vitamin pill," he says. "Calcium, iron, magnesium, copper—hell, I don't know what else. Just about everything you need to make your teeth and bones grow strong."

"You sound like an advertisement."

He flings a handful of slime in her direction. It oozes to the ground almost at his feet, but she's not one to back down. "Oh, yeah?" She reaches into the tank for her own ammunition.

She lobs her slime, but again, it splats on the ground before it touches him.

"This stuff is gross." Looking at her hand, she wipes it dry on the seat of her jeans. "Ick."

He whistles for Ratso. "Come on, let's go for a walk."

He leads her up into the canyon. The walls loom over their heads— "How high are those?" Erica asks, and Dave surmises, "About sixty feet"—and the air grows colder where there is no sun. The heels of Dave's boots sink in the sand. They have gone about a hundred feet, when Ratso scampers up behind them, running as fast as he can, his tongue hanging out of his mouth.

"Look at him!" Erica says in surprise. "Has he ever been lost out here?"

"No—hell, not this knucklehead. Wish he would be."

"You don't mean that." Her breath grows labored as they move through sand that piles deeper and deeper on the floor of the canyon. "Where are the rest of the cows? Are they up here?"

"Probably not," he says. "There's three other windmills. Dad checked two of them last night."

"So will we check the third?"

"We'll see what kind of daylight we have left."

The canyon has started to narrow, the carved and striated sandstone walls closing in. "Knock on that wall."

"What?"

"Knock, knock, like you're telling a joke."

She raps her knuckles against one of the sandstone walls, eliciting a hollow, dead sound. "Ouch, it's sharp. Sounds like I'm knocking on Styrofoam or something. What causes that?"

"It cooled from magma," Dave explains, "then got carved by oceans and rivers that ran through here. It's light, lots of air pockets and stuff in it."

"We learned about that in school. Igneous rocks."

"Well, you're up to your igneous in it now."

She snorts at the corny humor. The canyon breaks off into smaller canyons—the behemoth rocks splitting into alcoves or nooks or overhangs or caves. Erica cranes her neck, trying to see into each. "What's up there?" she asks, or "Have you ever been up that one?"

"Go up there and see," he encourages. "Just watch out for rattlers."

"What?"

"Rattlesnakes. They like to sun themselves on the rocks." She recoils, her expression stricken. "Oh, hell," he says. "I'll go with you. You'll know one if you come across one. It'll tell you."

She finds her way into breaks between the formations, at times squeezing through openings no bigger than a foot, and calling back her excitement: "Oh, you have to see this!" or "Isn't this great?" Dave follows, running his hands along the sandy-sharp walls. Rocks form into lavish, jutting shapes—a series of horizontally-striped pink spindles here; a blood-red pile of mushroom-like boulders over there; lopsided chunks of columns that look like a melted Greek Parthenon; sheer walls of scarred and furrowed rock. Here and there, a hardy scrub of sage pokes out from a sandy ledge, clinging for its life.

He scoops up a handful of sand and offers it to her. "Feel this."

"It's like talcum powder," she says. "It's soft."

"Most of the time it has more grains to it, but where it's been sifted and broken down for so long, it's like this." He rubs his fingers together, but microscopic specks still glitter on his skin. "Look at that. It's got quartz and mica and other shiny stuff in it."

She looks at her own fingers. "I'd rather have this on my hands than that goop from the water tank."

He laughs. "When we were kids, we used to come up here and play almost every day in summer."

"You and who? My dad?"

"Me and my brother, Butch." He looks at his fingers one more time, then wipes them on his pants. "He died when I was about twelve."

"Here?"

"No, he fell under a train in Cheyenne. He was nineteen and gone by then. Never knew if he was just drunk or it was suicide."

"Everyone here seems to have one of those kinds of stories."

"It's a tough place to live."

Dave breaks away from the main canyon into a narrower one. Climbing over rocks and through holes and crannies, he leads her upward toward a formation that juts into the sky. It is made of two piles of bulbous, pink and black striped rocks—each the size of a house—that are separated by about ten feet at the bottom. At the top, the fat crowns of the rocks lean in against one another.

"Look at this," he says. "We used to call them Kissing Camels. Looks like two heads with humps coming together in a kiss."

Erica puffs a few times, while Ratso chews at a thorn in his paw. "Okay," she agrees.

He climbs up the formation, using a series of holes that have been carved into the sandstone. Erica follows, and he reaches down a hand to help her up the last few feet.

"Did you make those holes?"

"Me and Butch did." Standing together on top of the rocks, he says, "Yeah, we played bandits, we played Indians, we camped out up in here. There's plenty of places to hide."

"Or get lost."

"You can see the windmill from up here," he says, motioning toward the south. The steel blades of the turbine reflect the sunset, dwarfed by the immense landscape around them. "This was always our favorite hoodoo."

"What?" she says. "Who—?"

"They call these rocks that are stacked on top of each other like a totem pole hoodoos." Seeing her raised-eyebrow skepticism, he says, "That's the name."

She laughs. "Hoodoo. You aren't joking?"

"Honest to God, that's what they're called. Now, tell me, apart from the windmill, what do you see?"

With one hand, she shades her eyes against the low-hanging sun in the west and pivots on her heels, turning in a complete circle. "Nothing. What am I supposed to see?"

"Wrong answer," he says. "Look again."

After giving him a mistrusting look, she turns in another circle. Dave's eyes follow hers to the ridges and tabletops and hoodoos and boulders that roll up from the sand-washed canyons of the Badlands, to the rise to the north that climbs up toward Pindall, to the verdant, pristine land that bowls out from their high perch into miles and miles of openness.

Erica stops when she spots a hawk in the sky. As she watches it, Dave watches her.

And he sees it. The realization on her face, the sudden awe that comes to her.

"Nothing," she says again. "There's nothing man-made for as far as I can see. There's . . . you can't see your entire ranch from here, can you? You can't see that far?"

"Sure you can, honey," he says quietly. "You can see a hundred miles to the south, that way."

"There has to be something else within hundred miles of here? Other farms or something?"

"Yeah, a couple of ranches. Vern Stacy's is actually just over there. See that clump of trees that look like they don't belong there? His house is in the middle of them. And the reservation's about ten miles that way. And there's electrical lines, too. They run along the road—see?—just over there."

"Oh, I see them, but nothing else. This is crazy!"

Her voice echoes from the canyon walls below—"crazy!"—and she yodels, "Hoodoo! Hoodoo! Hoodoo!"

Dave starts as the words arc and bounce back to them. Ratso, who was left behind at the base of the Kissing Camels, barks wildly, and a flock of birds—horned larks or something—scatters. A couple of cows bawl from the direction of the windmill.

"I think you just hoodooed every living thing within fifty miles," Dave remarks dryly.

Erica laughs, and he hears what he has wished for more than once: Renee's laugh, Renee's wonder and joy at the beauty of the land, Renee's voice telling him that she loves what she sees as much as he does.

On a Friday night, he comes home early from work. Erica's car is in the driveway, but she isn't in the trailer. He heads toward the barn, but stops before he has gone far. She's standing at the corral, her feet on the bottom rail of the fence, lifting her enough so that she can lean toward Rain. She's stroking the horse's neck, and he can hear the soft murmur of her voice.

He leans against the side of his pickup. He should tell her, he has to tell her. *That's the horse that threw your dad. My horse killed your dad.*

Something furious sweeps up inside him. He wants to tell Erica to get away, to grab her arm and shake it and say, You're a fool, you don't know what the hell you're doing. You're a stupid little girl with a romantic dream that has nothing to do with what's real. He dumped your mother without even a backward glance, then married the prettiest goddamn woman in town and left her, too. With Marguerite's money, he could have done anything he wanted, moved a thousand miles away and never looked back, free in a way that nobody else in this God-forsaken place can be. He could have been what everybody thinks he was. But he left us with nothing, nothing.

Instantly, remorse wells up in his lungs, his throat. Erica is doing what he has not in almost a year. Touching Rain, petting her, talking to her.

Walk over to her, he thinks. Say to her, You have to understand how much you mean to me, how much I've come to love you. Like my own, like my own . . . heart.

But he can't. He can't reason, he can't act, he can't do anything but dream again and again and wake in the morning as dead inside as he would have been had he been thrown in that field during the Derby.

He turns back to the trailer. Inside, he turns on the television. Sitting in the recliner, he pops the top on a can of Coors.

THIRTEEN
PERSPECTIVES OF YELLOWSTONE NATIONAL PARK
PART II
44.11N 110.55W

Every day, I'm caught in traffic no matter where I travel. On my way to work, I join the line of cars that crawls around the right-hand turn leading from the Yellowstone Highway to Main Street proper. On my way home, the left-hand turn lane leading to the highway backs up for two and a half blocks, while motor homes vie for parallel parking spaces in front of the boutiques. Parking is slim at the Wickiup, too, where Marguerite offers ready-made sandwiches with miniature bags of potato chips and cans of pop in something called the "Camp Pack." Her quilts vanish from The Daisy, sold to out-of-towners for a fortune. The Morning Glory Motel hangs out a NO VACANCY sign every evening around nine, and even Robyn blocks off a section of the Rambler's parking lot with a hand-scribbled sign that reads: MOTEL GUEST'S ONLY.

It's July, and you can hear the cash registers ding up and down Main Street.

On a warm, windy night, Lex comes into the Rambler. I haven't seen much of him since that cold night in March, but I know that for past three or so weeks, he's been up in the Park, leading graduate students in a seminar on field work. He flashes his toothy grin at me, and I react like a sixteen-year-old girl. My heart va-vooms, and I'm twitchy, every nerve in my body set to go. Robyn puckers a low whistle and makes a fuss of checking the glasses for cleanliness—something she's never done before in my recollection—as Lex settles at the bar near us.

I serve him a Dewar's and a smile. We've barely covered the greeting and the small talk when he asks, "Want to go to Yellowstone tomorrow? You and Jason, both."

"Didn't you just come from there?"

"Yeah." He shrugs. "But we'd be all alone, except for Juli and Jason."

"In July?"

"You've never been to Yellowstone with me. I have the keys."

"The keys to the National Park?"

"Yes, ma'am. I have the keys to the National Park."

Such mystery is enough to entice me.

Lex picks us up in a rough-and-ready Ford Bronco that is peeling paint and rust. When he opens the passenger's door for me, it squawks in protest. I see that the interior of the Bronco is stripped down and bare. Knobs are missing, the floor has no mats, and the seat upholstery is split. Everything seems broken—even the windshield is cracked.

"Hop on the Tour Bus," he says.

"This is a little different from the air-conditioned Grayline buses that pull into the Wickiup."

"That's because where we're going is very different from where the Grayline buses take their cattle—I mean, passengers."

Jason climbs into the back seat and is greeted by Juliana. She wears a bright green billowing blouse, and her hair is pulled back into a girlish ponytail, tied by a green ribbon. Tossing a sweet smile toward me, she says, "Hi, Mrs. Brock."

"It's Shari," I say.

"Okay." She jets across the wide backseat to adhere to Jason, like a piece of scrap metal pulled to a magnet.

Lex settles behind the steering wheel and maneuvers the Bronco from our driveway. "Vern found this for me last January. My real car is—"

"The Camaro," I say, in a sudden rush of insight. "You drive the Camaro, don't you?"

He laughs sheepishly. "I told you I have a weakness for muscle cars and women who sing the blues."

"If you ask me, the two are pretty compatible."

"That's good news," he says. "Very good news."

True to his word, Lex has the keys to Yellowstone. Long before we reach the main gate, we break away from the caravan of sputtering recreational barges and turn onto a little-traveled dirt road that burrows through a field of sage toward the pine apron of the Grand Tetons. The sharp spines rise before us, granite-blue against the brilliant sky.

"You know, the Tetons are the only mountain range in North America that has no foothills," Lex reports.

"So that's what makes them so dramatic," I say.

"Yep, they rise right out of the valley floor."

We come to a metal gate sealed with a thick chain weighted with a clot of padlocks. From the visor of the truck, Lex pulls a set of keys and tosses them into the back seat to Jason.

"Do the honors for us, Jason," he says. "Green lock."

"Take the bear spray!" Juliana insists.

We all scan the flat, open spaces. A bear would have to mount a mighty ambush to take us by surprise. "I'll fight them off," Jason flips back, and hops from the truck.

As Jason opens the padlock, Lex tosses a saucy grin in my direction. "Told you. I have the keys."

"So, how do you come across a set of keys?"

"Key-Mart, of course."

And, of course, I have to laugh.

Jason waits for the Bronco to pass through before he secures the gate and comes back. He keeps the keys, and I have a sense that none of this is new to him. When we reach a second gate several miles down the road, Jason again hops out to open it. As we pass through, Lex says, "This area used to be populated by beavers. But when the natural predators were eliminated by the Park Service and the elk population exploded, the elk ate the sapling trees and drove away the beavers. So another animal disappeared from the Park—along with wolves, lynx, wolverines, cougars—and the riparian habitat turned to sage when non-native trees like tamarisks took over and soaked up the water."

He delivers the information in the tone of a college lecturer who is not particularly concerned with whether anyone is listening. Juliana certainly isn't. She's craning her neck to watch Jason lock the gate, as if she's afraid he'll hightail it into the wilderness. Across the sagebrush flats, fifty or sixty pronghorns graze. A few sun-brushed heads bob with curiosity at our arrival, but most remain unperturbed.

"What we really need are wolves," Lex adds.

I laugh. "That's something you don't want to say around Pindall."

"Exterminating the wolves left nothing at the top of the food chain. It's caused havoc since. As for the ranchers, it's the age-old question of who or what was here first."

"Tell that to the Shoshone."

Jason rejoins us again, and Lex drives on. Dust fans out behind us, obscuring the way back to the civilization. The road deteriorates into a single track through unculled trees, tangled undergrowth, and granite boulders. Hope rises in me that we have gone beyond where anyone else has ventured, that we have reached the new, the unexplored.

"Will we be the only ones up here?" I ask.

"Maybe," Lex says. "Although you can get here without the keys. Backpackers do it all the time. They're the tough ones, who've lived for weeks on gorp, with only a Swiss army knife, a canvas tarp, and a John Muir reader in their backpacks."

"Where do they come from?"

"The closest you can leave your car and register with the Park Service is about twenty-two miles back." He brakes and shifts the Bronco into four wheel. "I usually carry extra food with me. They're always starved."

The journey grows bumpier, and the Bronco fights the terrain, rocking and jouncing, heaving us here and there. Finally, we come across a clearing where mist rises out of a field of sinkholes, mudholes, and steaming pools. A few scraggly pines surround the thermal plain, but mostly it's just muck. Farther back, beyond the heat, the forest resumes in earnest, with thick growth and shadowy depth. The scent of sulfur permeates the air, and the steam wafts warm and heavy toward us.

"We're here." Lex pulls the emergency brake and turns off the engine. "This is where I work. Paradise with a stench."

We scatter from the Bronco, stretching limbs that have been idle for too long. As I kick a few times to get the blood flowing in my legs, Lex opens the tailgate and pulls out a square card table, which he sets up directly behind the truck. Jason weights it with a rock he hefts from beside the road. Lex opens a squat black box and gently lifts out a microscope.

"You thought of everything," I say.

"This isn't a day off for me. I'm working." He plops a wide-brimmed hat on his head. "Come on, you're my assistant."

"Me?" I shake back my hair and put on my cowboy hat. "Didn't you just have an army of graduate students helping you?"

"Yeah, but you're prettier." He secures the microscope on the table. Unfolding a metal chair, he says, "You'll enjoy it. You'll see."

As Jason and Juliana head into the trees, armed with bear spray and cascades of jingle bells tied to Juliana's belt loops and sneakers, Lex and I set off into the thermal field. We wade treacherously near the boiling water, balancing on wet rocks and ledges or traversing the pools on narrow, makeshift boardwalks that Lex and his fellow researchers have cobbled together. He points out the bones of animals mired in the bubbling mud pots and bleached skinless by the ferocious water.

"This isn't a place you want to come after you've had a few," I observe.

He laughs. "We try to put up as few structures and make it as temporary as possible." Looking across the field, he adds, "It's so perfectly balanced this far from the tourist hordes."

"Have you ever found trash up here?"

"Not twentieth century trash. But the Native Americans cooked their meals in these pools. Just wrap the meat in a skin and throw it in. In a few hours, you had a roast."

"Didn't it taste like sulfur?"

"Maybe, but it was well-done."

I laugh. The pools strike a full palette, from dirty gray to brilliant, unrepentant red. With a stick, Lex gently pushes aside the brackish green growth that floats on a small, steaming pond.

"Look quick," he advises.

Beneath the scum, the water is the vivid orange of an Easter egg, beautiful and pure.

"So what makes some of these pools blue and others red or orange?" I ask. "Some of them even have rings of different colors."

"Good question," he says, as if he is addressing one of his students. "The temperature of the water determines what kind of bacteria colonize. Some bacteria flourish in one-hundred degree water, others in much hotter conditions."

"So you know by the color what is growing where."

"Pretty much." He leans down for a closer look at the orange pool. "And the stuff that grows over it isn't there just by chance. One type of bacteria supports another—the mat protects what's beneath it—in this system. It's called archaea, if you're interested."

"I like that word. It sounds old and mysterious."

"And it's both—an age-old secret of our earth. There's a theory that there is more life in the crust of the earth than anywhere else, including the oceans." He pulls the stick from the water and tosses it aside. The grayish slime creeps over the opening, hiding the colored water from view. "Those few moments of exposure ought to have wiped out a colony or two."

We continue on our way. The mist wafts across my face, drying in the wind, while the sun blazes overhead, prickling my back and neck with sweat. Flies and mosquitoes flit around my head, and I swat at them without much success. My hair grows weighty and wet beneath my hat, and the ends string in the humid air. My clothes stick to me. The smell of rotten eggs lodges in my nostrils and sticks on my tongue as if I'd been eating them. Lex looks just as bedraggled, his denim shirt stained by sweat under the arms and on the back, the knees of his jeans daubed with mud.

He touches my arm to stop me. "Look, a killdeer."

The bird runs helter-skelter on the mud beside the boardwalk. She peeps as she scampers, like a child's toy fueled by battery. Every once in a while, she drops a wing and drags it pitifully. She's a deceiver, a charlatan, trying to make us believe we can catch her while she craftily leads us from her young. "Where's the nest?" I ask.

"We must be pretty close."

"You have to be kidding. Wouldn't her eggs fry?"

"They're probably in one of the grassy patches where it's not so extreme. What better incubation than a sauna?" He steps closer to the bird, and it shies into the sky, circling our heads with its plaintive, whirring call. "They live on the flies that breed in these thermophyllic communities."

"Thermo-what-tic?"

He looks at me as if he's tempted to say what has come into his head, but he says gravely, "Thermophyllic."

I laugh anyway. "What a difference a vowel makes."

"You're no better than my Biology 101 students." He nudges my arm with his elbow. "They're giggling before I even open my mouth."

I nudge back. "Do you study the thermo—"

"Watch it—"

"—thermophyllic flies, too?"

"No, but someone does. There are a number of us working up here. There's the USGS, there are the Park Service biologists, there are guys from the state, and from the environmental agencies, and a whole bunch like myself, from the universities or private institutions. Montana State's lucky—it has one of the most respected programs—although the University of Wyoming boys think they're better."

"What are you all looking for?"

"We gather biological and chemical information. Who knows what secrets these pools hold? Keys to new medicines or chemical interactions or evolution. Just last year, an enzyme extracted from a synthetically grown batch of *Themus aquaticus*—which is found right here in these pools—was found to help in DNA research. It's all the stuff of the future, but someone patented it and made millions."

"It wasn't you, was it?"

"Would I drive a Bronco held together with baling wire if it was?"

I laugh. "So now everyone's in the hunt."

"More or less." Squatting beside a noxious pool, he uses a hook from his backpack to grab a metal ring that's barely visible above the surface of the water. He lifts a metal rack clearly labeled "Montana State U." from the muddy, bubbling mess. "Slides," he says. "They've been here a while, to allow colonies to form. Now comes the test. Getting these back to the truck before the growth dies."

"Won't even a second of exposure kill it?"

"I'm usually pretty lucky." He lifts the cooler. "I get enough living organisms to identify what's swimming around with what. It's a pretty primitive method—it's been used since the sixties—but it allows me to learn some things right here, in the field."

He gathers slides from two or three other pools, placing them carefully in the cooler. Then we rush back to the laboratory on the road, Lex cradling the cooler to his chest to keep it stable. Sitting at the table, he draws a slide from the racks with tweezers and places it under the lens. As I watch him adjust the focus, I say, "Our father used to take us down to the school on the weekends. Me, Lance, and Amy—do you remember her? She must be about your age."

"Sure, she was in my grade."

"Dad would set up a series of slides and we had to guess what they were," I continue. "He'd use coffee, spider legs, dust bunnies—whatever he had found that morning. By the time I took his class in high school, I could identify just about anything through a lens."

He fiddles with the knobs. "You know, I nearly flunked your dad's biology class."

"How'd you manage that?"

"Maggie Ostler was my lab partner." He shakes his head. "I couldn't think of anything but how short her cheerleading skirt was. Wow." Standing, he says, "Okay, here's your chance to prove your ability with a microscope."

"Oh, I probably shouldn't have bragged."

"Probably not. What do you see?"

I look through the eyepiece, while he writes something in a spiral notebook. Beneath the lens, greenish-speckled oblongs float vaguely in the dim light. "Ummm," I say. "Moldy jelly beans."

He snickers. "Let me see."

He leans down and peers through the lens. I can smell the warmth in his hair, the salty moistness of his skin. He wears some kind of aftershave or deodorant, musky and clean, but its freshness has been washed away in the bright summer day.

"They're *Synechococcus*," he says. "But I'm not sure what those googly-eyed things are."

"What googly-eyed things? I didn't see anything else."

"Look again." He makes another notation in the notebook. "They're the ones that don't look like moldy jelly beans."

I snort, but return to the lens. "Oh, there is something else. They're a little more . . . they have . . . um, googly eyes—"

"Told you so." He places a new slide under the lens and brings it into focus. "Now, look at this. What do you see? This is a Rorschach slime test, my dear."

I focus on long tendrils spreading out from a central nucleus. They sway back and forth, a choreography of grace in their last moments of life. "A field of waving grass."

"Very good." Lex takes a glance. "*Chloroflexus*."

"*Chloroflexus*," I repeat, the word new and light on my tongue. "Do you know how to spell all these words?"

"Most of the time. Not right now. Right now, I'm shaky on how to spell googly-eyed."

He is looking at me, and I think: I could touch him, I could kiss him. But I don't want this afternoon to end up in the pile of wreckage that my date with Ronald did. Not able to trust myself, I ask, "So what do you learn from the data you collect?"

He squints into the lens. "We're trying to determine which bacteria thrive with which, which are mutually exclusive. And of course, the big mystery is how they exist in such violent, inhospitable conditions in the first place." Waving toward the misty field, he says, "To be done properly, it really requires a much larger lens than your standard car trunk microscope. We need the big lens at the lab."

"I'd like to see it."

"Would you now?" He asks this in such an intimate way that I blush—foolishly. "You'll have to go with me to Bozeman sometime."

"How do you get them there if they die so quickly?"

"Oh, I do all the preparation and fixative folderol, and most of the time it works, if I can keep them at about sixty-five degrees. But it takes more patience than I have just now." Peering into the microscope one last time, he adds, "Yup, these creatures are just about gone. You witnessed their last hurrah. About time, too." He stands abruptly and reaches for blankets and a picnic basket tucked into a corner of the cargo hold. "And now, the best part of this job. Long breaks."

We seek out a shady patch of grass tucked beside an ancient Ponderosa pine. Above, clouds float across the turquoise sky. Lex spreads one of the blankets on the ground, and then digs around in the food.

"Should we wait for the kids?" I ask.

"Naw, we'll just ruin our appetites and beg for forgiveness later."

I watch him with unwarranted anticipation, as if he's going to pull a five-course meal from the basket. Instead, he comes up with a Tupperware container of strawberries dipped in chocolate. As he shakes the ice from it, we giggle, as if we're naughty children.

Lex dangles a strawberry. "I believe Juli labored over them for quite a while last night. We should relish them."

I take it from him and bite into it. He reaches over and runs his thumb below my lower lip. My heart heaves-ho, and electricity quivers through my mouth and tongue. I instinctively lick my lips. "Strawberry juice," he says simply.

He takes off his hat and sunglasses and lies back on the ground. I follow suit, resting my head on my hands. The sun dapples us, and a sweet-smelling wind blows from the trees behind us, keeping the sulfuric stink of the pools at bay.

"When I'm up here," he says, "I feel I'm at the beginning of time. It's just me and the elements, the energy, the earth. Nothing else exists. I have no past, no future. I'm without complication. A grateful observer, a piece of the great serenity."

"I know more when I'm outside," I admit.

"What do you know?"

"Everything." The answer rings with more energy than I intended. "But it isn't real knowledge—I'd never remember the names of the googly-eyed things. It's more a fullness of . . . heart, maybe, or spirit. A broader sense of being. Like you said, a great serenity. Brad used to say that a man can be bigger where he's smaller."

"Maybe that is truer knowledge than the names of bacteria." Lex stretches, shifting his neck from side to side. "I was married once, you know."

"You were? When?"

"In San Francisco. Where you wear flowers in your hair."

"What happened?"

"They always wilt."

"No, I mean—"

He lets the joke go with a snicker. "Oh, we were both young, amazingly stupid, ridiculously selfish. She thought I should give in to her every wish, and I thought she was encroaching on my freedom. It was the stereotypical bog, nothing new or interesting. It lasted seven months— six months too long, by our reckoning."

"I'm sorry—"

"Don't be," he says. "It wasn't anything like what you had."

But now I wonder exactly what I had. Brad was always on his way to another place, determined not to be pinned down, and I wasn't always wishing him a fond farewell. How much time we'd wasted in that tug-of-war. The stereotypical bog.

"What are you thinking?" Lex asks.

I scramble. "As a kid, I used to lie in my bed and feel the world spin beneath me. I really thought I could feel it, whirling through space, carrying me along with it. Dad told me that it spins at a thousand miles an hour, give or take a few hundred, and we just whisk along with it. I loved that idea, I found it so comforting. Close your eyes. Try to feel it."

He closes his eyes, and I join him, but there's definitely something wrong. I'm not comforted, I'm not lulled. In fact, I can't concentrate enough to tell if the earth is moving—it could have stopped for all I know. All I can think of is Lex. He is so close to me that I can't tell how much heat comes from the sun and how much from his body. When my eyes flutter open, I find he's lying on his side, head propped on one elbow, watching me.

"Did you feel it?" I ask, a little breathless.

"So that's what causes the whirling in my head," he says. "I thought it was you."

He leans forward and kisses me, a tender kiss, a kiss that demands nothing. I touch his face with one hand, and he delivers a second kiss that has more promise, one with more lip, tooth and even a hint of tongue. My misgivings peel away into pure, delighted desire. I'm ready to kiss again—oh, I want to kiss him again—but he stops, putting space between us.

"What do you think Jason would do if he saw us?" he asks.

Desire flickers into disappointment. "I don't know," I concede. "I don't think he's ready for me to . . ." My voice trails off.

"You know, I like Jason." Lex settles back on the ground. "He treats Juli pretty well."

"Have you brought them up here before?"

"A couple of times. But they're more interested in researching their own biology than in listening to me talk about Yellowstone's."

"I suppose every motherly antennae in my body should be bristling with warning. Danger, ahead. But right now, I'm just glad Jason has someone."

"Hey." Lex takes my hand. I curve my fingers around his, and he clasps his other hand over mine, locking it in his warmth.

We lie side by side, completely still, completely silent. My head is—truly, this time—spinning, and there's a luxuriant rush in my heart. This all feels so bright and bold, so sweet and fresh. Right now, being alive and in Yellowstone National Park is all I could ever want.

A voice from beyond jars me from my jubilant trance.

"Mom," Jason calls. "What are you doing?"

Jason and Juliana stand in front of us, their faces shaded by the sun behind them. I jerk upright—Lex, too—and blink against the brilliance of the day. Apart from looking annoyed, both Jason and Juliana look rumpled. One of his shirtsleeves is slathered with brownish pine sap and needles. Juliana's Indian summer hair, meticulously brushed and tightly restrained this morning, now falls around her shoulders in a tangled heap. Her jingle bells, so strategically placed on their departure, tinkle from the pockets of her jeans. My motherly alarms clang louder, but this is not the place or time. The birds and bees will have to wait.

Juliana kneels down next to the picnic basket and sorts through the disruption Lex caused when he pulled out the strawberries. "Did you eat already?"

"No," I say. "We just—"

"We had a snack," Lex admits.

Juliana unloads the fare from the basket. She brings out fried chicken, potato salad, pickles, chips, and the strawberries. She has brought along a pretty arrangement of flowered paper plates and napkins and plastic forks and knives. She's even included a bud vase. She commands Jason to find a flower fit for the occasion. Amazingly, he complies, wandering off into the trees, minus the bear bells.

"Did you eat the strawberries?" Juliana demands. "They're for dessert."

"Come on," Lex says to me. He grabs my hand, choosing the scalding heat of the thermal plain over Juliana's scolding. Traipsing along the boardwalk, he waits until we are out of earshot before turning to me. "That was a narrow escape," he says.

I put my hands on either side of his face. I don't care that the air stinks or that thermophyllic flies buzz near my ears. I don't even care that my shirt is plastered against my back or that a strand of my hair is pasted across my forehead. Lex's cheeks are hot, boiling along with the landscape around us. Or maybe it's my blood, or my thoughts, or my heart. Amid the belching, steaming pools, where the *Chloroflexus* and *Synechococcus* and googly-eyed things simmer and swarm, I kiss him the way I want to.

FOURTEEN
VESPERS

Six months after he arrives in Pindall, Ronald is a stronger, saner man. He is freed from the grim tangle of his divorce and custody battle, although not from his longing for Craig. He has successfully fled the tree wars of Oregon. He drinks less here, with some exceptions, than he did in Portland. He watches little television, even though he has a satellite dish bolted to a concrete pad behind his house. He drives through magnificent scenery between Pindall and Jackson for the simplest of reasons—to visit a doctor, to buy clothes, or to search for gourmet products.

He is a happy, happy man.

He tells himself this every day.

He has adjusted to the altitude, strengthening his sea-salt lungs until they no longer ache at the thinness of Pindall's air. He wakes at four to stretch, and once the dawn outlines the black bluff to the east with dove gray, he traces a wide arc around Pindall, running about five miles through forest and meadow. The route that Shari recommended takes him straight up the mountain and over the first sun-dazzled crest, where he greets the day long before it reaches Pindall proper. From there, he emerges into a sprawling meadow of bristled grass and wildflowers.

It is a beautiful place, the kind that might grace a calendar—if it were in any state but Wyoming, where such beauty is overabundant. A stack of wind-carved boulders marks the western end, and the eastern end disappears into saplings that represent the beginning of the Bridger-Teton National Forest. Beyond the saplings, mature trees meld into the blue-black darkness of dense forest.

It's here that Ronald does most of his running, and it's here, where the forest envelops him, that he starts to forget that he is a happy, happy man. Here, shadows shadow him, trees groan and creak as if trying to speak, and inanimate objects seem to move in the dim light. Most of all, he hates the lurking silence that pulsates and howls in his ears. It sets him on edge, for only something far bigger than he is can shatter it.

He runs prepared to do battle, however. He wears heavy, tightly knit clothing and carries a pack from which protrudes a rugged, thick walking stick. Bear spray rests in the pocket next to his heart, and he has the ubiquitous bear bells attached to his sneakers. He has memorized the advice from a handful of pamphlets printed by the Department of Wildlife. The litany of potential threats rumbles through his head as he runs.

DEER can lash out with hooves or antlers. BISON are large, swift, and unpredictable in temperament. Even WILD TURKEYS can run at speeds up to 30 miles per hour.

Good God, turkeys.

Which reminds him of the men at the mill.

They're never friendly, never forthcoming, and what's more, Ronald knows they laugh at him behind his back. In April, he had posted a sign-up sheet for a spring softball league. Get together a couple of bare bones teams, play a few games at the weedy field in Asa Pindall Park, and see what happens. Surely it would boost morale and bring the community together.

Six men signed up, including Joe DeMajio.

Assholes.

BLACK BEAR: Alert the bear to your presence. Sing or talk softly as you back away. In the case of an encounter, make noises and stand your ground. Throw stones or small sticks. If attacked, yell and fight back.

What is this piss-poor place, anyway? Oh, it pretends to be the gateway to Yellowstone, but it is really just a blank spot in the road between two national forests. He despises the pickup trucks that tie up traffic and the good-old-boy camaraderie in the aisles of the Wickiup. He hates the women who think that a man with a job—no matter how demeaning it is—is the equivalent of a man with a future.

Ronald, on the other hand, is well-educated. A bachelor's degree from the University of Oregon and an M.B.A. from Portland State. Years in the management training program at Cascadia Northern. He embraces Total Quality Management and managing in one minute and swimming with sharks. He reads the high-class thrillers of Tom Clancy, James Clavell and Robert Ludlum, as well as respectable non-fiction about the

Camelot years and Israel. His musical tastes run to jazz and classical, his taste in art from Brueghel to Warhol. He knows a good deal about wine, a competent amount about painting, a smidgen about architecture, and *un peu de Francais.*

So, how in the hell did he end up in Pindall?

GRIZZLY BEAR: Grizzlies will attack if their territory is threatened. Slowly move or back away from the bear. Don't yell. If the bear approaches, climb a tree, if possible. If attacked, play dead. Lie on your stomach with your hands interlocked behind your head. Do not make any noise that will lead the bear to think you are not dead.

He is deep in the trees now, no choice but to press forward to the end. The path takes him about three miles southeast of Pindall, just to the mouth of the canyon, where he meets up with a steep grade that leads out of the forest and down to pavement. Civilization at last—even if it is the highway to Riverton. He crosses the road near the mill, all the while scanning the chain-link fence around the property for sabotage or damage.

His eyes rivet at the spot where Elise perches each day near the entrance. Sometimes she arrives at about the same time that he is emerging from the forest. Then, concealing himself in the shade of the pines, he watches as Darnell Hillyard, dressed in green army fatigues and black boots, emerges from a military jeep to scout the situation. Every morning, he makes a general sweep of the area, surveys the mill buildings that sit a quarter-mile away up the drive, peers up and down the highway. Then, seemingly satisfied that no enemy assault is likely, he unloads the chair that Elise sits on during the day and her cardboard signs. Only then does she appear, a princess taking her throne.

And then something happens that touches Ronald in a deep, formless way. Darnell lingers, he loiters, he jabs his hands into his pockets, brings them out again to hang loose at his sides. He seems lost, unable to simply crawl back in the jeep and drive away. All the while, he talks with Elise— as if they haven't just shared a ride, as if they don't repeat this ritual every day, as if they don't live together. They talk like old friends who have sighted one another on the street and are delighted by the prospect. Watching them, Ronald is certain that Elise and Darnell are not lovers; there's nothing of the itch and sting of passion in their movements.

Not so with Jason Brock. When Jason hangs around, he scuffles, paces and squirms with hopped-up-on-hormones teenaged angst. Ronald has considered calling the county sheriff about Jason—little bastard, it'd serve him right. But, if he has Jason hauled off as a nuisance, then why not Elise? Besides, it wouldn't take Jason long to figure out who turned him in. The kid's lethal enough as it is.

Jason and Elise talk when they're together, shifting poses in a way that reminds Ronald of a nineteenth century flipbook of photos. Flip, they lean toward one another, heads conspiratorially bent. Flip, they sit face to face, serious and soft. Flip, flip, they wave hands, ardent and quick. Flip, flip, flip—they laugh, and laugh, and laugh. Through high-powered binoculars that he keeps in his office, Ronald zooms in on their faces and wills himself to read lips. What in the hell do they have to discuss? He once grew so intrigued by them that he lost track of time, missed a meeting, and was discovered by his secretary spying out the window, binoculars glued to his eyes and an ungainly bulge in his trousers.

Try to avoid MOOSE if possible. If confronted, don't throw anything. Raise your hands over your head and spread your fingers. Hold your arms still, don't wave them, so the moose thinks you are bigger than it. If charged, get behind a tree and run around it, for a moose can't turn as quickly as a human. If caught, get on the ground, cover your head and stay still.

But today Ronald is either early or Elise is late, and the gates to the mill stand open and unchallenged. He runs hard up a slight slope behind the mill and over the last hump on the way back to town. From here, he can see Pindall's houses. What a mess they are—ramshackle doublewide trailers staked to the side of the hill with corrugated tin-roof carports tacked to one side; dog runs built of splintered snow-fencing; broken-down cars. Chicken coops, 55-gallon drums for trash, a rusted school bus or two with the name of the school blacked out. Naggy horses graze in tiny, manure-caked lots. Nearly everybody owns a pickup truck with a dog in the bed. Everybody owns a gun.

Occasionally, he encounters Mary Flying Eagles up on this ridge. Mary rides her horse to town every morning and poses for snapshots with tourists to make her living. In the late afternoons, she loiters near the Wickiup or other businesses in town, hoping that someone will be generous. Ronald often sees her in front of the liquor store—a place they both seem to frequent.

One day, two cowboys—the kind who jerk calves from cows with tractors, and ride horses with mouths bloodied by gag bits, and date women who were pretty before the abuse—had been coming out of the store at the same time.

"Jesus." One of them eyed Mary. "Is that old hag still alive?"

Mary had stared straight ahead, completely still. The cowboy lit a cigarette, flicking the match at her. It landed near her moccasin.

She did not move.

"Christ, she's made 'a wood," the first cowboy said. "Old wooden Injun."

"Give me that." The second cowboy took the matches. Striking one, he dropped it on Mary's moccasin.

"Yer foot's on fire, Pocahontas," the first cowboy said.

"Hey, hey," Ronald had said. "Leave her alone."

The two looked at him, sizing him up.

"Piss on it," the second cowboy had said, and they walked away, climbing into a pickup truck that had a roaring diesel motor. Leaving a stink of blue smoke behind, the driver gunned the truck out of the parking lot.

Ronald had bent down and swept the match from Mary's foot. Black ash stained the soft leather. "You shouldn't put up with this," he said. "You should call the cops."

She made no reply. Ronald looked around for her horse, a pinto, which was gobbling nascent tulips from the garden in front of the Chamber of Commerce, just across the street from the liquor store. Nearby, a sign over a metal trough read: HORSES WELCOME. HUMANS SEE THE BARTENDER.

"That's my Joe," she said, and Ronald turned back toward her in time to catch the full bitterness of her next words: "He's the only man I ever knew worth feeding and caring for."

Mary Flying Eagles was once beautiful—Ronald could see that. She carries all the noble features of her Shoshone lineage, the aquiline nose and preternaturally high, defined cheekbones. Her black hair has no gray. But she is Old Testament old. And she emits a smell that isn't entirely wholesome. He suspects it's the traditional costume. Anyone draped in that much animal matter could hardly help but carry its scent.

"What do you drink, Mary?" he asked. "Jack?"

Her nod was barely perceptible. When he came out of the liquor store, he had offered her a brown, paper sack. "This should keep you for a while," he said.

"You're a nice white boy," she said. "Such a pretty, nice, white boy."

She had leaned toward him, probably to see better, and touched his face with fingers so callused they scratched. He stepped backward, and she immediately resumed her stiff, straight-backed, dead-faced pose. He has not spoken to her since.

MOUNTAIN LION: Make plenty of noise. Stop or back away very slowly. Never look directly into its eyes. Cats interpret direct eye contact as aggression. Do all you can to appear larger. Carry a walking stick. If you are confronted, throw stones or wave branches or your arms. If attacked, fight back.

Back in town, he crosses Main Street beside the Methodist Church and cuts through the auto graveyard behind Vern Stacy's garage to climb to his house at the pinnacle of Pindall. He keeps his gaze straight ahead as he passes the chalet of his neighbors, the legendary monks. A few weeks ago, Ronald had sat outside his house and listened to their merrymaking. After a couple of hours—and more Crown Royal than he should have— he'd gone to their door and pounded on it. "I'm going to tell the whole fucking town about you," he'd screamed.

The giggling stopped. Finally, one of them answered the door, serenely silent. His silver-gray hair swept with Hollywood glamour across his forehead, and even in the blinding porch light, his eyes were brilliant, sapphire blue. Behind him hovered a much younger man who resembled a folk art Mexican Christ—all angles and gauntness and hair seemingly chopped by a dull knife.

The impasse went on until Ronald gave in. "Oh, shit," he had said. "Just forget it. Never mind. I . . . just forget it." And he'd staggered down the hill to his house, tried the door, and discovered he'd locked himself out. He slept that night in the back seat of his BMW. The next morning, he discovered his house keys in his pants pocket.

Above all, in any encounter with nature, KEEP CALM.

He reaches his house and, having survived another run, he reminds himself that the best part of the day is still ahead. After he showers, he spends extra time primping. When he finally climbs into his BMW, he looks good. He smells good. In Portland, he charmed. And even though it is closer to eight o'clock than it should be, he takes time to stop by the mill gates. Elise has arrived in fine form, he sees, her lawn chair folded out, her skirt draped over her legs. Her hair hangs loose down her back.

"How are you this morning?" he asks her.

"Fine, thank you."

On the road, a car whistles by—passing in one Doppler-esque horn honk that leaves Ronald pondering whether it was in support of Elise or of him—and he instantly devises his pretense for stopping.

"How many cars are passing by here these days?" he asks her.

"Around two hundred."

"One way or both?"

"Both. There were more going toward town than going south."

"Well, that's good," Ronald says. "Good for the town. Good for the economy."

"But not for the environment."

Before she can go further, he asks, "What's the fewest you've seen?"

"Three."

"How cold was it that day?"

"About fifteen degrees."

He shakes his head—in mock disbelief, in gosh-darn admiration. "You know," he says. "I've been wanting to find a time when we can sit down together and talk. Would you be willing to meet with me tonight?"

As she digests his words, his blood darts as if it might just shoot out of his fingers and toes. Every fiber tenses in his body. Right now, he wants this more than he has ever wanted anything.

"All right," she says.

Elation—and not a little surprise—flows through him. Did she actually agree?

"The restaurants here are limited," he says. "Why don't you come to my house? I'm a good cook. I'll make fettuccine Alfredo. I'll fix salad, too."

"That's kind of you. I'll bring bread."

He gives her the address of his house and fixes the time. As he drives toward the administrative building at the mill, he thinks: I am truly a happy, happy man.

Elise arrives at his door carrying a loaf of freshly baked bread nestled in cheesecloth. She has changed from the clothes she wore this morning, but her basic uniform is the same—graceful skirt, simple long-sleeved top, and jean jacket.

"Let me take that," Ronald says, cradling the warm bread. "Come in."

She follows him into the galley kitchen, where hand-cut fettuccine from Jackson bubbles in boiling water on the stove.

"Did Darnell drop you off?" he asks.

"He did."

He offers her a drink. "Anything from grapefruit juice to Vodka."

"I'll have juice."

As he pours, he becomes aware of the way she lounges at the door, leaning against the frame, one hip jutted out, her left arm crossed and her left hand cupping her right elbow. He catches the scent of soft skin and hair—lilac, lavender, something that makes him think of tiny, purple flowers—which sends a thrill through him, making him bold and talkative.

He cooks with a flourish. He tips the pans, disappears behind columns of steam, chops and tosses the salad with elan, all the while keeping up a *Going My Way* narrative of his boyhood in British Columbia and college days and travels.

She answers any questions he asks in simple syllables, holding back, as if she doesn't want to commit herself. She makes no offer to help with the meal. Ronald senses that she is as tightly-coiled as he is, and that their nearness in the steamy kitchen, where hands and bodies might brush, would be too much. At least, that is what he hopes.

At last, they are seated at a well-set, candlelit table near the windows in the great room, two glasses of Ronald's best California white wine within reach, Elise's bread sliced in thick, voluptuous chunks by his gourmet knife.

"Enjoy." He waves his hands over the feast. In this proximity, Elise just across the table from him, her lightly freckled face purified in the candlelight, he feels too restless to eat. He wants to suck her nipples to craggy tightness through the black knit of her top or to cup his hand in the warmth between her thighs and feel her plump against his palm.

Instead, he serves salad. "Tell me about yourself," he says. "I've told you about all there is to know about me. I'm a simple guy, with simple tastes and pleasures. Pretty straightforward."

"I was born in the San Fernando Valley, but we lived in a number of places as I was growing up," she says. "I left home at seventeen with a boy I'd met the year before. We settled in Berkeley for a while, and we were part of it all—drugs, free love, radical politics. But it didn't work out. We split, and I moved to Maine. That's where I learned about deforestation."

Carry a walking stick.

"You know," he says. "That's not what we're doing here. Our mill only contracts about six fellers—"

"You've told me this."

"Then what is your objection?"

"Don't you read your own company's brochures?" She leans forward, crowding her glass of wine. With one hand she steadies it. "Cascadia Northern Mills consumes worldwide resources. It isn't just here. It's in Canada and Central America and Asia. Do the people in Costa Rica, say, even understand what's about to happen to them? Or does Cascadia Northern come in and offer them enough money so that they're blinded, because for the first time in their lives, they can afford first-world 'luxuries' like shoes and baby formula and aspirin?"

"I don't think you're entirely wrong," Ronald says. "But look at the people here. Fifty to sixty men work at the mill. Men with families and obligations. They're Americans, and as such, have the right to decide how to use their natural resources—"

"The earth's natural resources."

In the case of an encounter, make noises and stand your ground.

"Okay, the earth's natural resources," he concedes. "But if the forests aren't managed, it will lead to catastrophe. You've heard of the pine beetle and how it is killing trees. If we don't do something about it now, it will devastate the forest, take out whole yields—"

"If they were to use pesticide, as has been suggested, it would take out whole species—"

"And, besides, Pindall's not like the big mills. It's more of a family concern. Grandfathers, fathers, sons—generations of men have been proud to work there. It's the town's only industry. The harm done to the forests is hardly notable, but the benefit to the local economy is remarkable."

"Who said the harm done in the forests is hardly notable?"

"This isn't old growth," he says. "Not like the Northwest. It's young trees, no more than a hundred and forty years old, and as such, easily reseeded—"

"A hundred and forty years! That's two human lifetimes! Surely you know that Cascadia Northern doesn't own a single acre of land. All the timber comes from public land. Land that's supposed to be for everyone—"

"In a way, our industry makes that land more accessible to everyone. At least, it allows more people to benefit from it. Cascadia's workers make enough to buy a home, dress their wives in halfway decent clothes, have children. No one has to sign their kids up for the free lunch program at school. It's not exploitation of the workers or of the earth. It's giving people purpose and a sense of pride in their ability to provide for their families. It's allowing them to keep this place as their home—"

"And to become victims of a paternalistic system that bleeds them of their life energies—"

If confronted, don't throw anything.

"It's not paternalism," Ronald protests. "It's reality. What other choices do they have? Besides the school district, no one in Pindall employs more than three or four workers. The Wickiup is the largest store in town, and I've only seen a couple of barnyard yokels working with that old harridan who owns it."

He means Jason, and he is tempted to name him, but Elise jabs at the noodles on her plate with a lethal fierceness that silences him.

"That's arrogant," she says. "You have a soul. Don't you worry about it?"

Becky had once accused him of something similar, but when? Before the divorce, when they had tangled nightly, yelling at one another until one or the other slammed a door? Or maybe it was during, when Ronald was in therapy, and Becky was gunning for him, suing for full custody? Or maybe it was after—who knew, who cared, who could keep count anymore?

Sing or talk softly as you back away.

Helpless, Ronald holds both hands out, palms up. "Please, Elise, eat. I had to pinch every last leaf of romaine from the Wickiup to find enough for a decent salad."

She pounces. "The woman at the Wickiup, whose name is Marguerite, is very kind."

"Is she, now?" Inspiration comes to him. "Of course, you probably know she's Jason Brock's grandmother."

"I know."

"What do you talk about with him? Is he an environmentalist?"

"I believe he leans in that direction."

And a little push over the edge would launch him right into crazy activism. "I understand that his father wouldn't work in the mill," he says. "And it left that family torn apart, because the father had to seek work elsewhere, and Jason's mother raised him more or less alone. The breakup of that family is more tragic than any loss of forest from the sawmill. That's what the mill offers. It keeps families together."

"That's absurd," she lashes. "The Brock family—more than any other—has been victimized by that mill again and again. Surely you're aware that Jason's grandfather was killed there. That's why his father would never work there. And Jason—poor boy, he's repulsed by it, but he's also drawn to it. So much family history, so many open wounds. He's never been inside, and he's both afraid and curious."

"Ah." Ronald has never before known the name of the man killed by the blade. "No, I didn't know about the grandfather. My God, what a legacy. The men in that family tend to die young and violently."

"But don't you see?" she continues. "If the mill didn't exist, the tragedy in the Brock family wouldn't exist either. Jason's grandfather might still be alive, and his father, too."

"You can't blame Brad Brock's death on the mill—"

"It's called Sawmill Days, isn't it?"

"That's reaching, Elise. Play fair."

"The entire culture here is structured around the sawmill." The tension in her voice lifts. "And everyone kowtows to it. Men need to learn that their primary purpose is to be fathers, to be present, and not to engage in the brutal machinations that force them to—"

Ronald leans back, not quite certain how to respond. For the first time that evening, Elise seems a bit incoherent. "I'm truly sorry about Jason Brock's family," he soothes. "I admire Jason's mother, Shari, to no end. She's been a good friend to me."

"Jason thinks you're romantically involved with her."

Throw stones and small sticks.

"No," Ronald says honestly. "No, I'm not. She hasn't quite worked out what she felt for her husband, and she has other things happening in her life as well. Anyway, I'm not willing to take on being a father figure to a troubled teenaged boy."

"Jason doesn't understand himself." Her face softens, her mouth growing pliant, tender. She plays with her wine glass, turning it by the stem. "He's so confused. He feels he has to follow in his father's footsteps in order to be a man, and he's completely unaware that the definition of manhood in this culture is utterly wrong."

Ronald makes no comment.

"I've tried to bring Jason to peace within himself. I gave him his first sexual experience, I believe."

Ronald's fork clatters against his plate. "You did what?"

"He doesn't understand that it's all right to express his feelings. He's mired in sorrow that he can't release."

"He's a kid. He's not legal, and besides—"

"He's a young man who needs to learn that it is all right to be sensitive and gentle. He doesn't know where he belongs, he doesn't know who to turn to. He needs to explore his heart."

"Then let a girl his own age take him on."

"A girl his own age would want candy and hearts and flowers. He would never be allowed to simply be his own natural self. He would never be allowed to simply *feel.*"

Ronald's mind twists and spins. Jason and Elise? When in the hell did that happen? Where did it happen? Surely not on that forlorn stretch of highway in front of the mill. Shit, what has he missed through his binoculars?

Above all, in any encounter with nature, KEEP CALM.

"Did you know that he tried to run me off the Yellowstone Highway one night?" he demands. "Did he tell you that?" He gives her the details, feeling a rush of fresh anger.

"How do you know it was Jason? Quite a few of the people around here are aggressive. It's something to do with driving a big truck."

"It was Jason, and his intentions were unmistakable."

Her mouth tightens, and she picks at her food, her face pained. Ronald shakily pours himself another glass of wine, wishing for Crown Royal instead. A double. No, fuck, a whole bottle.

"Do you actually live with Darnell Hillyard?" he blurts tactlessly.

"I live in a cabin on his property. I don't share a house with him."

"How did you come to be involved with someone like him?"

"I wasn't aware you knew him well enough to pass judgment on him," she says haughtily. "Darnell and my mother graduated from Cal Tech together."

"I suppose he didn't major in something like Interior Design."

"He was an engineer."

"Does he have a family?"

"Most everyone does."

"Does he have an arsenal?"

"Don't worry," she assures him, sweetly evading his question. "He has no grievance against the mill."

"You don't understand." He considers a rare stab at honesty. What could it hurt? "I saw a man killed when his saw hit a tree spike. I know what happens when social protest turns to fanaticism."

Compassion flickers across her face. "You shouldn't have to live with that specter haunting you every day," she says gently. "Why not do the right thing and quit? Why not be rid of the horror?"

"It's not as simple as that. It's all I know, and it's a good living. A great living, in fact. I was born into it—my father was a sawyer. It's in our blood up in B.C."

"Nothing's in our blood. You were just taught wrong. Otherwise you would honor your instincts."

Do not make any noise that will lead the bear to think you are not dead.

"Come with me," she says. Puzzled, he rises and follows her to the fireplace. "You're a good person, but you have no idea what's inside of you."

She crosses her arms and lifts her knit top over her head. It falls on the floor. Her breasts are full and tipped by round pink nipples.

"What is this?" Ronald asks, but forgets his question as soon as the words are spoken. "God, you are beautiful."

She kisses him, nothing held back, hands clasping his shoulders. He finds her lips, her tongue—still tart with dressing—and her teeth. He takes it all in—my God, this was easy—until he realizes that she has put her hands on either side of his head and is urging him to kiss her neck. He teases her breasts with his tongue, feeling the swift wrinkle of the skin, her sharp inhale of breath. Kneeling, he nuzzles his way down her ribs toward her skirt. She slings one leg over his shoulder. He runs his hand up her calf, rummages around until the folds of her skirt give way, then follows the curve of her thigh upward. Her pubic hair is coarse and curled, a thick mat around his fingers. She moves backward, slipping into the easy chair. Bringing her skirt up around her waist, he kisses his way up her thighs.

She tugs his shirt from his pants and unbuttons it partway, until he grows impatient and sheds it for her. Her hands are demanding and firm on his chest and shoulders. She reaches for his belt and the zipper on his pants, and he straightens up so she can slip her hands inside. He sucks in his stomach, feeling so full, so stiff and eager that he cannot wait.

"We need to go where there's more room."

He leads her to the master bedroom and turns down the feather-filled comforter and sheets. She drops her skirt, lies back, and watches as he finishes the work she began on his pants.

Do all you can to appear larger.

Later, it all comes back to Ronald. He had pictured himself as the seducer, as the spider who trapped the fly. He would be the one in charge. But after all the weeks spent plotting how to get laid, this feels nothing like it. He whispers, "Why?"

"What are you asking?"

"I don't understand. Why are you doing this?"

"Is that so important? Stop thinking. Just feel."

There is no satisfaction in that. The air lies stagnant and still outside the open windows. The comforter that covers the bed even in mid-July is too heavy tonight. He pushes it aside and greets her body just as muted music drifts down from the house up the slope.

"What is that?" Elise asks.

"It's the monks up the hill," Ronald says. "It's odd, they don't speak in public because of a vow of silence or something, but they carouse half the night."

"Jason told me about them."

Damn Jason. Well, at least in this, Ronald has the advantage. Surely Jason has no idea that the monks speak in private. He listens to the music and laughter, swelling in rich, joyful cadences. "I wonder if it's some religious ceremony."

"Vespers."

"What's that?"

"Evening prayers."

"Sounds like too much fun for prayer."

Elise lifts herself on one elbow. "What bliss to save your entire being for your lover, and direct all your energy, all your verbal power, all your vision to him or her only."

"Yeah," Ronald snorts. "I had a wife who saved all her energy and verbal power for me. Every bit of hate she was capable of."

Elise places a finger on his lips. "Let it go. Don't spoil the energy we've created. Trust your feelings. Trust me."

She arcs her way down the bed, kissing his nipples, running her tongue down his sternum, tonguing his belly button, and takes him into her mouth. The sure strength of her lips and the coy flick of her tongue send a current of heat through his groin, ribs and heart. He reaches down and pushes the hair away from her face so that he can watch her in the half-light.

As release builds in him, his head clears, as if he has come into a vast openness, a place of freedom. Everything spins away, realigns itself with ferocious clarity and brilliance. Something comes from his throat—a sob, a scream, a growl, a laugh—but when it finally reaches its apex, it can only be described as a howl.

From the meadow above his house, his cry is answered. A ripple of sound curves lightly upward, a thin strand of silver, like tinsel or lightning, free of the heavy weight of Ronald's burst. It wafts on pure, hollow pitch, then rides down the scale, down into the valley to Pindall.

With a jerk, Ronald frees himself from Elise's mouth. "Good God, what was that?"

She wipes her lips with the back of her hand. "It sounded like a wolf!" she exclaims. "I don't think it was a coyote. They aren't that powerful."

"A wolf? There are no wolves here. They're extinct."

"Darnell has always claimed there are wolves in the Park. He's seen them. Call it again!"

"I didn't intend to call it in the first place."

Elise rises and goes to the window, peering out, her body glowing in the ethereal light. "A wolf! To make that connection with the universe! With the wildness of the land! How glorious!"

Ronald lies with eyes open, hands clammy, heart clamped in a knot. He cannot bring himself to move.

Shit, wolves.

FIFTEEN
WOLF PACK

Pindall is still buzzing about the wolf's howl when Sawmill Days kicks off on Friday evening. A band of Shoshone has come into town and camped out in the meadow; two researchers from the Park Service have settled into the Morning Glory Motel; and kids down in the town howl like coyotes and play Wolf Hunt, charging after one another with sticks or toy guns.

The Friday night street dance features The Lonesome Doves, a girl band from Riverton. As they croon Reba and Barbara and Loretta, most of Pindall's population frolics behind a roadblock that separates Main Street from the Yellowstone Highway, and Pindall from the rest of the world. The band wails away in the parking lot of the Wickiup, and for three consecutive blocks, Pindall's storekeepers and artists hustle customers from beneath red and white striped awnings. The carnival grinds away at Asa Pindall Park.

Nobody has heard the wolf again, but by ten o'clock, when the dance has wound up into a rootin'-tootin' stomp, that single howl is enough for Johnny Hart to stagger down memory lane. Johnny can tell you real stories. About the time he slipped into a bubbling pool up in the Park and his boot just suckered up into a scalding leather oven and burned his pinky toe into a purple plug. And about the time a moose charged him as he was snowshoeing and shooting the gol-durned thing point blank between the eyes just riled it up. Tonight, though, there's only one story he wants to tell.

"With wooves, it ain't like coyotes," he tells Robyn Ruggles. "Coyotes, you cut off the ears for the bounty. Naw, with wooves, you brung in the kill. They'd string 'em up one after another at the ranger stations. If you got a she-woof with pups, you'd bring 'em all in, and they'd let the tourists play with the pups before they drownded 'em."

"Think it was a wolf howling the other night, Johnny?"

Johnny's rheumy eyes blur. He sees forest and night and so many stars that you could imagine the multitudes of heaven winking the message of Jesus's birth. A wolf, still alive and running wild in the Park, outsmarting all them government dudes and their guns. If only Marie knew.

"When wooves run," he says, "it's just black shadda. No sound, just shaddas that stretch until they ain't even there anymore." He drains the cup. "I used to have a pelt or two."

"You traded them to Walt for your bar tab."

He hangs his head. Even the good Lord can't keep him sober. Forty years, he's read the Bible every day, gone to church every Sunday, prayed. He even attended one of them AA classes at the school with some of the young bucks from the mill. But he's always thirsty. "I used to have a rifle," he laments.

"Well, when you find it, you owe us that, too," Robyn says.

After enterprisingly applying for the sole temporary liquor license awarded this year, Robyn has established The Old Ramblin' Wagon, which is literally a dilapidated buckboard that Walt dragged in from a ranch south of town. Kegs of beer drip in the bed—3.2 only, according to the permit—and leave a sour pool on the pavement. Rope cordons off the legal drinking range, beyond which no alcohol can be carried, a fact that Robyn frequently announces at the top of her lungs. Dennis Farrell, that little pissant of a police chief, has warned her that she better stay within the law's boundaries tonight. In fact, Robyn's main competitor is the Methodist Church, which is offering free lemonade and Popsicles from a folding table on its lawn. In the blaze of July heat, the Methodists have attracted quite a teetotaling crowd. Anything free, and this town becomes a hog lot.

She notices that the keg's getting low. Climbing into the buckboard, she yells, "Hey, Shari, come over here a minute."

Shari has been talking with her sister, Amy, who is visiting from Fort Collins for the weekend. Dave Phillips watches them from where he leans against The Old Ramblin' Wagon. Now there's a pretty picture. You could almost swap one Johnson girl for another, except Amy's got horn-rimmed glasses and shoulder-length hair she's frosted blonde and a veterinary degree. He had looked her over once, after Brad and Shari married, but she was too young and too smart for him. So Dave married Diane, who only stayed with him long enough to make him miserable.

He feels an elbow in his ribs and finds Donna Rae Griffiths, who has just slipped back to the dance with Jack Hardaway. Donna does a jiggling cha-cha while Jack works on zipping his fly. He's so drunk he can't find the tab, which doubles them both over with laughter. Finally, he spits out, "I gotta find Joanne and the kids," and leaves Donna with a peck on the cheek.

"Don't let her slug you again," Donna yells after him.

She bums a cigarette from Dave, but can't steady her hands enough to light it. Her face is etched by forty years of misfortunes, her hair overdosed on chemicals. She has five kids, but Dave's never slept with her. Once everybody's taken a ride, the bronc's too broke to buck.

"Dance with me." She leans into him, her chin dug into his shoulder, her arms cinched around his chest.

"How much you had to drink?" he asks, trying to keep her from toppling him.

"More'n you, I bet. You still dry?"

"For now."

"You hear that wolf the other night?" she asks. "I ain't heard a wolf in twenty years."

Dave had heard it as he was sitting in his pickup outside the Rambler, just waiting out the night.

"Me and Brad saw one up in Canada," he says. "It moved like a bullet."

"Ah, Brad." Donna Rae lets out a sour-smelling sigh. "He used to light up this town when he come back. Ain't a woman whose heart didn't lay down and roll over for a scratch when he smiled at her. He never had eyes for nobody but Shari, though."

"Yeah, but you got the rest of the boys in town, Donna Rae."

She laughs. "Excepting his other wife, or whoever the hell she was."

"Hey, hey," Dave says. "She was nothing of the sort."

"Well, she had to be somebody at some time," she argues. "His daughter tell you anything about her?"

"No," Dave lies. "Not much."

"You running in the Five-Kay race tomorrow?"

He laughs bitterly. "Not me."

"Lordy, that's about the stupidest thing they ever come up with. I guess Little Miss I'm-Too-Good-to-Live-Here will be there, since she's the one thought of it."

Dave says nothing. Tomorrow, while Erica runs the 5K Derby, he and a posse of men will be in the meadow. They'll ride a slow dirge across the field until they reach the spot where Brad fell. Then they will break into a full gallop and finish the race for him. Dave hasn't said anything to Erica about it, although he isn't sure why. Maybe it's because he'll be riding Don Wheeler's mare. Not Rain, never again Rain.

"Come on, Dave, swing," Donna Rae urges. "You're dancing like you got a cob up your poke."

He spins her out, pulls her close again. Her body is starting to feel pretty good against his. The leaking taps at The Old Ramblin' Wagon are starting to look mighty inviting.

Marguerite sits alone in The Daisy, drinking Macallen, a taste she acquired from a British admirer whose name she can't remember just now. Good grief, it's a sad thing when you start to forget your lovers' names. The Wickiup is closed to give the Boy Scouts a chance to sell cans of pop that she donated, and it's dark and quiet, except for the music of The Lonesome Doves resonating from outside. It was Marguerite's idea to hire an all-girl band, a paean to Wyoming's always having known that women can be just as tough as men.

She eyes this year's Celebration Quilt, hanging on the wall in front of her. It is a crazy quilt of yellows that range from fabric so ashen that it appears nearly white to the brilliant hues of the golden kernel of wheat to the shine of fresh straw.

The sight of it takes Marguerite back to a moment after Brad's death when she walked outside the firehouse, where they had taken him, and encountered Dave Phillips. Dave was with his horse—the horse that had thrown Brad. His forehead rested against her sweat-stained neck. His hands gripped the saddle pommel, his fingers tangled in the horse's white-yellow mane. His body spasmed, wrenched by sobs.

"I'm so sorry, Marguerite," Dave choked. "I'm so sorry. She's as good of horse as any. As good as Shiloh. Jesus Christ, Jesus Christ! I'm sorry, I'm sorry—!"

His anguish spooked the horse, and it shied. Dave jerked away in the opposite direction and vomited again and again in the empty street.

Marguerite could not think, she could not speak. The horse was a beautiful palomino. Where sweat had darkened it, it was the color of honey, but where the sun struck the coat, the color washed away into silvery-golden aura. This, this was the animal that killed her son?

A noise outside the door of The Daisy captures her attention. Marguerite looks up to see Erica standing halfway inside the coffee shop. The girl's face is completely shadowed by the brim of her oversized cowboy hat.

"Hi," Erica says. "What are you doing?"

Good Lord—what must she think, finding her grandmother sitting in the dark, drinking alone? Marguerite leans back in her chair, as if to distance herself from the booze. "Where did you come from?"

Erica laughs. "Melissa let me in before she locked up."

Waving toward the counter, Marguerite says, "Get yourself a cup and join me."

"What are you drinking?"

"Scotch."

Erica rummages around behind the counter for a Styrofoam coffee cup, which she sets in front of Marguerite. "I haven't learned how to drink here yet," she confesses. "Columbus is barely above sea level. I can drink all night there. Here, it's one and I'm three sheets to the wind."

"A lot less oxygen at seven-thousand feet." Marguerite pours a finger into the cup.

Erica lifts it, then mockingly toasts. "Look out stomach." She takes a sip and grimaces. "Ugh, I've never learned to like Scotch."

"You don't have to drink it."

"But you are," she says simply.

The words jumpstart Marguerite's heart. It's one of Erica's talents— she can make Marguerite almost believe that she is perfectly content, that the scattered pieces have fallen into place, that healing happens. Across the table, Erica takes off her cowboy hat, and Marguerite sees that her hair is parted in the center and styled just like her own. A thick braid curves over Erica's left shoulder, a crook of hair at the end. Marguerite's lips curve upward as she pours another shot.

"You probably shouldn't drink too much," she says. "You're in training, aren't you?"

Erica coughs down her Scotch. "I used to take finals after a night of drinking." She tries to laugh, but it comes out as a squeak. "I think I can jog around town after one." She sobers. "I'm sorry, Grandma. I didn't mean to get you involved in this."

She's referring to the 5K Derby Run; Marguerite's vote at the Town Council meeting was the one that broke a tie and changed the town's history forever.

"I'm involved in most everything that happens in this town," she says. "I'm used to it."

Erica's gaze falls on the Celebration Quilt. "How much do you think your quilt will sell for?"

"Five hundred, maybe." Marguerite shrugs. "Maybe more."

She reaches out and touches it. "Well, whoever buys it will be lucky to have it."

Marguerite watches the girl stroke the soft fabric. Just like Erica, whoever buys it will see a pretty quilt, a menagerie of yellows. But when Marguerite looks at it, she sees the coat of that devastatingly beautiful horse, glistening under a brilliant sun, and remembers her dead son.

Up in the meadow, Jason takes a hit from the reefer that Russ passes to him and slumps against the sandstone boulders of the Honeycomb. He's stoned, man, so stoned that the Shoshone camp across the meadow is receding into a fine haze. It's not very interesting, anyway—no peace pipes, no tomtoms, no *Man Called Horse* shit. They're just sitting around talking and drinking. He takes a slug of Captain Morgan, and his eyes roam toward the dead darkness of the forest. He's waiting—just like they are—for the wolf.

The night he heard the wolf's call, he was making out with Juliana at her house. They had just tumbled off the couch, and one of the clasps from Juliana's discombobulated bib overalls whacked against his front tooth.

"Ouch, damn it." Jason rubbed at his tooth, his pants down around his ankles, the belt caught under his left calf. His boxer shorts were twisted, the fly pulled open like a pocket.

"Ahh, too bad." Juliana sprawled lushly on top of him. She kissed his neck, nibbling at it as if it was day-old cotton candy, and that's when he heard it. Without warning, he dumped Juliana off and scrambled around, pulling up his pants and searching for his shirt.

Yet when he reached the meadow, it was deserted. No sign of a wolf or any other animal. Just wind and night and the moon overhead. Jason had been sure that if he waited long enough, or looked hard enough, or wished deep enough, he'd see it and it wouldn't hurt anymore. He wouldn't think of his father all the time or of how much he can't undo. If he could just see it, it would be a sign saying, Go ahead, be free, forget, live your life.

"This is so fuckin' boring," Terry complains. "Fucking Indians, why don't they just stay on the reservation if they're just going to get fuck-ugly drunk?"

"Let's see." Russ stands and pulls down his pants.

"What are you doing?" Jason asks.

"WOO-woo-woo-woo!" Russ shouts in pure Hollywood rhythm. "WOO-woo-woo-woo!" He moons the Shoshone, waggling his big butt at them.

"Oh, fuck, run!" Terry chokes on the smoke in his throat, and Jason catches the roach clip just before it hits the ground. They scatter down the hill, dodging through back yards and around parked cars, running toward the carnival. Terry's shouted laughter echoes up the hill, and Russ yells, "We got 'em on the warpath now!"

Jason stops near the Ferris wheel, gasping for breath, and drops the roach clip into the pocket of his shirt. Jamming his hands in the pockets of his jacket, he finds the hood ornament from Ronald Dailey's BMW, which Terry had pried off earlier. As he turns it over in his hands, he feels a sudden sickness in his heart. What is the point of all this? It doesn't change anything.

He flips the ornament like a bottle cap toward a trashcan and saunters through the carnival. A roller coaster with Chinese dragon cars bumps over rickety hillocks. Teacups whirl on a tilting platform, and metallic rockets spin above the ground. A carousel with elaborately carved wooden horses spins on one end of the lot.

He spots Juliana and her friends at one of the carnival games. The high school football captain, Cody Crane, shoots at a wooden duck that dodges and scoots its way around a pond, while rainbow-striped fish jump and an eagle occasionally swoops down. Each time Cody hits a target, a goofy electronic melody beeps and lights flash, and the girls scream. The carny inside the booth leers, "You ladies able to do that all night?"

"Oh, Jason, I'm glad you're here," Juliana beckons him. "Look." She gestures into the chasm of her enormous purse. "I have Jello shots. Mandy's mom made them for us. Reach in and get one quick."

He sucks a Jello glob from a Dixie cup, as the girls dip their hands into Juliana's purse. He thinks of the half-smoked doobie in his pocket. "Let's get out of here," he says.

"Okay." She unloads the purse on one of her friends. "Let's go up to my house."

Ken and Brodric have ridden nearly all the rides at the carnival. Ambling through the garish lights and pushy kids, Ken munches on kettle corn and Brodric hoists a tower of cotton candy. They nod and smile at passers-by, but never speak. Pindall's rumor mill is somewhat-right about them: Ken attended seminary in his younger days. Now, cloaked by darkness, he squeezes Brodric's hand as they climb aboard The Zipper.

Brodric's cotton candy whisks away as they whip forward, then backward, and they laugh aloud. On the night the wolf howled, seemingly just outside their front door, Ken had felt as certain as he ever has about the path his life has taken. As Brodric—so much younger, so undaunted by mortality—had whispered excitedly, Ken had spoken again with his Creator: Oh God, how can one reject all earthly pleasures, and ignore soul-ravishing beauty, and flesh that feels, and a heart that doesn't falter, but beats faster and faster and cannot be willed to silence? How can one find sanctuary in the spiritual, when the earth is so lovely?

He clasps Brodric's hand against his chest, fusing it with his heart.

Macky Bain checks in at the Shoshone camp, not entirely welcome, his navy polyester pants and blue shirt an eyesore amid the tanned hides and beadwork.

He's patrolling tonight with a quartet of county sheriff's deputies. Both the Morning Glory and the Rambler are filled, and there's a rendezvous of mountain men in the grassy lot behind Rob Grenville's. Earlier, a motorcycle gang cleared out the Silver Spur for its own private party in a mistaken belief that this is Sturgis, but Macky set them straight. The temperature is in the mid-sixties, one of those rare, mind-boggling nights when the wind has spared the day's warmth. It's downright hot for Pindall, the kind of night when kids ride minibikes into oncoming semis on the highway; fires spark in the dry needles beneath the pines; and tourist brats sink in the deep end of the swimming pool at the Morning Glory while their parents are screwing in the room.

Macky's real name is Mackay, after his Scottish father. He's not even a reservation Indian, born in Gillette. But with his mom in and out of rehab and his dad vanished as soon as he found out he'd spawned a half-breed, Macky was sent to live with his grandmother on the reservation.

Scrawny and graceless, he fought his way through school and, at five foot seven, ended up playing basketball for his high school team, which was known as the toughest and roughest in the state of Wyoming.

"You hear the *tam apo*?" his aunt Glenda asks him. The beads shimmer like gems on her robe. "He's come back."

Wolves are sacred to both Macky's peoples. The Celts carved the wolf into their rings, amulets and stones. The Shoshone believe the wolf is God, and that the white men killed off the wolf to curse the Shoshone. For years, there's been talk of bringing the wolf back to the reservation. For nearly a century, the Shoshone have beckoned God back to His land.

"You had any trouble?" Macky asks Glenda.

"Some kids, acting stupid. They ran away."

"You let me know."

Someone starts to sing, a low chant that whispers with the swaying trees and rustling grass. In his police uniform, with holstered gun and babbling walkie-talkie, Macky joins in.

Ronald and Elise can view Main Street and the carnival lights from behind the sliding glass door of Ronald's house, which provide them with plenty of ambient light. They've elected not to illuminate the house, mostly so that no one can glimpse Elise's presence there. It's romantic and dark—a perfect combination, Ronald thinks as he navigates his way toward her, wine glasses in hand.

"Cheers." He carefully hands her the wine. They have spent the time since her arrival, only a couple of hours ago, in bed. There seemed to be no question, when she appeared at his door, of where they both wanted to be. All week long, they've ogled each other in passing at the mill, and he has spied on her through his binoculars for more hours than Cascadia Northern can afford.

"Are you hungry?" he asks, kissing her hair. "I have some leftover chicken porta—"

"I don't eat meat."

Of course not. A brilliant red pinwheel bursts in the sky over the bluffs east of town, the start of the volunteer firefighters's annual show. "Oh, here we go," he says.

"I've never understood the appeal of fireworks," she says. "It's very detrimental to the environment, and animals hate them. To do that here, where there's so much wildlife—"

The wolf. He has not heard the wolf since the night it answered his call, but my God, the town has gone berserk over it. The mystery of the howling wolf was the headline in the *Pindall Press* this week.

"What do they think they're watching? A reenactment of war?"

He hugs her from behind, drawing her into the circle of his arms and brushing her hair aside so he can kiss the tender spots on her neck. "Does everything have to have a political message?" he asks. "It's a redneck hootenanny, for heaven's sake."

She reacts just as his expects, trying to wriggle out of his embrace to confront him. He seizes the opportunity to slip his hands into her loosely tied robe. With his thumbs, he rubs gentle circles around her nipples until she quiets. "I'm riding on the Cascadia Northern float in the parade tomorrow." He teases her neck with quick light kisses. "Perhaps you should protest that."

"Maybe I will."

He lifts his face in surprise. "You mean to spend the night in my bed and then go down and protest the float I'm sponsoring for my employees?"

"Yes."

He laughs. "Do you have a permit?"

"I need a permit for free speech?"

"You need a permit to march in the parade."

"Then I'll get one."

"It's ten dollars, Elise," he warns. "Rich fare for some of these folks. And for you to disturb the peace—"

"It's a parade. It's not a peaceful event to begin with."

He trails a row of kisses over her shoulder. "If you like," he says, "I'll buy the permit. Cascadia Northern isn't about to squelch free speech in America. In fact, we invite dialogue with those who—"

"You'll sponsor me?"

"It would be Cascadia Northern's pleasure."

"I'll buy my own permit, thank you."

She turns fiercely, and roughens up his lips with her own. Laughing, he moves backward to the couch, drawing her down on top of him, thrilled that she enjoys this game of cat-and-mouse as much as he does. What a glorious woman.

The dance on Main Street is winding down, and Shari is wearing out with it. It's been a tough night for her. Between so many condolences for Brad's loss, and so many memories, and Robyn's belligerent kegs, she feels like a balloon that has deflated, squealing pitiably as it goes.

All around her, people are talking about that crazy wolf. Someone says that the wolf's howl is the loneliest experience on earth, but she knows far worse: the half of the sheet that never warms in a bed too big for one; doors that never open or close unexpectedly; the day she took off her wedding ring before she mucked out the horse stalls and, afterward, did not put it on again.

She's just opened another package of plastic cups when Lex strolls over to The Old Ramblin' Wagon, wearing his best grin. Robyn lets out a "Wowzers," and the blood in Shari's head does a cannonball right into her toes. Her heart pumps frantically, trying to reclaim it.

Lex greets them, then strikes up a conversation with Shari's sister, Amy, who is visiting from Fort Collins. After they run down the list of "whatever happened to" their sixteen classmates, he grins at Shari, looking as if the night has just begun. "Come take a spin with me," he says.

Shari wipes her hands on her beer-soaked apron and inspects her drenched boots. Robyn's kegs have a nasty habit of spitting. Her perfume tonight is Eau de Coors. "I'm so sticky, I doubt I can move," she says.

"Doesn't matter," he says. "The pavement's covered with cotton candy and gum and worse."

"I'll take care of things here," Amy offers.

Shari takes Lex's hand. The band rolls into a laid-back instrumental of "San Antonio Rose." She lays her left hand on his shoulder, and he pins her right hand against his chest. She's aware—too aware—that the denim of her jeans feels too hot and heavy, and the flimsy knit of her tank top too revealing. She's aware, too, of the well-worn cotton of Lex's button-down shirt, of the heat of his skin beneath.

They plunge into a stream of Friday-night-feel-good couples; water-pistol-armed kids; chew-chomping, girl-flinging cowboys; and the Higginses, an elderly couple who share a single walker because Mr. Higgins is too stubborn to admit he needs one. Lex is right. The pavement doesn't allow much lightness of foot. It may as well have been washed down with glue.

"When are you coming up to Yellowstone with me again?" he asks.

"Whenever we get another chance."

"Any time you want," he says. "I found something new that day. Something I hadn't registered before—"

"Besides the googly eyes? What was it?"

"Oh," he says. "Those were actually a strain of *Sulfolobus*. In case you were wondering."

Shari laughs. "I have been wondering. *Sulfolo*—"

"*Sulfolobus*," he says. "But I wasn't talking about bacteria."

He kisses her forehead, and a thumping starts up in her head, pushed through by the electric bass of the band. It forms into words: I want I want I want— She's ready for the long journey of the past year to end.

The leader of the band yells, "Who wants to go faster?" The crowd whoops, and the fiddle bounces into a lively two-step.

Lex shifts, so that his hands are both around her waist, and she has a grip on each shoulder. "Can you feel the world spinning now?" he asks.

"Nope," she says. "This time, it's all you."

They sashay around, counter-clockwise, avoiding the Higginses, who have refused to give up, and the kids, who have broken into frenzied, caffeine-and-Popsicle-fueled dashes. Folks hook arms and thunder past in staggering herds. Lex twists and turns, and Shari lets herself be whisked along, her body supple and free, but they break apart, and are forced to clop around, arms around each other's waist, just a step or two ahead of the lethal conga lines.

"One more time!" The band leader shouts. "Pick it up, girls!"

"Hold on." Lex takes both Shari's hands again.

It's polka run amok. Shari's ribs ache from laughing, but she tries to hang with Lex's hand. The fiddler launches into a crazed shinnying up the strings. The notes turn to screech, but she keeps plying the bow. The crowd goes wild, urging her on, jumping and clapping, whistling and yeehawing. Lex and Shari pant into the madness, their arms around each other, shirts beaded to their backs by sweat.

The fiddler crests the violin's neck with her left hand. She gives two quick saws of the bow at stratospheric pitch, then, with exceptional tenderness, releases a single, sweet note to close the song.

And somebody lets out a high-pitched wolf howl.

Lex hugs Shari against him, and she feels the dampness of his shirt, tastes the saltiness of his neck. The crowd stampedes toward the beer wagon, driven into parched, insatiable beer-lust. Lex puts his hand on Shari's arm. "Donna Rae's over there now," he says. "Come with me."

They travel against traffic—along with the Higginses—away from downtown and the festivities. Shari's still winded from dancing. Her clothes have the consistency of soggy washcloths, and "San Antonio Rose" plays in her head. They leave the vending area, and the street quiets considerably. Bypassing his house, they go to the garage. Without clicking on any lights, Lex leads Shari up the stairs to the loft.

"Sit next to the window," he tells her. "I'll be right there."

She sits down and leans back against the desk, relieved to be out of the open air, and the relentless noise, and the milling crowd. On the ridge to the east of Pindall, the volunteer firefighters set off the first blast of the fireworks display. A red starburst hangs over the town, then plummets into the pull of gravity.

From somewhere behind her, Lex produces a bottle of chilled red wine and two long-stemmed glasses. He uncorks the bottle and pours. "For you," he says, handing her a glass. "To googly-eyed *Sulfolobus.*"

She laughs. "And to *Syne*—whatever it was."

His glass clinks against hers. "And to googly-eyed sin."

She drinks, still smiling. A green cascade lights up their toast with a hearty boom.

"I thought this would be the perfect place to watch the show," Lex says. "Away from everyone."

He shoves the window up and settles close to her. A fresh breeze— not yet cold—carries the burnt-sulfur smell of fireworks. Tinny music from the carnival tinkles aimlessly. A couple of families have camped on the lawn of the Methodist Church, the kids doing cartwheels and somersaults. After every explosion, oohs and aahs seesaw on the air. Somewhere a car horn blares, and someone howls like a wolf.

"Did you hear the wolf?" Shari asks. "Was that what it was?"

His glasses reflect the falling cascade from outside. "At first, I didn't think so. I had to ask myself, where would it come from? For it to come down from Canada, it would have had to dodge hundreds of human settlements, and wolves aren't that fond of people."

"It's strange. You said the Park needs wolves to balance it again, and here comes one."

"I didn't expect my wish to be granted," he says. "When I heard it, I was reading this deadly dull government study of Yellowstone that basically compacted the Park into a postage stamp." He refills his cup. "You know, America's got a wonderful gift for sameness. Living in California taught me that. Everybody said, oh, we're such individuals. But if you weren't as uptight and politically correct as the next guy, they didn't even give you a second glance. It was the most homogeneous place I've ever lived. Thank God for Wyoming."

Shari laughs, spilling her wine on the shag carpeting. "I'm sorry," she says.

Lex lazily retrieves a towel from the desk. "Happens all the time."

"I was at Marguerite's when it happened," she says. "We went out on the porch, thinking it might howl again, and about two minutes later, Jason ran by, on his way to the meadow."

"Was he thinking he'd see it?"

"That was the idea," she says. "He'd been down here—at your house, I guess. When he went by, Marguerite—well, you know how she is— decided to take care of it. She pulled her shotgun out of the closet and went up there after him."

"Who was she planning to shoot?"

Shari laughs. "I asked her that. I told her that wolves are an endangered species, and she said 'So are the menfolk in my family.'"

She laughs, but this time, it feels like tears. Lex puts an arm around her, gathering her close to him, but her mouth runs on, independent of her thoughts. "The last thing Brad said to me was 'See you in Jackson.' He planned to win the Derby and take home the purse and the free night's stay in Jackson. And I didn't even say anything . . . witty or smart. I just laughed it off."

"You couldn't have known."

She screws up her courage to say something that she has never confided in the past year. "They say," she whispers, as if afraid the revelers on the Methodist church lawn might hear. "They said that he died instantly. That he didn't suffer or call out or . . . need us. But how do they know? How do we know that there wasn't something? A flash in the air, or a touch, like a butterfly's wing, or . . . something?"

She bites her lip. Here she is, so tired of hearing about Brad, and dreading all the ceremony and hoopla tomorrow, and now she can't stop talking about him. All the words she's kept silenced for a year well up in her, ready to erupt like some geyser in the National Park. "I'm sorry," she says.

"Oh, Jesus, Shari," Lex whispers. "It's all right."

His lips touch her forehead, and she lifts her face. Just as he's about to kiss her, she lays her fingers on his lips. "I shouldn't be here," she says. "Not tonight."

He moves away. "It's okay. I won't—"

"What do I do, Lex?" The words spill. "Where do I go? How do I do it? I'm so afraid—"

"Of what?"

"I don't know," she confesses. "If I think about Brad day and night, is that wrong? If I don't, is that wrong? I don't know what's best for me, or for Marguerite, and Jason's just . . . beyond me."

"You'll work it out," Lex assures her. "But not tonight. Not this weekend. It's not the right time just now."

His words settle her down some, and she wonders what she has done or hasn't done or asked for or hasn't asked for now. But Lex is right. This weekend is an endurance contest.

"Well, anyway," she says, trying to pull herself back together. "Marguerite went up to the meadow, and—this is what Jason told me later—stood there with her arms crossed over her chest, cradling that shotgun. Jason said she looked like an old Shoshone bent on vengeance, all silhouetted and dark against the night sky, her braid flapping in the wind. He said she scared the bejesus out of him, more than any wolf would have."

Lex laughs—thankfully—and she manages a couple of hiccups. Outside, the night is still, conspicuously barren after the booming of the fireworks. Only the carnival music plays, the same tired phrase over and over, and the words start up in Shari's head: I want I want I want—

From the church lawn, a child shouts, "He must be reloading!"

"We'll assume he's talking about the fireworks," Lex comments dryly, and Shari laughs.

Thank God someone is dry-eyed and sane around here.

As the sun reaches Pindall the next morning, Johnny Hart snores in the back of the The Old Ramblin' Wagon. He crawled in last night, too tired to wend down Main Street to his room above the Greenbow. When Robyn found him, she threw a tarp over him to hide him from Macky Bain. No reason for poor old Johnny to be hauled off to detox again. Besides, it's usually Walt who bails him out, costing them fifty bucks a pop.

Mary Flying Eagles coaxes her Joe down a trail that leads from grittier, colder ground. Even though the temperature will reach seventy today, she's in full fur and feather, her face a gnarled knot of brown. It will be a good day for her, the tourists paying five dollars each to pose their little ones in panty-wetting terror next to a real, live, full-blooded Indian. She rides past the Shoshone camp in the meadow, not even turning her head. Oh, there's family there, all right, but it has been too long. Too long since they told her, You married a white man who beat you and cursed you, who got you with child and then abandoned you, You brought this shame on yourself, We cannot help you.

"*Da-men bai sogopi da-me gewainore, gewainore,*" she whispers.

Our old earth, we are fading away, fading away.

Ronald sprints over the crest of the mountain to find the meadow—which he has come to think of as his meadow—flush with people. At one end is a make-shift camp filled with Shoshone dressed in skins and beads; at the other, a gathering of horseback riders who appear to be trying to arrange their horses abreast, like a cavalry unit. In the middle, a few spectators have gathered in the not-yet light of day. The air is eerily still, no wind, no sound from any of the assembled parties. Ronald bounces on the balls of his feet. Oh, good God, this isn't some re-enactment of a legendary battle or something, is it?

He is tempted to call to the Shoshone, Don't bother! You'll lose! Again! But his curiosity quickly lapses. Turning, he runs over the embankment to his house. He goes directly to the bedroom, where Elise lies, one freckled shoulder outside the blankets. Sitting on the bed, he kisses it.

She raises her head, sleepy and sexy. "Are you back so soon?"

He pulls his sweatshirt over his head, unties the drawstring on his sweatpants. "Why go out there when I can be in here with you?"

When the riders start their long, slow procession across the field, Shari sees that they are all there. Dwayne, Tommy, Jerry—the boys that Brad grew up with, and hunted and fished with, who helped him build the house, and who have dug her out of the driveway or jumpstarted the truck time after time.

Her breath catches in her throat as she spots Jason, mounted on her own LilyBelle. Astride a horse, he reminds her of Brad—the confident seat, right hand at his side, reins in his left. His legs are long and strong, his shoulders and back straight. His chest and arms look sturdier, a man's body. He wears his hat low over his eyes, making him mysterious and handsome. Something in her hurts so badly that she nearly bends double.

Lex, who stands a respectful distance behind her, takes her elbow, keeping her aloft.

"I'm okay," she whispers.

"Are you sure?"

She nods, and his grip loosens.

At Pindall Consolidated School, a shot from a starter gun marks the first annual Sawmill Days 5K Derby Run. Erica is in the first wave of runners to trot around the school's track and out onto Lakota Street. Anita, Darcy, Jenny and some of the other young mothers jog beside her.

"This is fun!" Darcy calls.

The racers climb upward, heading for Ute, the highest street in town. It was agreed that the steepest ascent would be at the beginning of the race. The course will carry them the length of Ute, and then flow down behind Vern Stacy's garage. On flatter land, the race will parallel the Yellowstone Highway as far as the Morning Glory Motel before doubling back to Asa Pindall Park for the finish.

When the runners reach Ute Street, they find a number of pickup trucks and horse trailers parked along the route. Erica trots along until she sees Dave's truck. Curious, she detours up the embankment that leads to the meadow at the crest of Pindall's slope. The runners behind her follow, spilling into the field and fanning out into the knee-high grass.

"I think we were to stay on the street," someone says behind her.

Erica doesn't retreat, and the others prance nervously, waiting for her to make a decision. From the far end of the field, horsemen are slowly wending their way toward them, twenty or so of them riding abreast of one another. In the middle of the pack, Dave sits astride a big-boned buckskin that Erica has never seen on the Phillips ranch. Beside him, Jason rides a petite black horse. They wear cowboy hats and western shirts buttoned up to their Adam's apples.

She feels a pinch at the base of her heart. Whatever is happening here has something to do with her father. And she has been excluded again.

Suddenly Dave kicks his heels against his horse and gives a great "Yaaw!" The others follow suit, their horses surging into a gallop. Behind Erica, runners scatter, dashing for the far edge of the field, fleeing into the trees behind them, or scampering toward the street.

She doesn't move, still caught in thought. By the time she realizes that she stands in the path of the riders, it's too late. There's nowhere to go. She freezes, afraid to move one way or the other as the horses thunder closer to her. One of the horsemen yells, "Watch out!" and she has a flash of Dave's stricken face as he sharply reins in his horse. The black horse heads directly for her, Jason bending low over its neck.

"Erica, move!" someone shrieks. "*Run!*"

At the last moment, Jason jerks the reins, and the horse angles away, passing within inches of her. She feels a rush of whipped-up wind on her face and catches the scent and heat of the horse. Clods of dirt kicked up by its hooves pelt her calves and thighs.

She whirls around in time to see the riders pull up at the fringe of forest that marks the end of the field. The horses jumble in confusion, and she hears a growl of anger or fear or disgust rise up from the men. At the same time, a feminine voice chides, "What do you guys think you're doing? You're going to kill somebody else!"

"You okay?" Dave calls to her. Beside him, Jason's face is hidden by the brim of his hat.

Erica doesn't reply. Springing toward the embankment, she runs.

SIXTEEN

HOODOO: A LOVE STORY

"What the hell were you thinking?" Dave demands. "You could have been killed. You never know what's going to happen with a horse."

Erica stands in the kitchen of the trailer, stirring Nestea into a pitcher of water. Dave sits at the kitchen table, smoking, his face gray, more aged than his years. The western shirt that was freshly ironed and perfectly buttoned this morning is limp and stained by sweat in the armpits. He carries the smell of fermented fear and drink.

"When a horse is coming at you, you get out of the goddamned way." He plugs the hole left by her silence. "Didn't they teach you common sense in Ohio?"

She turns to face him. "Why didn't you tell me they were going to hold a memorial for my dad? I should have been there."

"It was for the people in this town who knew your dad."

She feels the sting: outsider, interloper, out-of-stater. Furious, she grabs two glasses from the cupboard and slams the flimsy pressed-wood door. "Where was Grandma? I didn't see her there."

"Marguerite's always busy during Sawmill Days."

"It was six o'clock in the morning," Erica protests. "No, she voted for the 5K, and everybody in this petty little place has to hang on to their petty little grudges."

Dave gets to his feet with a forceful backward shove of his chair. "Maybe you ought to think twice about what the hell it is you're doing here."

He jabs his way out the front door and slams it behind him, leaving Ratso skittering through the trailer, trying to catch up with him. As Ratso comes to an abrupt halt at the closed door, Erica blinks back tears. After her escape from the meadow this morning, she had run—but not to join Anita or Darcy. Going directly to her grandmother's house, she let herself in through the unlocked door. By then, Grandma was gone, her car visible in the Wickiup parking lot. As Dane and Amory tried to lick her into happiness, Erica had sat on the living room couch and sobbed.

She hears Dave's truck grind out of the gravel driveway. She paces as the ice settles in the tea, wishing she had somewhere to go. But there's nowhere to hide here, no refuge. The highway goes either to Pindall or into the emptiness that leads to Riverton. And beyond Riverton, there's more emptiness. Finally, she pulls on her boots and goes outside, Ratso at her heels.

At the barn, she finds Rain drinking from the water tank in the corral. The horse lifts her head and ambles over with her goofy, heavy-footed stride. Erica reaches out and strokes the velvet muzzle, the flat cheekbone.

"Oh, God, Rain," she says. "Why am I here? Why don't I just leave?"

But she knows why. There is nothing for her in Ohio—Natalie and Royce aside—a useless college degree, no job prospects, her mother gone forever.

"I've got to get out. I've got to just give this up and get out! It's stupid, so stupid to stay where you're not wanted! So incredibly stupid!"

Rain tosses her head, forcing Erica to renew her attentions. "You know how I feel, don't you?" Erica says. "We should run away together."

Possibility comes to her. Why not? Why not run away with this beautiful animal, this sweet thing? A cool breeze sifts up from the creek bottom, bringing the smell of green grass and waxy cottonwood leaves warmed by sun. The freshness makes Erica restless and defiant.

She opens the corral gate and goes into the barn. Rain and Ratso follow, curious as always about her doings. She goes to the sawhorse with a blanket and saddle thrown over it. A bridle hangs from a nail on the wall, cobwebs mating the various parts together. She fingers the end of a rein, trying to remember everything she learned about horses during riding lessons at camp. "Is this yours?" she asks Rain. "Does it fit you?"

It takes her longer to saddle and bridle the horse than she expects. The saddle is more cumbersome than the light eastern model she is used to, and she checks the cinch a number of times, not sure what is too tight and what is too loose. The stirrups—set for Dave, she assumes—need adjusting, too. Fortunately, Rain stands still, her flesh quivering now and then, as if with excitement. Erica's heart is no quieter, flittering in her breast. Her mouth feels dry, and her throat is tightly keyed. She's never done anything like this. Even driving across America to Wyoming did not feel so bold. As she slips the bit into the horse's mouth, she asks, "Want to go for a ride? Want to see the world?"

Rain neighs in response.

"Then come on. Let's get out of here."

After letting herself out of the corral, she mounts Rain and rides into the Badlands.

She follows the track that Dave uses when they check cattle, closing the barbed wire gates behind her. Ratso puffs along behind, his tongue hanging out, loving every moment. Erica, too—it doesn't feel awkward to sit astride a horse, it doesn't feel foreign. She doesn't feel winched apart by the horse's girth beneath her, and the mechanical jounce of her body as Rain shifts her weight from hoof to hoof doesn't unseat her. Instead, something new opens in her, another reality coming to light.

"Let's go," she says, urging Rain into a trot.

When they reach the windmill, Erica slides from Rain's back. At once, she wobbles, feeling spread-eagled and stiff. "Oh, oh," she says to the horse. "Land legs." She hobbles along, keeping a tight grip on the reins— she does not want to lose her means of transportation back to familiar ground. But Rain follows her to the water tank with the same easy calm as she does in the corral. With one hand, Erica scoops the moss that collects near the pipe that joins one tank to the other. She rinses her hand under the cold water that spurts from the pipe in rhythmic intervals.

Shaking her hand to warm it, she says to Rain and Ratso, "Come on. Let's go see the Camels."

She rides up the canyon. Time has barely scraped this part of the world. The striations in the rock run horizontally above her head, clearly defined in black, white, pink, and every shade of red imaginable. Petrified wood scatters across the sand, washed in from some primeval forest that disappeared an eon ago, smooth brown shot through with red and opal-colored veins. Opaque, flesh-piercing black obsidian from the volcanoes reflects the rays of the sun. Erica picks up the sharp shards and puts them in her jeans pockets.

She comes to the Kissing Camels, but doesn't climb to the top. Instead, she dismounts and sits at the base of the rocks, her back against the knuckle-bruising Styrofoam husks. Idly, she runs her fingers through the talcum-powder sand.

One year ago today, her father died. Are the rights to his memory off-limits, like some movie script that is copyrighted? Do they belong only to the people who knew him? She closes her eyes and listens. The silence in the canyon is so profound that it beats with energy of its own. She strains to hear something, to arrive at some determination.

"Oh, Mom," she whispers. "I wish I could talk to you."

Rain nudges her, and Ratso ambles over to her. She reaches out to pet him and notices that her hand sparkles with mica and quartz from the sand.

"Look at that." she says. "Nature's glitter."

In this incomprehensibly vast land, everything shines.

When Dave comes home that evening—not particularly late—Erica is waiting on the cinder block porch of his trailer, Ratso beside her, Rain brushed down and in the corral. Dave climbs slowly from his pickup, as if his joints ache more than Erica's leg muscles do. He sits beside her, patting Ratso absently.

"Is it hot inside?" he asks.

"No, it's cooling down."

He fiddles with the radio, and Reba McEntire's "Little Rock" blurts from the speaker. Lighting a cigarette, he says, "Sorry about this morning. Guess I was just letting off steam."

Erica doesn't answer right away. At last, she asks, "Is everyone still mad at me?"

Dave shrugs. "It'll blow over."

She looks out at the barnyard, where everything—from the trampled grass where the sheep gather to the battered machinery—looks worn out. She feels the same.

"Have you been at the Rambler?" she asks.

"At the rodeo."

"Oh, yeah." She has forgotten that Sawmill Days is still in full swing, with the Saturday night rodeo and ice cream social and the auction of the Celebration Quilt. "Did you ride in it?"

"Naw." His boots scrape against the concrete as he shifts his weight. "I'm getting too old for that."

The night closes around them, the wind from the west blowing the hair off Erica's face. Coyotes yip, sounding as if they are just beyond the circle thrown by the barnyard light. From near the farmhouse, Louise's dog, Frank, woofs. Ratso growls.

Dave continues, "I wish I could have . . . I should have . . ."

Erica feels the despair radiating from him with the smoke that he breathes from his mouth.

"I wish it would have been me," he says at last. "Last year."

"How would that make it right? It shouldn't have been anyone."

He doesn't answer, but takes another draw on the cigarette.

"Was the ride across the field your idea?" she asks.

"Not entirely. We wanted to do something, but we didn't know what for a long time. Finally, we decided to run the race for him."

No wonder they resented the 5K so much, Erica thinks. It had nothing to do with Brad Brock, no connection to his—or the town's—reality. How can someone run a race in cowboy boots? In the steel-toed boots that Dave and the others wear at the sawmill?

Something comes to her—a memory from this morning. As she fled from the field, she had nearly collided with Shari, who had grabbed her arm and asked if she was hurt.

Shari had looked terrified, haunted, as if she had just relived her husband's death in meadow. But Erica had broken free of Shari's grasp without speaking—or did she speak?—intent only on escaping.

"Did you see Shari tonight?" she asks. "How is she doing?"

"Didn't see her. She's been spending a lot of time with Alex Stacy lately. That's okay. Good for her, I guess."

The conversation dies, the radio cuts out, and the coyotes howl again. Ratso lurches into barking, earning a "shut up" from Dave. For some reason, Erica knows that this is the wrong time to mention Rain to Dave, to properly ask him for permission to ride the horse. Tomorrow will be better—or maybe it won't.

"Why didn't you tell me what was going to happen this morning?" she asks.

"I don't know," he says. "Shari and Jason . . . it just, it didn't feel right." He looks up at her. "I don't want to hurt them any more."

He may as well have said it: She, more than Brad Brock's death, is the cause of their pain.

"I'm going in," she says.

"Okay." Dave grinds his cigarette under his boot. "You all right?"

"I don't know," she says honestly. "What about you?"

"Sure," he says weakly. "Always."

From the library, Erica borrows a children's book on the Badlands. She studies the colorful photographs, memorizing the name of each of the structures: pinnacle, spire, toadstool, mesa, butte. A castle is a large, block-shaped rock; a monument is a lone pointed rock.

"Did you know that the Kissing Camels is a caprock?" she calls to Dave, who is in the kitchen cooking dinner. The smell of spaghetti sauce, made with elk rather than beef, fills the trailer. Erica sits on the couch, her bare feet atop Ratso, who sleeps beneath the coffee table. The trailer door is open, the wooden screen door allowing the cooling breeze of evening in while barring the entry of the skinny, lurking cats.

"Not a hoodoo?"

"Still a hoodoo," she says. "But the top is a caprock. And what you call a gully is actually a wadi."

"Wadi you know," he says.

She laughs, but her attention falls on a paragraph that reads: "If you hike into the Badlands, it is important that you build a *cairn* (see photo) of rocks and other debris at the mouth of each wadi you enter and wherever you make a turn. This way you will not become lost. When you leave the area, knock down the cairn so that others will not become confused and lose their way."

She thinks about cairns the next time she rides Rain. It's a good idea to mark her path, to leave a Hansel-and-Gretel trail not of bread crumbs, but of durable matter. Slipping from Rain's back, she piles whatever she can find—rocks, bones, driftwood, tumbleweeds—into a marker. It's a sorry looking thing—not at all like the cairn in the book—but when she passes it on her way home, she murmurs, "Thank you," as if the cairn is her guide, as if it possesses some spirit or power.

She starts riding every afternoon that she can, dressed in a long-sleeved shirt, jeans and boots, her hat on her head to shade her face, a cowboy bandanna around her neck. She may look like an extra from *Bonanza*, but she knows this is the only way to protect herself from the brutally hot sun in the canyons. She carries canteens, too, and a metal bowl for Ratso, and she is careful to stop at every stock tank to allow Rain to drink. As the days of August pass, she rides deeper and farther into the Badlands, beyond the windmill, beyond the Camels, where there are other canyons, coves and nooks to be explored.

She loves it all—the feel of Rain beneath her, the horse's muscles shifting and contracting to carry her along; the way Rain pricks her ears when she sees something that interests her; the heat of the summer that punishes the canyons, only to be swept away by an unexpected, cool breeze; the way Ratso trots along behind horse and rider, tongue lolling out one side, nose wrinkling at the smells.

One day, in a canyon far beyond the Kissing Camels, she discovers a testament of the settling of the great American West: the epitaph JOSIAH BAKER 1873, carved meticulously into the sandstone. In the silence, the name echoes through the canyon, just as if it had been shouted. She expects to see Josiah camped next to his Conestoga wagon, a rabbit turning on a spit over an open fire. But there is no other evidence of human life.

She rubs her fingers over the letters. 1873—more than a hundred years have passed since Josiah Baker walked through this same canyon. Has anyone been here since?

"What is your story, Josiah?" she asks. "How did you feel when you first saw this place? Were you scared out of your mind or were you awed by it? Did you take a few minutes to look around and appreciate the beauty before you"—she touches the letters—"defaced it?"

The question strikes her as funny, and her laughter echoes up and down the canyon. Rain neighs from where she grazes on the sparse grass, and Ratso pauses in peeing on every bush or rock in the canyon long enough to bark.

"Quit," she growls, imitating Dave, but her voice, like his, carries no threat.

At the base of the wall, she unloads the treasures she has collected, piling them in a memorial cairn. The sun pecks at the flecks of mica, obsidian, quartz and chalcedony in the sand and rocks.

"Rest in peace, Josiah," she says. "Wherever you ended up."

She sits beside the cairn for a long time, wondering if Josiah Baker reached California—a likely destination—or if he died somewhere along the route. Starved or frozen to death, or scalped, perhaps, or eaten, maybe by the wolves that used to roam this area or maybe by Wyoming's version of the Donner party. She can sense his—or someone's—presence in this canyon, just on the periphery of her consciousness. This is a land of ghosts.

Josiah Baker, the Shoshone and Arapaho and others nearly decimated by Manifest Destiny, the bison, elk, lynx, wolves and other animals that are now extinct, beings that once had voice but can no longer speak—they gather here, they live on in some intangible form in these canyons.

She closes her eyes. She is insignificant here, nothing, just another piece of organic material in this enormous stew. And yet, she can feel her soul spreading, traveling along the sandy bottoms of the canyons, touching upon the walls, skimming the sky, becoming something greater and stronger and freer than she has ever imagined.

One afternoon, Erica goes to The Daisy for iced coffee. The Closed sign hangs on the door, but she pays it no mind. Grandma has told her to help herself whenever she wants. Today, she finds she isn't alone in The Daisy. Jason stands on one of the white, wrought-iron soda tables, wrestling with a quilt that is hung on a dowel mounted only a couple of inches from the ceiling. He's not quite tall enough to reach it, and the table heaves beneath him, rocking back and forth, the metal of the uneven legs grating on the tile of the floor.

"Hi," she says. "What are you doing?"

She expects no answer, so she isn't surprised by the beats of silence that pass as she helps herself to a cup. At last, Jason begrudges, "I'm getting a quilt for Grandma."

"Did she sell one?"

"I don't know." His voice is swallowed in the sensuous red fabric that he's trying to heft from the dowel. Evidently the quilt is caught on something between dowel and wall. "I guess."

He stands on his tiptoes and strains upward, one hand against the wall. The table wavers to and fro, moving an inch or two.

Erica balances it by laying her hands flat upon it. "I saw you in front of the mill the other day," she says. "Are you a protester?"

He grunts. "No."

"Yeah, I've never been into that either. My mom was—Vietnam and women's rights and all that. It was part of being an American back then, I guess."

Jason makes no reply. The table rocks again, and Erica presses her thighs against it to steady it. Jason curses as he tries to pull the heavy fabric free.

"How did she get those quilts up there?" she asks.

"There's a ladder in the back."

"Why don't you get it?"

"Because then I'd have to put it back."

His tone is ripe with disgust. Erica doesn't bother to point out that the physical effort involved in carrying the ladder to and fro would be much less than jostling around on a table. Safer, too, and—oh, hell, this isn't Royce, someone she has every right to fuss about.

She steps back from the table, and it rocks violently. Jason glowers down at her. "What the hell?" he says. "Are you trying to kill me?"

"Isn't that what you were trying to do the day you rode that horse across the field at me?"

"What?"

"Weren't you trying to kill me?" She bites back the bile that rises up in her. She's surprised at how quickly and powerfully it has come on. She wants to scream—*he is my father, too.*

"Why were you standing in the middle of the field?" Jason asks. "That was really stupid."

"Not as stupid as trying to run someone down."

He jerks at the quilt until Erica is afraid he might rip it.

"Were you there when it happened?" she asks.

"When what happened?"

"When our dad died. How did it happen?"

He peers down at her. "You want to know what I *saw?*"

"Sure, why not?"

When he speaks, his voice is muffled by the cloth of the quilt. "I wasn't there."

"Where were you?"

"I was here. Grandma locks up during the Derby so all her employees can go to it. But I was short of cigarettes that day, so I was down here getting some."

She ponders the confession, taking some time before she says, "You were stealing from your grandmother?"

He gestures toward her cup. "Just like you are now."

"She told me I could help myself," she says easily. "She didn't mention cigarettes, though."

"Well, now you know. I'm a dick, just like you thought."

"I don't think that. I just feel sorry for you."

He balks. "Don't feel sorry for me—"

"Give me a reason not to. Every time I see you, you're doing something crazy. Trying to ride me down, skipping school, and—why don't you just get the damned ladder and do this the way a normal person would?"

"Why don't you fucking shut up?"

She laughs, a veteran of sibling quarrels. "Can't you come up with anything better than that?"

Jason doesn't answer—evidently that is the best he has to offer—and she feels a flash of impatience. She wants something from him, although she doesn't yet know what it is. Not an apology or reconciliation, but something that she can latch on to, something that reveals who he really is.

"Does Grandma know where you were that day?" she asks.

"I don't know."

"She probably does," Erica says easily. "Not much gets past her."

The quilt comes loose. Without warning, Jason drops it. Erica bats at it as it falls on her head with a surprising heavy loft.

"Thanks a lot," she says.

"Sorry," he says insincerely. He jumps from the table, then straightens the chairs, adjusting them until they form a perfect square around the round table. Erica can imagine Grandma giving instructions to her employees about the matter: Chairs must be equally spaced . . .

"So what would you do if I told Grandma what you tried to do to me on the day of the 5K?" she pokes.

His eyes flicker sideways. "Go ahead, I don't care. You can't prove anything."

"So, there is something to prove. That's a confession right there. What if I told her what you were doing when Dad died?"

"You're a bitch—"

She laughs. "Didn't anybody ever teach you how to fight?"

"Give me the quilt."

She makes a show of meticulously refolding the quilt. "Do you hunt and fish like our dad did?" When he doesn't answer, she adds, "I don't believe in it. I think it's wrong."

"There's nothing wrong with it." He rises to the bait. "I suppose you think it's like Walt Disney out there."

"I just don't think an animal is much of a match for a high-powered rifle."

"That's something a city girl would say."

"And that's what I am," Erica says proudly. "What's your excuse?"

"Give me the quilt."

She takes a step backward. "Answer me. You're willing to kill your sister, but you won't kill an animal? Did our dad know that? Did he know you were afraid?"

A sound like a punctured tire—"f-f-f"—comes from his mouth, but he swallows it, probably to stave off more ridicule. On his face, Erica sees a chain of emotion: shame, sadness, anger. She knows she has scraped something bare in him, and she's ready to fight it through.

"You're afraid of me, too, aren't you?" she asks. "I haven't done anything to you."

"Maybe I don't know how to fight," he wings, "but I know when somebody's trying to screw everybody else. You ruined that day. You fucked up what was supposed to be an honor for my dad. You made everybody forget about him and think about you. Are you proud of yourself? Are you happy?"

His bitterness surprises her, and she falters. Jason takes advantage of it. "Why won't you leave us the hell alone?" he asks.

"Is that what you want? To be left alone, so you don't have to be decent to anyone?" Her anger surges forward. "Well, that's fine with me. Grandma loves me, and that's all that matters to me."

He kicks a chair out of his way. "You take the fucking quilt, then. You can give it to her."

He's gone, the door of The Daisy banging behind him, before she can speak.

In the Badlands again, Erica rides Rain farther than she ever has. As she travels, she passes by cairns that she has built in the mouths of canyons, like welcoming beacons, or in the depths, where the walls guard them like secrets. The cairns no longer serve to guide her around the Badlands, and they aren't memorials, either, like the heap of rocks near Josiah Baker's name. She plans them, she sculpts them, she treasures them, anticipating their appearance the next time she rides past them. She thinks of them by the most elemental of names: Red

Rock Cairn, Black Shard Cairn, Wood Cairn, Metal Cairn. She offers them up to—who? God? the Great White Spirit? Mother Earth?

She carries with her a pair of saddlebags that she found in the barn to hold what she finds along the trail: feathers, driftwood, ribbons of furred sage, wildflowers, even a fuzzy rabbit's tail. She collects bones—skulls, legs, ribs, teeth that are stripped clean and bleached white—by the handfuls. She grows greedy over rocks, picking up chunks and slivers and everything in between and storing them in the saddle bags until the leather bulges and she starts to worry about the added weight on Rain's back. She discovers manmade objects that have arrived with spring floods—old cogs from machinery, rusted logging chains, a fender from a car. If she cannot carry it away, she builds a cairn around it.

Today, she rides in what Dave calls the "back pasture," although it, like every other place on the ranch, is a labyrinth of gullies, pinnacles, spires, toadstools, castles and hoodoos. At the windmill, she stops—as always—for water.

This windmill is different from the others. It is sunken, the round metal of the tank walls rising only about two feet from the ground where she stands. When Dave first took her there as they were checking cattle, he told her, "It's in the new style."

"How many styles can a watering tank have?"

"You girls have new fashions that you have to fuss with. Us ranchers, we got new ways of grazing and watering to think about." He laughed at his own joke. "This tank's dug into the ground, so it's more like a lake or pond. Cattle lower their heads to drink, like they would at a natural water source. The only metal is in the sides. The bottom's made of sodium bentonite. What they use in kitty litter."

"You have a stock tank filled with kitty litter?"

"There's some pretty big cats in this territory." He laughed again. "It's the newest, greatest thing, a natural sealant. But I tell you what. It was hell getting that thing to seal. Took twice as much bentonite as they thought."

"Who thought?"

"The water men."

"Like mermaids?"

"You think crazy sometimes," Dave teased. "No, well drillers. Hell, that well was trouble from the start. Well witcher missed the spot. We had to go down halfway to China to find water."

"Well witcher?" she had asked. "One of those guys with the pronged stick?"

"You ever seen that done?" Dave glanced at her. "Pretty fascinating."

"Isn't that a wives's tale? I mean, it has the word 'witch' in it."

"No, we've always had our wells witched. It's just about always worked."

"But this one was wrong. Who's crazy now?"

He shrugged tightly. "Never said I wasn't."

The algae growing in the sunken water tank is different from that in the other tanks. Because of the bentonite, it forms in stringy, loose pats that look as if someone has half-melted little pink marshmallows on the top. It has the consistency of meringue.

She scoops it out with the palm of her hand. She has learned to love the cold of the water, the pang that it sends to her elbow, the rust-like smell of it. Shaking the excess water from her hands, she unscrews the lids of her canteens and fills them with water from the pipe. For some reason, the water that pours into the stock tanks is better than the water that comes from the kitchen tap in Dave's trailer. It's the purity of it, she thinks, the elemental rawness—straight from the ground, not filtered through faucets or refrigerators.

Swinging into the saddle, she rides into a gloriously deep and winding canyon. The walls are pocked by secret coves and cubbyholes opened and deepened by erosion, and the hoodoos and other stack formations have the about-to-tumble-down look that leaves her breathless. About half a mile into the canyon, she comes across a bedraggled barbed wire fence that once stretched from one wall to the other. Weather-blasted stumps of fence posts lie in the canyon bottom, toppled by time and shifting sands. Rusty barbed wire, once taut on the posts, spools on the ground.

She slides from Rain's back and follows the broken line of fencing. Who would try to build a fence across here, a fence that would divide the canyon in two? It strikes her as funny—as ridiculous, in fact. Man trying to carve out boundaries in a land so immense that nothing can be clearly envisioned. She has seen a plat of the ranch, its shape blocky and squared-off, and she's heard Dave speak of quarter-sections and even of townships. It seems so futile, so meaningless.

Lying near the wall of the canyon is a gnarled fence post, its rough sides spackled with lichen. The post's bottom has rotted away, and it has fallen with one straggling strand of barbed wire looped around it. The wire is vicious and rusty, the barbs flattened triangular pieces of steel that narrow into sharp points.

"Well," she says aloud. "Let's see what we can make of this."

She drags the old fence post to the very center of the wadi. Digging a hole in the easily-sifted sand, she stands the post upright. The barbed wire whips around it, like arms, extended forward and slightly curved, twitching in the wind. It looks like a variation on a Christian cross, or a human figure reaching forward.

She adjusts the barbed wire a bit, shaping the opposing strands into a full-on, rounded embrace.

"This is Strong Woman's Cairn," she says, to Rain, to Ratso, to the ghosts and gods, to Brad Brock, to her mother. She thinks of Jason. The words he spoke to her still echo in her head: *You made everybody forget about him and think about you.* They hurt yet. Is that really what she had intended to do?

She packs rocks and bone and anything she can find to keep the post upright. The sand gives way easily—she can see why the fence fell down—and she searches for more debris to bolster the post. As she is dragging a piece of driftwood across the ground, she hears Ratso growl.

She whirls, searching for the bear or puma or rattlesnake that has found her at last. The hair on Ratso's back ridges into a spine, and his growl becomes a bark. Rain neighs, dancing her weight from one foot to another. Erica looks down the canyon, her vision blurred by her panic. My God, she is so far from anything she knows, and she is helpless, caught here in this steep-walled canyon.

A rider approaches on horseback. The horse is a brown and white pinto, a Little Joe Cartwright horse, but the rider is harder to see. Its clothes, its face—everything blends into the reddish, tan landscape of the Badlands. It moves lightly, like the ghosts she has conjured in her own head. Around the hooves of the rider's horse, Erica sees dark shapes that contort and shift. She squints, trying to identify them, but they slip from her vision whenever her focus alights on them. They are shadows, she thinks, tricks of the eye—they have to be, don't they?—yet they flop or scamper or *something* away like actual animals might.

Ratso barks viciously.

"Hush!" Erica snaps. Rain tosses her head, and Erica grabs the reins. The horse's hooves shuffle nervously, and she rears back her head, trying to pull away from Erica. "Stop," Erica says. "Rain, it's all right."

The rider comes closer. Erica sees that it is a woman whose face is wrinkled and browned by the sun to the same color as the hoodoos around her. She is Native American, dressed in the traditional way, in buckskin, with beads hanging from her braids.

From the pommel of the woman's saddle hang a couple of rabbits and something that looks like a fox. A rifle pokes from a scabbard. The woman's eyes skim over Erica and stop at Strong Woman's Cairn. She reins in the paint horse and circles the cairn at a slow walk. The horse's hooves churn up the soft sand, leaving a darker ring of slightly damp sand.

"This yours?" the woman asks.

"I built it," Erica stammers. "But . . . am I on reservation land?"

The woman makes no reply. "You've made the others, too?"

"Yes."

Another circle. Then the woman pulls one of the rabbits from her clutch near the pommel and drops it onto the pile that surrounds the fence post. When it lands, Erica can see that it is not freshly dead, but skinned and tanned.

A chant rises from the woman's throat. "*Da-me Apa nanamburu, Da-men biya namburu nareyizinore. Niam biya nareyizinore, Niam biya nareyizinore.*" She looks at Erica and says, "Our father's steps, Our mother's, flying up"—she motions upward with her hands, palms toward the sun—"flying up to the sky. Do you know that?"

Erica hesitates, uncertain.

"Your mother, your father—they died?"

"Yes," Erica breathes. "I'm Erica Brock."

The woman rides over to where Erica holds Rain. The horse jerks again, and Erica grasps the reins with both hands, struggling to hold on. Leaning from her saddle, the woman gazes into Erica's face, her ancient eyes tracing eyebrows and cheekbones and lips. She smiles—Erica can count her remaining teeth on one hand—and touches Erica's cheek, the dead calluses of her fingers prickling the soft skin.

"*Im-pate,*" she says. "Daughter."

She pulls up the reins and clucks the paint horse a couple of times with her soft-booted heels. Erica watches in silence as the woman rides down the canyon, the strange, life-like shadows nipping and flipping along with her.

She mentions the encounter to her grandmother on the following Sunday as she sets the table for lunch. "I met a Native American woman the other day when I was out on the ranch," she says. "She was wearing traditional dress, and it looked like she'd been hunting."

"That's Mary Flying Eagles," Grandma tells her. "I think the Phillipses have always let her hunt on their property."

"Oh, that's good." Erica lays down spoon, fork and knife. "I thought I was trespassing on sacred Native American soil or something. I wouldn't want to be disrespectful or anything. I'm glad she was the one who was trespassing."

Her grandmother snorts. "Who do you think that land belonged to before Louise's family showed up and claimed it as theirs?"

"I was so flustered by her that I forgot my name. I said I was Erica Brock."

Grandma gives her a look that makes Erica think she is in for a scolding, but she says, "Well, it's about time, don't you think?"

"What?"

"Do you want to take your father's name?" Grandma asks. "Either casually or legally."

Erica laughs in surprise. "Would you let me?"

"I believe you're old enough to change your name to Sunflower Starlight, if you want."

"I'd like that," Erica says, then corrects, "Not Sunflower Starlight, that is."

"Wise choice."

Erica throws her arms around her grandmother's neck. Her grandmother's hands come up and rest lightly on her back, as if she is unaccustomed to embracing, but Erica holds fast. What she said to Jason was true: This, right here, is all that matters to her.

SEVENTEEN
IN THE EYE OF THE STEEPLE

Jason has had a bad week. School has been back in session at Pindall Consolidated for five weeks, and Jason has received ample encouragement to attend from any number of sources. A stern phone call from his Grandma Jackie and Grandpa Bill in Phoenix, a funny-serious scolding from his aunt Amy in Fort Collins, ardent vows from Juliana that she can't bear a day inside that school without him, a judgmental sniff from his grandmother, and a recitation of the dire statistics about high school dropouts from Robyn, who is one herself. "They grow up to be no-good-niks," she concluded.

"Why didn't you finish high school?" he challenged her.

"I married Walt when I was fifteen." She trailed lazy cigarette smoke through the air. "He left to fight the Japs two days later."

"So are you a no-good-nik?" he asked, earning a thump on the head from Robyn.

Today, Jason has once more skipped school. His mother has started driving him, but this morning, the pickup wouldn't start and she had to call the school and ask them to radio the bus driver to stop along the Yellowstone highway. Once delivered to the school, Jason had slipped in one door of the gymnasium, where a bunch of seventh graders were shooting hoops, and out the other. Now he saunters down Main Street past the Greenbow Boutique, with only a passing concern as to whether Robyn or Walt might spy him from the Rambler. If they do, so be it. He'll be long gone by the time somebody goes to pick up his mother and bring her to town.

As he passes the Greenbow, he glances at the second-story window of Johnny Hart's apartment. It's too early to wake Johnny from his boozy burrow. As always, Tiger sits in the window, watching the street below. Recognizing Jason, he stands and rubs against the window, meowing. The cat knows who feeds him.

Jason peers into the window of Rob Grenville's shop. It's that breathless moment between tourist and hunting seasons, when Pindall tallies up one boom or bust and readies itself for the next. As a result, no one is there. Curious, Jason wanders inside, triggering a chime that plays the first phrase of "Dixie."

"Be right there," a voice calls from the back.

He bypasses stands burgeoning with rifles, crossbows, and fishing rods; circular racks crammed with camouflage and winter overalls; cases of binoculars, bullets and traps. In the back of the store is the glass case that holds his father's knives. With tight throat, he counts how many are left. Three. At the beginning of the summer, there were five. When these are gone, there will only be the few left at home and the unfinished pieces in the equipment shop.

"Hey, Jason." Rob appears, with hair on seemingly every part of his body. "Seein' about the knives?"

"Yeah."

The knives are Bowies, not fillets like the one his father gave him, or four-inch-blades like the one his mother keeps beside her bed. They are grand, monumental, irreplaceable. These are his father's last creations. So beautiful, so lethally sharp, the blades so highly polished, the artwork so perfect and exact. One is scrimshawed with the paw print of a puma, another with an eagle feather. The third, the simplest and most beautiful, has a black bolt of lightning slashed into the highly polished antler. The etching is rough and bold, wicked. All carry the trademark, BB, his father's initials.

Rob fingers one. "Every once in a while, someone comes in here who can't resist 'em and is willin' to pay what I'm askin' for them. I won't take a dime less than what's listed there."

Jason reads the tags. Hundreds of dollars. "Do you tell them he's dead? That there aren't any more?"

"Now, Jason, you wouldn't want me to do that—"

"What about giving them to me," he says, suddenly, boldly.

"What?"

"Let me take them back"—he nearly says 'home'—"to my mom."

"Is that what Shari wants?" Rob furs out, just like a threatened cat. "I give her every penny I make from these, Jason, don't think I don't. It's a good chunk of change, while it lasts. I ain't makin' a profit from this."

"Okay."

"She's never said nothin' to me about it. What'd she say to you?"

"Nothing," Jason says. "Never mind."

"If she feels she ain't been treated fairly, have her come see me. I can show her the books. Every penny goes to her."

"She didn't say anything about it." Jason backs away from the counter. "She doesn't even know I'm here."

Rob seems somewhat mollified. "Well," he says. "If she wants them back, tell her to come see me."

Jason slips out the door. What an ass Rob is.

He lights a cigarette and skulks along the road to the mill. The day is one of those brilliant, glassy fall days when you know that the weather will break soon and the wind will hit hard. The aspen have dropped most of their leaves, and hay trucks roll through the canyon, bound for dude ranches in Cody and Jackson. The too-blue-to-be-true sky seems higher somehow, already eclipsed by winter's approach.

Jason comes around the curve that divides town from mill and stops dead in his tracks. Sitting before him on her lawn chair is Elise. On the ground beside her is Juliana.

His heart takes one frantic, sidelong leap before a new fury surges through him. What in the fuck does Juliana think she's doing? What right does she have to sit there like she and Elise are friends or something? Damn it, he wants to see Elise. He needs to see her, he needs to talk to her before his chest collapses on itself or blows sky high. He throws down his cigarette butt and grinds it into the ground.

"Jason!"

It's Juliana's voice. She hails him again, and he reluctantly walks toward her.

Juliana's dressed as she always is—sweatshirt, tights, anklets and boots. Her hair is pulled to the very crest of her head and held by a thick band. It tumbles downward from there in a kinky tail. Elise's long, silken skirt drapes over the edges of her chair, and she wears a black button-down sweater. Her copper hair frames her face before it drops straight to her shoulders. Her feet are bare and slim, her shoes kicked away.

"I'm writing a paper called 'The Most Interesting Person I Know,'" Juliana chirps happily. "Lex said I should talk to Elise, and Mrs. Rayhill let me come down here and interview her during class. Where were you this morning, Jason?"

Jason meets both of their inquiring gazes. "I didn't make it," he says belligerently.

"What are you doing here?"

He scrambles for an answer. "I'm going down to Dave Phillips' place."

"Dave?" Juliana looks down the highway, as if searching for the man himself, then says brightly, "Oh, to see Erica?"

Ah, fuck it. He'd forgotten that she lives there—as if it's possible to forget her. He hasn't seen her since the day she cornered him in the Daisy, but he has been sucker-punched by her accusation. He hadn't intended to kill her when he rode that horse at her, but *he could have.* He could have, and then she'd be gone, and things would be back to normal. Except, they wouldn't, because his dad would still be dead. It exhausts him to try to figure it all out.

"Stay and talk," Elise says, and the tenderness in her voice lures him back. "I haven't seen you in so long. How are you? How's your horse?"

The mention of the day in Disney Land makes his neck burn. It seems so long ago, when he was another person—somebody who burned with desire, not rage. "Listen," he says. "I have to go."

He tromps on, as if truly committed to going to the Phillips ranch. Once a curve cloaks him from their sight, he lights another cigarette. What is it about this town? Every time he has something that might be special—his father, Elise, those knives—it gets taken from him.

Jason scrambles up the embankment from the highway and cuts through the trees, heading toward Pindall via the tall, rocky butte to the east. Elise and Juliana are probably laughing their heads off right now about how stupid he is.

Or, they're talking about his dick. The very thought makes him ache.

He and Juliana have been screwing since the night of the street dance at Sawmill Days, after they smoked what was left of the doobie. But Juliana is not who he sees when they are together. He envisions Elise—in the nude, in the shallows of the lake, her breasts so round and soft, her hands held out to him. The first time, he came after about a minute and a half.

"Was that it?" Juliana had asked.

The past few times, he has refrained from thinking of Elise until the very last, possible second, when all hell and fire and creation and shit break loose from him. Juliana has been kinder since. They usually do it at the Stacy house, while Lex is up in the Park. Juliana was a virgin, which surprised Jason. He thought she'd been around.

The worst part of it, though, is that his mother knows.

Last weekend, she came into his bedroom and asked him pointblank if he and Juliana were having sex. When he protested, she said, "I was only a few months older than you when I got pregnant. It took both your father and me by surprise, because we thought we were too smart." She was not at all embarrassed by this bald admission, as far as he could tell. "What sort of protection are you using?"

"Juliana knows when it's safe." He swallowed a couple of times, trying to rid his mouth of the taste of week-old hot dogs.

"Maybe, but you don't." She didn't even bother to scold him or ground him or, at the very least, tell him he would rot in hell for his sins or go blind like any normal parent would do. "Lex is going to talk to Juliana about seeing a doctor, but you need to get some condoms before you two do it again."

"God, Mom, don't say it that way—"

"What do you want me to say? It all boils down to the same thing."

"All right, I get it." He shook off his revulsion. "The pharmacy counter's locked."

"Well, then, ask your grandmother."

"No way," he said. "That's disgusting."

His mother's lips curved in a faint smile, but she remained stern and cool. "Then I'll ask her."

"Please, don't," he had begged.

"She doesn't need to know they're for you."

She was nearly out the door by the time he figured out what she'd said, which nearly made him puke. The next day, when he returned home from school, a box of Trojans was sitting on his bed.

Jason's anger with Juliana abates enough for him to keep his date with her that evening. Thunderheads have gathered by the time he clocks out at the Wickiup and walks up the block. The Stacy house is his only refuge. He cannot go to the Rambler. His mother has already accosted him about missing school, confronting him in the storage room at the Wickiup.

"Why are you doing this?" she had demanded. "One day, only one day I can't drive you to school, and you ditch—"

In response, Jason had knotted his work apron and picked up the list of jobs his grandmother had left for him, studying it fiercely.

"Talk to me," his mother pleaded. "Tell me why."

He has told her a million times. There's no point to school, no purpose, no goal. "Why do you care?" he'd blasted. "It's my life."

"Don't you give me that," she'd fumed. "Were you down at the mill again? What do you do down there? It isn't right, it makes everyone nervous—"

"Yeah? What do they think I'm going to do? Figure out how stupid they are—?"

"This is your home, Jason. This is our town. Grandma's a leader in this community, and your dad was loved here. And every night I hear about what you're doing from somebody. I don't need that right now."

"I'm really sorry I'm here on this earth getting in your way—"

"You act as if it's wrong that I want what's best for you. You're only hurting yourself by doing this—"

"You used to let Dad do exactly what he wanted. You never tried to stop him. You always just let him go, and then we never saw him. He didn't stick around his 'home.' His 'town.' He didn't even stick around his 'wife' or his 'son,' but went out and had a daughter."

It was a cheap shot, but by then, the argument had attracted the attention of the produce manager, Bob Haynes, who had barreled into the storage room at the sound of their voices and just as quickly left.

"Jesus." His mother seemed to shrink in front of him, pulling inward like she had been clobbered. "I have to go to work. We'll talk later."

After she left, Jason had had to blink a number of times before the to-do list came into focus again.

Now, Juliana opens the door dressed only in a red bra and panties. She throws her arms around his neck and kisses his lips and cheeks with giggly passion. "Come in quick before anyone sees!"

Gruffly, he barks, "What in the hell were you doing at the mill today?"

"What were you doing?" she shoots back. "Why weren't you in school? If you get kicked out, Jason, you're gonna be really, really sorry. Besides, if I want to talk to Elise, that's my business. I wrote a really good paper on her during math today."

"What did you talk about?" he asks, heart pounding.

"What do you think? She's so smart, and she cares so much about the earth and—"

"Why Elise?" he lashes. "Why not your brother or your uncle? Why not Mrs. Rayhill?"

"She's a teacher! How interesting could she be? What's your problem, Jason? Elise is there every day. Probably half the town knows her by now."

That's what he's afraid of. Who else has Elise befriended?

"I could have chosen Erica," Juliana snips. "But it was too far to walk to the Morning Glory during class. She could have told me all about coming here—"

"I'm going," Jason says, turning to leave.

"Don't be mad." She crosses her arms over her breasts as if she realizes how ridiculous she looks. "Come on, Jason, you don't want to leave."

It's true—he doesn't. "Then shut up. I don't want to hear about her."

"Fine," Juliana agrees.

He follows her up the stairs. The Stacy house is one of those creepy old grandma houses, built in 1890 or something. Every wall is plastered with hideous, flowered wallpaper, and the closets all look like a long-dead great-uncle could be stowed amid the overboots. Tonight, Juliana has chosen for their tryst to take place in the spare bedroom next to Lex's, rather than in the living room or her bedroom.

"This room looks over the driveway," she explains as she opens the door to yet another flower-choked room. "Lex is down at the Rambler. We'll hear him, if he gets home early."

"Did he tell my mom about us?" Jason asks. Lex has never caught them in the act, but he's discovered them snorting like steam engines a few times.

"What?"

"Does he know about us?"

"Maybe." She turns down the flowery bedspread. "What's wrong, Jason? Don't you like Lex? You better, because he really has it bad for your mom."

He does not want to think about his mother. "Whose room is this?" he asks, noting the floral quilts on the two twin beds with distaste before walking to the window. He finds himself eye to eye with the steeple on the Methodist church across the street.

"The twins, Caroline and Leah. They're both gone now."

"Who came up with all these flower designs?"

"My mom always wanted a big garden." Juliana sits on a bed, her breasts popping out of the scarlet bra. She shoves a strap back up on her shoulders. Her panties are, incongruously, virginal white. "But you can't grow much here. So she planted her garden inside. Me and Lex decided not to change it."

"It's weird."

"That's really rude, Jason," she flares. "How'd you like it if your mom threw out all your dad's stuff?"

"She has," he says bitterly. His mother has sold the outfitting equipment and trail horses and pack mules and his father's new Ford three-quarter ton, even though money hasn't been any more of a problem for them since his father died than it was before. They don't have much, but they don't need much. So why should she sell the knives at Rob Grenville's? Why not keep whatever is left of his father, what little there is? He adds, "I'm next."

"What do you mean?"

"Never mind."

"Then come over here," Juliana orders.

Jason fingers the wrapped condom in his pocket. There's no easy way to do this. "We have to use this," he says brusquely, pulling it from his pocket.

"What is it?"

"A rubber."

"I told you." She sounds exasperated. "I know when it's safe. We learned all that in seventh grade."

"Yeah, but I don't." With some belated gratitude, Jason cops his mother's line.

"Don't you trust me?" Juliana demands.

"Oh, come on, Juliana. Accidents happen. I'm one of them."

"So am I," she retorts. "I'm seven years younger than my sister, Cammy."

"Well, then, let's just follow family tradition and fuck up our lives."

"Your life, maybe. My parents loved me. They called me Angel Surprise."

"How do you know that? You told me you never knew them."

Juliana's face puckers. "Why are you being so mean?" Pouting, she folds her arms across her breasts. "I don't know how to use those things."

"I do," Jason lies.

It's not as simple as it seems. The condom is slimy and wadded up inside the mint-sized package, and Juliana has the finesse of a debarker at the mill. She keeps up a steady stream of complaints: the medicine smell of the lubricant turns her stomach, and she can't slide the ring to the base, and she thinks she may have torn the thin skin with her Godzilla fingernails. Jason keeps wilting in the face of her displeasure. When, at last, the mission is accomplished, his penis looks like the bag of giblets that his mother pulls from the Thanksgiving turkey every year.

Juliana laughs.

Jason pulls his knees to his chest. "Do you want this or not?"

"Jeez, Jason, what is wrong with you tonight?" she asks, but she giggles again as soon as the words are out.

A bright light assails Jason's eyes. It comes from the steeple across the street. He squints into it, and spies a figure standing beside the bells. It's a man dressed in winter gear. He wears a hat pulled low over his eyes. The rest—his expression, his hands, his mouth—are washed clean by the light. Still, Jason recognizes his father.

"Holy crap!" he explodes. He grabs for his shirt and jeans, stuffing himself into his underwear without removing the sagging condom. He jams his feet into his shoes so hard that the heels breach beneath his weight.

"What's wrong?" Juliana cries. "What's going on?"

He clatters down the stairs of the Stacy house and darts across the street to the church. The wooden sign, replete with the history of the church, rests on a grassy patch in front of concrete steps. Jason knocks into it, sending up a ringing screech from its hinges as he runs up the steps to pull at the front door.

It's locked.

He circles the building. There is a side entrance to the one-room church, between the rows of pews and the altar. It's also locked. Leave it to Pindall—not a soul in town locks their front door, but the church is a fortress. Angrily, Jason bangs the door back and forth against the jamb. With a loud crack, the door gives way, and Jason falls inside without the least bit of grace.

He hurdles a metal gate at the base of the bell tower and thunders upward. The stairs are creaky and wooden, wrapped in a gnarly spiral.

The whole rickety structure heaves beneath his weight. At the top, behind a ramshackle door, is a tiny landing, spacious enough for one person. Jason plows through to stand just below the carillon.

The landing is deserted. The wind blows through the open arches of the steeple and whistles between the loose, weathered boards. Lightning snaps in the western skies, illuminating not only the barrel-sized mouths of the bells, but straggly swallow nests mudded into the pointed gable. Black tar made up of decomposing leaves, bird shit, and dirt smothers the floor. It's obvious no one comes up here. A tangle of electric-chair-worthy wires snakes down one wall and through a hole in the floor.

Jason leans weakly into the arch, trying to catch his breath and still the dizziness in his head. What had he seen? Was it his imagination? He tries to revive the vision of his father's face, but now he sees only shadow and blinding light, black angles and fuzzy gray.

The uneven tails of his shirt, buttoned incorrectly, flap in the wind. Thunder rumbles lazily over the forest. Defeated, he winds down the treacherous staircase to the church below. At the bottom, he climbs over the metal gate. A "NO ENTRANCE" sign clanks against the rungs.

"What are you doing?"

Jason whips around toward the altar. Lex is sitting in the first pew. The dim light beneath the cross renders his face nearly as blank as that of the man in the steeple.

"What the—?"

"That staircase was condemned about ten years ago," Lex continues serenely. "Imagine that—it's damned, while the souls who come to pray here are saved."

"Why are you here? Was that you up there?" He wonders if Lex was trying to see into the darkened bedroom across the street. Was he spying on them? Trying to catch them at it?

"Pastor Marty has me keep an eye on things," Lex replies. "Juli told me you'd come over here."

A million more questions pour into Jason's head, the most pressing being: Was Juliana dressed when Lex saw her? Had she had time to smooth the bedclothes and close up the spare bedroom and put on something besides that bull-baiting bra before he walked in?

"You don't have any malice in mind for the good Methodists, do you?" Lex talks as if this is Sunday brunch. "Theft, arson, murder?"

"It's a fucking church, for Christ's sake," Jason remonstrates, and the words echo through the sanctuary, the evidence of his blasphemy reaching God's ears more than once. Too late, he realizes that Lex is teasing. He flops down into the pew opposite Lex, the aisle between them. "I thought I saw my dad," he breathes. "Up there. In the steeple. Was it you?"

"It wasn't me." Lex mulls over Jason's confession. "Juli says she's seen our parents walking through the trees, up on the pass where they were killed. She says they're walking hand in hand, looking straight ahead, intent on their business. They never look at her or attempt to make contact. I've never seen them myself."

"So you don't believe her?" Jason's heart sinks.

"Who am I to say?" Lex shrugs. "Mark Twain wrote that every activity that humans enjoy has been left out of heaven. Sex, drinking, smoking, gambling. Up there, everybody sings or plays a harp or praises God endlessly. On earth, Twain says, a place like that would be empty in two hours. So if my parents want to walk around in the forest or your dad wants to visit the steeple, who can blame them?"

Jason wants to laugh, but he has forgotten how. "Did my mom send you to find me?"

"No, I came home to get a book that she might like."

"She's really pissed at me."

"I don't think she's as pissed as she is worried." Lex resettles, raising a wooden squeak from the hundred-year-old pew. "Do you want to talk about it?"

"No," Jason says automatically, but all the same, words flow from his mouth. "Why did you come back?"

"It's funny. When you've been away for a few years, you start to think maybe this isn't such a bad place after all." He stands. "Why don't we go over to the house? We can talk more where it's warmer."

"I think I broke the door of the church," Jason admits.

"Yep, you did. So you'll be back tomorrow to fix it."

Outside, Lex strolls through the darkness toward his house, evidently expecting Jason to follow like a lamb. But Jason loiters, unsure of what he's started and unwilling to face Juliana and the mess he left behind. From the middle of the street, Lex calls, "Are you coming?"

"No," Jason says. "I guess not."

"Do you want a ride to the Rambler?"

"No."

"So where will you go?"

"I'll be okay."

Jason hikes up the hill to the meadow. Only the neon glow of lightning illuminates it. Waves of grass, the color of sleep, sway eerily before him. There is a clear-cut path through the field, but he saunters into the thigh-high growth. Surely if his father could appear in the steeple, he can come here. Jason raises his hands, palms skyward, in a gesture worthy of Elise, to try to call his father's spirit to him.

Suddenly, at the edge of the forest, Jason spies a dark, loping shadow, graceful and silent. The wolf. He bursts up from the grass and runs toward it. As he does, he catches another from the corner of his eye, flying alongside him, matching every stride. A second wolf? When he jerks to a halt, panting, nothing is there. Ahead, he glimpses another shadow, hightailing it into the trees, and another, this time to his right. They make no sound, leave no impressions in the grass. The meadow swarms with them, swelling here, twisting there, all around him. Yet each time he swings or whirls or leaps to capture a clear view of one, he sees emptiness.

"Come on!" he screams into the wind, but the words are blown back into his face. He stops running and clasps his arms around his waist. His sides are aching, and his lungs feel seared with a hot poker. "Come on!"

He waits for them to return, whatever they were—spirits, demons, hallucinations. Why is it so hard? Everything escapes him, even the stuff that's only in his imagination. When sleety rain cracks open the sky, he slogs through the thick grass and treads the slippery path down the hill. Seeking shelter and warmth, he heads for his grandmother's house. Without knocking, he lets himself in.

She sits on the couch, a quilt in her hands. "What are you doing here?" she asks, by way of greeting. She looks at him over granny glasses. Her braid is coiled at the nape of her neck.

"I don't know." Jason sits on the couch beside her and scratches Dane and Amory, who slobber in welcome. He doesn't dare tell his grandmother about the creatures in the field or about glimpsing his father in the steeple. She is well grounded in reality. Solid as granite and twice as immovable, his mother has called her.

The quilt she is making is of pinks and purples, but not normal shades of either. The pinks have the velvet loft of a wild rose, the purples those of the larkspur. Wyoming colors, his grandmother would call them.

"Have you had dinner?" she asks.

"I don't want any."

Unlike his mother, who would leap to her feet and insist that he eat something wholesome and hot, his grandmother acts as if she doesn't give a shit. This is why he loves her. She never assumes that she knows better.

Jason watches her needle wend in and out of the luxurious fabric. The stitches lie even and fine across layers pinned together with colorful bubble-headed pins. His grandmother's fingers, laden with turquoise rings, arch over the fabric with strength and absolute control. Her steady, tireless sewing, so delicate and sure, brings a pang to Jason's heart. Something nameless, something that murmurs of the windswept dark, and the elusive shadows, and the figure in the run-down steeple.

"I miss Dad," he says, his eyes still on her hands. The needle pauses on the purple cloth. "I really miss him. I think about all the stuff I've screwed up." Tears roll from his eyes. "I've really fucked up."

"It's not that bad, Jason," she says.

"You like her better than me, don't you?"

"What?"

"Erica." Saying the name sends a pierce of pain from the base of his neck right down to his groin. "You like her because she's not screwed-up or stupid like me."

His grandmother lets a tick of silence pass by. "I have two grandchildren, Jason, and I have enough love that I don't have to choose between them."

His throat tightens. He doesn't think he has ever heard his grandmother say the word "love." It's something he's always known, something he's never needed to hear, and it is painful to force her to say it.

"She's your sister," Grandma says. "Shocked as we all were, I won't turn my back on my son's daughter, just as I'd never turn my back on you. As far as I'm concerned, the two of you are equal."

"But he wasn't even married to her mom," he explodes. "He didn't even care about her, and now here she comes, trying to make everybody like her. And everybody does. They're always saying she's so nice—"

"I heard that you and your mother had a knock-down drag-out in the back room of the store today. What was that about?"

"It doesn't matter," he says. "She thinks I'm a fuck-up, they both do, and they're right, I am, and it's no use pretending—"

Suddenly, he's sobbing, his body wracked by long, shuddering cries from the very deepest part of his abdomen. Why is he so helpless, so lost? Why can't he just pick up and go on, like his mother wants, like Juliana wants, like Erica can, like everyone seems to expect?

His grandmother's arm encircles him, and he throws himself face down into the soft, rich fabric on her lap. The cloth smells crisp, like fresh grain. For a long time, he cries, his chest breaking open again and again, as if the sobs have ripped away his ribs and left his lungs and heart exposed. The straight pins in the quilt rake his cheeks, and he gathers up bunches of cloth, clenching his fingers around the satisfying bite of the sharp points. He feels his grandma's hands on his head and shoulders, and running up and down his back.

He cries until there is no more. Burrowed in the soggy cloth, he lies motionless, unwilling to resume. At last, he finds the strength to release the cloth and sit up. When he does, one of the long, steel pins snags his cheek and skims across from his nose to his temple. He wipes away the tears and blood with a palm that is pricked and raw.

"I didn't get any on the quilt, did I?" he asks.

"The quilt doesn't matter." She folds it up and lays it aside. "Let's get you cleaned up."

She rises and moves down the hallway to the bathroom. The dogs huff along behind her. Jason follows, puppyish and needy, but stops at the door of his father's old bedroom. It's been a long time since his father lived in this house, and his grandmother mostly uses the room for storage. A twin bed still graces one corner, a small, child-sized bureau another, and an old trunk presses against a wall. Jason wanders inside and sits on the bed. Boxes are piled in front of the closet doors, a few with opened flaps. Behind the stack, Jason glimpses a single, black marble eye. He shoves the boxes aside until he finds a pronghorn head, fully mounted on a trophy board. He thinks of the stuffing where the brains used to be and wants to cry again.

"Here." From the doorway, his grandmother waves a wet washcloth.

He sponges away the blood from his cheeks and hands.

"What's this?" he asks. "I've never seen it."

His grandmother sits on the bed. "Oh, I don't know. One of your dad's projects, I guess. Erica must have found it somewhere."

"Erica? You're letting her go through his stuff?"

"She's looking for something that belonged to her mother."

"She's not taking stuff, is she? It's mine—"

"I'm not letting her take anything."

"Why does everybody like her so much?" he asks. "Why doesn't anybody see what she is?"

"What is she?" Grandma asks coolly.

"She's a—"

But he can't say it—he won't—in front of his grandmother. He knows how she would see it, how the whole world seems to see it—that he's the one who is jealous and angry and stupid. Besides, he can feel the waning of his heart. He's tired, and he doesn't want to talk about this anymore, and he doesn't want to fight against Erica or his mother or anyone anymore.

"Erica isn't that different from you," Grandma says. "She had to grow up in a hurry when her mother got sick, just like you've had to grow up in a hurry this past year. Too much of a hurry."

Jason strokes the pronghorn's hide, the color of newborn rust. The sturdy hair resists his fingers. "Why didn't I listen to Dad?" he laments. "Why didn't I do what he wanted me to do? Why didn't I go with him when he asked or spend more time with him when he was home?"

"Because you were young, Jason," she soothes. "And part of being young is that you believe that time is endless, and there will always be another chance." She strokes his hair. "And part of growing up is learning that it's finite, everything's finite. It can end. It does. But we have to keep living on."

Jason touches the cold, sightless marble eye, smooth and slick beneath his fingers. If only he knew how to live. But like a condom, living isn't as simple as it sounds. It's slippery and ill-fitting and ugly and a whole lot of trouble.

"Can I have this?" he asks.

"If you want. Have your mom pick it up for you tomorrow."

"I want to take it now." If he doesn't take it now, Erica might get her hands on it. Rearranging boxes, he gathers the pronghorn in his arms, his arms slung around the neck, the backboard pressed against his chest.

"It must weigh fifty pounds," Grandma protests. "Let me give you a ride."

"That's okay. I can get it."

Jason wanders out onto Pindall's streets, his hands buckled under the pronghorn's brisket. Almost at once, the decision seems foolhardy. The rain has stopped, but the wind is whipping, and the clean smell of frost is in the air. It's downhill to the Rambler, and Jason's feet slip on the loose, muddy gravel. Occasionally, he's forced to drop the head and wipe sweat from his face.

He is halfway to the Rambler when a car speeds around a corner and aims directly for him. Its headlights, low to the ground, blind him so that he only hears the gritty, desperate skid of tires on dirt. Asshole, Jason thinks. Who the hell drives like that?

Ronald Dailey climbs from the car and rushes forward, his face ashen in the light of the street lamp. "Good God," he says. "Has there been an accident?"

Jason resettles the pronghorn in his arms. Someone else is in Ronald's car, a solitary head backlit by the street lamp. Not his mother, he prays, please not his mother. But if it were his mother, she would have beat Ronald out of the car.

"Did something happen?" Ronald demands. "Do you need help?"

For a moment, Jason doesn't understand. Then he shifts the head. "It's dead," he says.

Ronald flounders. "You mean it's . . . you didn't just kill it?" His voice rises roughly. "Your face is covered with . . . I thought you were hurt."

And what would you care? Jason wants to lash. Asshole, stupid drunk, always after his mother like she's some country bumpkin who can be dazzled by a city boy's fast car. "I'm taking it home," he explains. "My mom's at the Rambler."

"All right," Ronald says, relieved. "Okay."

He climbs back into the BMW and pulls out a safe distance before creeping away. As the car passes, rage overtakes Jason. He hefts the pronghorn over his head, like a primitive warrior with his kill. Ronald swerves wildly, as if afraid that Jason is going to lob the pronghorn right through the windshield. In the light of the street lamp, Jason glimpses the passenger, whose face, until now, has been obscured.

It is Elise.

EIGHTEEN
LOVING YOU

Driving back from Lander late on a Saturday afternoon, I come across a sheriff's car straddling the dotted line of the road, lights flashing. The deputy, who is not much older than Jason, poses in the roadway, his belt weighted down by the paraphernalia of law enforcement. He looks wound up, ready to make his mark.

I roll down my window. I've stopped on the last flat stretch before the canyon. The Badlands are at my back, Pindall still nine miles away. I can't see anything ahead but tight curve and solid rock wall. "What's going on?" I ask.

"There's a protest at the sawmill," he says. "We're asking that only folks who have to travel the canyon go through, just to keep traffic down."

Since it's November, this seems a bit officious. Anyone on this snow-packed road has to be headed toward purpose.

"I live on the west side of Pindall," I tell him. "On the Yellowstone Highway."

"Okay, go on through. Just keep it slow. Watch for people on the road."

I'm expecting a mob, an onslaught on the mill. Camera crews, maybe, from the local station up in Cody, or the news helicopter from Jackson. And sure enough, when I round the last corner and come out of the canyon, I see that the protest has attracted quite a crowd. Two sheriff's deputies, a throng of pickups parked helter-skelter along the road, making it one lane, even the ambulance. A goodly number of the weekday shift—Jerry Whistledorn and his crew—have gathered in a surly knot directly across the road from the mill entrance.

It's the protesters who are hard to pinpoint. I can see Elise—her hair flames even in the overcast light—but it seems that only five other eco-minded souls march before the mill, carrying signs that are not nearly as clever as Elise's. There are two men and three women, dressed as you'd expect environmentalists to dress. One woman wears a beret, another a pair of silvery sunglasses. One man wears—in this weather—Birkenstocks with argyle socks and shorts. Parked nearby is a blue Econoline van with peace symbols and doves painted on it.

I spy Ronald's BMW across the road from the mill's driveway. He leans against it, arms folded over the tan raincoat that he's never abandoned, even in the harshest of temperatures. I veer off the road and park. Tucking my down-filled coat around me, I lower my head, walking into the wind.

"Shari!" he calls. "Come to join the party, I see."

"What's going on?"

"It's the Save the Forests Society or something. Anyway, they're here to rescue our trees."

"Oh, so Elise is part of an organization."

"No." His gaze alights on her. "I got the call around noon that they were here, and we came down."

I'm not sure if Ronald realizes what he's just said, but it smacks me clearly enough. I've heard the gossip at the bar, and now, his eyes confirm everything. He's dreaming on the scene, almost doting.

"So what's Cascadia Northern going to do?" I ask.

He straightens up, remembering his official capacity. "I'm here to observe, make sure there are no incidents, engage in civil discussion if they desire. We encourage dialogue with all who wish to explore our mission and purpose."

His recitation reeks of the corporate handbook. Across the road, Elise is engaged in less than civil discussion with Birkenstocks. He gestures in wider and wider circles, until I suspect that he is documenting the ruin of the entire world because of our little mill. Neither he nor Elise seems to notice that the wind is picking up, the clouds moving in, and the temperature plummeting. By the end of the day, we'll have snow.

A red Ford F-150 bears down on us from the south—someone else let through by the efficient deputy. Dave's truck doesn't quite pull off on the side of the road, as much as it bucks to a stop, the engine dying with a cough.

Giggling, Erica spills from the driver's side. Dave climbs out the passenger's side. "You can't park in third gear," he laughs. "You gotta shift down."

"I thought I did."

"You little knucklehead." He catches the keys that she tosses toward him. "What's going on?" he calls to Ronald.

While Ronald explains, I nod toward Erica, who smiles her hello. Her dark hair is caught beneath the multi-colored scarf that is wound around her neck, and her straw cowboy hat has been replaced by furry earmuffs. She's the spitting image of my husband—something I register with a jolt every time I see her.

"Where the hell did they come from?" Dave asks Ronald.

He is silenced by Jerry, who strides toward us with such force that his boots kick up sand and pebbles on the asphalt. The men who follow him are no less determined. They forge a righteous circle around Ronald, their breath creating a haze in the cold air.

"What are you going to do about this?" Jerry demands.

"There's not much I can do," Ronald admits. "It's peaceful, and they aren't trespassing on company property. As long as they stay within the law, all we can do is wait it out."

"You can't let her get away with this," Jerry snaps. "You can't let her start bringing in every fucking hippie who can't find a job—"

"As I understand it, this group is usually in Washington state," Ronald says tightly. "They were just passing through today."

Jerry's glare burns across the highway. "Go home!" he shouts. "Get the fuck out of here!"

"Jerry!" Ronald says. "Don't. They have rights—"

"Why don't we have rights?" A couple of growled "yeahs" accompany him. "Seems like just about anybody can waltz in here and stake a claim to this place and we can't say shit about it."

It's a direct jab at Cascadia Northern. With calm disdain, Ronald says, "I think you just did."

Jerry huffs, still itching for a fight and disappointed that Ronald has taken the high road. Noticing me, he flings, "Where's Jason today? Why isn't he here, sitting with his little girly friend? Why don't you do something about it, instead of letting him get away with it? If Brad was still alive, he'd beat some sense into that kid."

I start. "Oh, come on, Jerry—"

Erica steps forward, her words overpowering mine. "From what I understand," she says, "my father wasn't the kind who would beat sense into anybody."

Her voice bristles with indignation, and if that isn't enough, she takes my arm. We're locked in solidarity now, standing ground that is ours. It's a heady feeling to have an ally, too. I'm tired of others appropriating Brad's memory for their own use whenever they want. I'm worn out by the stories and the eulogies and the tears. I'm fed up with having my life—and Jason's—measured by the compass of Brad.

Jerry's eyes narrow, as if he will call her out, but Dave chuckles, "You tell him, honey."

He winks at me, and I see Ronald's gaze flick between Erica and me as he figures out who she is.

Ronald turns his attention back to Jerry. "Don't forget that the deputies aren't just here to keep them"—he nods toward the protesters—"in line. They'd be just as happy to haul you in, too. I don't want Cascadia to have any trouble over this, you hear me? Now go home. They'll be gone in an hour. Sooner if we just ignore them."

"But she won't be," Jerry growls, glancing toward Elise.

"No, she won't," Ronald says. "But that's her business. Not yours."

Jerry grumbles, and for an instant, I think that it is all going to be settled right here, along the highway. Ronald's body tenses, and his usually genial mask slips away, revealing a dark, moody scowl. Some of the others look ready to grab him by the throat. It doesn't so much frighten me as make me feel a bone-grinding weariness.

"I need to go," I say, unconcerned whether anyone hears me. I pull away from Erica and turn my back on all of them, heading toward my pickup.

She hurries along behind me. "Can I ride with you?" she asks. "We were on our way to the Wickiup."

"Sure, but I'm not letting you drive."

She laughs. "Let me get my things from Dave's truck."

I climb into my pickup to wait for her. When she joins me, she carries a backpack. Settling into the passenger's seat, she says, "I'm sorry that happened. Who was that guy, anyway?"

"Jerry? Oh, he'll quiet down. He's just a big blowhard."

She shakes her head. "That mill seems to run the town. I'm glad my dad never worked there."

"It's about the only thing there is to do here," I remind her. "So I guess it does run the town."

As I pull out onto the road, I look straight ahead. I don't glance toward Ronald, or Elise and the mill, or Jerry and his churned-up crew. This isn't my battle. Soon, we've cleared the crowd and are traveling on open pavement. Snow starts to fall in big flakes that slop onto the windshield. Erica looks out the window, studying the scenery as if she's never seen it before. I don't let my eyes flicker from the road. But as the pavement disappears beneath the tires, I feel every emotion I've ever had bubbling inside me. I have to say something.

"Why are you going to town?" I ask.

"I have some film to drop off." She hesitates. "I want to apologize for the way I interfered in Sawmill Days. It wasn't very . . . respectful of the people who live here."

Her words take me back to that day in July and the memorial ride for Brad that ended in mayhem. I wonder if we'll ever let him rest in peace.

"I'm just glad no one was hurt," I say.

The conversation stalls until we reach Pindall's city limits.

"I've been taking pictures around Dave's ranch," she says.

"Oh? Of the cattle and whatnot?"

"No." She laughs again, but this time it sounds tinny and young. "I . . . it's something I started doing during the summer. I started building cairns in the Badlands."

"Cairns? What are those?"

"Piles of things that I find. One day I found where someone by the name of Josiah Baker had etched his name into a canyon wall, and I left this pile of rocks at its base, and then . . . well, it's become sort of an obsession with me. I collect stuff and build little towers with it."

"Josiah Baker," I muse. "That must be one of Louise Phillips's ancestors. She was a Baker."

"Is that so?" she asks, delighted. "So he didn't go on to California. He stayed."

"So you take things that are lying around the canyons and build these . . . cairns?"

"Yeah, it sounds kind of pointless, I know, but it's amazing what's out there."

She tells about the car fender lodged in a sandstone wall that became part of a cairn when she couldn't budge it, about the bones of dead animals in the canyons—cattle, coyotes, birds, rabbits, deer—and the rocks that she uses in her cairns.

"After a while, I decided I wanted to take pictures of them," she says. "So I bought a really nice Canon SLR at David's Variety. I didn't like the way they looked with color film, so Grandma has started ordering black and white film into the Wickiup for me."

"That's nice of her."

As we pull into the lot of the Wickiup, Erica offers, "Do you want to see my photographs? I brought them to show Grandma."

"Sure," I say.

She lovingly pulls a leather-backed photo album from the backpack. Inside, she has placed black and white photos of her cairns on the left side of the page, each titled with a handwritten caption beneath—and pictures of Brad on the right. My heart, which has been jostled around enough for one day, takes another hit.

"What's this?" I breathe.

There are pictures of Brad as a boy with missing teeth, as a teenager with a sunken chest that has not yet filled out, as a hunter, a fisherman, a friend, a son, a father, a husband. There are photos of Christmases and Sawmill Days, of birthday celebrations in Dave's trailer or at our house, of Brad and his clients, of him with his horses, with Shiloh. I'm in some of the photographs, and so are Jason and Marguerite. Erica has compiled a record of Brad's life.

She is talking. "Dave told me I could keep any pictures I found of my dad in his stuff, and one night, I started to match the photographs with the cairns. Something in each of the photographs corresponds to something in the cairn. At least in my mind. There's really no logic to it. Just a feeling."

I flip another page, and another, unable to speak. I have never seen these photos, although I remember most of the occasions on which they were taken. But my thoughts are frozen, my tongue unable to produce anything coherent. I'm stunned again by enormity—of his loss, of her existence.

"You don't think it's silly, do you?" she asks.

I'm forced to speak. "Not at all," I croak. "Has your grandmother seen this?"

"No, you're the first. I haven't even told anybody about it, really." She stops, then presses on, excited and sweet. "It feels timeless out there. Like everything could exist at once, or not at all. I love it when

I find that the cairns have changed. An animal has dragged off a bone or something's fallen under its own power. Something new has been created, but it isn't new at all, because it's just part of what was always there. Does that make sense?"

"Yes," I say, my voice soft and weak.

"Oh, good. I've been afraid that I'm just crazy."

"Your dad"—the words feel foreign, but I stagger on—"Your dad had a belief that nature holds the things we offer in its balance. These things that you've picked up have been in those canyons for a long time, And they'll stay there for a long time, even after the cairns themselves are gone. Like an echo"—I falter—"or a memory."

"Look at this one."

She shows me a cairn that begins as a pile of rock on the ground. An old fencepost emerges from it, strands of barbed wire still stapled to it and whipped outright. In the shades of black and white, the post is charcoal gray, the barbed wire a wicked black streak against dove-gray sky.

She's paired it with a color snapshot of Brad and me. I am sitting at a table in the Rambler, wearing my work apron. My chin is cupped in my hand, and I'm gazing at the camera with neither smile nor frown, but with eyes that snap in the flash of the bulb. Brad stands behind me, hands on my shoulders, grinning. He is dressed in blue jeans, plaid cowboy-cut shirt, and his hat.

The handwriting beneath the photo of the cairn reads: "Strong Woman's Cairn."

"Dave says your love was like fire and fire," she says. "He told me that when two forest fires burn into each other, they flare up into a great, beautiful flame that swallows up all the air so no one can breathe." She pauses. "I think that's so beautiful."

Her words take the breath out of me. Evidently she doesn't realize—as Dave must—that when fire meets fire, everything is consumed, until nothing is left. It just burns itself out.

"When did he say that?"

"Oh, I don't know. One night when we were talking."

I look again at the photo. In my own face, I read my longing for Brad, my desperate desire, that crazy wild need that I always felt for him.

"I'd better go," I say weakly. "And you'd better get inside. The Wickiup will be closing in a few minutes."

"Oh," she says, crestfallen. "I was hoping you'd come in for a cup of coffee or something. I thought Grandma might join us." As an afterthought, she adds, "And Jason, too, if he's here."

"Another time," I say. "Jason's at home."

"Did I upset you?"

"You shook me up. But it isn't a bad thing. I just . . . thank you for showing me your pictures."

"Are you sure you won't stay—?"

"Not right now."

"I'm sorry," she says. "I wish . . . well, I wish things would have gone better between us."

She climbs from the pickup, leaving me alone. I sit for a long time, not sure what to do. My instincts call me home, where Jason is. I want to see him, to sit beside him, to share the words that shore up our wrecked lives—Are you hungry? Did you feed the dogs? What's on TV tonight? But there is someone I need to visit first.

The cemetery lies at the far western edge of Pindall, past the Morning Glory Motel, a mile or so up a dirt road from the Yellowstone Highway. It's on a gentle slope that overlooks town, near the boundary of national forest. I park beside the Brock plots. Brad's grave still looks unreal to me, poorly placed beside his pioneer grandparents, his unfortunate father, a few others. The dirt has sunk down now, and pasture grass has taken it, but it still feels raw.

Thoughts rampage in my head: What have you done to me? Leaving me alone with . . . I don't know if it's a mess or a gift. I don't know what you'd want me to do, what you'd want me to say, and I'm tired of doing it without you.

I stay until the night is full of wind, and my hands and face tighten into numbness, and the tears that have streamed down my face have turned salty. When I can stand it no longer, I climb into my truck. The cemetery lies between Pindall and home, but when I come to the intersection, I cannot bring myself to make the left-hand turn that will take me up the highway. Finally, I turn right and drive to Vern Stacy's Autobody and Garage. The lights from the loft blaze in the windows, and the outer door is unlocked. I creep unheard up the stairs.

Lex types on an electric typewriter at the table. The notebook in which he records his observations rests to one side. Occasionally, he squints at his handwriting, and I imagine him coming across an entry written during drizzle or twilight. Blowsy jazz plays from the stereo. When I say his name, he wheels around.

"You look like you've seen a ghost," he says, looking none too calm himself.

"Several of them, in fact."

His chair squawks as he rises from it. "What's wrong? Come in and sit down. My God, you're freezing. Your hair's soaked. Did your truck break down? Did you walk from somewhere? Jason said you went to—"

He puts one solicitous arm around me, but I have another agenda. My hands on his shoulders, I seek his lips. He responds with an introductory offer peck, still talking, but I'm greedy. I deliver a kiss that's tongue, and bruising lips, and shared spit, a kiss that says, Kiss me in a way that forces me to say yes. Wrap me up in your arms and refuse to let me go. Think of me—no, make me think of myself as a woman. Not as someone's left-behind wife. Not as a widow.

"I don't want to be alone," I whisper.

I can feel the surprise in his arms and his hands, too light on my back. His mouth is still full of questions. He steps back, frank assessment in his eyes. "Give me one minute to close up here," he says. "Less if I can possibly manage it. We'll go over to the house."

I sit on the top step, overlooking the garage, and blow into my hands to warm them. Behind me, Lex clicks off the typewriter. The music falls silent in mid-wail.

"Where's Juli?" I ask.

"She's out at Vern's." A book slams, a drawer whooshes shut, the lamp snaps off. Nylon rustles as he slips into his parka. "He and Sandy went on a marriage retreat this weekend and left Juli in charge."

"I'm surprised Jason didn't ask for the truck tonight."

"Oh, no, she's having a slumber party with about six other girls. He's better off in hiding." He touches my shoulder. "Let's go."

At the base of the steps, he switches off the overhead lights and locks the door. Outside, the snow whips around us. We don't touch as we hike to the house, but stay separate, independent. Lex's house is a narrow, turn-of-the-century two-story, with a parlor to the right of the foyer, and a dining room to the left. Directly ahead are the steps that lead to the bedrooms.

"You want a drink?" he asks.

"Not yet."

Wordlessly, we climb upward. My palms itch, my mouth is dry and tight. I'm shivering, although I don't know whether it's from cold or nerves. On the landing, we pass a bedroom that reeks of pink—Juli's, I presume. Flowers are everywhere—on the wallpaper, in a vase on the elegant table at the top of the stairs, in pictures on the walls.

"Why don't you take a shower?" Lex stops at a bathroom that is as pink and flowery as the bedroom. "Get warmed up."

"That would be good."

"Wait here." He disappears into a bedroom at the far end of the house and comes back with a towel and a terry cloth robe. "Take your time."

I follow his advice, letting the water wash over me, trying to get away from the sense that my bones are frozen. After I dry off and slip into the robe, I exit the bathroom in a cloud of steam.

Lex hails me from the bedroom. "I'm here."

In the wavering light from outside, I can make out heavy, solid furniture against patterned wallpaper and a wide sleigh bed covered by a thick, dark comforter in the room. He sits in an armchair near the tall, latticed windows. "Still okay?" he asks.

"Still okay."

He stands and kisses me, no mistaking his intent this time. His fingers tickle against my neck, skirting beneath the collar of the robe. He smells the same as his robe, musky and sweet. He urges my body upward, so that I'm better positioned against him. I bring my crotch up to rub against his, the hard denim seam of his jeans against the softness of the robe. His hands slip inside onto the bare flesh of my back, hot and demanding. I pull him up against me, my hands in the back pockets of his jeans, my fingers curved hard against him.

He groans, and the sound seems to echo in my own throat, jolting my stomach and thighs. My blood's rushing—everything's rushing and burning and tingling—as it hasn't done in nearly two years.

He pushes the robe from my shoulders, and it slides downward into a heap. We tug at his clothing, peeling away the layers.

"What do I need to do?" he asks between wet, urgent swipes at my lips. "I may have some condoms—"

"Don't talk, Lex."

There's only one way to stop his tongue, and that's with mine. Lex likes to kiss. Long, sloppy, where-did-my-lips-go, kisses. He keeps on kissing, too, moving to my cheeks, my jaw, beneath my ear lobes, down my neck. When his lips touch the hollow of my collarbone, the sensation is so strong that I jump. I'm a volatile substance in his hands.

"Easy," he murmurs. "We have a long way to go."

"It's been so long," I force out. "It feels so good—"

"That's right."

His words settle me, and we both seem to realize that the night has only begun, that our intentions are unwavering, that the urgency of the night is ours to play with, not to try to overcome. He moves to the bed, sitting on the edge, where he can kiss and nip and tongue-tease my breasts. I offer him one, then the other.

Coaxing me closer, he pulls me down on the bed beside him. We're back to mouths—lips and tongues and sounds deep in our throats, our own wild, guttural music. Slipping his hand between my legs, he cups me, and my wetness melds to his hand. When he slips a finger inside me, I brace my hands on his shoulders. A slow burn spreads through my body. He has the right touch, the right pressure, the right rhythm to make me dance along with him. I let him go on until I know I can't keep it up. "Lex," I breathe. "I don't want to come yet."

"Here," he says, tucking a pillow beneath my hips. Kneeling beside the bed, he kisses his way up my thighs, his face sinking between my legs. His lips tug at the tender flesh, his tongue probes inside, then circles flat and firm up against me.

It doesn't take long to finish what he started with his hands. Abandon builds in me, and I can't stop it. It is a wild and nervy thing, a flare that makes the insides of my arms tingle and my legs flush with warmth. My body arches in a cascade of pleasure, and I hear the wordless singsong of my cries. Delight bolts through my abdomen, careens off my heart, and shoots into the back of my throat so that the top of my mouth pulses.

"Lex," I say. "Lex." And I giggle, as silly as a teenager.

With one last loud, slurpy kiss to my thigh, he lifts his head. "That was good, I take it."

"Did I kick you?"

"I ducked."

He climbs up on the bed. His mouth tastes of my tartness now. I kiss the slope beneath his ear, then trail my tongue across his collarbone. Nudging through the hair on his chest with the tip of my tongue, I tease first one dark nipple, then the other. His arms fall away, revealing his entire body to me, and I flick my tongue through the hair that leads to his navel.

Reaching down, I curve my fingers around him. He's long and smooth, pumped so full of blood that the skin feels satiny beneath my fingertips. I swoop my lips up and down the length of the hard ridge. It slips into my mouth with a clean, earthy taste. I tease with my tongue, a blind woman taking the lay of the land. At last, I tighten my lips and draw it outward. With a gasp, he settles back and lets me play with him until I feel him moving toward the brink.

He tugs at my shoulders, coaxing me back to where he can kiss me. I put him between my legs and hold him firm against me, just to feel him close. Moving against him, I rub his hardness against my every crease and curve.

"Let me do this," he begs.

Lying on my side, I open my legs. He slides in, and I revel in the sense of fullness, my body relieved from wanting and withering.

"Go slow," I whisper, and he complies. My hips tighten, my back arches, the muscles inside of me lift with their own instinctual eagerness. I hook one leg over his waist. His mouth is moist and hot against my skin.

He keeps a steady rhythm, but I can feel how much he wants to lapse into abandon. I close my eyes and enjoy—the power, the vulnerability, the sweetness, the anxious need. All that I've missed so much.

"Shari," he breathes, and I say, "Go ahead."

He rolls suddenly, carrying me with him, so that he lies on his back. Without breaking apart, I straddle atop him. Every nerve sparks when he thrusts. With every breath, I cry out, a little stronger, a little louder and more wildly. He puts his hands on the back of my thighs and brushes the spot where he enters me with the tips of his fingers. Sensation whirls up my body, from the soles of my feet to the part in my hair.

Lex cradles my hips in his hands, pressing me against him, his thrusts rapid and short now. My hair falls over my eyes, catches in my mouth, and I crumble with my face against his neck. He turns his head and finds my tongue with his. Our kisses are clumsy, uneven, hit and miss in the rocking of our bodies and the tangle of my hair, but neither of us cares. Lex calls out, heaving beneath me, his mouth against my cheek. He shudders one more time before he collapses in a shaky, panting stillness.

We melt into a warm bundle, our bodies quivering every so often with remembered pleasure, our parts tangled together, and neither of us up to sorting out what belongs to whom.

"I'd forgotten," I whisper, and nip at his lips.

"Not much, you haven't." With mock gentility, he adds, "What have you forgotten? I'll be glad to demonstrate it for you."

"How good this feels."

He pushes the hair back from my face. "Sex is like spring. All winter long, you can hardly wait until spring. You think you know what you're missing. But then, when spring comes, it's so much finer than you'd ever imagined."

"Oh, I can imagine a lot."

"Oh, don't worry. So can I." He runs his hand down my cheek. "I'm glad you're finally here. This town's too small to sleep around in, but, man, the nights get long."

I kiss his neck. Lying in his arms, it's possible to pretend that there is no world outside, that I've never been alone or sad or hurt. The heat between us simmers down to warmth, and I gently lift off of him, reluctant to break the bond. His arm comes up around my shoulders as I roll beside him, and I lay my head in the hollow beside his neck. His fingers play up and down my body, and I skim mine down his breastbone.

"So tell me why you came here tonight," he says.

I tell him about Erica's photograph album. "She's so much like her father in the way that she puts the world together."

"I think that would be a comfort to you."

"I don't know," I say. "I'm a little shaky on what's comforting and what isn't just now. She said she wished things would have gone better between us. It made me feel . . . terrible."

"It's not too late to change it, I guess."

"I know." I speak with my lips against his neck. "But I just don't know if I have the guts."

He strokes my hair. "How long have you been thinking about us? About this?"

"Since that night at the Rambler when you brought in the Escher book, since that first afternoon up in the Park, since five minutes before I came here."

He plays with my hands, running his fingers into the sensitive crevasses between my knuckles. "I knew the minute I saw you at Vern's garage, lusting after my Camaro. I'd never given a Pindall girl a second look—sexual fumblings in high school aside—but I couldn't get you out of my head. And, damn, who can forget a woman brazen enough to steal somebody's calendar?"

I laugh. "Guilty on all counts."

"Can you stay tonight?"

"Sometimes when things get weird and wild at the Rambler, I stay with Robyn and Walt. Jason won't think anything of it. I'll call him."

"Good." He pulls the down-filled comforter and blankets around us, seeking refuge from the cold. "Stick with me, honey, and something's sure to come up."

His voice is soft and sly, and I start to laugh. And laugh and laugh. I don't know if I'm on the verge of tears or if this is true hilarity. Whatever it is, it feels good.

Jason sounds sleepy and annoyed when I finally call him—an hour and another romp later. I wonder how he can be oblivious to the giddiness in my voice.

"I didn't think you had to work tonight," he says.

"We'll talk tomorrow." I'm not ready to share the truth. "Call Grandma if you need anything."

He easily accepts it. Even when—or especially when—I tell him I love him, his voice drags with boredom.

I wash up in Juli's fragrant bathroom and return to bed. For a long time, with Lex warm and solid beside me, my eyes seek the light on the church steeple. It's all right, I think. I can do this. I loved my husband. Fire and fire, abnormal breathing, and all the rest of it. But love is too hard to find, too slippery to hold onto, too rare to waste.

Deep in the night—or is it morning?—Lex and I let go of one another and sleep.

I awake to a pounding in my head that sorts itself into a four-tone melody. With a start, I sit up. Cold air wings under the blankets, and Lex groans, "Church." A gray tortoiseshell cat curled near his feet shoots me a look of ferocious contempt.

I'm wide awake, washed by the morning sun streaming through the window, mesmerized by the rhythmic swing of the bells and this new place. The wallpaper reveals itself in daylight to be a rich, elaborate Victorian print with nosegays encased in velvety scrolling. A solid maple armoire soars from floor to ceiling, and a mirrored dresser and hefty bureau fill the angled spaces beneath the dormers. The comforter we lie beneath in the sleigh bed is a deep, purplish maroon. It's an elegant, rich room.

"Does this happen every Sunday?" I ask.

"That I wake up beside a beautiful woman? Not for about the past four years."

"The bells, this early."

"Oh, God, yes." He rolls onto his back, unwillingly awake. "And we used to attend every Sunday." The cat pads up to Lex, then leaps from the bed when I reach out to stroke it. "When you live across the street from a church, there aren't a whole lot of excuses for not going. My mother didn't accept any."

"We never went to church." I drag a finger across his chest, tracing the collarbone from shoulder to shoulder. "My father used to lecture us at the dinner table about scientific method, while my mother told us bedtime stories taken from the Brontes. Religion just couldn't compete with all of that."

He laughs. "I still believe in the essence of what I was taught as a kid. But I reserve the scientist's right to be dubious about the details."

"Such as?"

"Such as the existence of hell." He punctuates the statement with a kiss. "Such as the definition of sin." Kiss. "Predestination." Kiss. "The creation myth." Kiss.

"So what's left?"

"I like Christmas."

He stifles my laugh with his mouth, his fingers creeping over the crest of my pelvis and into the warmth between my legs. Within minutes, we chime with the same rhythm as the frolicking bells.

It's silent outside by the time we shake ourselves out from beneath the covers. The service has convened. While I dress, Lex goes downstairs to cook. Pulling on my jeans and sweater, I marvel at myself. I'm not full of regrets, I'm not feeling guilty, I'm not twisted up inside or confused. Just a little sore between the legs.

When I join him in the kitchen, he stands by the stove, toggling a cast-iron skillet, barefoot and dressed in jeans and an unbuttoned shirt.

"Can I help?" I ask.

"Nope, just sit there and praise my culinary skills."

As I sit down, the cat pads across the kitchen table and flops down by the sugar bowl, tail snapping.

"That's Pandora," Lex says. "Juli's cat. She comes by her name honestly."

I reach for her, but she twists away from me. "Friendly sort," I remark.

Lex steps away from the stove, leaving the bacon frying and the eggs scrambled. Placing his hands on either side of my face, he tips it up and asks, "Happy?"

"Yes," I say, speaking into his kiss. "You?"

"Oh, boy, you better believe it."

We eat, talking of here and there, of nothing at all, of everything at once. Yet as the minutes tick by, I find myself falling prey to a post-coital clamor as strident as the Methodists's bells. I know I can't return to the luxury of Lex's bed until I've thought it all out. After our third cup of coffee, I say "I should go soon. Jason will be wondering."

He glances up from his cup and asks bluntly, "It's not me, is it?"

"Well, actually, it's something you did." I reach across the table for his hand. "I need to think all this through."

"Wouldn't it be more fun just to do it again?"

I give him the laugh he expects. After we clean up the kitchen, I head upstairs to use Juli's pink bathroom. Halfway up, I lean over the banister and call, "Lex."

He comes from the kitchen, a dishtowel in his hands.

"Come see my pool."

"Should I bring my trunks or are we skinny-dipping?"

"It's a thermal pool on my property. It's dark green in winter, but when the sun hits, it turns emerald green."

"Oh, that kind of pool." He puts damp hands on mine. "I'll come see it." He cranes his neck, fishing for a kiss. I bend further. One of his hands snakes up onto the back of my neck, and all of a sudden, the kiss is more tongue than lip.

"Lex—"

"Go," he says. "I won't keep you."

We walk together through five inches of new snow to retrieve my truck. Lex starts it with a couple of roars to the engine, and then climbs out to scrape the ice from the windshield for me. I wander toward the church, where the Methodists have revved up into a raucous hymn. Marty Huttman, the pastor, has a flare for Dixieland, and he's at it full force this morning. "I am weak but Thou art strong," the congregation sings. "Jesus, keep me from all wrong. I'll be satisfied as long—"

And I join in, "As I walk, dear Lord, close to Thee."

The words bubble out of my mouth, as if I'm the featured singer and the whole choir has built up to my solo. The notes echo in the icy air, and I glance behind me to see if Lex has heard. But he's still digging at the stubborn ice with all he's got. Joy wells up inside me. My voice sounds unexercised, but there's still intonation, pitch and intention to it.

There's still music.

NINETEEN
LETTER TO BRAD
I

I didn't want to leave things the way they were the other night. I'm sorry you left before we sorted it out. You know how much I love you, and always will. But when you said that you wanted to do right by me, all I could think was that it wasn't right for me.

You know I would never want to hurt you. But you have to understand that what I said the other night had nothing to do with you. It's just that I want to get out of Wyoming, and marrying you would mean I never could. I want to see other places, and to get an education. Maybe I'll come back to Wyoming, but for now, I need to go somewhere else. Somewhere bigger, maybe, or just different. If I don't leave, I'll go crazy. Haven't you ever felt that way? Like it's all too stupid, too dull, like you'll die of boredom? You talk about how big Wyoming is, but it's tiny too, for someone like me, and I just can't stay here, I can't, I can't. I HAVE TO BE FREE!

I'm crying as I write this, you've probably guessed. I want you to know that I will raise our baby with lots of love and caring. I want to name it Eric, after my father. Dad has told me that he will make sure everything is taken care of, and Mom has said she will help with whatever I need. I promise you, I won't do anything that would hurt the baby. I will bring it up in the most loving way I can. But I have to do this for myself—

Erica finds the letter in the crawlspace under her grandmother's house, a hole three feet high and lit by a bare light bulb that is clipped to a floor joist. It is in a box of old bank statements and embarrassingly bad report cards from Pindall High School, and it rests with three other letters from Lael Sheridan, all of them creased into origami beneath a high school yearbook. Erica bends them back and forth, trying to flatten the folds. She reads this one—surely, the last, the most important—in a hunched position near the light bulb, her shoulders aching, her nose running from the dust she has stirred up in her search, her knees raw from crawling.

This is it, she thinks. This is the letter that proves all she has claimed. She will show it to her grandmother and to Shari and to Dave. She will shove it in Jason's face, shouting, See, see? I am who I am, and he was who I said he was. You're the one who is trying to make him into someone else.

She wriggles her way out of the crawlspace and onto the laundry room floor, where Dane and Amory, who have both been peering into the hole in curious concern, wag their tails and lick at her ears. She pushes the dogs away, saying, "Stop it, you old sillies," and reads the letter again.

That is when she realizes how callow her mother's words sound. To refuse to marry, to name her baby without consulting its father. *I HAVE TO BE FREE!* With this letter, Lael Sheridan not only relieved Brad Brock of any obligations, but stripped him of any participation in his daughter's life. Erica puts her face in her hands, ignoring the canine noses that poke at her. She has never thought of it this way before; she never questioned her mother's actions. But now she wants to say to her, *We could have been a family, I would have known him. I wouldn't have had to fight my way into this place. And I would have known Grandma, who I love—I love her so much. She would have been a part of my life forever. And maybe he wouldn't have died—*

She pulls herself up off the floor, replaces the trap door that leads to the crawlspace, and goes into the kitchen, the dogs at her heels. At the kitchen sink, she washes her hands and splashes water on her face. Looking out the window at the Wickiup below, she thinks of her grandmother, working in her office, and Jason, probably out on the floor. She thinks of Shari, undoubtedly at the Rambler at this hour of the afternoon. And she knows she will not show the letter to anyone. What would it change, what would it fix? Wouldn't it just make Lael Sheridan seem selfish and cruel?

This is what she came to Wyoming to find, this, her mother's voice, her parents' past. What she didn't count on was that it would break her heart.

TWENTY
WHEN SPRING COMES

I'm breaking the ice on the horses' water trough with an axe when Lex drives into the barnyard on Monday morning. We haven't talked to each other since I left him yesterday, but if he had as much sleep as I had last night, he's been thinking about Saturday night for the past twenty-four hours. As the dogs bark and circle his beat-up Bronco, Nick and Dutch peeing on the back tire, I straighten up and push back my hair, letting the axe rest against my legs.

Without even a greeting, he takes the axe from me and finishes the job with a couple of sharp blows that calve a bevy of ice floes. Shiloh and LilyBelle and Old Adam mince around, the silly fools, acting as if they haven't had fresh water in ages. Lex hoists the buckets I filled and dumps in new water, raising a cold steam.

Then he turns to me with a smile that lights my socks on fire. "Hey, there," he says.

"Thanks," I say. "The tank heater's on the fritz again."

"Bad timing."

"Really bad timing. You think it could have done this before it got so gol-durned cold."

We both study the trough, as if an answer waits there, and I realize I'm shy, tongue-tied for the first time in years. I don't know whether to acknowledge what we did with stolid adult frankness or to ignore it, as I would a kid who keeps interrupting the adults who are talking. Or I might just giggle—nerves and girlish flightiness released.

Lex saves me. "I've come to see your pool. Is the invitation still open?"

I laugh, relieved. "Come on."

We walk around the house and down into the field. Yesterday's powdery snow has been braised by wind into icy crust. Walking is hard—I lift my feet up out of the holes they've sunk into just to break the snow again with the next step. The dogs spin out around us, light enough to walk across the crust.

"I just took Jason to school," I say, gasping for air between steps. "We have a deal with Assistant Principal Hamilton now. I walk Jason into the school, and Mr. Hamilton meets us and walks him to his first class. It's pretty crazy."

"But he'll graduate, won't he?"

"That's the promise."

"Then it's worth it."

I can feel my heart pounding and my blood pumping in a double time Sousa march, and it isn't just from exertion. I'm wondering what comes next for us. I was so brash on Saturday night that I'm not sure what I'll do for an encore.

We move into the trees, the silence broken only by our labored breathing. When we come to the pool, I see the edges are solidly covered with a filmy glaze of translucent green ice. The center, as always, is open and bubbling, refusing to give into the below zero temperatures. Steam wraps around it, nearly obscuring our view of the water.

"So what's in there, Dr. Stacy?" I ask.

He squats down along the edge to peer into it. Ice crystals float through the air and lodge in his hair, on his beard, and on the shoulders of his coat.

"It looks like you have a right nice algae population there," he says.

"Algae?" I protest. "This whole area is filled with googly hoochy-doos that make somebody a million bucks, and I have algae?"

"Hold your horses." He laughs. "There are probably hoochy-doos in there, too. I'll bring some slides out when the weather's better and we'll find out."

"Leave it to me to be stuck with run-of-the-mill pond scum."

He eyes me, his lips pursed and his eyebrows lifted in censure, and we both start to laugh. Standing, he puts his arms around me. I do the same, although with the bulk of our down-filled jackets between us and our hands sheathed in gloves, it isn't so much an embrace as a stiff-armed joining.

"So how have you been?" he says. "Still thinking it through?"

"Nope, I'm finished with that, although I'm still thinking *about* it."

"And what have you decided?"

I kiss him with lips that are warmed by the heat from the pool on one side and chilled on the other. Laughing, he says, "As much as I would love to continue this conversation, it's just too cold for me."

"Let's go back to the house."

"Race you."

We tromp a few clumsy steps into the snow before we're both winded. Katie bounds happily, and Dutch and Nick strike out on a bark-fueled, canine chase. Lex grabs my hand, and we walk side by side through the trees and the field to the house.

Inside, we pull off gloves, hats, coats and boots as the dogs shake off the cold. Lex pokes at the fire in the wood stove while I fix tea. Padding around in his stocking feet, he inspects the house, checking out the chinking between the logs, taking in the view out the cathedral window, and running his hands over the river stone that Brad mortared into the wall behind the stove. "This is a pretty place."

"Thank you," I call from the kitchen.

He walks to the piano and flips through the sheet music that I bought from Evelyn Drew. Picking up a sheet, he chunks out a couple of treble bars on the piano. "This is serious stuff," he says. "Do you sing this, too?"

"I try."

"Why haven't I ever heard you?"

I carry the steaming cups across the floor to the coffee table. "Because nobody in the crowd ever yells, Sing 'Ah, Mio Cor.' It's always 'Mr. Bojangles.'"

That sets us to laughing, ridiculously, uncontrollably. I fall back on the couch, bringing up my knees, my feet on the cushion. He sits beside me and rings my ankle with his hand, tugging it gently, beckoning me to him. I jet over onto his lap, arms around his neck, the tip of my tongue catching the tip of his.

"I worried all last night that it would be sleazy if I came to visit you so soon," he says between kisses. "But, oh, my God, I was lonely."

"And I wondered all last night where in the heck you were."

"Did you, now?" He settles into a long, serious kiss. "Can we go somewhere warmer?"

There is only one place in the house that is warmer than the couch in front of the fire, and that is the upstairs bedroom. I've left it unchanged.

The headrest and footrest of the bed are those that Brad hewed from raw log, and there are no curtains or shades on the east window so that the sunrise colors the room. A quilt that Marguerite made from fabric the rich color of autumn—aspen gold, the reds, purples and oranges of spent grasses, the dark green of the pines—drapes over the bed.

Lex's voice breaks through. "If you're not ready—"

But the sheets have been washed and the spare pillows tossed aside for a long time now. Brad's side of the closet is empty, his clothes donated to the Mormon clothing bank. I no longer wake at night to listen for his breathing. I don't seek the smell of his hands or soap or sex in the blankets. I don't cry that often anymore.

"Sure." I take Lex's hand and lead him up the stairs.

He hovers in the doorway, taking in the room. "Hey," he says. "Look at that."

Moving to the nightstand, he lifts the alarm clock. Beneath it is the Escher print that I took from the calendar in Vern's garage. He turns it over in his hand, revealing the month of September, 1982.

"If you're good," he says, "I might buy you a decent print of this. Maybe I'll even get you a whole calendar of your very own. One that's for the current year and everything."

"How good do I have to be?"

"Let's see."

He lifts the sweater and thermal top I'm wearing over my head, and I slip open the buttons on his shirt, working my way downward as he works his way up. He sheds his shirt, and pulls his long-sleeved undershirt over his head. We fumble with each other's jeans—always tricky—until we can at last kick them away. The rest of our underwear, long and otherwise, falls away in impatient tugs.

Leaving our clothes in a cold, soggy pile on the floor, we crawl under the blankets.

And it turns out to be all right. It turns out to be wonderful.

When I come home from work on Friday night, I find Jason and Juli on the living room couch watching a rented movie. Juli lies with her head in Jason's lap, a throw pillow clutched in front of her face. Only her eyes show.

"Jason chose the movie," she says.

"The killer's name is Jason," Jason says. "Cool, huh?"

I sit down in the recliner. It was a long evening at the Rambler tonight. Dwayne Black and Jesse Mount tore it up again, still at it over the fact that Sarah Dale left Jesse for Dwayne twenty years ago, and Walt's grill went up in flames. A storm dumped heavy snow on the roads, and it took me twice as long to come home as usual. And now, on the TV, a killer in a hockey mask is chasing teenagers through the woods. He catches up with one and proceeds to make mincemeat. Juli hides her eyes behind the pillow. I close mine as well.

Jason's whisper brings me back. He's pointing at Juli, who has fallen asleep while the kids on the television scream and dodge. Her t-shirt has worked its way up so that a crescent of skin shows, whitish-blue in the reflection from the screen. Jason's fingers play across her ribs onto her stomach, and I think: How did he learn to caress a woman? When did he learn? I want to say to him, You were supposed to have a father who came home one day and announced that he was tired of wandering, who would teach you to chop firewood and talk to you about girls. You were to have a mother who wasn't always having to scold you and choke away your freedom. That's what I wanted for you.

Jason shuts off the television with the remote, and the house is quiet, but for the shiver of half-burnt wood in the stove and the yawn of the log walls, always shifting with heat or cold. The silence seems to surprise us both. We look at each other, then at Juli, then at the blank screen.

"What should I do?" Jason whispers.

"I don't want you out on the roads," I say, my voice low. "I'll call Lex and tell him she's staying the night here."

"Okay." He moves out from under her, holding up her head until he can stuff the throw pillow under it at about the same height as his legs. He pulls a quilt from the end of the couch and tucks it tightly around her, sealing off her body from the cold air, leaving only the pretty moon of her face. His face is soft—lips twitching in a smile, as if he just wants to give in and be tender but he's afraid that it will cost him too much.

And I think: He'll be all right. Whatever happens, he'll be okay.

I stand and go to the kitchen, and Jason follows me. He sits on one of the bar stools at the island.

"Why didn't you just stay with Lex tonight?" he asks.

I wince. I haven't yet had—or taken—the opportunity to talk to Jason about it. "I guess you probably know that we're, um—"

"Doing it?" he jabs. "Jesus, Mom, everybody knows. Mrs. Whistledorn asked me if your truck was broken down again. She saw it in front of Vern's last Sunday morning."

"What did you tell her?"

"I said I didn't know."

"She knows better than that. What did she say?"

"She kind of laughed and said okay."

So everybody does know. I want to protest: Lex and I are unattached, consenting adults. We have every reason, every right. But this is Pindall. "So how do you feel about it?"

"What?" he says.

"That Lex and I are . . . doing it?"

"I don't know." He mulls it over. "So will you marry him?"

I laugh shakily. "What?"

"Will you guys get married?" He waves a hand toward Juli. "If you do, she'll be like my sister."

We both look toward her. She is sleeping deeply now, her mouth slightly open, her breathing growing heavier, headed toward a snore. In the half-light of the living room, her face is angelic and soft.

"I think one unexpected sister is enough," I say, then bite my tongue. I had no intention of introducing Erica into the conversation.

His face is already darkening, though, tightening into its usual scowl.

"I'm sorry," I say. "I shouldn't have said that."

Surprisingly, he doesn't storm away. I take the opening I've been given. "But I've started to think Grandma might be right," I say. "If we just accept Erica, it will be a whole lot easier."

"Why don't you and Grandma just adopt her then?"

"We have to talk about this at some point. She's been here almost a year. She's not going away."

"If you and Grandma wouldn't have been so nice to her, she would have left—"

"I haven't been particularly nice to her."

"Yeah, but Grandma—"

"Grandma does what she wants, and you know that. She's just like Dad. She's just like you." I consider. "So's Erica."

"Why does everybody take her side?" he demands. "Why doesn't anybody just say no? No, she can't be here, no, Grandma can't give her Dad's stuff—"

"What?"

"Grandma's letting her go through Dad's stuff to see if she can find anything that's her mom's."

"She is?" The image stops me for a moment. "I wonder what she expects to find."

"That stuff's mine."

My eyes go to the pronghorn head that is leaning up against the living room wall. Jason dragged it into the Rambler a few weeks ago and insisted we bring it home. It has been propped up in a corner ever since, as deserted and forgotten as it was at Marguerite's house.

"I doubt there's anything of value in the stuff that Grandma has," I say.

"You think that matters? You think I'm going to sell it?"

"Shh, you'll wake Juli."

"I don't care! Why doesn't anybody ever say what happened to us was wrong? Why does everybody keep telling us to get over it?"

"Because we don't have a lot of choice. What can we do? Tar and feather her and ride her out of town on a rail?"

He folds his arms, closing himself off.

"It was just a matter of time before she came here," I say. "Dad probably knew that. He must have figured she'd catch up to him someday."

"Then why didn't he tell us?"

"I still don't know that."

I could tell him: I have recounted every minute I can remember from the night I met Brad to the day he died, searching for an answer, digging for a clue, trying to figure out if I said or did something that made him feel he had to keep it a secret. I've found nothing.

"Let's talk about you," I suggest. "What are you going to do?"

"What do you mean?"

"You're a senior, Jason."

"Grandma said she'll make me Assistant Manager if I graduate."

I recognize a bribe when I hear one. "Do you know why your dad used to work away from home?" I ask. "He always said that he couldn't stand to work where he would have to call his boss 'Mom.'"

It takes Jason a minute to digest my words. "So what do you want me to do? Ditch Grandma?"

"I want you to think about what it would be like to be working for her in ten or twenty years."

"You've been at the Rambler about that long—"

"What's that got to do with it?"

"You didn't go to college. You didn't leave town."

"Nope," I acknowledge. "And you know why I didn't."

"Yeah, but now you want me to quit and let *her* have the store!"

I calm myself by running a glass of water from the tap. "I don't think Erica's the kind to stick around a small town and mind the general store."

"She would if she thought she'd get something out of it."

"How can you say that? We've given her nothing—I don't even speak to her unless I'm more or less forced to—and I don't think Grandma's offered her anything either. She hasn't come here out of ill will. She's come here to find her family, to find *us*. We can't deny her that."

He jumps from the stool, and it tips, crashing onto the tile floor. From the couch, Juli calls, "Jason?"

"Oh, come on, Jason." I lose patience. "You can't spend the rest of your life being mad because of the raw deal you think you've—"

"I'm going to bed," he announces to both of us.

I close my eyes, waiting for the inevitable door slam. Once it rocks the house, I wonder if this will ever end.

Juli sits up, tousle-headed and lovely. Her blond hair hangs in loose curls around her face, and she has a child's dream-blessed sleepiness in her eyes. She looks around as if she's forgotten where she is. "Where's Jason?" she asks. "What's wrong?"

"You can sleep here tonight," I say. "The roads are pretty slick. I'll call Lex in a while."

"Okay," she agrees, lying down again.

"Do you want another blanket?" I move to the closet, where I keep a stack of Marguerite's quilts. Taking another to her, I spread it over her feet. "Is this okay?"

"Thanks," she says. "Goodnight."

I stay in the kitchen for a few more minutes, waiting for her to drop off again. For some reason, I want my conversation with Lex to be private—as private as it can be when the phone is on the kitchen wall.

Finally, I pick up the receiver and dial. Sinking down onto the cold tile floor, I sit with my back against the island, as far as I can be from Juli.

Lex answers right away.

"Weren't you asleep?" I ask.

"Not yet. I was reading."

"What were you reading?"

"The *Canadian Journal of Microbiology*. It's a page-turner."

I laugh, but he catches something in my voice and asks, "What's wrong?"

"What's always wrong?"

"Jason again?"

"Every time I try to talk to him." Quickly, I add, "Cheer me up. It's two-thirty in the morning, and I haven't even taken off my boots."

"I'll talk you out of them," he offers. "And whatever else you want to remove. I can help you slip, slide, caress or rub whatever you're wearing right off."

"For a college professor, you do talk dirty."

"I'll have you know I'm a pillar of respectability." Lapsing into Groucho Marx's voice, he adds, "And I have a respectable pillar, too."

I cover my mouth with my hand. "Your sister is sleeping not more than ten feet from me, and here I am laughing like an idiot." I steady myself. "I think she'd better stay here tonight. I'm not letting Jason out of here with the truck."

"That's fine," he says. "I wish I were there."

"I wish you were, too." I wrap the phone cord around my finger. "By the way, the secretary at the school asked Jason why my truck was in front of Vern's last Sunday. So there's not much sense trying to keep quiet about us."

"I didn't know we were."

"We aren't." I correct myself. "It's just my small town reflex kicking in, I think. Trying to keep everybody out of our business."

"I don't care who knows. I don't care what they think."

I wonder how much I care. Sometimes I forget that people in other places make choices and moves and mistakes without everyone watching. Sometimes—especially on a night like tonight—I find it hard to even imagine somewhere else.

"Hey," Lex says. "Did I lose you?"

"I'm still here. Just thinking."

"About what?"

"About how living in Pindall is a little like being one of your googly-eyed things under a microscope."

"I figured that out fifteen years ago." He laughs. "I really do wish we were together."

"Don't try it. Take it from someone who has driven that road through just about any weather—it's bad out there."

We lapse into small talk. As the minutes tick by, I realize how desperately I don't want to hang up. When I do, I will have to go up to bed alone, and tomorrow I'll wake up alone.

After we finally say our goodnights, I go to the cathedral window on the west side of the house. It's dark, but I can hear the wind howling and the snow strafing the glass. Even though it's only November, I'm already thinking about spring.

East Pindall

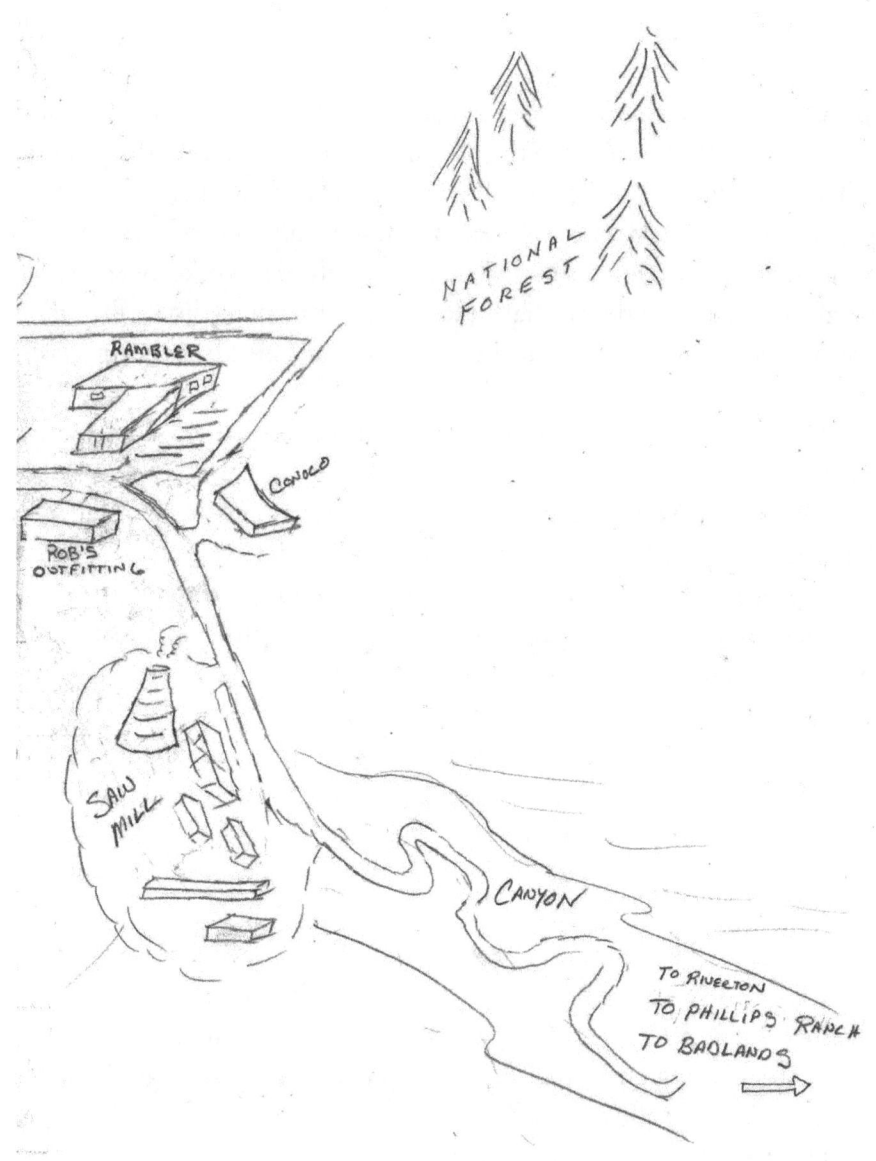

1988

TWENTY-ONE
RONALD, RUN

Cascadia Northern sends a Quality Control Analyst to Pindall in early March, almost a year to the day since Ronald took over the position of General Manager at the mill. The kid's name is Tim Etherton, and he is more or less half Ronald's age. Fresh out of the University of Washington's M.B.A. program, Tim has ideas. He plans a Saturday workshop, at which team-building activities will take place: brainstorming a list of five items you and your coworkers need when stranded on a life raft; relieving stress by learning to juggle; falling backward into your coworkers's arms.

Do that, Ronald wants to tell him, and these fuckers will let you hit the floor.

Oh, how naïve Tim is. How can you boost production when the trees have gone from a DBI of seventeen inches to thirteen? How can safety be improved when Cascadia Northern isn't willing to spend a dime to upgrade the antiquated equipment? And how do you build a team from men who were sold out for pennies on every Cascadia Northern dollar? Ronald has grown immune to their belligerent, beery stares. In fact, when Tim speaks to him, he suspects that his expression mirrors theirs.

To make matters worse, Save the Forests—which, Ronald has found, has no validating association or society attached to its name—still protests along the highway in front of the mill. Far from moving on, its leader, Andy Shenk, has declared the closing of Pindall's mill as his primary focus. Every morning, the Econoline van which they call the "Peace Wagon" dumps between three and fifteen protesters at the gates. Shenk leads them in ringing cowbells at the cars that enter and leave the mill and chanting and singing old songs from the Civil Rights era. He himself speechifies through a bullhorn five or six times a day. His modus operandi is far noisier than Elise's dignified signage.

Tim has ideas about them, too. "I hear that they rally around the redhead," he says as he peers out the window of Ronald's office on Friday morning. "What's her name?"

"Elise Martin," Ronald says tightly.

"What's her story? Is she some bored local housewife who reads the crap she gets in the mail from the Sierra Club? What does she need—a job, some education, a good lay?"

Ronald taps a pen on his desk, driving his anger into the wood. "I think she's highly educated, and I don't believe she's easily intimidated," he says coldly. "She's not local and she's not affiliated with Andy Shenk's group."

"So you've talked to her?"

"Yes, I know her well."

He hears the tremor in his voice. Now that Save the Forests has usurped Elise's position, Ronald no longer stops to chat with her in the mornings on his way to work. They meet each other only in the dead of night, coming together with a ferocity that tries to put Andy Shenk and Jerry Whistledorn and Tim Etherton and the whole messy situation at bay. It rarely works.

"Well, maybe I can make an impression on her," Tim says confidently. "I'll talk to her, see if I can rid you of a problem."

Ronald breaks the pen.

The afternoon grows cold and choppy, and by the time Ronald leaves the mill, a front has brought in driving sleet and snow flurries. At the gates, he notices Elise alone at her post. She's poorly dressed for the unexpectedly vicious weather, in only a sweater and one of her signature skirts. Her hair hangs in sodden strings around her face.

He brakes and rolls down the window. "Where's Darnell?"

"I don't know." Her redhead's skin, vulnerable to cold, has turned a pale indigo, and her lips are, shockingly, the color of a plum.

"Where are Andy and his clowns? Weren't they polite enough to offer you a ride into town?"

"I chose to stay."

"For God's sake." Ronald's annoyance spills over. "Get in."

"Now? You don't mind?"

Ronald leaps out to toss her lawn chair and her rain-smeared posters into the trunk, while Elise climbs into the car. "You're going to kill yourself, doing this," he scolds her. He can smell her drenched hair, her reeking wool sweater. "Catch pneumonia or something. And all for nothing."

"It isn't for nothing."

"Did Tim talk to you?"

"Who?"

Relief floods through Ronald, just as the vents hint at warm air. He flicks on the heat. Obviously, Tim never ventured outside the mill's doors. "No one," he says.

Elise touches his wrist. "Can you take me home? I need dry clothes."

"I'll give you some. Or, perhaps, you won't need any."

"The energy's not right, Ronald," she says, even more quietly than before. "You can't make love when you're angry. You need to purge your soul."

A good fuck would do just that, he thinks, but he says nothing. Following her directions, he turns onto the Yellowstone Highway and speeds west, out of town.

Darnell Hillyard's property is farther out than Shari's, perched on the full pitch of the pass, and on an even more impossibly rutted dirt road. In fact, it really isn't a road at all. When, at last, they arrive at the chain link gate, night has fallen in its full, gloomy depth. The BMW's headlights shine through the diamonds of fencing into a shimmering oblivion of snow.

"You live all the way up here?" he asks disbelievingly. "And you come to Pindall every day?"

"Yes." She slides out and circles the car to press a code into an electronic lockbox outside Ronald's window. With a grate of raw metal, the gates open. Ronald pulls through and watches in the rearview mirror as the gates, radiant red in the car's brake lights, slam with finality. He switches off the blasting heat, aware of sweat in his armpits and sticky hair on his forehead. It's fucking Alcatraz up here.

Elise directs him through dense forest to a clapboard ranch house generously rigged with floodlights. A traditional, lofted barn sits forlornly off to one side, fronted by a phalanx of military jeeps. Spotlighted in the trees is an honest-to-God military tank, its cannon aimed directly at his car.

"What in the hell is that?" Ronald asks.

"Darnell designed them at one time for the government."

"And they gave him one? They just handed it over as a token of thanks?"

"I don't know," she says in a pained voice. "It's his life, not mine."

Ronald pushes on the accelerator. As the car nears the house, a pack of dogs hurtles from the woods to snap at the wheels.

"Shit!" He hits his brakes to avoid mangling them, and they wheeze and bellow, frenzied by blood lust.

Elise calmly rolls down her window and calls a command in a language Ronald does not recognize. The dogs subside into muted snarling.

"Drive past the house," Elise instructs. "My cabin's up the road a bit."

The bit turns out to be a good length of muddy track. The barnyard disappears into the sleet-dulled night as Ronald eases the BMW along, trying to anticipate ditches and drop-offs, expecting to high-center. Every once in a while, a warning bark resounds from outside the car. The dogs remain constant companions.

A bare bulb shines above the door of Elise's cabin, yellowish through the flapping windshield wipers. Ronald starts to open his door, but, with pounding heart, remembers the dogs. Just then, headlights illuminate the interior of the BMW. A jeep screeches to a halt behind the car. Someone jumps from it and rushes the passenger's side.

All Ronald can see is a semi-automatic assault weapon cradled in rough hands.

Elise rolls down her window and speaks serenely. "Hello, Darnell. It's just me."

The glowering face of the legendary Darnell Hillyard appears. Beneath an oversized hood, Darnell has a graying mass of curls and skin as pale as a death row inmate's. He wears a Lenin-like goatee that sports an off-centered white streak.

"Who's that?" he pants. The dogs punctuate his words.

"Darnell, this is my friend, Ronald." Elise gestures across the car. "Ronald, this is Darnell Hillyard."

"Are you with the CIA?" Darnell demands.

"He's just a friend," Elise soothes. "He was kind enough to bring me home."

"I wanted to come get you," Darnell says. "But they called again."

"That's all right." Elise's voice rings with sweetness.

Ronald doesn't dare move. He barely breathes. He prays that Elise's calm and reassuring tone will make Darnell forget he's carrying a fucking Uzi.

"There's someone in Berlin," Darnell says. "KGB. They put me on it."

Ronald twitches despite his resolve to play dead. What has he stumbled into? Langley West? He calculates how he can swing the Beemer around and flee this madhouse. Just push Elise out and hit the accelerator, the dogs be damned.

"They don't trust me in the agency," Darnell reports. "Because of Fiona. And now this Eric Stinnes has gone and stirred it all up again."

Somewhere, Ronald has heard these names. Somehow, he knows this story.

"I may have to go to Berlin." Darnell straightens, and the gun appears clearly in Ronald's field of vision. He swears to God that Darnell's finger is curved around the trigger.

"We're going in now," Elise says easily. "I'll talk to you tomorrow, Darnell."

Darnell's face disappears, and Ronald hears his scratchy voice snap in the foreign tongue. The dogs scramble away. Within seconds, the jeep's headlights twist out of the BMW's rearview mirror. "What's going on?" Ronald asks.

"Don't worry. He's harmless."

"Harmless? Aren't those kind of weapons illegal? And what the hell was that about the KGB?" Recognition clicks in Ronald's head just as Darnell's taillights disappear down the forest track. "Those were characters in a Len Deighton novel," he protests. "What does he do out here? Play Spy Vs. Spy?"

"Why must you be so judgmental?"

Elise whips the words at him as she climbs from the car. For a moment, Ronald remains motionless. What are in those books? Endless scenarios of assassination, sabotage, destruction, warfare, detonation, clandestine killing, outright murder, torture, and mutilation. Shit, they're primers for the psychopath. Forgetting the threat of dogs, Ronald prudently locks his car doors and sprints into the cabin.

The cabin is a single room, more or less, with a shed-like bathroom and kitchenette tacked to one end. An ancient, squat woodstove consumes most of the livable space. Near the door leading to the bath and kitchen, a brass bed is luxuriously adorned with a voluptuous quilt. On the other side of the stove are a desk, an easy chair and ottoman, and a three-tiered wooden bookcase. Elise's elegant clothes rest in a pine armoire beyond the sitting area.

"These cabins were part of a dude ranch that was here in the twenties and thirties." Elise explains as she prods the embers in the woodstove into nascent flames. "It went to ruin, and in the sixties, Darnell acquired it before he went to Vietnam."

"He's a little old to have been drafted along with the eighteen year olds."

"Let it go, Ronald. It's not your worry." She rises from the stove and rubs at her arms, still encased in the wet, wool sweater. "I have to take a shower. I can't get warm."

"Go ahead." Ronald honorably puts aside the suggestion that he join her. Before she disappears into the bathroom, he asks, "What language do the dogs understand?"

"I don't know. Darnell taught the words to me."

It's probably best not to dwell on it. There is no television, no radio, no stereo, not even a telephone. What does Elise think she's doing? How can she feel safe returning to this nuthouse? How can she sleep at night with Hillyard just down the road?

A mighty clank and a feeble hiss from the other room announce that the shower has sprung to life. Still shaken, Ronald dares a peek into the kitchen, but quickly retreats. No gourmet cooking will take place in that hole, with its electric stove and pint-sized refrigerator.

He sizes up Elise's books. Works on eastern religions, Tibet and utopia rest amid the ubiquitous Edward Abbey and Rachel Carson. A book entitled *Spiritual Surrender: The Tragedy of Capitalism* by Dr. Aaron Malcolm, Ph.D., Bennington, catches his eye, its back cover graced by a photo and biography of Dr. Malcolm. Dressed in a checkerboard shirt and exuding the hearty robustness of a lumberjack, he leans against a tree in Rockport, Maine, where he lives with his wife, Elise Martin, and his two children, Whitney and Elijah.

So he has stumbled on a bit of her past. Ronald sizes Aaron Malcolm up and decides that the good doctor has nothing on him, in looks or physique. Flipping through the pages of preachy, socialistic diatribe, he finds, "The only way for the average American worker to save his or her soul from the greedy maw of capitalism is to revolt. Tear down the banks, factories, retail malls, car dealerships, or computer outlets, where the toiler earns a pittance for honest work and a pot of gold for his bosses. Rebuild the workplace with dedication to equality for men and women, senior workers and apprentices, and Afro-Americans, Chicanos, and Asians. Revolution is the only satisfactory avenue to change."

Beware, young Tim Etherton.

Ronald stows the book on its shelf. Wandering to the window that overlooks the front porch, he scans the darkness. The BMW is already buried beneath thick snow. He may be snowed in up here. As long as Elise is here to protect him, as long as she knows the guttural grunt to enchant the dogs, as long as Darnell stays away—*far* away—well, then he should survive the night.

He glances down at the desk beside him. An envelope addressed to "Ms. Elise Martin" at a Jackson post office box lies in plain sight. The Sacramento return address announces in bold, black lettering, "Davis Martin Trust." The envelope looks just large enough to contain a check.

Oh, isn't this rich. No poor little tree hugger, Elise. No live-in-a-cardboard-box, wear-rags-from-Goodwill, protein-starved vegetarian. But hadn't he known? He nearly laughs out loud, but a wash of bitterness makes him swallow painfully. Elise, who rails against capitalism and paternalism and misappropriation of the world's resources. Elise, who speaks of the cosmos and karma and holy energies. Nature's daughter, who takes from the earth only what she needs, who insists that everyone else do the same.

Where does a trust fund come from but filthy, anti-earth, anti-humanitarian, anti-woman capitalism?

She comes from the bathroom, wrapped in a Turkish cotton robe, her face once more the color of cream, her hair in a drunken twist over one shoulder. "That's much better," she says. "I can feel my fingers and toes again."

Ronald speaks abruptly. "I should go."

She stops in mid-stride. "Don't you want to stay?" she asks. "What's wrong?"

"I need to go back to town."

"What happened? Did Darnell come by? Don't worry—"

He gestures toward the desk. "You're a fucking trust fund baby, aren't you? You don't need to work, so you find some stupid sorry town in Wyoming and make it your mission to educate the ignoramuses. God, I should have known you were just playing us all."

"That is not true and you know it. I believe in what I'm doing."

"Oh, yeah. Let's use Daddy's money to become archenemy number one to a bunch of yokels who can barely read. Go back to Malibu or Carmel or wherever your beachside villa is. Leave us alone."

"You have no idea what you're talking about."

"You've always said that about me," he says, his voice slipping from his control. "But I'm just one of them? Isn't that what you think? Isn't that why you've never shared one single piece of information about your life? Isn't that why you never answer my questions?"

"You're making too much of this."

"Too much?" he shouts. "It means a whole hell of a lot to me, whether or not it does to you." He stops, his chest painfully squeezed. "You're not supporting Andy Shenk and his bunch, are you? You're not bankrolling them?"

"What does it matter? This is about us—"

"Answer me!"

She sits on the bed. "They needed somewhere to stay. I told them I'd cover the cost for their camping spot at the KOA as long as they felt they needed to be here."

"Jesus Christ," he pants. "Why would you do that to me? I'm barely hanging on, I've barely had my head above water since I came here, and you do this? Why? My God, why?"

He jerks open the door, not waiting for an answer. The snow, whipped by the wind into lances of ice, stings his face and hands. Desperately, he explores the door of the BMW with his fingers to find the keyhole. At last, he manages to unlock it and hurl his body inside. He starts the car and flicks on the wipers. Hitting the gas, he reverses into something that gives a hollow metal clang. Without stopping, he guns the car down the track, now sticky and slick. The car slides wildly, spins in the ruts, threatens to pitch headlong into the thick trunks of trees. All he can see is a spiral of white, the snow breaking against the headlights. He has no idea if he is on the track or if he has breached a gap in the forest. At last, the car weaves into the welcoming glare of the barnyard.

Dear God, what if Darnell opens fire on him? What the hell—it would be a perfect end to this nightmare.

When he reaches the gate, he brakes to a faltering, fishtailing halt. The chain link stretches before him, impregnable. There's an electronic lockbox, but when Ronald reaches for it, he hears the dogs rushing the car.

He jerks his arm inside and rolls up the window. Two German shepherds brawl in the headlights, tearing at each other in their excitement. A baying beast lunges repeatedly against the car, its claws strafing.

He is trapped.

He lays his head against the steering wheel, trying to drown out the scream of the dogs. He wants to cry, he wants to leap from the car and slash at the dogs until they break beneath his anger. He wants to do the same to Elise. He should have trampled her dainty skirts or sweaters. He should have ripped Aaron Malcolm's book into confetti. He should have laughed.

He does not know how much time passes before she appears. She emerges from the darkness, and the dogs quiet. The stocking cap on her head is crowned by snow, and she glides as if she were on skis. He rolls down the window.

"I'm not a fraud," she says. "I believe in what I'm doing—"

"Then why aren't you at some major production site?" he shouts, and the dogs bark angrily in return. "Why aren't you and Andy in Seattle or Portland or BC? Why aren't you in the Amazon trying to save the fucking rain forest? God knows you've got the plane fare."

"You've come here for reasons of your own. So have I."

"Are you running from the law?" he demands. "Are you a saboteur? Greenpeace? NRAG? What kind of monkeywrenching are you into? Fiddling with brakes? Bombs?"

"You know I don't believe in violence—"

"I witnessed it! I saw what you self-righteous fools do! That feller— that spike turned him into a bloody pool! It was horrible, he didn't even scream, it just ate him up—"

"You need to leave that world, Ronald. It's unclean, it's impure—"

"Don't talk to me about impure. You're a capitalist, sweetheart, a rich spoiled capitalist. Stop pretending to be anything else!"

Elise has started to shiver again. Evidently the warmth provided by the shower has evaporated in the wind. Her face looks bluish and sickly.

"Darnell's my father," she says, and even the dogs hush at this revelation. "I came here because of him."

She floats the words on the blistering snow. He looks up at her, silenced, but her face fades from his sight. A moment later, the gates trundle open. Ronald rolls through and waits for the grind of metal on metal before he leaps from the car. Spared from the teeth of Darnell's killer pack, he rushes the fence. "Elise!" he shouts into the whirlwind. "Elise!"

Not even the dogs respond.

He wakes in a rut of twisted blankets and lumped pillows. The clock says it's nearly noon, but the calamity of the night before reverberates in his head. Two and a half hours back to Pindall, guessing where the road might be. A detour through a ditch somewhere. Some redneck cowboy jerking the car out behind a pickup truck that spewed so much exhaust, the snow turned black. A fifth of Jack Daniels drunk straight from the bottle.

He rolls out of bed and goes to the bathroom. His mouth tastes of chewed-up bark. In the kitchen, there's day-old coffee in the pot, which he warms without regard for the rainbow film of grease. Looking over the deck, he sees that last night's blizzard blew through Pindall—at a lower elevation than Darnell's property—with very little consequence. Only an inch or so of snow lofts in most places. The sun has even broken through the clouds.

Fucking stupid place to live.

He dresses in his warmest clothes and dons his running shoes. He needs movement and release. He needs to purge his soul. It's not as cold as it could be outside, although frost crystals dance in the breeze. The path across the meadow itself is fairly dry, not yet thawed to mud.

What a fool he's been. He knew that she had money, that she was playing games. He knew that she was just a Valley Girl playing wood nymph, and that a sob story from Jason Brock or Andy Shenk would snag her like a fish in a net. He knew he could trust her about as far as he can trust himself. So why is he so angry? Why does this feel like old-fashioned, snake-oil duping? Why is it such an intimate betrayal?

Because he has played straight with her. Because he thought they were in this together, partners in contempt for this pathetic place that has no future or even much of a present. They were the ones laughing.

And after all those hours he's spent with her, deep inside her, holding back until the hunger for everything his life is missing becomes so great that he lets go, and she fills him with a powerful peace. "Why?" he has asked her. "Why are you here? Why am I here?"

"We were meant to share this point in the universe."

"No, but why?" he asked again. "Why here? Why this moment? Why didn't I meet you in Portland, where we could have at least gotten a good cappuccino?"

She had laughed without answering. Typical Elise.

He jogs into the thin, scraggly growth just before the true wealth of the forest. The path grows shadowy, glazed over by patches of snow and ice, and the wind bitter. Snow lingers yet on the low-lying branches of the pines. The cold swells up around his ankles, and the wind whistles. He had not intended to run this far, but something draws him further. He needs to reclaim himself from the murk in his head.

So Darnell is her father. My God, the mystery of genetics.

To his right, he spies a shadow in the trees. He swerves just as it jumps at him, and his shoe slips in the muck. Unbalanced, he falls, sledding across the veneer of ice until his back slams against a pine tree.

Pain rampages through his leg. He scrabbles on the ground, as if he can simply crawl away and escape from his own body. His vision darkens, and he vomits.

He has to get up. He tries to lift himself with his arms, but lightning shocks travel from his tailbone to his neck. My God, he has to move. The wet ground, the coming darkness, the freezing temperature. He reaches down and pulls his right leg forward, clenching his teeth against the agony, but his foot remains nearly perpendicular to his ankle. His left leg feels numb, but he forces it into service and starts to drag himself forward. If he can only reach a level spot, clear of pinecones and debris, he can stand and wobble back to his house.

He is sure of it.

The wolf finds him late in the darkness, after he already knows that he will not survive. Its eyes appear above him, as bright as a chunk of sky. He tries to cry out—Get away! Get away from me!—but hears only a buzzing in his ears as the wolf rolls him onto his back and starts tugging at his leg.

Don't touch me, please don't kill me, he begs.

Be still, the wolf replies. It won't hurt as much.

Ronald screams, but it's too late. He's being dragged, jostled, pulled asunder. He tries to call out to Elise, to tell her that this broken wad of flesh is his, but he sinks, instead, beneath waves of darkness.

And bobs back to the surface. Into warmth and the white light of day. Lying on his back, he feels drowsy and secure. When he raises his head, though, it splits with pain, and he drops back. Everything begins pulsating, the daylight turned into the strobe of a disco. He slowly maneuvers his head to the left.

Lying next to him is a dark-haired young man.

Ronald twists up suddenly and unleashes all the fury in his body. Pain crashes through his leg and pulverizes his back. "Oh, my God," he moans through lips that do not open.

"Don't move." The voice comes from his right. The white-haired monk lies next to him. "Don't move. We splinted your leg and ankle with a cardboard box, but it's not stable."

"What are you doing?" Ronald demands as indignantly as he can. Good Lord, surely he hasn't become one of *them*?

The monk rises, moving gingerly to avoid jostling Ronald. He is stark naked, and with razor-sharp insight, Ronald realizes he is, too. He reaches down to cover himself, but his hands are useless, uncoordinated. The old monk dons a robe and says softly, "Brodric."

The younger monk stirs and covers his bare skin with blue pajamas. He glances unsmilingly at Ronald, then fades away, as if he were simply a phantom of light.

"We came across you yesterday evening." The old monk leans against the closet door. "Fortunately, Brodric had seen you leave. When you didn't return . . ." He does not finish the sentence.

"I was attacked by a wolf," Ronald mumbles. "It jumped out of the trees at me." His tongue feels engorged and numb, too fat to work. Did he actually speak?

"Your ankle is definitely broken. Your leg may be as well. There's some frostbite on your hand."

"My leg," Ronald remembers. "I fell, I think."

"By the time we found you, you were severely hypothermic."

"Why am I here?"

"You wouldn't have survived the trip to Riverton last night. So we warmed you up in the most tried and true method known to man. Body heat."

Brodric returns with a tumbler of water. Cautiously, he sits on the bed next to Ronald.

"Drink," the old monk urges. "You're dehydrated."

With a tender hand, Brodric lifts Ronald's head and holds the glass to his lips. Ronald sips, but he cannot move his tongue or swallow. The pain jags through him again, and vomit rushes up in his throat. He waves the glass away. Brodric remains seated on the bed, a shy hand on Ronald's.

"I didn't think you spoke," he croaks.

The old monk laughs. "My name is Ken. Brodric is the one who realized you'd been gone too long." He adds, "It's Ronald, isn't it?"

He nods as darkness starts to sweep over his vision again.

"So, Ronald, shall we get ready to go?"

At the nearest hospital, seventy miles away in Riverton, Ronald's ankle is repaired with steel pins. His broken thighbone is reset, and his back, which has suffered deep contusions, is stabilized. An IV in his arm drips life-giving fluids back into his veins. His frostbit fingers are treated with warm-water baths. Two stitches seal his torn lip.

No one on the medical staff believes he has been attacked by a wolf. "There's no big, bad wolf in these parts, doll," one nurse tells him. "Maybe an old bear come out early. But if a bear'd found you, you'd be missing a part or two."

Ken and Brodric stay with him like maiden aunts, leaving the hospital late in the evening and reappearing early the next morning. They bring him fresh bouquets daily, fashioning his room into a floral masterpiece, much to the nurses's amusement. During the week of Ronald's stay, and through his surgeries, Ken does all the talking, while Brodric remains true to his vow. Ken contacts Tim Etherton at the mill, he informs Robyn—and therefore, the rest of Pindall—of Ronald's condition, and he consults with the doctors as if he were Ronald's kindly older brother.

"You're so good to do this," Ronald tells Ken.

"You would do the same for us," Ken replies.

Ronald is not so sure.

He returns home in a nest of blankets that Brodric prepares in the back seat of Ken's Suburban. His leg is in a cast that will stay on for eight weeks. They travel back to Pindall along the highway that passes through the Badlands and into the canyon. Ronald eagerly eyes the mill, but today is Sunday. Elise is nowhere in sight.

As Ken pulls into the driveway, Ronald surveys his scarred BMW, parked askew on the cement pad. What a wreck. A smashed front turn signal. The back fender dented by whatever he had clobbered at Elise's cabin. Scratch marks down the driver's door, gratis Darnell's Hound of the Baskervilles. Inside the house, Ken and Brodric fuss over him, making certain that he is comfortable on the sofa with books, magazines, his painkillers, water, his crutches and a remote controller for the television.

"Is there anything more that we can do?" Ken asks.

"Yes," Ronald says. "I need you to find someone for me."

She comes late that night. The headlights of the car that delivers her streak across his living room, where he is watching some mindless movie on television. She slips inside the unlocked front door and sheds her coat and boots, then drops a rucksack on the floor.

Her greeting is cool. "I'm glad you're all right."

"They found you." Ronald tries to straighten himself up. "I didn't know if you would listen to them—"

"Ken's a very gracious man," she says tightly.

They both look at the *pièce de resistance*.

"My leg probably looks like a road map," he comments. "Two surgeries on the ankle alone, and possibly one more in the future."

"Will you run again?" she asks.

"I don't know." Sensing the metaphorical aspects of the question, he quickly adds, "I guess it depends on how it heals."

She walks to the sliding glass door, her back to him. "I was at the mill every day last week."

"I wouldn't have expected you to act differently."

"Nor, I suppose, can I expect you to."

"I'm sorry, Elise." His words are as sincere as he has ever been. "I was wrong."

She doesn't scold. Neither does she acknowledge the apology. He forges ahead. "Tell me about Darnell." Softening it, he repeats, "Tell me about your father."

She doesn't answer right away, but stares out at the night, as if she no longer trusts him. At last, she says, "He and my mother married right out of college, but it didn't work out. Darnell moved to D.C. and took a job with the government." She pauses. "I rarely saw him. He never called or wrote. I didn't know then that he was living all over the world, in one secret capacity or another. I thought he had just forgotten me."

"So he really was a spy? I never would have believed it."

"I don't know. He can't talk about it." The pain in her voice is palpable, yet she does not vary her soldier-like stance at the window. "My mother is a wanderer, a free spirit. We lived in India, England, Japan, on the coast of Italy. She went through a series of men. She liked to marry, but didn't like being married. The money—the trust—is hers."

Ronald decides not to touch on the open sore of the trust fund. "How did you come to reconcile with Darnell, then?"

"I was living in Maine when I saw him again. Aaron—my husband—was having his first book signing in New York, and Darnell came. It was just after Vietnam." She breathes in, a ragged slice of air. "He was so different from what I remembered—what little I remembered. He jumped at anything, he couldn't cope with the noises and people. He told me he was moving to a place that the government had set aside for him. When I came to visit a couple of years ago, I didn't see how I could leave him."

Her breath has made an oval cloud on the glass. Ronald cannot see her expression, but he is touched by this fragile creature, this doe in the woods. He rubs at his cast. Somehow, even though he cannot touch his leg, the motion is comforting. "Does anyone else knows he's your father?" he asks.

"Marguerite," Elise says. "Marguerite Brock."

His hand ceases in mid-circle. "Does Jason know?"

"I don't think so. Why?"

"I think it would be dangerous knowledge in the hands of a teenager. You never know who he might tell."

"What would it matter? No one's going to bother Darnell."

"Then why have you kept it a secret for so long?"

She reconsiders. "I guess it is to protect him. From their . . . eyes, from their nasty words, from everything that I experience every day." She rubs at the condensation on the window. "I'm tired of this, Ronald."

Tired of what? he wonders. Of the eco-pretense? Of Andy Shenk's hubris? Of Darnell's dementia?

"All this sneaking around," she says. "That was my mother's thing, not mine."

Of course, she is tired of the one thing he has no intention of changing. "What do you want?" he asks. "It would be foolhardy for you and me—"

"Why shouldn't we?" She turns away from the window, her eyes lit orange by the fire. "Wouldn't that prove something to them? That it doesn't need to be strident discord, but can be amicable—?"

She has left him again, gone off to that place he will not follow.

"I have no desire to transform my private life into a public crusade," he says staunchly. "Besides, they would never see it as anything but a slap in the face." Unable to resist needling, he adds, "And what would your new friend Andy say about me?"

"Let it be."

"But now that Shenk et al. is here, it means less than it ever has. They're tawdry, they're sensationalist. They want the attention for themselves, not for the cause."

"You've always thought what I do is pointless—"

"There's a wedge between us, Elise, that's never been there before." Bitterness rakes his voice. "We're on opposite sides, we're enemies. We've played right into their hands. It's become as contentious as they wanted it to be. As this entire town has always thought it should be."

She turns back to the window, and the cloudy oval on the glass swallows the reflection of her face. She is still for so long that he half-believes that she is gone, and only a shadow remains. At last, she asks, "Do you need anything?"

"Will you stay with me?" He pleads, adding, "Please."

Shari arrives on Wednesday evening, bringing with her the smell of stale smoke and a crinkled brown bag from the Rambler. She swings into his living room with her sweet, shapely body decked out in a loosely knitted sweater and Wranglers tight enough to squeeze the blood right into Ronald's groin. Another spring blizzard is raging through Pindall's lonely streets, and she shakes snow from her hair before she bends to kiss his cheek.

"How're you doing?" she asks.

"Not bad at all." He is stationed, once again, on the couch, his leg propped on a pillow on the glass coffee table. He's just taken his painkiller, and the world seems nicely hazy and warm. Shari, especially. He's reluctant to release her hand.

"You shouldn't do battle with Wyoming's weather." She knocks on his cast, as if for luck. "It always wins."

"You're not working tonight?"

"I'm a free woman tonight." She holds up the brown bag, which gives off an aroma of greasy potatoes and shoe-leather beef. "Robyn and Walt sent you this, fresh off the grill. And their best wishes." She sets a bottle of Jack Daniels on the coffee table. "The guys from the mill sent you this."

"With their best wishes?"

"Don't be greedy." She takes the food to the kitchen, and calls back to him, "There's trouble with the kid from headquarters who's taken your place."

"Tim?"

"They don't like him. They were asking me when you'd be back."

"Things must be pretty bad if they want me back."

"And those protesters," she continues. "They've been getting really aggressive, I guess, blocking the road and stuff. It's kind of a mess. Or so I've heard."

"I plan to go to work next week."

"Well, then, you're warned. They're on the warpath." She pops her head around the corner. "Want me to make coffee?"

"Yes," Ronald says. "Although I'd rather have the Jack."

"Not with this line-up of pills." She whistles. "You must have cleaned out the pharmacy counter at the Wickiup."

She returns just as Elise, who had come in drenched and cold from her post by the mill, steps out of the bathroom. Elise has showered and dressed in silken pajamas and a robe.

Shari looks Elise up and down, and Elise glances toward Ronald, questioning. He hastens to make introductions.

"I just put on coffee," Shari says, claiming her territory.

"That sounds wonderful," Elise replies.

Ronald is growing sleepy. The women's faces grow distant and distorted, their voices like vinyl records played backwards. They crowd around him, asking him questions that melt in his mind. Elise, well-attuned to the routine, finally helps him hobble into the bedroom. Shari fluffs the pillows and turns down the blankets on his bed.

Why couldn't he have awakened between these two, rather than between Ken and Brodric? As he lies back, mellowed by their coddling, he watches Elise shed her robe, which floats to the floor like a cloud, and coax her pajama top over her head, freeing her pink-nippled breasts in a perfume of lavender and satin. Shari, not to be outdone, slips off her sweater and unhooks a surprisingly matronly white bra to reveal breasts as beautiful and bountiful as Elise's. The two women laugh at their daring striptease, then come together, Elise's bow-shaped lips against Shari's tilted smile. Their tongues, pink and delicate, touch with supple insistence in a full-lipped kiss. Elise's long tapered hands drift up Shari's arms to caress her breasts. Shari smooths work-roughened fingers through Elise's glorious hair and kisses her temples and cheeks. They sink into a dark, warm mist at the foot of Ronald's bed.

When he wakes, it's deep in the night. All the lights are off, and he is alone. Where did Shari go? Where is Elise? He can't quite remember what happened after they started kissing. Damn it all, don't tell him he dozed through *that*. He wriggles into a sitting position and gathers his crutches, then stumps toward the living room. Someone laughs, and Ronald finds the room lit only by a roaring fire. Elise and Shari are seated on the floor before the fireplace, fully clothed, their heads bent over his notebook of sawing patterns.

"Only a man would want to make something square out of something that's naturally round," Shari says.

"That's why you should always see a woman gynecologist," Elise quips.

The joke sends waves of laughter through them, and Ronald, suddenly wide awake and heartily disappointed, shrewdly notes an empty wine bottle on the coffee table. Another, on the floor at Shari's side, holds only enough for a single glass. It's his best wine, too. One of them—heiress or barmaid—knows her vintages. The Jack Daniels remains untouched, although the food from the Rambler has been devoured. All that's left are greasy wrappers and a crust of bun.

"Hey," he says, slightly annoyed.

Elise rises unsteadily to her feet and deposits the notebook on the coffee table. "You're awake!" she sings. "You've been sleeping for hours."

Shari rises and stretches, her body as sleek as a cat's.

"I hope you don't mind," she says. "I'm stuck here. My truck won't start. There's already eight inches of snow on the ground and it's blowing to beat the band. Jason's at Marguerite's, so I think I'm going to stay put."

"Fine," Ronald agrees absently. "That's fine."

"I told her she could borrow something of mine for the night," Elise offers.

Heaven help him, Shari in Elise's diaphanous underwear.

As Elise helps Ronald settle on the couch, Shari topples drunkenly into the easy chair. She throws one leg over the armrest, her foot clad in a thick, white sock that Ronald suspects might have once belonged to her late husband or to Jason.

"We've had the best time," she says, and Ronald holds his breath, hoping at least to hear about it. "We've been gabbing like girls at a slumber party."

"Were the two of you in my room?" he asks.

Without answering, Elise secures his leg on the pile of pillows. "Shari knows Darnell."

"Sure enough," Shari says. "Darnell taught my husband to shoot. Brad had the best aim of anybody I've ever seen. He was so steady, so controlled. So exact. Darnell's a wizard with guns."

Elise sighs, doe-eyed and sentimental at this inane tidbit. "He's such a dear man."

Good God, Ronald thinks. Is Elise claiming her affiliation to Darnell, or did the topic simply arise in passing? Certainly, this is daughterly solicitousness. Maybe it's not a lark for her, after all. It's just possible she is sincere. About everything.

"I really hope I'm not imposing on you," Shari says. "I didn't realize Elise was here—"

"You couldn't have known," Ronald says.

"Well, I should have figured it out. It's pretty common knowledge."

Ronald glances toward Elise, but she looks away. It was stupid of them to think they could keep it a secret, in a hillside town where every street is visible from below.

A knock sounds at the door. Shari and Elise look at each other in surprise, as if it might be a vengeful mob, but neither moves.

"Can someone get that?" Ronald asks.

Elise rises. "It might be Ken and Brodric. Ken said they'd stop by later."

Again, Ronald suspects that much has happened while he has been drugged up and in bed. He hasn't seen Ken or Brodric since the day they delivered him home from Riverton, although they have brought over fresh-baked pies and a plaster saint for "healing energy" that looks to Ronald to be a Friar Tuck knock-off.

It's Lex Stacy and Jason at the door. They stomp into the house in a blast of arctic air, banging snow off their boots and brushing it from the shoulders of their coats. Whatever erotic games might have unfolded with Shari and Elise are only the stuff of fantasy now that the Hardy Boys have arrived.

Shari fairly dances over to Lex and gives him a hug. He kisses into her hair, one of those aimless smacks that lovers share after the novelty has worn away. So, Ronald thinks, Shari is not as alone as he believed. She runs a swift, motherly hand down Jason's arm. He scowls in return.

"We came to get you, Mom," he growls.

"I don't know what's ailing your truck," Lex adds. "I'll have Vern take a look at it tomorrow."

Jason continues to scowl as Elise introduces herself to Lex and invites them in for a cup of coffee. Shari goes to the kitchen to make or reheat or wherever she left off with the coffee before Ronald's nap. Lex introduces himself to Ronald and sits in the easy chair. Jason sullenly slings himself into a wooden chair that Elise has brought from the dining set and glares at Ronald.

Elise fawns over Jason, asking him about school and his job and his horse, for God's sake. He answers in monosyllables, his eyes flitting nervously around the room. Casing out the joint, Ronald fears, planning how he can bludgeon him over the head with the fire tongs, or stuff his body up the chimney, or—

Elise turns to Lex. "How is your sister?"

"She's just fine," he replies. "She fell asleep before we decided to come up here. I know she'll be disappointed she didn't get to see you. Thanks for helping her with her English papers."

English papers? Ronald thinks. What does Elise do in front of the mill all day?

"Juliana has a new soul," Elise says. "It's pure and bright and kind. See that she stays that way."

"How's the tow business tonight?" Ronald asks Lex. "I'd guess it's pretty steady, eh?"

"I really don't take much part in the garage," he says. "My uncle handles most of it."

"So, what do you do?" Elise asks, with a polish worthy of the swanky estates of California. She sits on the couch beside Ronald, her feet tucked beneath her.

Shari comes from the kitchen and perches unsteadily on the armrest next to Lex. He settles a hand on her thigh. Ronald glances at Jason—does he mind that his mother has a lover?—but Jason is staring at the fire.

"I'm doing research in the Park for Montana State University just now," Lex replies.

Ronald's interest is piqued. He has always assumed Lex was a mechanic.

Elise's interest flares as well. "What environmental implications are you exploring?"

"Quite a few," Lex says. "The Greater Yellowstone Area is one of the world's few unspoiled thermal ecosystems. Most have been turned into spas and holiday resorts. We're lucky to have it so well preserved."

And they're off, discussing natural regulation, the health of the Park's 10,000 thermal features, and Lex's dissertation—dissertation! Ronald yelps—on Glacier National Park. Lex talks in paragraphs, rather than sentences, then, as the night sprawls, in tracts. Shari serves coffee to everyone in steaming mugs, then looks on dreamily, in no hurry to be rescued.

This is how it should be, Ronald thinks. Late night company, nowhere to go, a pleasant amount to drink, intelligent discussion. Forget Elise's crazy father; forget Tim Etherton's jacking around the mill, chasing a vice presidency; forget Andy Shenk and the Peace Wagon; forget the broken leg and the wolf and groveling in the forest and near-death. This is the point in the universe where he wants to be.

Until he notices Jason's face. Jason watches Elise with angry, lovelorn eyes, his mouth drawn up in a pinched, silent cry. When his eyes meet Ronald's, they blaze with hatred.

TWENTY-TWO
DAY AT OLD FAITHFUL

For the past month, Jason has carried a secret. Riding on his right hip in a sheath clipped to the belt loops of his Levi's is the knife that was designed and decorated with lightning by his father. It is the final creation of Brad Brock.

Jason credits Johnny Hart for the return of the knife. Johnny collapsed on Main Street, only feet from the door of the Rambler. The ever-vigilant Macky Bain and the firefighters took him to Riverton, where he spent a few weeks in the hospital. He was then sentenced to the Sunny Acres Nursing Home.

When Jason learned of Johnny's fate, he went to the Greenbow Boutique, below the room where Johnny lived, and asked about Tiger.

"Danny and I cleaned out Johnny's room a couple of days ago," Judy Christensen, the owner, told him. "What a job that was! Poor old Johnny, he just couldn't keep up with it all. We took grumpy old Kitty home with us."

So Jason had missed out on getting Tiger, despite all that stolen food, and Johnny's rotten breath, and those stupid stories about blowing away every animal ever to set paw or hoof in the American West. After all that, Tiger—now bestowed with an even worse name—had gone off to live with the rich folk. He felt betrayed, the loser in a custody battle. Leaving the Greenbow, he had started down the street, past Rob Grenville's.

That was when the urge hit him to go inside and look again at the three knives his father had made. Seeing Rob occupied by customers, Jason had slipped to the display case and found that only one knife remained for sale in the case. After a few more seconds, he realized that the sliding glass panel behind the counter was unlocked and slightly ajar. With a simple reach and a quiet jimmying of the door, he had helped himself to what was his anyway, leaving the index card that read "Knives by Brad Brock, local legend" abandoned on the grubby white felt.

Now, on a Monday morning in early May, as his mother drives him to school, Jason fingers the knife under his shirt. Graduation is three weeks away, and by all accounts, he'll wear cap and gown and shuffle across the gymnasium stage with his fifteen classmates to pick up a diploma.

Even so, he would give anything to avoid walking into that school again. Two weeks ago, he broke up with Juliana. Actually, he never told her. He simply started ignoring her at school, eating lunch alone and smoking afterward on the patch of butt-strewn grass designated "Smokers's Square."

Juliana confronted him in the dirt parking lot after school. "What's with you, Jason?" she had asked. "What did I do?"

"I don't know," he said. "Nothing."

"I thought things were going good," she said. "I mean, you didn't complain much whenever we were in bed. Was that all you wanted me for?"

"Listen, I don't want to talk about this."

"Well, I do. Why don't you come over? Lex is always gone now, with your mom."

"See that's just it," Jason said, grabbing an easy out. "Since Lex and my mom are screwing, it's like incest for you and me to do it."

"That's gross!"

Suddenly, she had started to cry. Not in any delicate, girly way, but in big, barking sobs that attracted the notice of the track team, which was practicing nearby. Embarrassed, Jason had stuffed his hands in his pockets. He wants to be free of Juliana, of her feminine tantrums, and overripe body, and needs and demands and hopes that he has no intention of fulfilling. She calls him late at night while his mother is at work and, since they don't have that much to talk about, ties up the phone line just breathing at him. She sneaks out of The Daisy when she's at work and follows him around the store. She tags along wherever he goes, then criticizes what he's doing. She makes him feel as if he can never do anything right.

Now, his mother brakes the truck in front of the school. "I have to take Ronald to doctors's appointments in Riverton," she tells him. "I may not be back until late."

"Again?" Jason asks. "Why do you keep doing this? I mean, is he even paying for the gas?"

"I don't know," she says vaguely. "He fell just beyond the meadow where Dad . . . It seems like the right thing to do. Christian duty or something."

"Christian duty? When was the last time we went to church?"

"Jason—"

"Never mind." He slides from the cab. "Have fun."

"Make sure you go inside."

"Jesus, Mom, I will."

"I'll see you tonight, then."

"Yup." He slams the door of the truck, and his mother signals to pull out. The truck stutters to a halt. Inside the cab, Jason sees his mother's lips form a quick, "Shit." She tries to start it, but with no success.

She crawls out and lifts the hood. Jason joins her, peering at the reworked, overworked parts. "Go on in," she tells him. "I don't want you to be late."

"I have a good excuse, don't I? I mean, you're blocking the bus lane."

His mother glances up at the traffic stalling behind her. "Shit," she says, this time loud enough for passing students to hear. An elementary school girl giggles, and Jason menacingly eyes her. His mother fumbles around inside the engine's greasy parts. "Try starting it," she orders.

Climbing into the cab, Jason complies, but nothing happens. He rolls down the window. "We should have kept Dad's pickup."

"Dad's pickup had payments due." She pushes back her hair, scuffing black grease across her forehead. "I'll have to call Vern. And somebody else is going to have to take Ronald to Riverton."

The disabled truck is attracting attention. One of the bus drivers has parked in the teacher's lot and is heading for them.

An idea comes to Jason. "Why don't you go inside and call Vern, and I'll walk up and bring Ronald down in his car?"

"Great," she says distractedly. "Great. We can just take his car, can't we? I'll tell Jan you'll be right back."

Jason slips from the truck just as the bus driver arrives, spewing masculine know-it-all-ism. The tardy bell shrills from the school's loudspeaker, and Jason realizes his wish has been granted. No school today. At least for a while. At least long enough for Juliana to be holed up in some classroom. And he won't have to face Terry and Russ either. A week ago, they had sauntered up to him in Smokers's Square and offered him a chocolate cherry shot full of vodka with Russ's horse syringe.

As Jason helped himself, Terry asked, "What're you doin' after graduation? Me and Russ already got jobs at the mill."

"You gonna live off your old granny?" Russ chimed in. "Man, you lucky shit. Must be nice."

Since then, both Terry and Russ have taunted him with calls of "Hey, bag boy," which have begun to sound like "fag boy."

When he knocks on Ronald's door, he is greeted by a cheery, "Come in."

Ronald stumps into the foyer, dressed in baggy sweatpants and a Portland State sweatshirt. The right leg of the sweatpants is cut off above his plaster cast. He looks like a gray Pillsbury doughboy.

He wobbles on his crutches. "Jason, why are you here?"

"My mom's truck died," he says. "She asked me to come get you and take you down to the school in your car."

"My car?" Ronald says warily. "Oh, I don't think—"

"It's either that or hitchhike to Riverton. The truck is dead."

"Where is she? Can I call her?"

"She's down at the school. I guess you could call her there."

"Surely she'll be here in a minute."

"She has to talk to Vern first about getting the truck towed."

Ronald chews at his lip. "All right, all right. At the school?" He hobbles back to a graceful, claw-footed table in the foyer. "Have you ever driven a BMW? Real gentle on the gas does it."

Jason rolls his eyes. Of course, he has never driven a BMW. He's never driven anything except his mother's junker pickup and his grandmother's boat of a Buick. Neither one has any flash, although Grandma's Buick can cut loose on long, straight stretches of highway. "We only have a few blocks to go," he reminds Ronald.

Ronald hands Jason the keys and closes up the house. Jason helps him into the passenger's seat, then politely closes the door. He angles the crutches into the nearly non-existent back seat, and climbs in himself. The Beemer looks worse for wear, kind of like Ronald himself, with broken turn signals and dents and scratches, and the hood ornament still missing.

"How'd you fuck up your car so much?" Jason asks as he adjusts the seat and the rearview mirrors. "You need to learn to drive, man."

Ronald's lips compress. Jason buckles himself in, pulling his shirt away from the knife at his waist to do so. The BMW purrs to life when he starts it, and jumps like lightning when he hits the gas. His heart revs with the motor. This is no driven-to-rust pickup or granny Buick. This baby moves.

"Take it easy," Ronald cautions.

The weather is golden, a spring day full of blue sky and the smell of budding aspen branches and plum blossoms. The air feels wild and quickened. He's halfway to the school when he suddenly veers west.

"What are you doing, Jason?" Ronald snaps.

Jason turns onto the Yellowstone Highway. It's too warm of a day and this is too hot of a car to waste.

"Where are we going?" Ronald demands. "Jason, what are you doing?"

His stomach lurches, his breakfast of coffee and toast heaving. His heart, jet-fueled by adrenaline and fear, thunders, and a hot flash runs up his spine, while a chill runs down. He twists toward Jason, but the boy's face is impassive. At his waist, readily accessible, is some god-awful knife that must be a foot long.

"Are you taking me to your place?" he asks. "I thought you said your mother was waiting for me at the school."

Jason doesn't answer as they speed past the Morning Glory Motel. Ronald spies Macky Bain's police cruiser parked in the lot, but there's no sign of the deputy himself. He's probably inside enjoying the All You Can Eat $1.99 Breakfast at Mona's Kitchen while a felony is taking place right outside the doors.

"Jason." His throat feels clogged with a river's worth of mud. "Let's talk about this. What is it that you need or want from me?"

Jason responds by shifting into overdrive. Thank God he knows how to drive a manual. Thank God he isn't grinding gears and popping the clutch.

"I've got some cash," Ronald offers. "I'll give you what I have and I'd be glad to help your mom out any time she wants."

"Wow, that's generous," Jason lashes. "What do you have on you? A buck fifty?"

Ronald clenches the arm rest on the passenger's door. Trees spin along outside the windows—even he's never taken this road at this speed. Within minutes, the turn-off to the Brocks' weather-washed logging road appears.

"Turn," he says. "Why aren't you turning?" He reaches for the steering wheel, but Jason clamps it tight in his hands. The opportunity to exit the highway comes and goes. Ronald's hope vanishes as well.

"Jason, please," he begs. "This is a bad idea. You can't possibly think that you can get away with this."

"Get away with what?"

Jesus Christ, Ronald thinks, what's he doing giving Jason ideas for crimes? His leg jerks, and his cast bangs against the bottom of the dash. Jason casts a sour look toward it.

"I know you don't like me," Ronald says. "I'm not from around here, and I'm not like your dad and the other guys you know. But I've never done anything to you that would make you want to . . ."

"To what?"

"I don't know," he admits. "Are you planning to"—he stumbles on the word "kill"—"hurt me? How smart would that be, considering that your mom and probably half the people at the school knew you were on your way to my house?"

There's no reply, and Ronald is reduced to pleading. "Let's turn around. It will be all right. I'll tell your mom we had some errands to run."

Jason doesn't budge.

The Shoshone National Forest welcomes them. Acres and acres of dense trees where a body can be dropped and lost for months, for years, forever. Miles of emptiness where a man can be cut to ribbons, slowly stripped of flesh, while his screams and blood are soaked up by the thick needles of the pines.

"Is this about your mother?" Ronald asks, still trying to reason his way out. "Believe me, Jason, I think she's lovely. I always have. I didn't hurt her in any way. Besides, she's seeing Lex Stacy now, isn't she? He seems to be a nice guy. Don't you like him?"

"You treat women like they're bimbos." Jason rolls down his window, and the sound of rushing air crackles through the car. "You've always treated my mom like she's some inbred, stupid country girl who'd just fall all over you, and you treat Elise like she's nothing."

"What makes you think that? When have you seen me do that?"

"Elise deserves better," Jason insists. "She deserves—"

He stops, and Ronald demands, "What does she deserve? Who?"

Jason's lips tighten.

"You have no idea what Elise and I share." Ronald's voice surges. "And you don't give either your mother or Elise credit for thinking for themselves. They're women, Jason. Brainy women, at that. Women who understand their own hearts, women with wisdom and strength."

The emotion in his voice stops him. He can feel it, raw, full, as if he's swallowed something triangular, or his own heart. When did Elise become his *raison d'être*? Lately it has been so difficult, sharing her with Andy Shenk and his minions, unable to trust either her or himself.

"You're full of shit," Jason says.

"Well, what are you full of?" Ronald's patience lapses. "Stupidity, that's what. Doing crap like this. And trying to run me off the road that night after I took your mom out. You could have killed us both. But do you know what? Your mom had already made it clear that night that she wasn't interested in me. The only time I kissed her—"

"Jesus, I don't want to hear—"

"The only time was to comfort her when she was crying over your dad. It was over between us by the time you chased me down that road. So if you'd killed me, it would have been for nothing. For nothing, Jason."

Jason grinds his jaw.

"When you do something this stupid," Ronald says, "at least make sure it means something."

His thoughts surge forward. Last Sunday, Craig had called, speaking in a quavering voice through eight hundred miles of telephone line. Surprised—Becky usually initiated and ended Ronald's communications with his son—Ronald had said, "Hey, cowboy, what's going on?"

Silence answered him, broken here and there by cheeping syllables as Craig tried to speak and then retreated.

"Come on, kiddo," Ronald coaxed. "Tell me."

At last, Craig managed, "Please, Daddy, can you come home?"

"What's going on?" he asked again. "Where's Mommy? Is she there?"

More sniffles. "She's in the kitchen making dinner."

"Okay," Ronald breathed out tension. "Okay, good. Why are you crying?"

"I don't like Mark."

"Who's Mark?"

"Mommy's boyfriend. He makes me do stuff I don't like."

Ronald's heart had stuttered, a pain racing through his chest. His breath did the same, and he had inhaled with a gasp. "Like what?"

"Go to bed early," Craig whined. "With no bedtime story."

He laughed weakly, relieved. "Well, that's not exactly cruel and unusual punishment."

"Or watch movies with Brandon while he and Mommy have private time."

Stupid bitch. "Who's Brandon?"

"Mark's son. Mark says Brandon is going to mop up the floor with me some day. He says I better get tough, because I'm a sissy boy."

"He calls you a sissy boy, huh?"

"Yeah, he's always punching at me and saying, 'Dukes up, baby,' and stuff. He punched my head on accident one time. Mommy laughed when I cried."

"Mark did this?"

"No, Brandon."

"And how old is Brandon?"

"Twelve."

Ronald had lapsed into panic, into crazed helplessness. What is Becky thinking, letting these thugs into her life? Doesn't she know Craig is the most important, the most precious thing she has?

Jason whisks around a final corner. "We're to the gates," he says roughly. "Ante up the three bucks."

The entrance booth to Yellowstone National Park appears ahead, a functional Park Service kiosk, staffed by a girl hardly older than Jason. She smiles widely as they approach.

"What if I tell them you've kidnapped me?" Ronald asks, sweat prickling the sensitive skin inside his cast. "That I'm here against my will?"

"You gave me the keys to your car."

"You have a knife in your belt."

Jason yanks his shirttail over it, hiding the sheath and handle under the cloth. He keeps one hand on it, as protective of it as he would be of his manhood.

The Park attendant comes to the car, her hands wrapped around brochures. She explains that their ticket is good for seven days. "Welcome to Yellowstone National Park," she beams in the voice of a ten-year-old. "I hope you enjoy your stay."

Ronald says nothing.

Jason floors the car, and they speed into the Park.

Traffic is eerily sparse—nothing like when he and Shari visited the Park last July—and Ronald begins to fear that he and Jason are the only two in this wild place. His leg itches violently, and he pushes his left foot against the floor of the car in a futile attempt to stretch it. He rolls down the window, craving air that does not smell of his own sweat and fear.

It's surreal—all this scenery, all this beauty. Around each corner, greater beauty appears—the new gold of the grasses, the crisp blue of the lakes, the heavy-bottomed clouds reflected in deep, still water. The smells of pine and snowmelt waft through the ventilation system. An eagle swoops through the sky to land on a lightning-streaked tree. Elk laze in the newly green grasses, their antlers lifted in elegant balance. The day resonates with serenity and pure, unspoiled light.

Jason pulls onto the one-way that leads to Old Faithful and parks the car toward the end of the parking lot, far removed from the other tourists's vehicles. For a moment after he turns off the car's ignition, they sit in silence, as if this parking space is their ultimate destination.

Ronald sizes up the knife. "Why do you have that? What's it for?"

Jason swings open his door. "Get out."

"Here?" Ronald shoots. "Sure." The place should be swarming with officials—Park rangers, gift shop attendants, custodians, tourists. Even now, Ronald could shout and bring someone to his rescue. How he'll enjoy seeing Jason's ass hauled off by the Park police, his hands behind his back, that knife stripped from his side.

Jason comes around and opens the passenger's door, and Ronald struggles to lift his cast and set it outside the car. Jason hands him his crutches. Ronald stands and leans back against the hood while Jason shuts the door. He's woozy, strung out by the lengthy drive, the cramped quarters, his own heart-altering fear, but he strikes out at a quick pace, determined and confident.

They bypass the Visitor's Center and join a throng of sightseers moving toward the observation area. Jason sits on the bench, with Ronald to the left of him. Stupidly—stupidly!—Ronald puts his crutches between them. With a quick movement, Jason swipes them and lays them to his right, where Ronald cannot reach them.

Ronald's heart stalls. "Jason, I need those."

"They're right here."

"Give them back."

"It's erupting approximately every sixty-seven minutes today." Jason reads benignly from the Park Service sign board. He checks his watch. "It should erupt in about two minutes."

"Give me my crutches."

Jason's eyes fasten onto the cone of the geyser, and Ronald scrabbles to try to stand. Finally, he falls back onto the concrete bench, exhausted.

As if on cue, the geyser begins to spit steam, and the plume lifts into the clear, blue sky. Around Ronald, tourists clap and whistle, snapping photographs and talking into briefcase-sized camcorders hoisted on their shoulders. Jason looks straight ahead, his face blank, his expression unaltered by Old Faithful's splendor. The three-minute spectacle seems to last for hours. Ronald endures it in silence.

The tourists wander away once the geyser stills, until Jason and Ronald are the only two sitting on the concrete benches.

Ronald slaps his knee. "Okay, Jason," he says in a voice that he hopes sounds both authoritative and non-threatening. "You've had your fun. You've seen the geyser, and I've missed my appointments. Let's go back."

Jason stares straight ahead. Without looking down, he picks up the crutches, plants them on the ground and stands. He positions them under his arms and leans heavily into them. Silent still, he hops off on them, his left foot cocked backwards.

"Jason!" Ronald yells, squirming across the concrete bench, trying to get close enough to snag the kid's shirt or trip him. He nearly loses his balance, and grabs onto the bench to steady himself. The surge of fear through his body kicks against his heart, and he puts a hand on his chest. Not a heart attack, too!

He watches helplessly as Jason shambles clumsily toward the path that leads into the Upper Geyser Basin.

What in the fuck is he doing? His heart has been beating like a marching band since they left Pindall. Once out of Ronald's sight, he folds the crutches under his arm, as breathless as if he had walked ten miles. He hadn't meant to come so far, or to drive so fast. But the farther he had gone, the farther he knew he had to go.

He expects the Park rangers to tramp over the hill at any moment, Ronald behind them, in a National Park Service wheelchair, shouting, There he is! Get him! He sees himself flung to the ground, a billy club jammed between his flailing legs. You want to lose your balls, kid? You want to sing soprano? Handcuffed, he'll be dragged back to the Visitor's Center to await the state police. Shit, he's eighteen, he'll do jail time for this, just moldering away in the penitentiary in Rawlins.

He walks to a thermal pool. A tiny geyser, only a few feet high, spits like a riled-up cat. The soil of the boiling plain before him has been seared to crusty sinter by the thermal activity. It's dead, lifeless for all intents and purposes. It looks like hell, all burnt and battered, but Lex would be able to discover all sorts of bacteria here. He'd point out a "soup" of this or a "noodle" of that or a "mash" of something else. When Lex talks bacteria, it becomes a feast.

Damn it, this earth spits up life like vomit. Why doesn't it do a better job taking care of it?

Jason spreads the crutches and ambles forward. Tourists—families with rambling kids, waddling elderly couples, hiking-booted nature lovers in overdrive—clear the way for him, as if he is a leper. He could use some of these on a regular basis.

But they're so damned tiring. His underarms chafe against the rubber, and he gives up again. With the crutches tucked under one arm, he walks, and walks, and walks, following the gravel path, flanked by roiling geysers. The stink of sulfur coats his nostrils until he forgets the smell of air.

He comes to the Morning Glory Pool. Famous once for its blue center and purplish hue, it is now stained an odious yellow. A sign informs him that the pool has been destroyed by man. Literally tons of trash have been thrown into it by careless and unappreciative visitors, which have clogged the underground natural vents and lowered the water temperature so that the yellow bacteria—identified by some Latin name Lex would know—have encrusted the pond. Only the water at the very center is still blue.

A family—mother, father, two boys around seven or eight, and a baby in a stroller—appears. Jason hitches the crutches under his arms and lifts his left foot, planting the toe of his boot on the path. They won't bother a cripple.

The boys rush ahead, competing to be the first to reach each geyser and shout its name, with thunderous echoes. "Fan! (Fan! Fan! Fan!)" "Mortar! (Mor-ter! Mor-ter!) "Spitful!"

"That's Spiteful," the mother sweetly corrects. "Not Spitful."

"Spitful!" The younger of the two boys spits toward the geyser.

"Don't do that please, Brody." The mother kneels to tend the baby in the stroller, who has started to cry. Brody blithely ignores her and spits at his brother.

"Come here, please, Preston," the father intercedes. He settles a hand on the child's shoulder. "Stay by me until Brody makes a better choice in his behavior."

Jason mulls over what a good whup on the seat would do for Brody's choice of behavior.

Preston takes refuge behind his father's leg and sticks out his tongue at his brother. Brody reciprocates, and they choose this behavior until the mother says mildly, "Boys, please don't do that."

Rebuffed, Brody wanders down to the Morning Glory Pool and comes to stand within a few feet of Jason. Without acknowledging each other, they gaze at the pool in tandem.

Something kerplops into the pool. Jason eyes Brody. The kid has pulled a plastic bag of coins from his pocket, and with nubby fingers, is digging in it for another.

He chucks a second coin into the water.

"Hey," Jason says.

The boy looks at him with deep brown eyes encircled by girlish black lashes.

"Read the sign," Jason says. "It says, 'Don't throw stuff into the pool.'"

The kid wings another penny. This one lands on the crusty yellow bank around the pool.

"That ruins the geyser," Jason explains. "See, it gets all plugged up. That's what it says here." He waves toward the information board.

"I don't care. They're stupid."

"So, you're going to ruin all this for everybody else, huh? For the whole world? What's your name? Brody? Is that it?"

"How'd you know?"

"Maybe they'll put up a sign that reads, 'Brody fucked this up for everybody else.'"

"That's a really bad word!" the kid accuses. "You shouldn't say that! I'm gonna tell!" He looks over his shoulder and bellows, "Mom!"

"You're a really bad kid," Jason replies.

"Shut up," Brody sputters.

"Come here," Jason coos.

"No."

"Come over here. I can't hurt you. I'm on crutches."

The kid creeps closer, hastily stuffing his bag of pennies into his pants pocket and holding the pocket closed with one tight fist.

"Here's a secret, Brody," Jason whispers, making his voice as threatening as possible. "You fuck things up, and you just fuck up your own life. And it stays that way *forever*."

Brody turns and screams, "Mom!"

He runs up the gravel path to join his family. The baby is crying steadily now, and both parents are engrossed in seeing to its needs. The father ignores Brody's tugging at his pants leg. "Brody!" he snaps at last. "Stop it now! I'm taking care of Hunter."

Brody grinds fists into his eyes, as if he is going to cry. For a moment, Jason feels sorry for him, caught as he is between his goody-two-shoes brother and the caterwauling baby. Brody casts a resentful look in Jason's direction. Then, damned if the little shit doesn't dig another penny from his pocket and lob it toward the nearest thermal pond. Jason shakes a crutch at him.

The family heads back toward Old Faithful and the air-conditioned buildings, where food, drink and toilets are readily available. Once again, Jason is alone at the Morning Glory. The sun is growing hot on his back, and he is sweating profusely under the arms. All he can see in the pool now is that fucking penny, a brown blemish ruining it all.

Annoyed, he drops the crutches and gathers them up under his arm, like a supplicant leaving the Pool of Miraculous Works. Cured.

When he pops back over the gentle slope and onto the concrete path that circles Old Faithful, he finds Ronald still perched on the bench. A blonde with rucked-up hair and eyes defined in Magic Marker sits beside him, engaged in animated conversation. Her ledge-like bosom, clad in filmy magenta, heaves when she laughs. Ronald coyly lifts a paper cup and sips through a straw. The blonde offers him food. Jason's stomach growls, gnawing on itself, and his mouth smacks with dryness.

The blonde smiles quizzically at Jason as he approaches.

"There he is!" Ronald blasts, almost happily. He is none the worse for wear, Jason notices, except that his forehead is beaded by sweat.

"You sure have been gone a long time," the woman shrills. "Old Faithful has erupted two—"

"Three," Ronald corrects.

"—times since you left. Your poor friend here! You took his crutches! What were you thinking? He couldn't move!"

"But I've had the best of company," Ronald oozes, and the woman melts under his charm. "I can't thank you enough."

She rises. "Now, what's the name of that town where you live again?"

"Pindall."

"Pindall." She puts a hand on his shoulder. "I will look you up, Ronald Dailey. Don't you doubt it."

"Thank you for your care, Lynda. I enjoyed it so much."

Lynda sings, "Don't you lose that phone number I gave you. Remember, Omaha's an hour ahead." With an accusatory glance at Jason, she swoops away, waggling her broad hips. Ronald waves to her as she heads to the Gift Shop.

"Make me puke," Jason says.

Ronald ignores him. "Have a nice walk?"

Jason slings down the crutches where Ronald can easily reclaim them. "These things hurt like hell under the arms. I'm glad I'm not so pissing stupid that I need them."

Ronald voice grows steelier. "Where'd you go?"

"To the Morning Glory." Jason sits where Lynda has just vacated. Something—either sun or her ample butt—has left the bench overly warm. "Did you know that the Morning Glory has turned from blue to yellow because humans have ruined it? Throwing pennies and trash and all sorts of shit into it."

"Lex studies those pools, doesn't he?" Ronald brushes crumbs from his sweatshirt. "Does he take you with him?"

"He doesn't work around here. He works where there aren't any tourists to spoil them."

"It must be interesting."

"Do you want to go up there?"

"I want to go back to town." Ronald's voice is silky and smooth, as if he is pulling the same scam on Jason as he did on Lynda.

Jason looks out over the dormant cone of Old Faithful. A crowd is gathering for the next eruption. "My dad used to bring me and my mom up to the Park for days at a time," he says. "We never came to places like this, where the tourists are. But during the really good times, the fall when the aspen changes or the spring when there are baby animals, he was gone. Guiding somebody around through the best days. He was never home when it mattered."

"I'm sorry."

"I don't understand it. People have kids, then leave them behind like they're pieces of shit." Jason thinks of Erica. "He did it more than once."

Ronald considers for a moment. "There are lots of reasons why parents can't stay with their kids."

"Name one reason that's good enough. Even dying is a cop-out." Jason pulls at a dirty piece of adhesive tape that is wrapped around the crutches' handles.

"Is that what you think your father did? Died on purpose? I doubt he wanted to die. I almost died, and believe me, I didn't want to."

"Did you think of her?"

"Who? When?"

"When you fell in the woods, dumb ass. Did you think of Elise?"

"I'd been thinking about her. The entire time I was running. We'd had an . . . argument."

"If it had been me, I'd have thought of her every minute, every second. I'd have given my soul to come back to her alive."

Ronald sits still, as if he is part of the concrete bench beneath him. He looks sad and small, and Jason realizes that no answer will come.

"I've seen her naked," he prods.

The instant the words leave his throat, he knows he has ruined what happened between Elise and him at Disney Land. Suddenly it's cheap, ugly, dead, stupid, what happened between them no better than the wrangling and gyrations he went through with Juliana.

Damn it, why does he always screw everything up?

"I know," Ronald says calmly. "She told me. I'm sure what happened between the two of you was wonderful. It would have to be. She is a wonderful woman."

"Do you love her?"

"Yes."

And that's it. Ronald offers no more. No gloating. No threat—So you better keep your fucking hands off. His expression does not waver, his eyes don't slide away to see where Lynda has gone. In fact, Ronald is looking out past Old Faithful, into some distance that Jason would have to strain to see. Jason feels tired, as if he will never be able to drag himself back to the car, to drive back to Pindall. He will be stuck here forever, with brats like Brody and bovine women like Lynda. He'll become what's ugly and stupid in this world.

"So tell me," he says. "Why did an asshole like yourself take a fall in that meadow and live, while my father died?"

Once the question is asked, Jason knows what this is all about. Like Brody and Preston, he is calling into the wilderness and hearing only an echo in response. Why did his father die, so stupidly, so unexpectedly, when the world is populated by dicks who pull through? (Why? Why? Why?)

"You don't expect me to answer that," Ronald breathes. "No one can answer that."

"Yeah, that's about it."

Old Faithful blows, and the crowd predictably cackles, whistles, and applauds. Cameras click and whirr, and video cams loop shaky footage that no one will ever watch again. Just as the geyser reaches its full height, Ronald says, "It must be hard sharing your father's memory with your half-sister."

Jason winces at the word, but Ronald's gaze is on the geyser.

Without waiting for an answer, Ronald continues. "What you have to realize is that love can never be exclusive. You can't ask someone to love only you—"

"What the hell does that mean?"

"I have a six-year-old son."

"Where is he?" Jason asks.

"Portland. My ex-wife has full custody."

"Why? Did you beat him or something?"

"No." Ronald makes a sound that Jason assumes is a surprised laugh, but which resembles a sob. "Never. I wouldn't . . . You see, you can't always choose what you want, you can't always do what's best. Sometimes you just have to do what it takes to survive."

"So do you call him?"

"Once a week."

"Once a week. That's great." Jason trains his eyes on the billows of Old Faithful. "When my dad was gone in the winters, I used to count the sunrises and sunsets. I'd think, maybe in ten more, he'll be home. Then, ten more. Then, five more. I'd always choose ten or five, because to think he'd be home in two days or the next day was just too stupid. I knew it wouldn't happen. Does your son do that?"

"I don't know," Ronald says tightly. "I know he misses me."

"Christ," Jason jabs. "You're more fucked up than I thought. Do you know what it's like? Every time Dad would leave, Mom would cry. They'd fight it out and then she'd cry. For days, sometimes. It wasn't so much the hunting trips—that's what he did—but he never stayed home afterward either. He'd go do some stupid job like the oil fields or the refineries, because he didn't want to be with us, he just wanted to be gone and—"

"Calm down, Jason," Ronald soothes. "It's all right."

"No, it's not! Because you know what? She stopped crying. That was the worst. She stopped crying after a while, because she knew she couldn't change him anyway. She just quit, she just fucking gave up and let him go. And then he goes and dies, and everybody says, just let it go, move on. They want me to give up, too, and just smile and say, oh, it's okay, it doesn't matter. Erica'd love that, the stupid bitch. Well, I say, fuck that, just fuck it, fuck them all!"

Jason pants so hard that it takes him a while to realize that someone is tapping him on the shoulder. "Excuse me, young man!" A woman hisses indignantly. "Your language is appalling! There are children here." She addresses Ronald. "You shouldn't let him talk that way, sir. It's a disgrace."

"Fuck off," Ronald replies. He leans closer to Jason. "Take me home."

Jason stands and hands Ronald his crutches. "Down in front!" somebody yells, as if a six-foot man can block the view of a hundred foot pillar. Neither Ronald nor Jason pays any attention. They hurry away, moving as fast as Ronald's stiff, blundering body will allow. Side by side, they find the BMW in the parking lot.

"You want an aspirin or anything?" Jason asks as he helps Ronald into the car.

"Aspirin doesn't quite do it."

Jason climbs into the driver's seat. The seat belt catches on the knife's hilt as he tries to buckle it. He pulls the knife from the sheath.

Ronald twists in his seat, looking like he's going to puke. He croaks, "Jason—"

Jason lifts the knife. "My dad made it. All by himself. You asked me about it earlier."

Ronald relaxes some. "It's beautiful," he says weakly. "He loved you very much, I'm sure. I know he loved your mother, just from the way she talks about him."

"It's stolen."

"What?"

"I stole it from the shop where he used to sell them."

Ronald shrugs. "It doesn't matter," he says. "You're not a criminal. You're not bad or a delinquent or anything else. You simply need to make peace with what's happened. That's all."

Jason fingers the blade as he glances toward the cars shuttling in and out of the lot. There's no happy ending, he thinks, but there has to be an ending. "She'd say that."

Ronald's voice sounds crimped. "Yes, Elise would say that."

Jason puts the car in gear and rolls toward Pindall.

When they arrive at Ronald's house on the hill, Shari and Lex rush from inside to greet them. "Oh, my God, you're all right!" Shari cries as she gingerly helps Ronald from the car. "I thought something had happened, and Jason had to take off for Riverton without telling anyone. Where have you been?"

"Nowhere," Ronald mumbles. He is sleepy and hurting badly after the day stranded on the concrete.

"I kidnapped him," Jason says flatly, pulling the crutches from the back seat.

"What?" Shari demands. "You what? What are you talking about?"

"It's all right, Shari," Ronald soothes. "It was a misunderstanding. It's over now."

"Are you all right?"

"Yes. Listen, I'm really tired. I need to get some rest."

They move slowly into the house, Lex holding open the door, Shari at Ronald's side, clamoring fear and relief, demanding information, scolding and pleading and soothing all at once. Inside, it is cool and dim with twilight. Ronald lies on the couch, unable to bear sitting for another moment. He asks Shari for his painkillers. She scurries about, seeing to his requests.

"Do you want me to stay here tonight?" she asks, kneeling beside him.

"No, I'm all right."

Lex clears his throat. "I'll take Jason down to my house."

"Can I go to Grandma's instead?" Jason asks.

"Fine," Shari says absently, and watches until the front door closes behind them.

Her face is ravaged by worry and heartsickness. It startles Ronald, and he reaches out and brushes his knuckles down her cheek, hoping to ease her pain. "Don't do that, Shari," he whispers, his heart twisted by her anguish. "It's all right."

She clasps his hand in both of hers. "Where did Jason take you? I'm so sorry."

"Don't worry about it."

"What happened?" Her voice is high-pitched and rugged. "What did you talk about? Did he say anything?"

"I don't know," Ronald murmurs. "Listen, I need to sleep. We'll talk tomorrow."

"I'll call Macky, Ronald," she says boldly. "I want Jason to take responsibility for his actions."

"Don't do that. There was no crime. Just . . . a mistake."

Shari considers his words, and he feels the weight of her unasked questions on his weary mind. Please don't ask, he thinks. Please don't. He would be tempted to tell how afraid he is. Afraid that he isn't healed, that he isn't a better person. Afraid that he doesn't love any differently. Afraid that it hasn't been a new beginning at all, just a protracted ending.

Instead, she asks, "Where's Elise?"

Ronald waves hazily. "She went home tonight, I think. I told her I'd be late."

"Will you be all right alone? I could go get her—"

He will cry if she mentions Elise again. "I'll be fine."

Shari bends over to stroke his hair and kiss his cheek. "I'm so sorry," she says again. "So very sorry."

After she leaves, Ronald gazes out the sliding glass door. The sunset reflects against the shoal of thunderheads on the eastern horizon, delicate orange against charcoal sky. Ronald watches the light fade until, once again, sky and earth are indistinguishable in the darkness.

§§§§§

Lex doesn't speak to Jason before he drops him off at his grandmother's house, but as Jason is climbing from the Camaro, Lex says, "Hey, just be cool, okay? Your mom's had a hell of a day."

Inside, Jason gives a quick look around to make sure Erica isn't there, then greets his grandmother, who is in the kitchen fixing a meal for one. She eyes him with the expression that makes her employees wet their pants, then freezes the piss before it hits the ground.

"Everybody's been looking for you," she says. "Where have you been?"

"Sorry I didn't show up for work. Something came up."

In the living room, he slings himself onto the couch and reaches down to rub the tummies of Dane and Amory, who dream on the rug in short, delicate yips. He is hoping that his mother will not murder him here. Surely his grandma's presence will slow her down some.

But when his mother skids through the door, Jason sees he has no chance. "Tell me," she begins. Then, as if she can't quite believe what she is having to do, she repeats in a deeper, uglier voice, "Tell me what happened before I blow my stack."

At the sound of the threat, his grandmother comes from the kitchen, a frying pan in her hand. The dogs rumble to life beneath Jason's feet and skitter toward the bedroom in cowardly retreat.

"I already told you," he mumbles. "I kidnapped him."

"Good Lord, what's going on?" his grandmother asks.

His mother ignores her, bellowing, "Why? He is my friend! What did he do to you?"

"I don't know," he says, and it's true. He can't seem to remember anymore.

"You don't know? Don't you pull that one on me! Tell me! Damn it, tell me what the hell you were thinking!" She slams her hand against the backrest of the couch. "I'm calling the cops."

"No!"

Jason's protest is echoed by his grandmother. "Shari," she says. "Calm down a minute. What exactly happened?"

Both of them look at Jason, and he swallows hard, feeling as if his mother has already strangled him. "When I got into the car, I just wasn't thinking," he says feebly. "And I started to drive, and then I realized we were on our way to the Park, so we went to Old Faithful."

"Old Faithful?" The frying pan in his grandmother's hand droops, nearly launching a half-fried egg onto the floor.

"And nobody stopped you?" his mother wonders. "Nobody helped Ronald? Good God, what is wrong with this world?"

"He didn't ask anybody, Mom. This fat lady fed him French fries."

His last statement silences both of them. The grandfather clock ticks steadily, and a car rushes by, gravel crunching beneath its tires. Dogs bark in the distance.

His mother half-shrieks, "All day long, I've been scared to death, thinking something happened to both of you. God, I thought you'd been in a car wreck and broken your neck, just like . . ." She covers her mouth, as if she's going to vomit.

"I'm sorry, Mom," Jason quavers, tears pricking his eyes. "What can I do?"

She turns away, crying, and his grandmother takes over. Her hand touches his shoulder, warm and paper-light, but ever so steely. "What in the world were you thinking, Jason?" she asks coolly.

Tears spill over Jason's cheeks, and he rams his arm against his face. "I'm sorry, Grandma. I didn't mean to upset everybody." When he tries to breathe in, it's a violent shudder. "Listen, Mom, he could have gotten away about a hundred times. He could have had every ranger in Yellowstone come rescue him. He didn't even try."

"This sounds like a joy ride to me," his grandmother suggests. "On both their parts."

"I don't understand." His mother plops down in the armchair, limp as a Raggedy Ann doll. "Tell me everything."

With both of them there, dodging the question is impossible. So Jason starts talking.

TWENTY-THREE
LETTER TO BRAD
II

So this is how it is.

I've been so damned lonely, so stupidly alone, and I've spent way too many nights longing for your voice and your touch and the sound of your breath as you slept and the smell of warm skin in the mornings, only to find myself with nothing. I never had enough of you when you were alive, so how can I bear having none of you for the rest of my life?

I can't do it, Brad, I just can't do it. I'm not meant to be alone, and I'm tired of fighting it. When you used to travel, I could imagine you somewhere, I could sense you, and I could carry on the conversations we'd been having in my own head. I could think, oh, I'll tell him the next time he calls, or when he's home again. Now, when I wake in the night, all I can think about is how quiet it is. It isn't that the night has grown quieter, it's that my brain—my consciousness, I guess—has become barer, more sensitive. I feel like something has scratched my heart raw.

I feel alone, too. Things have been muddy between your mom and me for a while now, and you can imagine that Jason and I haven't been too friendly since his kidnapping escapade. I didn't call Macky or the sheriff, mostly because Ronald didn't want me to, but also because I was scared that the Park police would get involved, but I tell you, I was furious with him. And ashamed, too. I just couldn't get over the fact that he'd done something so stupid, and of course, everyone in town knew about it. Walt even made up a drink called "Day at Old Faithful" that's really just a sloe gin fizz that goes right over the lip of the glass and onto the counter. That's earned him a lot of laughs and me a lot of ribbing, and the guys from the mill, who aren't too fond of Ronald to begin with, just love it. And it's all at Jason's expense.

But what I want to tell you doesn't have anything to do with that. It's this—I think I'm falling in love again. It's not the same as what happened between you and me. It's not so quick, so furious. Maybe this is the way adults fall in love—I don't know—with a slow, comfortable rhythm that grows into something that they all of a sudden can't do without. And here's the thing—it's just don't-give-a-damn wild fun with Lex. I'm doing things I never dreamed of—tootling through mud pots at Yellowstone guessing at the names of bacteria or singing an Italian aria in my western "make the 'r' as hard as you can" accent while he listens. One day he showed me his doctoral dissertation. He wrote it on microbes in glacial ice in Montana, and I read some of it as we lay in bed. I wondered aloud why he'd done so much work with ice, then come here, where it's all heat. He said he preferred fire to ice and he'd show me why. Then he started to seduce me, first mimicking the movements of glacial ice, and then the movements of magma. I mean, it was a just silly game—something I'd never want anyone to know about—but it made me think, this is what I want. I want to be happy again. I want to laugh again, I want to see that things are funny again, I want to be able to say I'm all right and mean it.

Everybody knows about us—Walt and Robyn, Dave, all the guys at the Rambler. They call him Scientific Slim and tease me about how much he talks, but none of them has been downright mean. Your mom knows, too, and even Jason. But he's more worried about our becoming one of those creepy, family-tree-with-no-branches families than about what Lex and I are doing.

Which brings me to Erica. I still don't understand, Brad, I still can't make heads or tails of it. Why didn't you tell me about her? Why didn't you trust me enough to let me know? I've spent hours trying to figure out if there were clues—when you went camping alone or riding up in the Park, were you thinking of Lael Sheridan? Were you wishing you'd done something different? Did you touch her the same way you touched me? Did you find the same pleasure—oh, God, that would kill me—with her as you did with me? I've tried to imagine it as a carefree teenaged fling, as something that didn't mean anything, but I can't, because our love was never like that. It was a done deal from the day we met.

Erica is so much your daughter. She has all your nerve and beauty and determination. I don't think anything can stop her—she's won over your mother so completely that she arranged for her to change her last name to Brock. So now she's claimed her heritage. And Jason and I just watch, silent, like those who've lost their voices.

But sometimes—and this is in the dead of night, when there is no one around to challenge me about it—I think she is our voice. By coming here out of the blue the way she did, she made us—or, at least, me—look again at who you were and what you were. If she hadn't come, we'd have remembered you the way the boys at the bar do and we would have just gone on nodding our heads and saying nothing, but she's flipped it all on its head. She's made us remember, really remember, whether it be good or bad. It's funny, but this terrible betrayal has given us something that is so much more real. It's given us the man that you were, the flesh and blood man who didn't always do what was right, but who I loved, oh, loved so much—

A tickle on my neck makes me start. I reach up to push away one of my dogs, and come into contact with something more solid. Lex kneels beside the porch swing, where I am lying. I brush my hand down the side of his face, and he says, "Wake up, sleepyhead."

"I don't think I was asleep," I say. "At least, I didn't mean to be."

"It sure looked like it to me."

I sit up and capture his face in my hands, exacting a kiss from him.

He laughs. "What a way to start the day."

"Want another go-around?"

He sits beside me. "Even better."

The sun warms my face. The chains on the swing squeak a lazy rhythm, and the dogs pant contentedly in the shade of the pines. In the corral, Shiloh whips his head a couple of times, trying to entice me to come pet him. My own LilyBelle bucks playfully across the corral, while Old Adam slurps at the water tank. It's one of those days when the clouds will float in the sky and the wind will carry the scent of pine and the sun's rays will never grow hot.

"How was Bozeman?" I ask. Lex has been away for a week, arranging his return to the university.

"Bozeman is Bozeman." He laughs. "But I'm looking forward to being back on campus."

"Did you find somewhere to live?"

"A nice little house on a peaceful street. Three bedrooms, two baths, nothing special. A garden level basement that will make a good office." He gestures toward a cooler sitting on the porch beside him. "Look what I have. Let's go down to your thermal pool and set these in and see what kind of critters come up from the deep."

We walk to the pond amid a three-dog escort. The grass in the clearing behind the house has sprouted beards in the mid-summer's warmth, and the seeds collect on the dog's backs and in our socks. Fireweed, lupine and paintbrush bloom in prolific waves. As we meander, we talk of wonderful nothings—the price of gas in Montana, how wet it has been this spring, and how hot it has been lately.

"There's a fire up around Moran Junction," Lex says. "It's pretty dry up there."

The pool in the trees is a murky bottle glass green today, the sinter surrounding it a flat crusty white. Lex opens the cooler and uses tongs to pull out a rack of slides. Immersing them in the pool, he says, "Everything's been sterilized, so we don't introduce any new bugs to your bugs."

"How long will you leave them there?"

"Two, three weeks. Long enough for them to get big and healthy."

"Any idea what we'll find?"

"I could speculate, but mystery is always preferable to conjecture."

"In other words, you have no idea."

"In other words, I have no idea."

Laughing, we sit down with our backs against a tree and our eyes on the pool, as if we can watch the bacteria colonize. After a minute, Lex pulls something that looks like a folded road map from the pocket of his shirt. "I have something else for you."

"What's this?"

I find a color brochure fronted by a photo of earnest-faced, open-mouthed singers dressed in nineteenth century garb. The group is identified as the Montana State University Opera Workshop. A second photo shows the MSU Chorale, the men in tuxedos and the women in long, black dresses. Flipping through, I find a description of the university's music school and community activities.

"Those groups sing the kind of music you want to sing," Lex says. "Art songs and that kind of thing. And they aren't all just for students. Some of the wives of the other professors belong to them."

"Wives?" I open another flap of the brochure. "Is that a proposal?"

"Actually, it's a proposition." He laughs. "I want you with me, Shari. Come to Bozeman with me."

It's what I've been waiting for, it's what I've been hoping for, everything opening before me. But the first words that come out of my mouth are, "Are you sure?"

"About us? Sure, I'm sure, but I'd like to know why you aren't."

"It's just, well"—words pour through my head—"living with someone gets dull fast. It's either wild nights and unhinged days, or stone cold nights and dreary days."

"Does it have to be? Can't it be a balance of something better?"

"I don't know." My words stick in my throat. "I sometimes wonder if—"

"Go ahead."

"Well, you once said that your marriage was a stereotypical bog, and I haven't ever been able to forget that expression." I bring my knees up and cross my arms over them. "Brad and I used to fight. A lot. We'd fight before he left, and then I'd sulk around the house until one or the other of us broke down and called and we made up. Then we'd fight again the next time he came home because he was only here for a little while. In between the fights, it was crazy—we wanted each other so much. But now . . . I don't know if we were really happy."

Once I've said them, the words feel like such a betrayal, such a rotten trick. Poor Brad—unable to defend himself against such treason. "I never wanted anybody else," I confess. "If he hadn't—"

"I know that, and it doesn't bother me." Lex touches my elbow, bringing us face to face. "But I don't want to come back to you, like he did. I'm not willing to drop by whenever I'm in town. I want to come home to you."

"Jesus, Lex—"

"Sorry if that hurts. But I'm not only thinking of myself. You need to get out of Pindall, Shari."

I know that, I've known that, it seems, for years. But now that it's been spoken, now that it could be a reality, it's like the genie that rises from the lamp—immense, all-powerful, frightening.

"Jason will leave," Lex says gently. "You know he won't stay. The Wickiup notwithstanding, there's nothing here for him, especially since Erica seems to be a permanent fixture."

His words make me wince, but he doesn't let it rest.

"There's nothing here for you, either."

I nod, the raw truth beating in my pulse. "I know."

"So you've thought about leaving?"

"Right after Brad died, it was all I thought about."

"What changed?"

"You," I say. "You were here."

I touch his face, and he starts to fiddle with my hand, tracing lines on my palm with a slowness that sends tingles up my arm. When his mouth enters into play, there isn't much I can do but surrender, and soon I've managed to unbutton his shirt and he's managed to actually remove mine. I'm on my back, with my blouse crumpled beneath me, and pine needles prickling my flesh.

Everything he does feels wonderful—from skimming his fingers up the insides of my wrist to the hollow of my elbow to his lips meandering along my jaw to his weight pressing me into the unforgiving earth. He traps my hands, my elbows bent, my palms helplessly skyward. Then he starts over with his mouth and tongue—kissing my jaw, the hollow of my throat, my collarbone, the rounded scoop of breasts that peek out of my bra, the thin giddy skin over my ribs. He works his way down to my navel, just above the waistband of my jeans. When he bites at the button on the fly, my eyes pop open and I lift my head.

Over his shoulder, I can see more steam than the pool has ever produced, shooting straight into the air. A moment passes before I realize that a geyser has erupted just beyond where we lie. "Lex!" I say, and when he doesn't respond, I pull free of his grip and shake his shoulder. "Lex! Look!"

"Bear?" he asks instinctively as he rolls away. Spotting the geyser, the scientist in him quickly overrules the lover, and he is on his feet, bounding toward the pool, buttoning his shirt as he goes. It takes me a little longer to retrieve my sappy, mud-blotched blouse and to stuff my arms into it. By the time I join him, he is squatting near the pond, beyond the blast of steam, his wrist across his knees to time the eruption on his watch. I kneel beside him.

"Stay on your feet," he warns. "I'm not sure what it might do."

"I've never seen it do anything in the nineteen years I've lived here."

"Right place, right time."

The geyser shoots about three feet in the air. The eruption is really no more than the equivalent of a fierce teakettle's, but the green water roils madly, creating tiny whitecaps as it churns. It's the ocean in a washbasin.

"What'll it do to your slides?" I ask.

"Probably nothing. If they get broken, I'll just try again."

Slowly, the geyser plays itself out, faltering to a couple of feet, then to one, then to a discontented burble. Both Lex and I laugh as the pond releases one last noisy gas bubble and settles back into its easy sway.

"Four and a half minutes," Lex says. "Watch out Old Faithful."

I swallow back emotion. "Do you think it will happen again?"

"It could happen again in four hours or in four years or in four hundred," he says. "Or never. We won't know unless we find some way to monitor it. When I get to Bozeman, I'll see what I can rig up." He turns toward me. "Hey, are you all right? You look shaken."

I am shaken, but not in the way that he probably thinks. This is not a matter of right place, right time, I realize, but of grace. I can't keep trying to second-guess the world—it hasn't worked so far—and I need to just let it go. I need to take my chances with living.

I press my face into Lex's shirt.

"Are you crying?" he asks.

"I think so."

He kisses the top of my head, folds his arms around me. "Wow," he says. "Second geyser of the day."

Laughing and crying at the same time, I lose myself in his embrace.

It's funny.

I've been thinking about going away since you died, but now that I actually have the chance, I'm not sure I want to think about it. Can I really stand to leave what I have here—the house you built, and the land, and the horses and dogs, and Jason, and your mom and all she's done for me, and Robyn and Walt, and the guys who'd do anything for me, and you lying in that stupid cemetery where you shouldn't be, not for another fifty years—to start a new life somewhere else? What if that new life doesn't work? Where will I be then?

But then, I think—if I stay, I will never heal because I'll be where memories of you greet me every morning and follow me through the day. They're like shadows that don't disappear when the lights go off. The love that you and I shared kept me breathing for years. It woke me up in the morning and I fell asleep at night with the knowledge of it and I miss all that so much. And I'm afraid—I'm terrified—that I won't be able to keep the memories of you alive enough to keep me waking in the morning or sleeping through the night.

It must be after midnight, but I haven't slept yet, although Lex has been out for a couple of hours. We spent the better part of the day waiting for the geyser to blow again, but nothing happened. Yet I'd like to think it meant something. I'd like to think it was the echo of the song I sang to you back when we first came up here, or the sound of your felling the logs and building the house during that beautiful first summer, or Jason's first wail after we brought him home from the hospital. I'd like to think it was a sign or gift or message—more than just the earth burping, which is what Lex called it.

I'm going to change, to become someone new. But I want you to know this: I'll never stop loving you even though I may love someone else. And you'll never be gone from me, although you're gone forever—

TWENTY-FOUR
CLOSURE

The phone rings, and Erica rolls over. The pink light of sunrise creeps through the cracked mini-blinds, and the breeze from the open window—the plastic sheeting has been removed—chills, even in mid-July.

The phone keeps ringing, and she stumbles out of bed. It has rung so many times now that she knows it is not Renee's weekly call from Minneapolis or one of Dave's friends. This is something else.

She answers with a dry-mouthed muddle.

"Can you come in and get Dave?" It is Robyn Ruggles, her voice juiced with self-importance and a long night of smoking.

"Where is he?" Erica asks stupidly. "Is he still at the Rambler?"

"They all are." Erica holds the phone away from her ear as Robyn shouts, "Okay, we'll see you later." She comes back on the line. "Get down here as fast as you can."

Before Erica can speak again, Robyn hangs up.

The number of pickup trucks in the parking lot at the Rambler resembles Friday night, not Saturday morning. A dented Ford Maverick sits helter-skelter on the loose gravel, and a truck with livestock panels noses up to the newspaper stand at the motel entrance. Inside, the Rambler is a mess, the tables strewn with bottles, glasses, caps and overflowing ashtrays. Chairs angle into chaos, and the bar is stained and slopped-on. A talk show plays on the radio, the voices testy in debate.

Robyn is right—most of the Rambler's regulars are still at the bar. Erica finds Dave at a table with five others. She knows them all: Eddie Fenton with his four-fingered hand; Dwayne Black in his bad boy black duster; stuttering Tom Prescott; Jack Hardaway, Tommy Dole. Dave sits with his chair cocked sideways, his hair stringy—he hasn't even bothered to comb it over the bald spot. The scent of already-drained-and-drunk alcohol lingers, exhaled along with cigarette smoke from their mouths.

Robyn hails Erica from across the bar. "Welcome to hell," she gruffs. She fiddles with a coffee machine, and the smell of the fresh brew rises up through the staleness of smoke and beer.

"What's going on?" Erica asks.

"If I let 'em out on the roads in this condition, I'll have Macky breathing down my neck." Gesturing toward the men, she adds, "They can tell you what's happening. I been hearing it all night."

Erica goes over to the table. "Hi," she says. "What's going on?"

They leave it to Dave to answer. "The mill closed. It was announced today, I mean, yesterday."

"Oh, no! It's gone?"

"Laid us all off." His voice twists in bitterness. "Cascadia Northern's pulling out. Stripping it down. Just like that. Seventeen years employment over."

"Twenty-two for me," Tommy chimes in.

"Why did they do it?" Erica asks. "They must realize what will happen to the town if the mill closes."

Dave snorts. "They don't give a rat's ass." As he stubs out his cigarette, he upsets the ashtray, raising a cloud of dust and stink from the table. He yanks his hand back. "Damn it!"

"It's okay," Erica says. "I'll get another one."

She takes an ashtray from another table and empties it in a trash can behind the bar, where Robyn is waiting for the coffee maker to dispense its last drops. "You ever heard anything like it?" she says. "Sons of bitches just take what they want. Half the town's going to be out of work now."

She trails Erica across the bar and pours coffee into the half-empty cups, then plumps down on a chair next to Dave. Erica leans against a nearby table, anchoring herself with her hands on the sticky wood top.

"Christ, surely somebody'd buy it if Cascadia Northern put it on the market." Eddie peels the label from an empty beer bottle. "That mill's been in business since the twenties."

"It's not an attractive site." Tommy mimics some nasal-voiced executive. "It's attractive enough for Cascadia to loot it and sell what they can."

His words die. The steam from the coffee is dwindling, although no one has touched his mug. On the radio, they're discussing the fires up in the National Park. "This is the result of poor management on the part of the Park Service," a commentator fumes. "This has been coming for years—" Robyn lights a fresh cigarette from the butt she's holding in her hand.

"Don Baker said he might go to Gillette to the mines," Tommy says. "Andy Hettrick's going back to cowboying up near Cody. His folks have a twenty-thousand acre spread."

"Yeah, he's a lucky fucker," Dwayne says wistfully.

"Maybe Simpson Bros. is hiring construction." The words leak from Eddie in tight, sad drops. "Or the highway department this summer."

"Yeah, but then you've got sn-sn-snow removal," Tom frets.

"Fuck that," Dwayne roars. "Miss one of them pole markers and you're off the edge of the pass. Look at Ray Stern."

"Damn, I wish Shari hadn't sold all of Brad's stock and equipment," Dave mourns. "I'd take up his old jaunts, see if I could get some of his old clients."

"You have Rain," Erica says.

Faces freeze against her. Bodies stiffen. It seems that time has stopped—even the radio statics out dead air. Finally, a rumble from Robyn's smoke-crazed throat breaks through. "What the hell, honey?"

With a jerk, Dave knifes back his chair, its legs grinding against the wooden planks, and walks out of the bar. Erica calls after him, "Dave!"

As the door of the Rambler slams, Robyn says, "Damn, Erica, what are you thinking?"

"He still have that nag?" Dwayne asks. "Jesus fucking Christ."

"What's going on?" Erica demands.

"Dave's horse is the one threw your dad," Robyn grunts. "Didn't you know?"

"No! No, I mean Rain, the palomino—"

"Shit." Eddie Fenton pushes back his chair and stalks out of the bar. Jack Hardaway follows him.

"Holy Mother of God." Robyn's voice is a coarse whisper. "Dave loaned the damned horse to your dad that day, and what does she do? She throws him, snaps his neck clean. How the hell didn't you know that?"

Erica whirls at a strangled shout from the bar behind her. Shari stands near the saloon doors that lead into the kitchen, her face tattered by despair. Beside her, Jason glares.

She flees to the parking lot. Not Rain, not that beautiful animal, that beloved companion! She opens the driver's door of her Honda so quickly that the metal squeals in protest. But as she starts to slide into the driver's seat, someone grabs her arm. She cries out, more in indignation than in pain.

"Why did you say that in front of my mom?" Jason spits, pulling her upright. "What in the hell were you thinking?"

"I didn't even know you were there!" She shoves him away. "How was I to know about Rain? No one ever told me—"

"Nobody ever tells you anything because you don't belong here! You have no business being here! Get out! Go away and leave us the fuck alone!"

Erica stumbles against the frame of the car, only its solid body preventing her from sinking to the ground. It couldn't have been Rain. Another horse, another palomino—

"There must be some mistake."

"Mistake?" Jason shouts. "You're the mistake!" He slams a palm down on the hood of the Honda with a reverberating ping of metal. "You come here pretending like it's no big deal, like you should have been here all along. But he didn't want you. He didn't care about you. He never even spoke your name or anything—"

"That's not true—!"

"You came here after he died because you knew that. You knew he would have slammed the door in your face if you'd tried to mess up his life the way you've fucked up ours!"

Her fury ignites. "He wanted me! He asked my mom to marry him. She's the one who said no. She's the one who told him to get lost. I have a letter to prove it—"

"What letter? What fucking letter?"

"From my mom to your dad." She feels a rush of righteousness. "I found it at Grandma's house. He'd saved it—"

"You're a lying bitch—"

"Yeah, and what are you? If she'd said yes, you never would have existed! You would have been somebody else, somebody like Royce, somebody nice. Not some small town screw-up who steals from his own grandmother! Not some ass who won't go to school! You would be somebody who was good enough and smart enough to be his son!"

Jason's face contorts into an agonized mask. He whips away, racing through the parking lot and climbing into Shari's rusted pickup truck. The motor starts with a roar, and the tires slide on loose gravel as he tears out of the parking lot, heading west.

Behind Erica, the door to the Rambler opens and closes. She doesn't wait to see who it is, but takes refuge in her car, spinning out of the parking lot in a cloud of dust. Turning left, she heads toward the canyon.

Nothing is worth this—this heartache, this season in hell. Jason's right, she never should have come here. She twists the steering wheel as she navigates the dangerous curves of the canyon, the road before her veiled by the tears in her eyes. And—oh, God—Rain!

When she reaches the Phillips's ranch, she makes the left-hand turn across the highway without looking, earning an ominous honk from an oncoming semi. Jouncing down the rutted driveway, she brings the car to a halt in front of the trailer.

In her room—in Renee's room—she tears at the drawers of the chipboard bureau and the little girl vanity. She throws her clothes on the bed, then goes to the bathroom and swipes her cosmetics into her arms. Whatever won't fit in her suitcase, she will leave behind. It doesn't matter—she just wants out. In fact, she won't even drive home. She'll go as far as Jackson and leave the car at the airport and fly out of this mess. She'll be home in less than twenty-four hours, with Nat and Royce, with Mike and Jeannie, his bride-to-be.

Yet, as she stuffs clothes into her suitcase, her gaze falls on the quilt on the bed. The conch design shimmers in amber against the cobalt blue background. There is no way to take the quilt with her, no way to wedge its glorious folds into baggage. She sits on the bed, shedding more tears than she has cried since she first learned her mother was going to die.

Who is she? Erica Wiegel, Erica Brock, both of them, neither of them? What happens when there is no place on this earth where you can be, where you are loved, where you are happy?

"What are you doing?"

Dave stands in the doorway, his face pale and drawn.

Erica wipes a hand under her nose. "I'm going home. I've got to get out of here. I never should have come." Bitterly, she adds, "My mother was right. This place is too small."

"I'm sorry I didn't tell you," he says. "I'm sorry, I'm so—"

He crumples against the door jamb and sinks into a crouch. "It should have been me! I should be lying in that cemetery with a fucking broken neck!"

"No," Erica says automatically. "No, you can't think that way."

"Don't you think I've felt it? Every day, every minute. And you living here, thinking it's all right—"

"It is all right."

"Jesus," he breathes out. "I'd do anything so that Jason and Shari didn't have to go through the hell they've been through—"

"Dave, don't," she pleads. "You shouldn't think this way!"

"They thought, at the Rambler"—his words pinch from his throat, raw and tight—"they said I ought to shoot her. Even Shari's dad told me to do it. That's what they would have—what any man would have. Jesus Christ, why am I so stupid?"

"Why didn't you tell me?" Erica asks through fresh tears. "You should have told me—"

"You came here, and you moved in here, into this room, and I thought, it's like having Renee here, it's like having a daughter again. I wanted to be what he should have been—a real father—what I should be for Renee—"

"What happened that day? I have a right to know."

Dave swallows a couple of times, his Adam's apple bobbing painfully. "He called me early in the morning. Said Shiloh had pulled up lame. I'd hurt my foot at the mill a couple of week before and was still on crutches, so, hell, I couldn't ride. I said yes, but I told him not to do anything jackass with her." He weeps, a raw, choking sob. "I shouldn't have said that, I shouldn't have—"

"You didn't know—"

"He was coming across that field, he was riding Rain the way I'd ridden her a million times. And she just twists, she just twisted to one side, and he went down . . . By the time I got there, he was already gone. He was already dead—"

"Did he do something wrong? Did somebody who was watching jump out at her? She wouldn't have done it unless she'd been scared or something."

Dave sobs, terrible, ugly sounds that seem like strangling. "I took away Jason's dad. I took him away from you. Sometimes I think I oughta just do myself in, because I can't keep facing this every morning—"

Erica drops to her knees beside him. "Whatever happened with Rain, it wasn't your fault. There must have been something else, something up in that field. Maybe nobody even noticed it or remembered it in the . . . in everything that followed. Maybe nobody even saw it—she's so sensitive, maybe she sensed something that no one else did. Maybe he did something wrong—"

"You don't understand," he mourns. "He had everything. Everything! He married the prettiest girl in town, and he built that house"—he looks up wildly, sizing up the trailer—"and he had people coming to him begging him to take them out, and he was making a bundle from it, you better believe it. He had everything, and I don't have nothing—"

"You have this ranch. You have Rain."

"Quit saying that! You don't know what in the hell you're talking about—"

"I do, too!" Erica cries. "I've been riding her. We've been miles together. We've spent hours together."

His head comes up. Tears have scored a trail down his face, the wrinkles around his eyes and mouth becoming grimy canals. "You? What—?"

"I've been riding her almost every day." Suddenly, she feels ashamed that she never let Dave in on the secret. "I didn't think you'd mind. You didn't have time for her, and nobody else cares about her—"

"You could have broken your goddamned neck! Just like he did!"

"But I didn't," she says. "I didn't, because whatever happened in that field was a fluke, an act of fate—I don't know—call it whatever you want—"

He mops at his face. "He was your father. You should hate her. You should hate me. I should have been honest with you. I should have said, it was me, I killed him, on the day you came here—"

She takes his hands. "Come with me, out to the corral."

With effort, she helps him to stand. He's wobbly at first, but she leads him into the barn. She's afraid to let go, afraid he might slip away and go after the guns that are so prominently displayed in his bedroom. Side by side, they walk to the corral, Ratso trotting behind, thinking this is another truck ride or jaunt into the canyons. In the barn, Erica pulls the tack from the sawhorse and gathers up the bridle.

As she saddles Rain, though, the full weight of what has happened comes to her. What really happened in the field? What if it is only a matter of time before Rain throws another rider? But no, this is Rain, this is the horse that has carried her through the canyons, who follows her when she dismounts, who loves the treks as much as she does.

Dave stands with limbs locked, his arms useless at his sides. Her foot in the stirrup, Erica mounts the horse. "See?" she calls.

"Get down," he begs. "I can't be responsible—"

"No, it's all right—see?" Erica rides Rain around the corral once. "You did a good job training her. She moves so well—I'd never really ridden a horse before, but she takes direction so easily—"

She offers her hand to him. "Come with me. Please, Dave. Don't be afraid."

She kicks her foot out from the stirrup so that he can pull himself up behind her. He moves slowly, like an old man whose joints hurt, or one who doesn't quite understand what he is doing. It takes so long for him to heft himself up that Rain grows nervous. Erica murmurs encouragement, not entirely sure that she is addressing only the horse. Once Dave is on Rain's back, he wraps his arms around Erica's waist, too tight, as if he is trying to stave off disaster. When he is settled, Erica urges Rain out of the corral. Ratso runs along behind.

They ride into the Badlands, into the dust and glitter of the ancient volcano's leavings, into the song of the birds—the meadowlarks's liquid slide, the mourning dove's dropping sigh, the hawk's keening, and the twitter of finches or towhees or whatever else nests in the thick pockets of sage. There is not much wind today, and the sky burns a breathless turquoise. Overhead, a jet carves a white contrail in the sky. Thirty-thousand feet, and yet Erica can hear it in the stillness of the day.

Dave's arms still clinch around her waist, so tightly at times that she can barely breathe. Yet as they ride, she feels the world opening up to her. She cannot be unhappy when she is on Rain's back, when she is in these canyons, in this beautiful place that has brought her so much joy. She knows things out here, things that can't be named, but can be seen, heard, felt. And she knows that she will take Dave not to the first windmill or to Kissing Camels, but far into the canyons, so far that the past will disappear and the future will not matter.

She makes no effort at conversation during the long ride. Neither does Dave, although she can hear his jagged breathing. When they reach their destination, she says to him, "Slide off. I want to show you something."

He dismounts, and Erica climbs down after him. "Come with me." She takes his hand as they walk to Strong Woman's Cairn. She keeps the reins in her other hand.

"What's this?" he asks, stopping squarely in front of it.

"It's a cairn, a . . . I guess you'd say a remembrance of something or a tribute. I've been building these in the canyons where you and your dad don't usually go."

"What? When?"

"In the afternoons, when I come home from Mona's. I saddle Rain and ride."

He takes one of the arms of the barbed wire figure and pulls it straight out. The graceful curve that has always defined the woman disappears. Erica nearly protests, but stops herself in time.

Dave says, "I don't . . . why do you do this?"

"I love it here, Dave," she says. "I love the land, I love these canyons—everything. I can imagine so much when I'm out here—even him. I know it's crazy, but I can almost feel him here—"

Dave fiddles with the barbed wire. "Where'd you get the post?"

"There's a fence up there that has fallen down."

"My great-great grandfather probably put it up. This stuff's a hundred years old." He tests a flat, triangular barb against his thumb, then looks down the canyon, struggling again with tears. "You, well, everything you said, it makes sense to me. I love what you are. You're funny and you're smart. Just like him. God, if you leave, I won't have nothing again—"

"I don't want to leave," she says. "But I realize now that I had no right to come here and turn everyone's lives upside down. Shari, Jason, Grandma—when I was driving here, I never thought about what would happen to my dad's real family." She swallows, thinking of her mother's letter. "Now I know it was selfish."

To her surprise, Dave laughs. "He can't have family that's more real than you. You have his heart. I knew it the first time I saw you. Nobody would stand up and make everybody in town stop and take notice like you have. Only he had those kind of balls—"

Erica says nothing, too touched to speak.

"You riled us all up good," he says. "It ain't a bad thing."

He squints at Rain, and she realizes that this is the first time he has actually looked at the horse. She gathers her courage. "Ride Rain," she says. "Don't be afraid. She won't hurt you."

With one hand, he reaches out and touches the horse's nose. Rain tosses her head, then brings it back down to him.

Erica lets go of the reins.

His movements are, again, agonizingly cautious. One hand reaches for the reins, then stalls, while the other moves toward Rain's cheek and nose. Minutes pass as he stands, as if paralyzed. At last, he runs his hand down her neck, his fingers trailing through her mane, and over her shoulder. He murmurs tender words—"hey, hey, come on now"—as he would to a woman. Finally, he puts his foot into the stirrup and pulls himself up on Rain's back. Taking the reins in his left hand, he simply sits. Erica doesn't perceive a command, yet Rain starts to walk. They move up the canyon, slowly, oh, so slowly, and then Dave brings the horse to a halt and turns back to Erica. Holding out his hand, he says, "Coming with me?"

"Not this time."

He looks down the canyon, and Erica sees what has been missing in him. On Rain's back, his spine is straight, his chin lifted. His face is no longer pale and featureless, his eyes drained. It is almost as if the vivid colors of the Badlands have lapped up into his skin, bringing it life, depth, and warmth. "Well, watch out, then," he says.

He kicks his heels a couple of times and shouts a great, "Yee-haw!" Rain takes off, weaving around Strong Woman's Cairn. Ratso chases behind, yapping wildly, but gives up after a couple of hundred feet and pads back to Erica, panting heavily.

Erica buries her face in Ratso's fur. "It's all right," she says, although she is crying again. "It's okay."

Already, horse and rider have disappeared down the dusty canyon.

TWENTY-FIVE
THE EIGHTH CIRCLE OF HELL

Fuckers, they had done it. Tim Etherton and his merry band of miscreants. They flew into Jackson and hired a car to drive to Pindall. Oh, there, they were—in crisp, button-down shirts, so suave and boffo, from the great city of Portland—looking down their noses at the mill, at Pindall, at Ronald in his short-sleeved polo and Cascadia Northern windbreaker, at his men in their scuffed work boots and threadbare flannel shirts.

Ronald had tried to argue. Sawmill Days less than three weeks away. Family celebration, 4-H fair, class reunions. Happiest weekend of the year, last hurrah of summer.

To which that dick, Tim Etherton, had replied: "And after that comes Christmas. Would you like us to wait until then?"

At noon, they announced the closing of the Cascadia Northern Mill, Pindall, Wyoming Installation to middle management. Just before the shift change, the rest of them found out. Ronald was forced to stand beside Tim as the young man announced, "We are here for you. We want to make this as painless as possible."

The men's eyes had nailed Ronald. Betrayal, anguish, blame, hatred. He had been unable to breathe, his chest warped by his own disgust. Every inch of his body had tingled. His leg ached. For the rest of the day, as he had entertained questions, giving imprecise, corporate-dictated answers, he had felt his heart beating slower, draining of blood. He could not forget the words Elise had once spoken to him: *the corporate lies you've been told to spread.*

He leaves the mill as the sun sets. The parking lot is empty, except for the rental car and his BMW. The machinery is silent, the great saws, the massive planes, the miles of conveyor belts stilled. No one sits at the gates—Elise, Andy Shenk and the others are gone.

It already looks deserted.

When he pulls into the driveway of his house, a jacked-up red pickup truck barrels in behind him. The truck's doors fly open, and two beefy figures swing from the chassis.

Ronald girds for conflict, but it is Jerry Whistledorn and his son, Russ. Jerry takes off his ball cap. "Hey, Ronald."

"Jerry, Russ." Ronald shakes hands. "Are you doing okay?"

"Some of us were wondering if there isn't something you can do." Jerry wads the cap in his hands. With each word, his voice grows tighter. "Some way we can demand a public hearing or a meeting to review the situation. It's not fair, what's happened to us. Isn't there something that would make them open it up for discussion?"

"I think it's all been decided by the brass in Portland," Ronald says gently. "I'm sorry."

"You see," Jerry says, "I've been there thirty-two years, and my boy Jeff's been there almost five, and Russ here just started."

"I'm out, too, Jerry," Ronald commiserates. "They haven't made me an offer."

He tries again. "Isn't there anything you can do?"

"I'm afraid not. The guys you saw today have a whole lot more say-so than I do. I'm sorry."

"Okay," Jerry concedes. "Thanks."

He and Russ turn toward the truck. As Jerry veers toward the driver's side, Russ mumbles something, the last part of which is, "too busy balling that whore."

And Ronald finds himself across the lawn, Russ's shirt collar in his hands. He slams him up against the door of the truck. "What did you say?" he screams into Russ's face. "What did you call her, you stupid little—?"

He is no match for an eighteen-year-old who is built like a fireplug. Russ sweeps his arms up and shoves Ronald away.

Jerry hauls around the truck, planting himself between Ronald and Russ. "Don't touch him again, Dailey," he warns, one hand on Russ's chest to keep him from going after Ronald. "Don't you come near him."

"Get off my property," Ronald snarls.

"It's not your property, asshole!"

Jerry opens the truck door and shoves Russ inside, then hustles around to the driver's side. He starts the truck and jams it into reverse, leaving a smoking trail on the concrete driveway.

Panting, Ronald listens as Jerry's truck travels down the hill to—where else?—the Rambler. Above the burr of traffic, he can hear it: Words, bitter and angry, being unleashed in the bars, in the shabby plywood homes, in the trailer park north of town, on the grand, bankrupt ranches beyond Pindall where a hundred years of family heritage hangs on the income of an hourly wage earner. Tears and grief and desperation rising in a firestorm of blame toward the crest of the hill, toward him.

He goes into his house and stumbles to the bathroom. A glance in the mirror reveals an unhealthy pallor, a mesh of crow's feet around the eyes, lips red and meaty. Not him, it can't be him. So used up, so drained, so flattened. So old.

He splashes water on his face. His body feels lifeless, his tongue parched. Making his way to the kitchen, he fetches a bottle of Jack and a bottle of Crown Royal. Sitting on the couch, he switches on the television and pours his first glass. Cackling laughter interrupts him—no one laughs that much in this town—and he glances up at the mugging, cow faces of Laverne and Shirley. He presses the mute button and takes a swig from the glass. He drinks until his muscles no longer ache, until the traffic down on Main Street thins, until the light of the day fails and the television illuminates the room with a bluish haze.

Later—how much he does not know—Elise arrives. She lets herself in, breathing heavily, as if she has run all the way from the mill. It is dark, and from the feel of it, the night has settled into broken-hearted weariness. He has finished the Crown Royal and opened the Jack, and he has gone from sitting on the couch to sprawling on it, his back against a pile of throw pillows.

Without turning on any lights, Elise glides across the room and sits on the floor. Laying her head on her arms, she leans against the couch beside him. Instinctively, he strokes her hair.

"How long have you known about this?" she asks.

"A couple of months. It was pretty clear when Tim Etherton came in March. We cut back the fellers late in May."

"Why didn't you tell me?"

He has no answer. He has kept it in, like a cancer, like the terrible secret it was.

"So you could tell Andy Shenk?" he stabs. "So you could all ring your cowbells and celebrate your victory?"

"But it's not a victory. Cascadia Northern hasn't been stopped. It hasn't even been slowed down. It's simply destroyed a beautiful place on this earth and ruined lives, and it will go on doing that. It's not a victory for anyone. It's a tragedy."

"All logging is an assault against nature."

"Don't." She weeps openly, her face hidden in her hands.

He lets her cry, ignoring his urge to comfort her. Whose side is she on now? What loyalties is she claiming?

"Don't worry." He takes a drink, swirls the glass, and drinks again. "Save the Forests can just move on—although they might not find another patron as generous as you. And you can just take Mommy's money and hike yourself off to another mill. After all, one mill's just like the other, isn't it?"

"Why are you doing this to me? I had nothing to do with what's happened—"

"No, you didn't," he reacts. "But don't think that Shenk won't take this and run. He'll write to—I don't know—Sierra Club or someone and claim responsibility for closing the mill. He'll capitalize on the destruction of lives, of livelihoods, of this town. It's his great prize."

"What he does doesn't matter to us—"

"Oh, yes, it does." He leans forward, urgent and forceful. "All day long, I've been looking at each one of the guys and thinking, this one is smart enough to find work elsewhere, but what will that one do? He has the mental ability of a sixth grader. And what will become of this town when sixty families—almost half the population—are set adrift, with no income, with no possibilities? They will never have what they've had in the past. It will never be the same for them, no matter what. Somebody like Shenk would never see the human cost."

"That's what we're against," she sobs. "The exploitation of—"

"Don't start that," he snaps. "Don't you get it? We have lost everything. I have lost everything. I'm nearly forty-three years old, and I've given the past twenty years to Cascadia Northern, and I don't know what the fuck I'm going to do now."

"We can start over, we can leave this behind—"

"And go where?"

The answer is clear to him—to a world *without*. How will he survive a world without the mill, without his job, without the prestige that it carries? Without Cascadia Northern and the pride he has always taken in being an executive there? How will he be who he is supposed to be?

"I thought I'd made it," he says. "My father was just a hard-ass son of a bitch. Worked in the mill all his life, never anything but a sawyer. Came home at night and beat the shit out of my brother and me. One time, he shaved off two fingers. Used to call it his trophy—"

"Ronald, don't—"

"And so I promised myself"—he bangs his empty glass down on the coffee table—"I promised myself I wouldn't be like him. And I made it. I was management, I was on the fast track. But after what happened in Oregon—"

He reaches to pour, but she puts her hand on his, preventing him. He grinds his teeth, but pulls his hand back, away from the bottle.

"How long have you been drinking?" she asks.

"How long have I been home?"

She lifts the bottle of Jack from the table and goes to the kitchen. He hears the pour of liquid into the sink. "What are you doing?" he calls, struggling to rise. "Damn it, bring that back!"

She steps around the corner with the drained bottle and flicks on the foyer light. He cringes with the instincts of a nocturnal animal, but then he sees a white bandage covering the right side of her face near the temple. The collar and shoulder of her jean jacket is spattered with brownish stains.

"What happened to you?"

She crosses her arms over her breasts. "I don't know."

Ronald wobbles to his feet. "Come sit down." He encloses her with his arm, and she lets herself be led to the couch. "Why didn't you tell me you were hurt?"

"Would you have cared? You're so hostile—"

"Elise," he soothes.

She takes a trembling breath. "They all went speeding by, all of them so angry, some of them shouting or flipping the bird. We had no idea what was happening. Andy—"

Ronald winces, but she continues. "Andy thought that maybe there had been a pay cut or lay off and—you were right—he wanted everyone to be strident and celebrate."

Her body spasms, and Ronald draws her closer.

"One of the cars cut the corner so close that I thought he was going to hit me. And they threw something at me—"

"Assholes! What was it? How bad is it?"

"There's a cut by my eye, so close it almost damaged my eye—"

"Do you have any idea who did it?"

"It was a cant hook," she says. "That's what Liz said."

"That could have killed you. Who bandaged it?"

"I had stitches at the emergency room," she said. "Andy drove me to Riverton in the van. When we got back to Pindall, I asked him to bring me here, and when he asked why, I told him the truth, and he called me a hypocritical bitch—"

Her words falter into sobs, and Ronald cups her beautiful face in his hands. His whole body is shaking, and he is suddenly inarticulate, incoherent, overcome. Wildness rends his head—he wants to make love to her, he wants to kill whoever did this, he wants to tear Andy Shenk limb from limb, he wants to slap her for her bullheadedness, he wants to retch. He gathers her against him. Her tears soak his shirt.

"You knew they'd come out of there with vengeance in their hearts," she whispers. "Why didn't you tell me when you first knew?"

"I couldn't tell you before I told them," he says, the words perhaps the most honest he has ever spoken. "I'm one of them, Elise, like it or not. I'd go back to the mill in a minute, I'd go back, and I'd take it all on again, if they'd give me the chance. If Cascadia called me tomorrow and offered me a place somewhere else, I'd go. I'd be there before dawn the next day, because that's who I am. I'll never change."

She pulls away from him, and he knows his words have stung her as deeply as her wounds. As she walks toward the door, he struggles to heft himself from the couch.

Stumbling into the coffee table, he calls, "Elise! Come back!"

"You will always be lost," she wings from the foyer. "Until you find the courage to honor your heart."

The door slaps shut behind her.

He slumps back on the couch. Why can't he just give in to her? Why can't he just surrender and say, I love you, save me? Why can't he forget who she is, what she is, and just lay his head in her lap and weep? It would be so easy to let go. But he knows he can't. He can't because she possesses secrets he will never know, and she can spew New Age nonsense and make it seem so true, so tempting and sweet. She believes and he doesn't, she sees and he doesn't.

He throws his glass at the foyer light, which she did not turn off, and then vomits down his shirt and on the rug. "Shit," he says. Weaving to the bedroom, he passes out on the bed.

Late in the night, a shot ruptures the air.

"Elise!" Ronald calls.

He rolls from the bed, and smacks his shoulder on the edge of the nightstand. The knitted throw that he pulled over himself girdles him. He cowers on the floor, not moving, breathing as shallowly as he can. Outside, tires rip on gravel as a vehicle skids away. My God, what are they thinking? Surely, surely, they could not be bent on murder. He sinks down into the darkness and into unconsciousness.

When he wakes again, he sees the wolf's blue eyes—brilliant enough to singe, even in the bright light that accompanies them. What has happened to him now? Is he in the hospital again? But the wolf? The woods? He jerks up, out of a dream of dark shadows, drowning in the terror of that night in the forest, his leg shattered, his hands and feet and face numb. His forehead smacks against the edge of the nightstand.

Ken reaches out a hand. "Come on, you need to get up."

"It was you," Ronald croaks, wedged between nightstand and bed.

"What?"

"The night in the forest." How could he have been so stupid? All that time, he had feared wild animal attack, so much so that he didn't recognize help when it came. Christ, what is wrong with him?

Ken unravels him from the blanket. Lifted to the bed, Ronald looks warily around him. The shades have all been raised, and daylight floods his bedroom. A fresh breeze blows from an open window somewhere, but it does nothing for the swampy miasma that hangs over him. He stinks.

"It's time you came back to life," Ken says.

"What time is it?"

"Nearly noon."

Brodric comes from the master bath, his hands clasped in front of him in true monkish fashion. Ken says, "Brodric has the shower running for you. Why don't you wash up?"

Ronald stands unsteadily and, helped by both men, limps to the bathroom, which is already steamy and warm. Ken closes the door behind him, and Ronald strips—he is still dressed in his grubby, puked-on clothes from yesterday—and revels beneath the hot water. He lifts his face up, dousing himself until the heat seeps from the water.

As he dresses, the smells of toast and coffee waft from the living room. Ken fetches plates and silverware, while Brodric brings in food from the kitchen. Ronald notices that the two have straightened up the living room, so that all evidence of the previous night's debauchery has disappeared. No more booze, no vomit, no trash. He sits at the dining table. "I'm sorry," he says vaguely. "I'm not usually . . ."

Without comment, Ken allows Ronald's feeble words to fade. If anyone knows the truth, it is Ken and Brodric. At last, Ken offers, "We heard that the mill had closed."

"Yes, very suddenly."

"Perhaps a quick end is for the best." Ken takes a jar from Brodric. "We brought our homemade chokecherry jam and Brodric's applesauce."

Ronald looks over the fare—English muffins, tomatoes, sausage, and the promised jam and applesauce. His stomach heaves with hunger—he has not eaten since yesterday. He helps himself with unsteady hands.

Ken pours coffee. "There was some upset last night," he says. "The passenger's window of your car is broken."

"What?" He drops half an English muffin on the floor, chokecherry side down.

"It's been shot out, I believe. Didn't you hear it?"

Ronald jags to the kitchen window and looks out at the car. A few chunks of glass cling in the window, but there's no escaping the message. He begins to sweat as memory floods his swollen brain. The fight with Jerry and Russ, the echo of the shot. Jesus Christ, Elise.

"Do you know where Elise is?" he asks Ken.

"Elise?" Ken's forehead furrows. "No. Why do you ask?"

"She was hurt. They had done something to her—"

"Good God. This is terrible."

Then, worse, he remembers what he said to her, and at once he knows: they went after her because of him. Not because of Andy Shenk or Save the Forests or her own Gaea crap. It was plain, stupid revenge.

"I have to find her," he says. "I have to tell her—"

"Let us help you," Ken offers. "We'll go get her—"

"No," Ronald says. "No, thanks. I'll do it on my own."

Darnell's property looks deserted when he arrives. Only the wind in the trees greets him as he runs up to the gate. He shouts, "Hello! Elise! Elise!" When no one appears, he goes back to the BMW and slams his hand against the steering column, furiously honking the horn. As the sound echoes through the trees, the dogs rush the gate, snarling and yelping. "Get back!" he shouts. "Stupid dogs!"

A moment later, Darnell's jeep careens into sight.

Darnell spills from the jeep, decked out in Mekong Delta finery circa 1969. With a brutal command, he silences the dogs, which collapse at his feet in submission. He carries a pistol at his side.

"What do you want?" he calls. "How did you know where to find me?"

Ronald steps up to the fence, into point-blank range. He keeps his arms at his side, his stance defiant. "Cut the Rambo shit, Darnell. Where's Elise?"

Darnell remains frozen and mute. His bloodshot eyes skiff up and down, checking, Ronald suspects, for a weapon.

"Did she come home last night?" he asks. "Do you know if she's all right?"

One of the dogs slinks forward, its rump rising like a tent. Darnell moves his hand, and the dog cowers. "What happened to her?"

"The mill closed yesterday. Somebody threw a metal hook at her. It hit her near her eye. Her face is cut."

"Bastards! Sons of bitches!" Darnell's face flushes a virulent red. "They better not touch her, they better not do—"

"They already have. Do you know where she is?"

"She spends Friday nights in town," Darnell says. "With her lover. Name's Ronald."

Ronald bangs his hand into the fence. "I am Ronald!"

Darnell raises the pistol so that it points directly at Ronald's heart, and Ronald runs for the BMW. He starts it with a roar. Shifting the car into gear, he takes off down the bumpy trail that leads to the highway.

But when he reaches the intersection, he cannot bring himself to turn left, to go back to town. He cannot bear to see it again, he cannot bear to finish it. On Monday, he will have to report to the mill to inventory equipment and finalize accounts. He will be in thrall to Tim Etherton and the boys, who will cluck their tongues in false remorse. It's for the best, Cascadia was losing money every day on this place, now you can go back to Portland, get a real assignment. He'll have to grovel for a new position, and it will all be dragged out again—the accident in the forest, the hours of therapy, the demotion. And where will they send him? Some cowtown in Colorado or Montana, some boondock in Washington? Another place where he is sure to fail?

He puts his head down on the steering wheel, pressing the backs of his hands into his eyes. He and Elise will never be able to live in a world where Tim Etherton and Andy Shenk and Jerry Whistledorn and jackasses like that rule. They will always be on opposite sides, put there not by choice, but by expectation.

When he lifts his head, he sees it. Across the highway, at the very fringe of the forest, stands a wolf. It is silver-gray, its coat thick and bristly, its eyes brilliant blue. It looks directly at him—not at the car, not at something beyond or behind him, but into his eyes. "My God," Ronald breathes. "My God."

A monotone squawk jerks Ronald out of his trance. He glances up into the rearview mirror, into the radiator of Darnell's jeep. Darnell hits the horn again, bearing down on Ronald's car.

The wolf vanishes into the trees.

Ronald twists the steering wheel, turning right onto the highway. He searches the pines, but sees nothing. He crawls along, holding up the tourists traveling toward the Park and earning a shouted, "Step on it, asshole!" from the driver of an RV behind him. Speeding up, he drives until the smoke from the fires in the National Park swallows the road.

It grows darker, the smoke dowsing all light. He can't see the taillights of the cars ahead of him, and the lights of oncoming traffic are feeble ghosts. Nothing seems real in this false night. He no longer feels as if he has a purpose or heart or even corporeal being. He presses on, letting it all go.

By nightfall—the true darkness—he has left the state of Wyoming behind.

TWENTY-SIX
A PRAYER IN EMPTY SPACES

The first indication that Marguerite has of trouble comes on Friday evening when Kaylee Bingham corners her in the diaper aisle. Kaylee's two preschoolers hang on the grocery cart, while the toddler rides with the diaper bag. "Mrs. Brock." Kaylee waddles forward, carrying her pregnancy in front like a boulder. "Can I talk to you for a minute?"

Marguerite has heard the question a hundred times, but she doesn't expect it from Kaylee. Both the Bingham boys, Keith and Kaylee's husband Marv, graduated from high school into the mill. They're good Mormon boys who take care of their families.

She reassures Kaylee as much as she can. It's no surprise, really. Howard knew years ago that the timber stands were disappearing. No surprise at all, and not once has the Town Council seriously considered alternatives. Instead, they've spent years haggling over Vern Stacy's junkyard.

At home, she closes the curtains and unplugs the phone. It's cowardly, but she needs time to think. Everyone eats, and no one can do without. She serves herself dinner from a Crock Pot that has been simmering all day, then returns to the living room to quilt. It's a little after ten—an hour that is usually peaceful in Pindall—when she hears Dane and Amory launch into a fusillade of barking. At the door, she calls to shush them, but they ignore her, tails wagging, both German shepherd noses poking at something they have discovered in the front yard.

"What's going on?" Marguerite asks. "Come on, now, get away."

Someone is sitting on the ground, just beyond the front gate. "Good Lord!" Marguerite jimmies open the stubborn gate latch. "What's wrong?"

Elise hunches on the gravel of the street. She is a mess—crying and dirty and clinging to the fence as a lifesaver. Dane barks ferociously, wagging his tail happily, while Amory licks at her ears.

"I thought I was all right," Elise says. "I thought I could walk down to your store and call Darnell—"

"Come inside." Marguerite hoists the girl to her feet. She shuts the front door squarely in the dogs's faces. "Here." She eases Elise onto the couch. "I'll get you some water."

The girl shakes her head. "If I could just sit here a minute—"

With a jolt, Marguerite realizes that the brown spatters on Elise's denim jacket aren't some artsy-fartsy New York design, but dried blood. She pushes back Elise's hair and finds the square bandage next to her swollen, nearly-closed eye. "What happened to you?"

Elise tells her, while Marguerite holds her hands.

"This happened today?" she demands. "At the mill?"

Elise nods with a painful swallow.

"Why didn't Darnell pick you up?"

"I stay with Ronald on Fridays and Saturdays." She looks around her, moving her head more than necessary, off-kilter because of her swollen eye. "Oh, Marguerite, I wish I could have done a better job here. It's such a simple message. Such a life-giving concept. All I wanted to do was to convince them they didn't have to live this way—"

"Do you know who did this?"

The girl hiccups into her hands. "I didn't really know any of their names."

"Well, the vehicle then. Color, model, license?"

"Oh, it stings when I cry." She swallows back her sobs. "I don't know. For two years, they've driven by me every day after work, and nothing has ever happened. At least, nothing like this."

"Do you want me to call Macky?"

"Not now," she demurs. "I don't want to think about it now."

"What about Ronald?"

"I just . . . no, I just came from there."

Marguerite says nothing. She knows Ronald only from the Wickiup, but he puts her in mind of the Cheshire cat—not much substance behind the grin. It's too bad a girl as precious as Elise has fallen for him.

"Can I shower, please?" Elise asks. "I need to be somewhere safe for just a while."

"Will you be all right in the shower?"

"I'll be fine. I need to get warm—"

As Elise showers, Marguerite worries. She cannot believe anyone would do this. Did they truly think Elise had anything to do with Cascadia Northern's decision to close the mill? She counts off the kids she has known since they were in diapers—Dave Phillips and the Binghams and the Whistledorn boys and on and on. She quells the urge to drive down to the store and shut it down, holding the town hostage until someone confesses.

Elise drifts into the kitchen, draped in a bunchy velour robe that she's borrowed. She looks like a renaissance queen bundled into fourteen yards of velvet—with the exception of her ankles showing three inches below the hem, and her wrists dangling from the sleeves. Her right eye tilts up at the corner into a swollen purple knot.

"Do you want me to call Darnell?" Marguerite asks.

"I don't want him to worry. If he sees me like this—"

Marguerite understands. Were Darnell to see her wounded, he would be likely to drive his tank right into Pindall.

"You don't mind if I stay here tonight?" Elise asks.

"Not at all. But we'd better put some ice on that eye. It's starting to look like an eggplant."

Elise lets out a whimper of a laugh. Marguerite wraps the ice in a clean dishtowel and hands it to her. Opening a kitchen cupboard, she says, "I have Scotch or aspirin. Which would you like?"

"They gave me a prescription at the hospital." She squints up through her uninjured left eye. "It's made me so sleepy."

"Well, we can take care of that."

She leads Elise to the bedroom opposite the hall from Brad's old room and next door to her own. As she clicks on the overhead light, Elise gasps.

The Celebration Quilt spans the spare bed. Marguerite had forgotten she had made the bed with it, simply to see the finished product. This year's quilt is a blaze of color. Starting at the end of the bed, symmetrical black, blue and orange flames of rich, textured fabric weave upward nearly the full length of the quilt. The colors mottle, metamorphose and mix, until at the top, an elaborately worked sun crests over the flames in blood red brilliance.

Elise begins, "That is the most stunning . . ." Words fail her, and she faces Marguerite, her haggard face alight. "You've created resurrection." She ventures a hand toward it, then recoils, as if afraid to touch it. "Oh,

Marguerite, you can't simply auction this off for $500 or whatever it is you usually get. This is too beautiful."

"Unless a well-to-do rancher from Jackson or one of our own absentee celebrity landowners drops in on the day of the auction, it'll go for what the townspeople can scrape up. They've always been generous."

"Within their means," Elise protests. "And their means will be sadly diminished this year."

"Well, you can be my guest now and sleep under it—"

"Oh, no, what if my stitches bleed or—?"

"Nonsense," Marguerite says firmly. "It's washable—they've finally come up with washable satin."

Elise laughs, but she acts almost frightened by the quilt. At last, she allows Marguerite to tuck her in, like a child. Marguerite brushes back the girl's hair, turns off the light. When was the last time she tended to someone like that? When was the last time she touched someone so tenderly?

But, of course—it was Shari, during the terrible nights after Brad's death.

Marguerite retires to her own room, washes up, and sits on the bed. Elise's remark about resurrection has shaken her. When the design came to her, months before, she had thought only of the bright red against the dark colors, which proved to be hell on her eyes as she was sewing. But resurrection, rebirth, rejuvenation. The question remains: whose resurrection is it?

She lies down and turns out the lights, but sleep does not come. Instead, she remembers 1964, when Darnell Hillyard swung into Pindall. What a brouhaha there was about Darnell's property in the national forest. He wasn't a concessionaire, with a twenty-five year lease, or a homesteader, with lifetime rights. He owned the land, paid in full. The deed was recorded at the county clerk's office, which prompted one town busybody—Marguerite has always suspected Robyn Ruggles—to write her congressman and demand why public land was being sold. He wrote back that no land had been sold, no money had changed hands, and there was no one by the name of Darnell Hillyard currently in the tax base.

Marguerite had met Darnell in the Produce section of the Wickiup, when she caught him standing directly behind her.

"Is it black or is it brown?" he asked. "Sometimes it shines dark as night. But right now, in the light, it's as brown as a chocolate bar."

She had no idea what he was talking about. All she saw were lettuce heads. But when she looked up, it was into blue eyes and a weathered face and a wild head of sandy-red curls, and she realized he had been standing there, watching her, for quite some time. Long enough to make her knees weak when he reached out and flipped a lock of her dark hair with his fingers.

"So pretty," he said.

Darnell took her up to his property and showed her around with a swagger that she knew was earned. He taught her to shoot, holding a handgun before him and blasting a full round into a target. When they retrieved it, the bull's eye had a single hole in the center, where all six bullets had entered. She could never achieve that, but Brad could after a few lessons. Darnell gave her a ride in his tank, jouncing over the rough ground, leaving chewed-up pine saplings in its wake.

"You're causing more vibrations than a hot geyser rumbling around in this thing," Marguerite had said.

"Maybe it'll heat up the Cold War," he said.

And they had laughed, while the tank blundered blindly forward.

But it was the barn that made Marguerite love Darnell. He took her to it on a fine spring day, when the sky was burning blue and the spongy white clouds looked as if they'd been put there for decoration. No longer used, the barn was on property near Cody. It was a monolith—a great two-story edifice of weather-darkened wood, which had turned every color from rich cocoa to gold to burnished black, like an eagle's feathers. A massive reddish tarpaper roof arched over the loft.

He took her through the dairy first. In the central part of the barn, a concrete floor lay beneath two long rows of milking stanchions, mirror images of one another, each capable of servicing a herd. Foot-long troughs in the floor about four feet behind the stanchions were for carrying away waste. A Dutch door led to the outside, into a corral, at the south end. At the north end of the barn, light shone through a narrow opening in the concrete barrel of the silo.

"The amazing thing about this," Darnell told her. "It was built in the thirties. They had to have used man-powered—or at the very least, gasoline-engine-powered—mixers for the concrete. There must be tons of concrete in these floors and the walls. It's an engineering marvel. All this concrete, all this symmetry and shaping. I haven't found a flaw yet. And that perfectly circular silo. Where did they get the forms?"

They peered into the silo through the gap, looking down at the floor spattered by bird droppings, and up at the blue sky beyond the high lip. Their voices echoed against the gray-white walls, and Marguerite breathed in a cool, rain-washed smell. Darnell climbed a few feet up the steel rungs that led to the very crest of the concrete giant. "See how they've embedded the rungs into the walls? Whoever built this knew what they were doing."

"Where's the family now?"

"Gone. Lost. I don't know." He beckoned her to follow him up the ladder. "Come with me."

He had saved the best for last. Swinging off the ladder, he led her into the lengthy loft, which was more than twenty feet high and equally wide. Empty now except for a few brownish bales of hay, the place was lit by four gridded windows at one end, two at the very apex of the eastern wall.

"Look at this," Darnell said in wonder. "Look at the framing. From the ridgepole down, it's round. Not segmented, like most barns." He circled his hands, carving an arch in the air. "Which means that those four by fours had to be warped to take on that shape, like in shipbuilding. Those are seven-foot beams. And each was perfectly vaulted, because the roof fits without exception."

The arc was beautiful, the beams curving from apex to floor. Roof and walls melded into one graceful continuum, with invisible joints. The roof was opaque from the tarpaper sheeting, yet on the wall opposite the silo, around the windows, sunlight pierced the horizontal spaces between the slatted boards, giving the impression of heaven unfolding right outside.

"It's a poor man's cathedral," Darnell said, walking toward the sun-sprayed wall. "Where God can find the lowly, and the lowly can find God."

Lying in the straw, they had talked as the sun traced a trajectory through the day, the light in the barn changing as it wended west. The darkest moment came at noon when the sun was far from the windows at the eastern end or the silo at the west. It was then that they made sweet, tender love.

But Darnell was recalled into service the following year, and Marguerite was left alone again.

It's nearly morning when she hears Elise rise from bed and tiptoe across the floor, stopping after every telltale creak. Dane and Amory snap to alertness where they sleep at the foot of the bed, but Marguerite hushes their growling. The girl goes outside, through the front door.

After a few minutes, Marguerite follows. She finds Elise on the porch, staring up toward Ronald's. The Celebration Quilt is draped over her shoulders like a cape. The sun rises on her left shoulder, while the flames angle across her back.

Elise half-turns to look at her. "I thought I heard something," she says groggily.

"It doesn't look like anything is amiss out here." Marguerite hears only the rush of tires of a late-traveling vehicle on the gravel streets. "But you'd better come in. They've already tried to do you in once today."

Elise laughs uncertainly. "I should go up there. I shouldn't have left him in the first place."

"Do you want me to drive you?"

"I don't know. I'm . . . confused."

Marguerite sits down beside her. "Probably the painkiller."

"I don't know what I'll do."

"I don't think anyone of us does."

"Ronald suggested that I leave," she says bitterly. "Am I just a fool, Marguerite?"

"No more than anyone else who is in love, I'd say."

"But you'd think—" She stops. "I thought . . . I thought it was something more, something real."

Marguerite reaches for her hand.

"Want to share the quilt with me?" Elise asks.

"Sure." Marguerite pulls it over her shoulders, the heavy loft already warmed by Elise's body. It's been years, she realizes, since she has slept beneath one of her own creations. She has kept the storebought bedspread that she and Howard used on her own bed. One day, she will make a quilt for herself.

Elise tilts her head and fixes Marguerite with her good eye. "Do you believe in God?"

"That's quite a question for this hour of the morning." Marguerite laughs, but offers, "My husband and son both died before I reached retirement age. That sort of thing takes the fear of God right out of you. In fact, God better be good and ready when we meet face-to-face. I've got some questions."

"Sometimes I wish I did," Elise says. "I envy those who can believe. But Darnell once told me that it's those who doubt the existence of God who are the deepest spiritualists. Those who blindly accept what they're told are the most spiritually deprived."

"That sounds like something he'd say." Marguerite says. "Or something he would have said at one time."

"He always tells me how good you've been to him."

That's it? Marguerite wonders. Nothing about the hours they had spent together, just talking and thinking? Nothing about the nights they loved each other? Lord, Darnell had read Nietzsche and Kant and Lacan and Jung—names that weren't heard within two hundred miles of Pindall. Pain cuts through her heart. Surely he remembers, she thinks. Surely he hasn't forgotten.

"He was quite the swain in his younger days," she says.

"Swain! I love that word." Elise half-laughs. "I don't see how I can leave him."

"I'm not going anywhere. I'll see to him."

"But he's leaving us."

Marguerite looks out into the night. How differently she should have done it—with Mateo, Darnell, maybe even Howard. She would have plunged in her hands again and again, filling them with as much love and life and joy as she could.

She lets the conversation die. Wrapped in the Resurrection Quilt, she and Elise watch the sun rise.

The next afternoon, Marguerite is called to the Wickiup for an emergency. She leaves Elise still sleeping in the guest room and goes to the store, arriving at the scene after most of her shell-shocked employees, who rubberneck at Darnell's steaming jeep rammed into the delivery doors. Darnell himself hangs half-in, half-out of the vehicle like a mangled G.I. Joe doll.

"Good Lord, Darnell," Marguerite says. "Were you trying to break down the defenses?"

"My brakes didn't work."

"Everybody all right here?" she calls to the assembled gawkers. No one answers. "Jesse, help him get that thing parked. Then you and Rick see if you can get the bay door open."

The men push the jeep backward into a parking spot, Darnell steering erratically and not at all helpfully. Green antifreeze snakes into the sewage drain.

"Mrs. Brock, um, Mrs. Brock." It's Melissa, the Saturday manager. "We have a Sysco delivery at four."

Marguerite utters a swear word that elicits a nervous giggle from Melissa. "Well, then, better hurry." She cuts the mirth short. "Keep me informed. Come on inside, Darnell."

In her office, she digs in her drawer for the bottle of Macallen. Darnell looks as if he could use something with a kick to it, and she could use a glass as well. Once he is seated, he launches into a shambling tirade about trying to find Elise.

"She's at my place, Darnell," Marguerite says. "She's all right."

"I've been looking for her for hours! Some man told me she was hurt—"

"She had to have stitches, and she has a whale of a black eye. Someone nailed her with a metal hook off a peavey yesterday."

"Bastards! I'm going to—"

"Sit down." Marguerite fills the glasses, trying to ignore the brutal clang of hammers on steel. God forbid they do more damage to the door. "Sooner or later, somebody will start yapping about it. We'll find out who did it."

"Then I'll—"

"I'll see it's taken care of."

He sizes her up, as he would an adversary. "All right," he agrees meekly. "Someone told me the mill closed."

"They're right. It did."

"She won't have anything to protest now." Darnell picks up his glass, but doesn't drink, only turning it in his hand. "Do you think she'll stay?"

"You should talk to her about it," Marguerite says gently. "I do think it's best if she keeps out of sight for a few days."

"I could be called away at any time, and she'd be alone."

Marguerite winces. Darnell hasn't left his woodsy nest for years. "Don't you think they could find somebody else to do your spy work? You and I, we're not young. Let the kids do the dirty work."

"Maybe," he says, embracing the idea. "Yeah, maybe."

Marguerite downs her Scotch. "Let's go get her."

Elise is lying on the couch in the living room of Marguerite's house when they arrive, her hands folded beneath her cheeks, the dogs snoozing on the rug beside her. The Celebration Quilt covers her legs and shoulders.

Darnell kneels beside the couch and pushes back her hair. "Are you all right?"

Elise's eyes drift open. "Darnell," she says groggily. "Can we go home?"

She sits up, gently smoothing back the quilt. She wears the denim shirt and stretch pants that Marguerite left out for her this morning, which drape shapelessly around her tall, lithe body.

"Your father's jeep has had a mishap," Marguerite says. "I'll take you home."

"We need to go by Ronald's first," Elise reminds her.

"He was looking for you," Darnell says.

"What?" Elise turns her good eye on him. "When?"

"Earlier . . . today."

"Then, we need to go up there."

"He won't be there," Darnell says. "He went toward the Park."

"The Park? Why would he go there?"

Darnell doesn't answer.

True enough, when Marguerite pulls up in front of Ronald's house, the BMW is gone from the driveway. After a few minutes of knocking at the door, Elise resigns herself, saying, "I'm ready to go."

It's a quiet drive through Pindall. Darnell sits stiffly in the back seat of Marguerite's Buick, while Elise occupies the front seat. It's starting to get dark, the sun slipping over the high ridges. The light is violent red, filtered by smoke into vivid beauty. Once they reach the national forest, Marguerite clicks on her headlights to see through the dim, smoke-washed twilight.

"I wonder if the Park will ever be the same," she says. "After all these fires."

Neither Darnell nor Elise answers.

Once they reach the compound, Marguerite opens the gates with the code that Darnell entrusted to her years ago. The dogs flood toward the car, but he rolls down his window and silences them. Marguerite bypasses Darnell's house and drives directly to Elise's cabin, where she helps the girl up the steps to the door.

"I'll come and look in on you in an hour or so," Marguerite says. "Is that all right?"

Elise wobbles a little. "Thank you so much, Marguerite. I don't know what I would have done without you."

Marguerite kisses the girl on the forehead. Thank God Darnell has such a decent daughter to look after him. She goes back to the car and drives back down the road to Darnell's house.

His house is an old farmhouse that was added to as the original family grew until it became a labyrinth. The floors throughout the house don't always align, so that toe-snagging ridges and swells in the wood planks loom beneath the lintels. Marguerite gingerly picks her way into the living room in half-light from the shuttered windows. Darnell snaps on a lamp, suffusing the room with yellow. A black-surfaced, walnut desk obscures the end wall, and towering bookshelves range along the adjoining wall. A Colonial recliner and sofa done in brown plaid pose against the opposite wall, with an olive-colored rug stretching between.

"I'm always glad to be home," Darnell says. "I don't like what's become of town. Too many people. Too much traffic."

He stretches out in the recliner, releasing the footrest with a thump. Marguerite sits on the plaid couch. A mangy brown bull terrier—not from the pack outside—moseys from the bedroom, grunts effusively, and collapses into snores at her feet.

"The world's filling up, Darnell," Marguerite says. "And those of us who like it empty are just going to be pushed aside. Nowadays, everyone who shops at the Wickiup seems to come from somewhere else."

"You and I came from somewhere else."

"Yes, but the statute of limitations on us has expired."

He chuckles, and Marguerite studies a series of photographs above her head. Fantastic places—the Forbidden City, the Taj Mahal, the Sphinx—emerge in clear black and white. "Where all have you lived?" she asks.

"Washington, Bangkok, Saigon," he says, ticking away on his fingers while eyeing the bookshelves. "London, Tel Aviv, Moscow, Budapest, Munich, Berlin, Belfast, Havana . . . " He stumbles, struggling to recall another.

"Havana?" Marguerite wonders if he is recounting the setting of each novel.

"There were some ugly places. So crowded, so noisy. Infested hotels and dirty women. Jungle and heat and . . ." His voice dwindles, lost in memory.

"How old are you?" Marguerite asks.

"Sixty-six."

"You're just a pup. I'm staring seventy in the face."

"Look a different direction."

Marguerite laughs, but quickly sobers. "What should I do, Darnell? Everybody in town needs to eat, but I can't just give it away. And food stamps are never enough, I've seen that plenty of times. I'm too old for this."

"We could go away," Darnell says, his gaze returning to the bookshelf. "They'd send me anywhere I asked them to. Anywhere we wanted to go . . ."

Marguerite waits for the flight of fancy to play itself out. "I'm pretty well settled here," she says gently. "So are you."

He nods a couple of times, his face grave, as if he understands her meaning. "Want some coffee?" he asks.

She follows him to the kitchen, which has a red and white checkerboard linoleum floor. Darnell fumbles with a Mr. Coffee on the counter, plugging it in, then unplugging it, then peering into its well. "I've used this before," he says. "But I don't remember how."

"Let me."

"Okay." Darnell excuses himself and wanders towards the back of the house. Marguerite plugs in the appliance, fills the basket with fresh coffee, and dumps water into the well. As the machine groans into action, she feels her braid lifted from her left shoulder. Darnell has returned, his hair slicked back and his face damp from a good splash. He fingers the braid, then pulls the band from the end and laboriously starts to loosen the plait.

"I want to see your hair," he says. "It was so pretty back then."

"That was a few gray hairs ago."

He combs the wavy strands with his fingers, gathering and releasing it in the same manner that she caresses fine fabrics. Her old heart does an uneven rub-dub at his touch, and her temperature goes up a good ten degrees. Oh, she's no girl, but that doesn't seem to matter to her pelvis, which has started to ache with something besides rheumatism, or her mouth, which has suddenly gone dry, or her breasts, which make a sturdy attempt to lift.

"It's still pretty. You're still beautiful."

Darnell arranges all her hair over her shoulders so that it trails down her back, then brings it forward so that it lies over her collarbone and breasts, framing her face. She catches a glimpse of herself in the window above the sink. Her hair floats with static electricity generated by Darnell's fingers, and the hard edges of her face are softer, gentler. For one moment, she believes that she is still young.

Coffee spits into the pot, and the machine huffs and puffs clouds of steam. After one especially ebullient burp, Darnell becomes distracted by Mr. Coffee and forgets what he's doing.

Marguerite reaches up and turns his face back toward her, her turquoise-laden fingers cupping his cheeks. "Come back to me, Darnell," she wishes.

At an emergency session of the Pindall Town Council on Monday night, the Council dickers over the fate of Sawmill Days. Given the sudden closing of the mill, it seems wrong to hold a celebration, but there are so many reservations already made and paid for, so many preparations underway, and the non-negotiable contract for the carnival already signed. Added to that, the fires in the Park are starting to receive national attention, reducing tourist traffic to a trickle.

In the end, the Council agrees that Sawmill Days will go on, but there will be no Derby and no 5K race. The air in Pindall has become so smoke-filled that physical activity is no longer recommended. Even the firework show on Friday night is canceled because of the thick haze.

It tires Marguerite to think about all of this. She's so worn out that when the phone rings on Tuesday morning, she answers it only after it rings too many times for the call to be another complaining citizen or broke customer. It's Shari, asking if they can meet.

"Sure, if you're game at this hour of the morning," Marguerite says. "But let's go somewhere."

"Fine with me," Shari agrees. "Think we can drive far enough to get out of the smoke?"

Before Shari arrives, though, there's a knock on the front door. Erica comes in without waiting for Marguerite to answer. She wears a short-sleeved maroon smock with the embroidered scroll over the heart that reads "Mona's Kitchen" and a broad smile.

"What are you doing here?" Marguerite asks in surprise.

"Kelly, Dawn and I were all scheduled this morning, and there are barely any guests at the motel," she says. "We were just going to squabble over tables, so I volunteered to leave. Are you on your way to the store?"

"Not yet. Shari and I are going out this morning."

"Oh." Erica's face falls. "Maybe I should go—"

"Why don't you stay?" Marguerite asks. "I want to show both of you something."

It's another quiet drive, with Shari in the passenger's seat and Erica, silent and still, in the back. Marguerite makes no attempt at conversation, but clicks on the radio to the local station, where there's talk that the Park Service may shut the gates—a move that would signal economic disaster for this area.

They don't quite escape the smoke when they reach the ranch in Cody, where the barn still stands, but it's only a whiff on the wind. Marguerite leads them into the immense loft. Shari stops dead-center, while Erica snaps photos with her camera.

"This is a piece of architecture, isn't it?" Shari pivots on the heels of her cowboy boots, taking in the arched ceiling, the light-porous eastern wall, bright in the morning sun, and the pine planks under her feet. "Who owns this place?" When Marguerite doesn't answer, she says sharply, "You do, don't you? I didn't know you were buying ranch land."

"Just this parcel. I bought it years ago when it came up for sale."

"How many acres?"

"Not enough to worry with. A few hundred, give or take."

"That's enough to rent for grazing."

"I don't need the money," Marguerite sits on an old three-legged milking stool that she found downstairs in the dairy. "Not yet, anyway."

"What do you think is going to happen?" Shari asks. "Almost everyone I know is out of work. Robyn's even threatening to close down the bar because she's afraid she won't get paid."

"Merrilee is saying the same thing," Erica volunteers. "She thinks she'll have to cut our hours."

"I suppose we'll figure out a way to get by," Marguerite says, feeling the familiar weariness in her soul. "Fill it up, Shari."

"What?"

"A place like this should have the acoustics of a great hall. Sing something."

"I haven't done any real singing since . . ."

"That's all right. I don't mind."

Shari seeks out the boxy patch of sunlight on the floor. She stands there so long, her back to Marguerite, that Marguerite begins to wonder if she is crying or praying. At last, Shari starts to sing "Amazing Grace," that all-purpose standard. Her voice falters at first, tentative and throaty, as if too much grief has collected there. By the second verse, though, the dulcet tones that are Shari's trademark emerge, sweet and pure and unforced.

Erica comes to sit at her grandmother's feet, and Marguerite lays her hand on the girl's shoulder. Shari's voice rises upward, moving through the barn with absolute clarity, so that by the time she has delivered four verses of the hymn, the final word floats back to Marguerite as a perfect, crystalline chime. Darnell was right. This barn is as sacred and elemental as any cathedral. She should bring him here, to see what he remembers, if he remembers.

When the last notes die away, Erica breathes, "That was beautiful."

"Where did you get so much talent?" Marguerite asks.

Shari turns around, wiping her eyes. "It's sort of a family mystery," she says. "The Johnsons aren't known for their musicality. They tend to be scientists." She glances at Erica, then addresses Marguerite. "I guess I should tell you, I'm going to Bozeman. At the end of this month."

The words strike at Marguerite. How did she not know this before now? But of course, she did. It has been coming since the day Brad died. There is nothing in Pindall for a pretty, young widow. Marguerite knows.

"Well, good for you," she says. "If I had a hot-blooded, long-haired, young scientist chasing after me, I'd take him up on his offer, too."

Shari laughs. "So you aren't upset?"

"Good Lord, do you think I'd be hurt if you had the chance to be happy again?" She stops to consider. "I'd be more upset if you didn't go. A man like Alex Jr. shouldn't inspire indifference."

"He shouldn't and he doesn't," Shari agrees. "But it isn't just that. I want to learn to sing."

"As far as I'm concerned, you already know how to sing."

"No, I mean classical music. Art songs, choral pieces, that kind of thing." She pauses. "I talked with someone from the music department last week, when Lex and I went up there to look at the house. Dr. Brenner—that was his name—asked me to sing for him. I was scared to death—as I said, I really haven't sung for two years—but I managed it. He said it's too late for me to be admitted to the program for the coming fall, but I could audit a couple of classes for free while I work on getting admitted as an actual student. I should be able to start in January."

"What did you sing?" Marguerite asks.

"'Oh, Danny Boy.'" Shari laughs as if she's embarrassed. "It was the only thing I could think of at the moment."

"That's a perfectly good song, as far as I'm concerned."

"It is," Shari admits. "But I would have liked to have wowed him with a song in French or Italian or something."

"Too rich for me," Marguerite says. "So you're going to college. How will you afford it?"

Shari's eyes flicker toward Erica. "I'll use what I have left of the money Brad had saved for operating expenses before he . . . That will keep me going for a while. And there have to be bars in Bozeman where I can work."

"Let me know when it gets to that point," Marguerite says.

"You'll love it," Erica offers. "All the thinking and reading and, well, just the learning. Will you major in music?"

"Music education, I think. I have to earn a living."

"What does Lex say about this?" Marguerite asks.

"He's like a kid at Christmas." Shari's eyes hone in on her. "What about you? What are you going to do?"

"I have business to finish in Pindall."

"The store? It's going to be so hard—"

"And other things. Don't worry about me."

"I'm staying," Erica volunteers. "I'll be here."

Shari eyes her, as if she is debating a reply, but Erica beats her to it. "I'm so sorry about the other day," she says. "I didn't know about . . . the horse. No one told me."

"What's this?" Marguerite asks.

Erica turns to her. "Last summer, when I started building my cairns, I started riding one of Dave's horses to get there—"

"I suppose you'd have to."

"I didn't tell him," Erica confesses. "I don't know why, exactly, but as it turns out, the horse was . . ."

Her voice trails away, and Shari fills in: "It was Rain."

Rain, the beautiful palomino. Marguerite feels something moving in her heart; it is grief, of course, renewed, but there's something else, too.

Lord, the vagaries of love—how they strip us of any defenses, of all our determination and our powers of decision.

When she speaks, her words are weak and thin. "You were riding that horse?"

"Yes," Erica says. "I was so lonely, I was so . . . angry after that day in the field at Sawmill Days. I had tried to be what everyone wanted me to be—or what I thought they'd want—and to make peace, but I just kept being shut out—"

No one responds, and it seems as if the three of them are caught, each behind her own berm of sorrow.

Shari breaks the silence. "You know," she says. "Your coming here has made me rethink just about everything I've ever done in my life. Everything. And I've realized that he was always more like your mother than he was like me. She went off to college and raised you just like she wanted, and she never looked back. We got married and settled down and tried to do it exactly like everybody else does it, but Brad never could. He never could give up what he had already promised to give up."

Marguerite hears the pain in her voice, sees the terrible cost of this admission in her face. Erica sits perfectly still, her gaze on Shari.

Shari continues, "I don't know—maybe it was my fault. I didn't give him the choice that your mom gave him. It didn't even occur to me to do anything but get married when I found out about Jason. I thought I had exactly what I wanted, then, and I expected him to feel the same way. He still could have walked away, I guess, but here—in Pindall—it would have made for a heck of a scandal."

"From what I've heard, he didn't want to walk away from you," Erica replies. "And, well, I've done exactly the same thing. Everything I thought about my mom was . . . well, now I'd call her a little selfish. She kept me from knowing my dad and from knowing Grandma. Don't get me wrong—I love her and I miss her so much—but . . . I don't think I agree with what she did anymore. I really wish I'd had what Jason has."

It's a raw, heartfelt declaration. Marguerite takes Erica's hand, which trembles as if the girl is crying. We have so little time, and so much is left to chance.

"You'd think with all the trying we do, we'd figure it out," Shari says.

"Are you in love with Lex?" Marguerite asks.

She laughs. "I don't quite know yet."

"Well, you'd better figure that one out. If you love him, let him know."

In response, Shari says, "I love you."

Erica echoes her. "I do, too."

The words bring tears to Marguerite's eyes. She has not cried in years, not even at Brad's death—someone had to take charge—and it hurts so badly to want to that she does not know if even her enormous willpower can prevent it. She aims for a diversion, patting Erica's hand, and saying to Shari, "Sing me another song."

Shari begins to hum, then drifts into a lilting "There'll Be Peace in the Valley."

Leave it to Shari to know exactly which song to sing and how to sing it.

TWENTY-SEVEN
RECKONING

Jason is smoking in the parking lot of the Wickiup when Lex rides by on a Harley. It's not one of those mean mothers, no *Easy Rider*, but it puts out a respectable chop all the same. Jason grounds out the cigarette, ducks his head inside the store, and calls: "I'll be back in a few minutes." If anyone hears, they don't respond.

He hustles down the street toward Vern's garage. From inside one of the bays, a testosterone-rousing blast splits the air. When Jason arrives, he finds Lex gleefully revving the engine.

"Man, where'd you get that?" Jason asks.

"Pretty cool, huh?" Lex looks as goofy as a kid, with his broad grin. "Vern came across it in a trade down in Lander. Guy traded this for a little Honda Civic Vern had on the lot."

"You have to be kidding. What a dope."

They fiddle around, Lex pointing out the features and Jason delighting in just touching it—the leather, the chrome, the handlebars. Lex revs it again, and its thunder assaults the rafters and swirls out the door.

"Are you taking this to Bozeman?" Jason shouts.

"It's Vern's, not mine."

Itching to straddle it, Jason minces around. "Would he sell it? Can you ask him?"

Lex laughs. "Whoa, Jason, your mother—"

"Mom can't stop me. I'm eighteen. I have my own money. Grandma just promoted me to Assistant Manager."

"Congratulations. That must feel pretty good."

"Yeah," he agrees, but his patience dissolves. "Where's Vern? Is he here?"

Lex straightens up, his head cocked as if deciding whether to fight or resign. After a long moment, he says, "He's probably in his office. Come on."

One hour and a quick driving lesson later, Jason roars out of the garage on the Harley. He storms the parking lot of the Wickiup just as his grandmother is loading sacks of groceries into her Buick. "What is this?" she asks coolly.

He climbs off the bike. "Vern gave me a good deal on it. He set up payments with me."

She leans against the open door of the car. "A good deal for you or for him? Watch out, Jason. Vern Stacy is one shifty son of a—"

He laughs and runs his hand over the leather seat. "Lex was there," he says. "He did most of the talking."

"And it's all on paper?"

He pats his chest pocket, where all the documents are stuffed in a wad. "Lex cosigned the loan."

"Did he now?" His grandmother lifts an eyebrow. "I wouldn't think a college professor would make that sort of loot. I wouldn't think an Assistant Manager would, either."

"I can't keep borrowing Mom's pickup forever."

"You'd better think about what you'll do this winter, unless Vern sold you a snowplow, too. Did you read the fine print?"

"Well, no, but Lex said it was standard."

"Next time, read the fine print. You'd be surprised what you're agreeing to." She gives the Harley the once-over. "It's a good-looking bike."

Her reaction delights him. Who would have thought she'd give her blessing? She looks as if she always knew he would ride a Harley Davidson into the Wickiup parking lot at the end of his fifteen-minute break one Wednesday afternoon in July, and she's really rather proud that he did. And all of a sudden, he realizes that it wasn't just his father's—and his own—instinct to thumb his nose at others and live a rangy, mixed-up life, but his grandmother's. Even though she's spent years making sure every dimwit in this town has something for dinner, she's never been one of them. Alienation is a family habit.

"Want to go for a ride?" he asks merrily.

"Do you know what you're doing? Do you have a license?"

"No."

"Ask me again when you've accomplished both those things." She shuts the car door. "Does your mother know?"

"Not yet."

She merely raises her eyebrows, indicating that he is a goner, but he knows that if his grandmother approves, his mother will follow suit, especially since Lex assisted in the deal. Luck is on his side this time.

"Where are you going?" he asks.

"Darnell's."

Elise. Jason's heart bounds—as if it wasn't racing fast enough after the teetering careen from Vern's garage to the Wickiup. He heard about her injuries at the mill, but he has not seen her, he has not spoken with her, he has not breathed in her scent in so long. "Can I go?" he asks. "I'll ride along behind you. My shift's almost over, anyway."

She agrees, and Jason shoots out of the parking lot on the tail of her Buick. They ease through town, but once they are beyond the city limits, his grandmother picks up a pleasant amount of speed, and Jason rides behind her past the Morning Glory Motel and the cemetery gates and the turn-off into his own home.

He can feel the power of the bike beneath him. It glides, it flows, it hums, even though his riding leaves something to be desired. The handlebars tug at his shoulder sockets, and a couple of times his heart snags as he leans too far. Yet the sound wells up on either side of him, cocooning him in a heady, joyous vibration.

They come to the national forest, where smoke shrouds the trees. His grandmother signals for about half a mile before she turns onto a meager, grassy strip. Jason follows her, bumping the bike through ruts, striving to stay upright. She doesn't make it easy for him, braking often and swerving around a broken tree limb across the track. He jams the brakes of the Harley too hard and wobbles behind her until she stops at a chain link fence.

"Park it here," she calls to him. "Come get in the car."

He settles the bike and crawls into the Buick. She looks at him critically. "Well, you made it this far without killing yourself."

"It's fun, Grandma. You have to try it."

She punches a code in the lockbox that opens the gates. As she rolls through, dogs run at the tires of the car, and Jason understands why he could not bring the motorcycle into the compound. He would have been torn to shreds. "Jesus, they're nuts!" he says.

She speaks some gibberish out the open window, and the dogs rush into the trees, seeking new prey. She drives toward a white clapboard farmhouse. "Grab the four sacks off the back seat," she instructs Jason.

She knocks at the door, then goes inside without waiting for a reply. "Darnell!" she calls. They round a corner into the living room, and Darnell Hillyard leaps from his recliner in front of the television set, his hands twitching nervously at his side. "I didn't hear you come in," he says.

Jason spies a pistol on the coffee table. Jesus Christ, what is his grandmother thinking, just walking in unannounced? Darnell could just as easily shoot her as wipe his ass.

"This is my grandson, Jason," she says, and Jason shifts grocery bags so that he can hold out his hand for Darnell to shake. "Jason, this is Darnell Hillyard."

Darnell looks as if he's entirely constructed of dryer lint, with his woolly, graying head and his unkempt beard and eyebrows. He wears a nubbly flannel shirt, which may have been plaid a century or two ago, and black pants.

He ponders Jason's hand, but doesn't offer his own. "Are you with the CIA?" he asks.

"Sir, no, sir," Jason barks, his rejected hand shooting to his forehead in a salute. "I'm with the Wickiup, sir."

Darnell stares. With an irritated humph, Jason's grandmother tells him to take the groceries to the kitchen. He dawdles as he unpacks the sacks, craning his neck to peer through the kitchen window at the junk collected on the storage porch. Surely there's a nuke or two out there. Or a body. JFK's cloned brain probably dozes beneath a four-foot-high stack of egg cartons, entrusted by LBJ to Darnell, who forgot where he put it.

When he returns to the living room, after snooping as much as he can, Darnell is paddling through some moldy war story that is as dull as the black-and-white films they show in history class. Jason shifts from one foot to the other, trying telepathically to summon Elise from the dark recesses of the house—where does she sleep in this wandering fortress?—and wondering when the war will be won and Darnell will finally shut up. At last, his grandmother interrupts, sliding the keys across the coffee table. "Take the car and drive up to Elise's cabin," she says. "I've got a couple of sacks for her on the floor."

Without even asking where Elise's cabin—or the attack dogs—might be, Jason bolts out of the house.

He finds Elise without much trouble. A jumble of cabins appears deep in the smoke-cloaked trees, one of which sports hummingbird feeders and a drapery of little square flags with Chinese writing on them. As Jason bounds up the steps, he hears the dogs baying and snarling from somewhere nearby. If Elise doesn't answer the door within seconds, he'll be dog meat.

She opens the door. Overjoyed, he hustles inside.

"I thought they were going to get me," he exhales.

"Oh, the dogs?" she asks. "Don't worry about them. I'm so glad to see you."

He starts to protest, but he's shocked by her appearance. It's so much worse than he had imagined. The right side of her face is a mottled purplish green, and a sizeable bump swells on her temple just beyond her eye. Her eyelid droops downward, as if pulled by tape. He stumbles into, "God, you look terrible. I mean, are you okay? How bad does it hurt?"

"It isn't too painful. Anyway, I try not to give it any power over my thoughts. Would you like some tea?"

"As long as it's not green."

"I'll let you choose." She peers into the bags he brought. "Oh, your grandmother sent muffins. Would you set those out for me?"

She busies herself in the kitchen, asking about his doings and his mother. He puts the muffins on the coffee table, then wanders around the one-room cabin, taking in one of Grandma's quilts on the bed, and the writing desk, and the books on the shelves. He spies the book by Aaron Malcolm, Elise's ex-husband, and flips to the back jacket, hoping that the professor is some dumb-looking weenie. But the guy has linebacker shoulders and perfectly straight teeth—and he's the one she married without seeing him beforehand. Jason stuffs the book back on the shelf.

"It's been so long since we've talked." Elise sweeps across the room, cups of steaming tea in her hands. She makes a second trip to the kitchen for honey. "Tell me what's happened in your life."

It's difficult to look at her without staring at the misshapen eye. As he tells her about graduation and working at the Wickiup, his anger grows. What if that cut leaves a scar? What if the eye never opens up fully again? Those sons-of-bitches who did this to her deserve to hang.

She laughs when he tells her about the Harley. "My first husband, Raj, had a Vespa. We rode it all over Berkeley. It was so much fun."

Jason hopes a Vespa isn't bigger than a Harley, and that Rog isn't the beefcake that Aaron Malcolm is. "Do you want to see it?" he asks.

He drives the Buick back to Darnell's, where he pounds on the door. No one answers. "Grandma, I'm taking Elise for a ride!" he shouts, then looks toward the car and shrugs.

Elise steps out of the car. "Leave the keys in the car. She'll know you've left if your motorcycle's gone."

"I just hope he hasn't chopped her up in pieces and put her in the freezer," Jason grumbles as he joins Elise to walk toward the gates, the dogs at their heels, as docile as poodles.

"That's unkind, Jason."

"But he's such a weirdo. You need to be careful. He keeps a pistol on his coffee table! He could blow away anybody who walks into the room. You or Grandma or—"

"Is that your bike?"

She operates the gates, and they exit the compound. Jason shows her the Harley, stroking it as if it were a treasured pet, then says, "Hop on." He's less steady with Elise's added weight behind him, and leaving Darnell's property via the grassy track is none too pleasant. Yet when he comes to the junction of the highway, Elise speaks in his ear, "Take me somewhere wonderful."

He panics, unable to think of anywhere to go. Disney Land—that pristine acreage—isn't accessible except by horse, and the Park is burning. Besides, it's after six, and darkness will fall in less than three hours. He spins out onto the highway, heading toward Pindall, and turns off on the logging road leading to his own house. His mother should have left for work hours ago.

He parks in the barnyard and fights off the ecstatic dogs, who circle and sniff and jump up against his legs. Nick and Dutch both anoint the Harley by peeing on the front tire. Katie bounces and licks and bounces and licks. "This is where I live," Jason says, as he pushes Katie away.

"It's beautiful."

They wend their way through the three jumbly dogs into the house. Recently his mother has undertaken a spring-cleaning that has turned into Armageddon. Boxes of Christmas ornaments pile in the armchair, and on the floor are yellowed stacks of the *Pindall High Pioneer*, the high school newspaper, each emblazoned with a grainy black-and-white photograph of his mother in a striped turtleneck and chunky hairdo above the caption, "Shari Johnson, Editor-in-Chief." His mom has hauled things from the house to the steel barn, and from the steel barn to the horse barn, and from the horse barn to the trash barrels, which smoke night and day. She's even wondered aloud whether Old Adam, Jason's aging gelding, will withstand one more winter.

"My mom's been kind of strange lately," Jason apologizes. "She's going to Bozeman with Lex."

"Lex?" Elise brightens. "I like him. And you don't mind?"

He shrugs. Even if he did object to Lex, he's not about to badmouth a guy who just arranged for him to own a Harley. "I don't think she likes being alone," he says. "She's not like us—I mean, my dad and grandma and me. She likes to be needed, and to do things for people, and take care of them. She'd probably die if she didn't have someone to do stuff for."

"That's beautiful, Jason. You have such a deep soul. Such a kind, understanding nature." She pushes junk aside until she can sit on the couch. "I really enjoyed that night when Lex and your mother and Ronald and I visited at his house. Do you remember?"

He recalls how much he hated Ronald then, a hatred that has evaporated. It seems so pointless now, such a complete waste of time. A son in Portland, and the big coward is hiding out here. "How is Ronald?" he asks.

"I don't know," Elise says stiffly. "I haven't seen him since Friday."

Jason realizes he has ruined the mood. Elise picks at a tray of fishing flies, rubbing them between thumb and index finger and leaving him at a loss. They just drank tea at her cabin, so coffee would be overkill. So would cookies, even if there's anything other than stale Oreos in the jar. Maybe he should show her around, and they might end up in his bedroom, where she'll say, I've always dreamed of being here with you, and . . .

"Do you want to go see Ronald?" The words simply drop out of his mouth without his brain's consent.

She glances up at him. "You wouldn't mind?"

Oh, crap, now he's done it.

Jason spins into town with Elise's arms tight around his waist. He takes great pains to drive safely and steadily, so that word doesn't reach his mother that he is a danger to himself or anyone else in Pindall. Ronald's Beemer isn't in the driveway. When Jason plants his feet on the concrete, broken glass crunches beneath his shoes. "What the hell?" he mumbles, but Elise has already vanished inside the house. He follows.

It's eerie in the house, with half the curtains drawn and the other half left starkly open, as if Ronald could not decide whether it was night or day. The main room smells of puke shrouded by air freshener. Jason fidgets near the fireplace as Elise wanders back to the bedroom. The neck of a bottle peeks out from under the couch. Jason crouches on all fours to retrieve it. It's Crown Royal. Unfortunately, it's empty.

He slips down the hallway to find Elise. She sits on Ronald's unmade bed, looking aimlessly around the room.

"What's going on?" Jason asks.

"I don't know." Elise frets with the plush bronze and black comforter that lists off the matching sheets and heaps on the floor. Elise and Ronald do it in this bed, Jason thinks, and suddenly wants to chop the whole tasteful ensemble to ribbons.

"Hello?"

The voice echoes down the hallway. Before either Elise or Jason can respond, the silver-haired monk enters, followed by his scraggly partner. Elise jumps to her feet. "Ken!" She kisses his cheek. "Brodric. How nice to see you both. What's happened to Ronald?"

"He hasn't been home since Saturday."

The monk named Ken speaks. Hypocrite, Jason snarls.

Ken tells Elise about discovering Ronald and about the broken window of the BMW. Jason keeps a sharp eye on the one called Brodric, wondering when he'll start yapping, but Brodric simply notes the empty whiskey bottle that Jason holds in his hand before he gives him a cold, hard stare. Elise explains that she hasn't seen Ronald since the night before Marguerite took her home.

Ken asks Elise about her eye. "You didn't see or hear anything that could reveal who did it?"

"No. Some of them yelled, but they'd done that before."

"I know who did it," Jason blurts, certainty blooming in his chest.

All eyes turn to him. "Who?" Elise asks.

"My friends Terry and Russ." Ken glances in alarm at Elise, and Jason quickly adds, "I mean, they used to be my friends before they became complete assholes." Brodric winces at the language, but Jason presses on. "They're really stupid, but they're mean, too."

Elise touches her wounded eye. "They're friends of yours?"

"They used to be," Jason corrects her. "I haven't seen them since high school." He speaks as if high school ended years ago, not six weeks ago.

"Do you think they could have shot Ronald's car?" Ken asks.

"I don't know." Jason could shit care less about Ronald's car. He wishes he had a cigarette. Ken annoys him. The old fart obviously believes him to be guilty by association. "Could be. They may have wanted to get back at both Ronald and Elise, since they were . . ."

"We are lovers, Jason," Elise supplies.

"Well, yeah." Jason hedges, then dives into it. "I mean, all day, he'd be trying to get the men to work harder, and then he'd come home to you, who wanted them to quit working. They must have thought that pretty underhanded."

"Why do men always have to politicize sex?" Elise explodes. "Why can't they realize it is a natural function, from deep within, without political implication? Just because he believed one thing, and I believed another, it makes us enemies?"

The last sentiment seems to be a question that no one dares address. Ken clears his throat; Brodric's glum, dumb expression remains unvaried; and Jason refrains from saying that, when he's having sex, he can't remember if he's Republican or Democrat.

"We'll let the two of you sort this out," Ken offers. "But if you need any help . . ."

Elise nods, and Ken and Brodric start to retreat down the hallway of Ronald's house.

"Hey!" Jason calls, and Ken turns. "Why don't you guys talk down at the store?" he demands. "I mean, it's bullshit trying to figure out what you want. It's rude."

Ken merely smiles and disappears, Brodric in his wake. With a snort, Jason sits on the bed beside Elise. "I'm sorry about Terry and Russ," he soothes. "They're just stupid jerks." He reaches over and pushes back her hair, uncovering the beautiful, unblemished side of her face. "I'm sorry about Ronald. You know, he wasn't so bad after all. Just really fucked up."

She laughs weakly.

Jason lies down and opens his arms to her. She moves into the circle of his embrace. He gently kisses the top of her head and strokes her hair. She settles against him, so warm and so unbelievably sexy. His jeans tighten down about two sizes, and every millimeter of his skin burns.

What do people think they're doing? Ronald's ditched her, and Darnell, rather than being the fearsome warrior, is stuck in 1942 or something, and Ken and Brodric are just dickheads. Why doesn't anybody stand up for her?

"Don't be sad," he says. "I love you."

She kisses his jaw. "You are so courageous. So honest and authentic. You have always lived by your own heart."

He pulls her closer to him.

He knows that this is probably the only time in his life that he will be in a bed with her. He knows that this is the one and only time that he could make love to her as a man—he isn't the boy who took her on the ride through Disney Land. Instead, he says, "I'll be back. There's something I need to do."

She opens her eyes, and says vaguely, "I'll wait here a while longer—"

Jason climbs from the bed and covers her with the fancy comforter, then leans over to kiss her cheek. Outside, he straddles the Harley. Starting it up, he rips away into the darkness.

It's not hard to find Terry and Russ. He spots Terry's white Dodge Colt as it circles the Morning Glory, on the prowl for tourist girls, and pulls out onto the highway, heading back to town for another cruise along Main Street. Jason follows warily, checking often for Macky Bain. Right as Terry pulls into the Rambler, Jason swerves dangerously close to him and speeds away. Terry follows, gunning the Colt. Once car and motorcycle have swung around the corner that leads into the canyon, Jason hogs the center of the road so that Terry can't pass him or come up beside him. An oncoming vehicle could take him out in a second. Still, Jason accelerates.

When the entrance to the sawmill appears, he whips in, sliding onto Sawmill Road. Directly in front of the locked gates to the mill, beneath the sign that reads WELCOME TO CASCADIA NORTHERN MILLS PINDALL WYO INSTALLATION, he kills the engine and waits for Terry to catch up.

Without shutting down either the motor or the lights, Terry bursts from the car. Russ rolls from the passenger's side. Blinded by the headlights, Jason can only see two faceless hulks.

"Whaddaya think you're doin', asshole?" Terry roars, then sneers, "Hey, it's Jason. Hey there, bag boy. What's it like being a grocery boy?"

"It's better than being out of work."

"That your bike?" Russ asks. "You can't buy a Harley by baggin' groceries. Your old granny get it for you?"

Jason folds his arms over his chest, afraid that Terry can see the furious pound of his heart. "You guys think you're so cool. Trying to run over a woman who's just standing there, minding her own business. Throwing a whatever the fuck it was at her—"

"What the fuck you talking about?" Terry demands.

"Elise!" Jason's anger breaks loose, bubbling up from some steaming cauldron in the pit of his belly. "Do you know what you did to her? There's this huge cut right next to—"

"Why's it matter to you? She's a fucking bitch—"

"Don't you say that about her! She's—"

All of a sudden, his body explodes. He can't see, he can't hear, he can't move or talk or breathe, but he can feel the ground solid and cold beneath him. Russ is on top of him, punching him. His face is being disassembled—jaw whacked off, eye socket jabbed. Each time he takes a breath, it's pounded right back out of him.

"Lousy fuckhead!" Russ shouts. "You know what she does? She sits there all day long with her stupid signs and then she goes and fucks him! She fucks that stupid Dailey! That's what your fuckin' girlfriend does!"

Terry hammers the ground with a tire iron, and Jason cowers, covering his head with his arms. Russ springs up and kicks, his boot connecting with Jason's ribs. A terrible pain in his gut lacerates him, and he chokes on something that tastes of iron and salt.

Terry aims the tire iron at the Harley, metal smashing into chrome and leather. "Don't!" Jason pleads, as the bike tips. Suddenly, hands yank him up and force him to move. He tries to get his feet under him, but they flop in the dirt.

"You better not tell anybody!" Terry screams at him. "You better shut up or this is just the beginning!"

Terry gives him a shove that topples him over the embankment into the drainage ditch. Jason lands on his stomach, his chest in the water from the culvert, his hands and face mired in mud. He vomits an ugly grayish pile onto the earth.

He curls in on himself, shivering in the chilly water. He gasps, trying to will air to enter into lungs that feel crushed. There's blood—he knows there's blood, how could there not be?

His eyes close, and in the darkness, he finds his father. He stands in the entryway of their house, newly arrived from some adventure. Jason's mom runs into his arms and does what she always does, each time his dad comes home. She tips back his black cowboy hat, so that the brim no longer juts over his eyes, and gives him a long, slow, deliberate kiss. Jason scurries toward his dad and hugs his legs, and once his dad has finished kissing his mom, he lifts him. And Jason does what he always does—he grabs for the brim of the cowboy hat and tries to steal it from his dad's head. But his dad is too quick for him, and holds him away, so that the hat is just beyond arm's reach. Finally, after several wriggling attempts, Jason comes close enough so that he can snatch the hat and plop it onto his own head. Then his dad hugs him against his shoulders, and his mother laughs.

The vision fades, and Jason sobs. He loves so many people—his dad, his mom, his grandma, Elise—and all he wants to do is tell them. He tries to gather them in his head, to call them to him, but a welcome, painless blackness takes him in its arms and shushes him.

"Come on, get up."

He hears the voice, feels the hands on his shoulders. Jesus—Terry and Russ, back for another round. He tries to wrench out of their grasp, but he can't move. Almost immediately, he pukes again, drool spilling onto the cold earth beneath his cheeks.

"Can you talk?" the voice asks. "Can you sit up?"

"Shit," he says. Everything hurts—his ribs, his face, his stomach and thighs. His mouth feels as if it is stuffed with a gym sock, and his eyes are pasted shut. "Leave me alone—"

"Come on, you have to get up."

The hands are jabbing at him, trying to lift him. When they come in contact with his ribcage, he lets out a shout and sits up.

"You have to get out of this water," the voice says.

"Okay," he says. "Help me stand up."

The hands do that, then draw his arm over their shoulders and walk him up the bank. He leans heavily—if he doesn't, he'll fall. As they scramble up the bank to the road, he shields his eyes from the glare of headlights.

"Lean against the car. Just rest a minute and catch your breath."

He pants, trying to coerce air into his lungs, but it feels as if they've been flattened, like burst balloons. At the same time, pain rips through his side, causing him to bend double.

"Steady now," the voice says.

And he recognizes it at last—it is the voice of the nightmare of the past eighteen months. Before him stands Erica. The car that is supporting him is her Honda.

"I'm okay," he says, even though his insides twist again.

"Get in the car," she says. "I'll take you home."

"I can't leave my bike."

"You can't ride it either."

"Yeah, I can. I'm all right."

"It looks like you've already had one accident tonight."

"That's not what happened." He limps toward the dented Harley and, in a burst of stubbornness, hauls it upright. Grabbing onto the handlebars, he manages to throw one leg over the seat, despite pain that ricochets up and down his back. "See? I'm fine."

"I'll follow you," she says. "Let's go to Grandma's."

"I need to go to Ronald's."

"Where's that?"

"Just . . . I don't need you."

To his surprise, she laughs. "I just picked you up out of a ditch. You need me."

He doesn't have the strength to argue. Starting the Harley, he manages to make it to Ronald's, with his teeth clenched and his breath shallow and painful. He parks the Harley in the glass-strewn driveway and slides off in a gummy pool. Erica parks her car on the street and shuts off the headlights. Together they walk to the porch, but at the door, he vomits again—how can he have anything left in his stomach?—and sags against the side of the house, his bones inching down onto the ground.

"Open the door," he says to Erica.

"Should I knock first?"

"No, he's . . . just open it."

Once again, Erica hauls him up and walks him into the house. It's dark inside, except for a single overhead light in the kitchen. "Elise?" Jason calls. "Hello? Are you here?"

"This is a nice house." Erica circles the great room, running a hand along the enormous rock fireplace in the corner of the room and pausing to look out the sliding glass door. "It doesn't look as if Grandma is home anyway," she remarks.

Jason collapses onto the couch, his left elbow pressed against his ribs. His body spasms as if his veins are frozen and locked.

"Look." Erica comes over to the coffee table. "There's a note."

She hands it to him, but he can't make his eyes focus on the flowing script. "Read it for me."

"'Jason, Ken and Brodric took me home. Thank you for everything. Elise.'" She lays the note on the coffee table. "Who are all these people?"

"Thanks for everything." He tries to snort in derision, but it comes out as a pathetic grunt. Thanks for getting the shit beaten out of him, for messing up his bike, for acting like a stupid ass once again. It was probably that damned old monk who talked her into going. He probably told her that Jason would bring back Terry and Russ to finish the job on her.

Erica is talking again. "—cleaned up, unless you want to call the police first."

"I'm not calling the cops."

"Well, then." Coming over to him, she jimmies him to his feet. "Alley oop."

In the guest bathroom, Jason catches a glimpse of himself in the mirror above the sink. His face is a mess. Bloody nose, bloody lip, his eye swelling and purplish. "Jesus," he breathes.

Erica picks up a silver-gray washcloth that looks as if has never been used. "Sit on the toilet," she instructs, and he does, acting like a little kid who has just scraped his knee. Soaking the cloth in the sink, she starts to dab at his face. The cloth stains to the color of rust, and she rinses it in the sink. He lets his chin drop toward his chest, and the rankness of puke and blood and sweat rises up from him.

"I stink," he says.

"Yeah, you do," she agrees, dabbing at his face again. "I doubt if what's-his-name would mind if you used his shower." She turns off the water in the sink and pushes back the curtain on the bathtub. With a quick twist, she turns on the water.

"I don't have any clothes," Jason protests.

"What's-his-name should have something you can wear."

"Yeah, like I'd wear anything of his."

She laughs. "What's wrong with his clothes?"

An answer demands too much energy, so Jason simply asks, "Why are you doing this?"

"Doing what?"

"Why did you stop at the mill?" He looks up at her. "Why are you helping me?"

"I saw the motorcycle. I didn't know it was you."

"Would you have left me if you'd known?"

"I wouldn't have left anyone." She dries her hands on a towel. "Back in Ohio, I was always patching up Royce."

"Was he in a lot of trouble?"

"A little bit, but most of it was because he played rugby."

"What's that?"

"Like football, but nastier." She eyes the steam coming from the shower. "Water's hot. I'll be outside if you need me."

She closes the door, and Jason fumbles around, trying to undress. His belt may as well be some kind of Chinese puzzle, and his fingers stick to the buttons of his shirt. When he finally slides the fabric from his shoulders, he finds a perfect imprint of a waffled boot sole outlining his left rib. Just the sight of it makes his stomach turn again.

But the hot water of the shower soothes him. The kinks in his neck and shoulders relax some, and the pain in his ribs ebbs. The shower comes stocked with Irish Spring soap and Pert shampoo, and he washes himself again and again, trying to rub out the stench of fear and ruin in his nostrils. When he's done, he opens the door of the bathroom and squints through the steam down the hallway before slipping across the hall into the master bedroom, where Ronald's clothes hang like dead men in the closet.

He emerges dressed in a polo shirt and a pair of jeans that are too short and too square for him. In the living room, the fireplace glows and

Chicago plays on the stereo. A stack of records balances on the turntable, ready to drop once Peter Cetera is finished. Jason hears Erica rooting around in the kitchen, but he's cold again, the warmth of the shower water already seeping away. Sitting on the couch, he tries to inhale the heat of the fire, but it doesn't seem to help. A minute later, Erica arrives, carrying two glasses and a bottle of Jack Daniels.

"There's not much to eat in there," she says. "But there's plenty of booze."

"That's Ronald for you."

She pours the Jack into the glasses. "Want some?"

He shakes his head, feeling another heave of nausea. Erica lifts a glass in a mock toast and then downs the whiskey without a flinch.

"Where'd you learn to do that?" he asks.

"From Grandma." She sets the empty glass on the table. "She drinks Macallen. Didn't you know that?" She doesn't wait for a reply, but forges ahead. "Who's Elise?"

He doesn't answer right away. "The woman at the mill."

"Oh, right." She swallows the Jack in the glass she had offered to him. "I've thought about stopping and talking to her on my way home from work, but I didn't know how Dave would feel about it. So who's this Ronald character?"

"He's the manager at the mill."

"Oh, the one you kidnapped. I can't imagine you guys are friends."

Her bluntness annoys him, and he shifts to alleviate the pain in his left side. "He and Elise are . . . well, lovers. That's what she calls it, anyway."

Erica laughs. "No kidding. A regular Peyton Place, as Grandma likes to say."

He shivers again, the cold driving into his bones. How does she know so much about Grandma? What has he missed out on? He crosses his arms and grips his elbows, wishing he had borrowed a sweatshirt or something from Ronald's drawers.

"Do you want to go lie down in the bedroom?" Erica asks.

"No." He doesn't want to sully where he and Elise were holding one another, where he might have made all his dreams come true, if he hadn't been such an idiot. "But there are blankets on the bed in there."

Erica disappears down the hallway, and he leans back and closes his eyes. He wants to sleep, to forget. He tries to squelch the niggling voice in the back of his head that is trying to push its way into an expression of gratitude toward Erica, but the Eagles have come on now, singing "Take It Easy." He lets his thoughts flow into the music until Erica spreads the down comforter over him. She drops a pillow on the couch cushion beside him. Gratefully, he inches down onto it.

"So why were you here with Elise?" She sits in the recliner. The footrest shoots out as she leans back, and Jason sees she has taken off her boots. "What were the two of you doing while Mr. Day at Old Faithful was gone?"

He tries to think of an out, but his mind is pulpy and loose. So he starts to talk, telling Erica about the days he ditched school to sit with Elise at the mill, about the ride to Disney Land, and the day in the Park with Ronald, and what's happened since. As he speaks, his words sound brittle, drained, as if he's telling a story that happened a hundred years ago or that happened to someone else. Yet when he's done, something lifts from his chest, from his aching ribs, from his sore shoulders. He feels relieved, almost peaceful.

"So does she love you the way you love her?" Erica asks.

"No, she . . . no. I couldn't hope for that."

"I don't see why not. So who are the guys who did that to her and beat you up?"

"Russ and Terry. Their dads work at the mill. Jerry, Russ's dad, is the Head Sawyer. That makes him pretty important around here. Or it did."

"Oh, I've met him," Erica says casually. "He's a jerk."

"He was one of Dad's best friends," Jason snaps.

"Yeah, and his son was one of your friends until tonight." She rocks back and forth in the recliner. "So what were you planning to do to them? I mean, for one thing, it was already two against one."

"I don't know," he says truthfully. "I just wanted to do what I could . . . for her."

"So you went off half-cocked? That's just asking for trouble."

Her voice sounds so much like Grandma's that he closes his eyes. When he opens them again, Erica no longer sits in the chair, but is fidgeting around the room, studying the painting of a wolf above the fireplace, and the hoity-toity art prints on the walls, and the books on the massive bookshelf. Jason realizes with a start how unafraid she is. She's never needed to fear, he thinks bitterly, she's always gotten exactly what she wants.

"You can leave, if you want," he says. "You don't need to stay."

"I know." She pulls a thriller by Nelson DeMille from the shelf. "What do you want me to tell Grandma and your mom about tonight?"

"What do you mean?"

"Royce used to get in plenty of scrapes, and Nat and I would figure out what to tell Mom and Mike."

"You'd lie to them for me?"

"We never called it lying." She flips through the book, avoiding his gaze. "Anyway, it's what sisters do for brothers."

"I don't know," he says. "They'll know anyway. That's the way it works around here."

"Not always." She tucks the book under her arm and walks to the sliding glass door. "Nobody knew about my mom and your dad."

Jason doesn't want to think about it, he doesn't want to have to go back to that place where she is always in his thoughts. But it's too late now. She has forced him to go back. "Did you really find letters from her?" he asks.

"Yeah, I found four of them. They're at Dave's, but I'll show them to you."

His stomach twists into the ball of pain that it has been in for the past year and a half. He hears her accusation again: *You wouldn't exist, and if you did, you'd be someone good enough and smart enough to be his son.*

"I found them in Grandma's crawlspace, like I told you," she says. "He offered to marry her, but she turned him down. She didn't want to live in Wyoming, and she told him she'd go crazy if she stayed." She presses her palm against the sliding glass door, then watches as the steamy imprint disappears. "So you see, it really could have gone either way."

Jason closes his eyes. She has always been there. She didn't simply show up. She was always there, before his father married his mother. Before he was born. She has always had the better claim, no matter how much he wants to deny it. And his father knew it all along, carried it with him to the grave . . . oh, Jesus, it hurts to think about it.

"What did Grandma say about them?" he asks.

"I didn't tell her. I never really intended to tell anyone. It slipped out that day that you—"

"Don't tell my mom," he interrupts. "It would kill her."

"There's something else I need to tell you. The reason I mentioned Rain that day at the Rambler . . . well, I've been riding her around Dave's ranch."

Jason's stomach rocks. "Why?"

"I love her." Erica turns away from the sliding door. "When I first came here, well, it was such a mess"—Jason hears the accusation in her voice—"I was so upset and lonely, and I needed a friend—"

He feels sick again, stricken by the sense that nothing can stop the slow slide of everything he is into oblivion. It seems like the perfect end to his life—battered to bits and finished off by Erica. But now she is talking about building things in the canyons, and her words catch at his imagination. He closes his eyes and listens as she describes towers of rock and wood and bone—things that he wishes he could touch just now, just to feel the comfort of their earthly weight.

"Why do you do that?" he asks. "I mean, all that junk is just going to wash away or fall over or something."

"I don't know. I started doing it, and it felt . . . like I'd discovered how to live in his world, how to be a part of it. Our dad's world, that is." She pauses, as the Eagles croon "Desperado," then says, "That's all I ever wanted, Jason. To be a part of his life."

"Me, too," Jason says, but the words sound weak and tear-filled.

"I'm sorry I said that to you, that day at the Rambler."

"It's okay. It doesn't matter."

"But it does. I shouldn't have been so cruel. I'm not really like that."

"That's okay," he says again. "I shouldn't have said what I said, either. I was just pissed."

Once he says it, he knows it's true. It's hard to hate, he realizes. It takes so much out of you, makes you so tired of yourself.

"You don't care about my riding Rain?" she asks.

"I don't know." He isn't sure this is the truth, but he doesn't have the energy to figure it out. "It's your life, I guess."

"Do you want me to take you home?"

"I don't think I can move."

"Then we should probably let somebody know where we are. Who do you want me to call?"

"My mom, I guess, but don't tell her what happened. She doesn't even know about the Harley."

"Oh, man, you've got some 'splainin to do," Erica says. "Is she home?"

"She's at the bar."

"So is Dave, undoubtedly. I'll call."

She goes to the kitchen, and he hears her dial the phone, but he doesn't listen to the words. She'll say what needs to be said; she'll do what needs to be done. He can trust her—after all, his life has already been in her hands. She comes back into the living room.

"So, give a yell if you need anything," she says.

"Yeah," he agrees groggily.

He sleeps—for fifteen minutes, maybe, or for three or four hours, or for days or years—and wakes with a full bladder. Hobbling down the hall to the bathroom, he sees a light in the guest bedroom. He finds Erica asleep in the bed, the pillows propped up behind her head, the bedspread pulled up over her teepeed knees. She wears heavy black-framed glasses, and the DeMille novel is tucked beneath her chin, spread open about a third of the way through.

"Hey," he says from the doorway. "Hey, you should get some sleep."

She stirs and mumbles something.

"Take off your glasses." He goes to her and takes both glasses and book from her and leaves them on the nightstand. "Want me to turn off the light?"

Another mumble.

He clicks off the lamp, while she snuggles down beneath the bedspread. At the doorway, he turns. "I never went hunting with Dad, because I never liked it."

The clock in the hallway ticks a few times. "I know," she says.

"How'd you know?" he asks, certain that he never confided in Grandma or his mother.

"I don't know. I just figured it out once I saw how much you were like me."

He leaves without replying, but her words follow him. If she is so much like their father, and if he is like her—the thought causes him to lean against the wall of the hallway, gripped by the need to weep. You can't fight over the dead. No one wins. You just lose over and over again.

"Are you okay?" Erica's voice is just a whisper.

He runs a hand under his nose. "Yeah."

"Listen," she says. "Why don't we go down to Grandma's early tomorrow morning and talk to her before she leaves for work? She'll be able to figure all this out. We're going to have to call the police sometime.

At least to report who attacked Elise—you don't want them to get away with that."

"Yeah, I guess not."

"It will be all right. We'll stick together."

"Okay."

He wends his way to the living room. Tomorrow morning—if she doesn't have a heart attack when she sees the two of them together—he'll ask Grandma to make Aunt Jemima pancakes, the way she used to when his mother left him overnight while she worked weekends until two, before he could take care of himself. Then the three of them will sit at the kitchen table and eat breakfast while Dane and Amory lick up syrup that has dripped on the floor and old Purdy wheezes. And even if his ribs ache and his head throbs and his eyes are swollen shut, it won't hurt anymore. It will feel natural, it will feel normal. Most of all, as Erica said, it will be all right.

TWENTY-EIGHT
THE SCENE OF LOVE

I

At the Portland Zoo, Ronald watches the giraffes. He stands back a few feet from the mob of children that presses up against the walls of the enclosure, vying for a better view. In the very front, Craig fusses with an Instamatic camera that Ronald bought for him, trying to capture an entire giraffe through a focus-hole the size of a dime.

Craig is all skin stretched taut over bone. He isn't a well-proportioned toddler any longer, but a lanky, knob-kneed seven-year-old. His teeth are coming in miserably crooked, and his lips stretch to close over them. Becky has told Ronald that Craig struggled to pass first grade. His teacher reported he cries too much.

Craig winds the camera, intent on the little gear, oblivious to the jostling kids around him.

Ronald wants a drink, but by God, he's not going to go that route. Not now. He showed up this morning at Becky's apartment, neatly shaven and dressed in Dockers and a polo shirt—just enough to whisper, but not shout, prosperity. He has gone to great lengths to present himself as a competent, confident man.

But he can't silence the rampaging voice in his head: Coward. You walked out on the men, left them alone to try to navigate through Cascadia's crap. You have the sophistication to do that, you have the smarts. They have nothing. And you walked out on *her*. Jesus, what were you thinking?

"I've got ten pictures left," Craig announces.

"Well, then, come on, cowboy," Ronald says. "Let's go hunt some elephants."

Craig jets to him, taking the hand that Ronald offers. "I'm going to take two pictures of an elephant," he says.

"Okay," Ronald says as they start along the path.

But once he had left Pindall, Ronald could not bring himself to turn the car around and go back. He had kept driving, pulled by panic and revulsion, by the percussive pound of his heart. The BMW had limped into some downtrodden town in Idaho—Ronald can't even recall the name—before it spectacularly overheated with a geyser worthy of Yellowstone issuing from beneath the hood. He had parked it on a sleepy residential street and stripped it of everything that indicated ownership. At the local Ford dealership, he offered cash for a Ford King Cab to a salesman who said he hadn't sold a vehicle in a year, what with the farm crisis and all.

Craig bounces toward the elephant compound and points the camera without even looking at the animals.

"Hold it steady," Ronald advises. "Make sure to move your thumbs back."

Ronald had called Becky last night to ask if he could take Craig to the zoo for the day.

"Why are you here?" she had demanded. "Why aren't you in Wyoming?"

"I have a couple of weeks of vacation."

"But you're going back?"

"Well, sure," he bluffed. "I've got a job, you know."

"You don't have custody, Ronald," she had barked. "You don't even have visiting rights. You should be damned glad I'll even let you come over."

"You're right," he said smoothly. "I have no rights. So come with us to the zoo."

"I have no intention of spending the day with you. In fact, you should know, I'm planning on remarrying. I've met someone, a great man, who has a son of his own—"

"Oh, yeah, I've heard about him from Craig."

"What?" Becky barked. "Have you been calling him when I'm not—?"

"How would I know if you're there or not?" Ronald said. "So, congratulations. Is this Mark anyone I know?"

"Yes," she said breathily, although he had asked only in spite. "Mark Jacobsen."

He had racked his brain to remember the face. Then he recalled—a V.P. at Cascadia, stocky, broad-shouldered, a man who grew a noticeable five-o'clock shadow by two in the afternoon. Jacobsen was promoted at about the same time as Ronald was sent to Pindall.

"I don't remember him as being very nice," Ronald had said. "And Craig told me he's pretty abusive—"

"Craig wouldn't know what that means—"

"Along with his charming son, Brian—is that the name?"

"You're an ass."

"Always the silver-tongued one, weren't you, Becky?"

Now, Ronald's heart doubles-down again. It will be only a matter of time before Becky learns of the closing of Pindall's mill. Perhaps she already has.

There's a dust-up in front of the elephant compound, and Ronald hears Craig say, "Out of my way, baby."

"Hey! Hey!" Ronald says, at the same time that the other kid's mother says, "Dakota, what's going on?"

Dakota rubs at his stomach, howling. "He hit me!"

"Did you hit him?" Ronald grabs Craig by the shoulder, which rises and falls with the boy's rapid breath.

The mother kneels and wraps her arms around her son, who cries into her neck. Looking up, she snaps, "You owe my son an apology."

"Is he all right?" Ronald asks, then adds, "Craig, you need to apologize."

Craig shrugs defiantly. "I don't want to."

"Tell him you're sorry," Ronald commands.

The boy's face tightens, his lips pressing together, and Ronald recalls the look of Jason's face on the day they went to Old Faithful. Knotted with pain and fury.

"Come on, Craig," Ronald says.

"Sorry," Craig says, his voice coated with sarcasm and contempt.

"That's just rude," the mother says. "What kind of son are you raising?"

She and Dakota—still crying—huff off, leaving the question stinging in Ronald's head.

He guides Craig to a nearby bench. "Let's talk about this," he says. "Why did you do that?"

"I didn't like him," Craig pouts. "He was stupid."

"How do you know he was stupid?"

"Because he was. He was a sissy."

Ronald's jaw tenses. "That isn't a nice word, and you don't hit somebody because you don't like them. And when someone asks you to apologize, you need to do it nicely."

Craig lobs the Instamatic camera. It strikes the concrete and shatters, shards bouncing onto the grass and under the feet of passers-by. A mother with a stroller steers around it, sending Ronald a look of disdain.

Ronald swallows back a surge of anger. "Why did you do that?" he asks. "You just ruined all your pictures."

Craig says nothing, crossing his arms over his chest and shrinking into himself. His lower lip trembles as if he will cry.

"Go pick it up," Ronald says. "Somebody is going to step on it and hurt themselves."

Craig does not move.

"Craig," Ronald says again. "Pick up the camera before someone steps on it."

"It's all baby stuff, anyway," Craig says. "Stupid."

Ronald jerks upright and walks to where the camera pieces lie. My God, what has happened to his son? He never acted like this when he was younger. As calmly as he can, he gathers up the broken plastic, then carries it to a trash can and drops it in.

"Let's go get something to eat," he says coolly.

For lunch, Ronald buys Craig hot dogs, chips, and soda. The boy gulps them all down, then complains through the ape exhibit and the big cats about his stomach ache. After about half an hour of whining, Ronald asks, "Well, then, have you had enough of this?"

Craig nods, his face crinkled into unhappiness, and they go back to the truck. As Ronald starts the engine, Craig asks, "Are we going back to Mommy's?"

"Sure," Ronald says. "I told her I'd bring you home by six."

"Will Mark be there?"

Ronald winces at the fear in Craig's voice. "I hear he and Mommy are getting married," he says, careful to eliminate expression from his voice.

"If you'd come home," Craig says, "you could marry her again."

Ronald lets the truck idle without shifting. "We won't get married again. She's going to marry Mark."

Craig throws himself onto the seat, arms over his face, and sobs.

Ronald reaches down and strokes the soft, white-blond head. His son, his flesh and blood. Tender, sweet, loving boy. "Hey," he says. "It will be okay."

The boy's sleeve slips up as he rolls back and forth in protest. On the inside of Craig's right arm, Ronald sees a yellow-purple bruise.

"What's this?" he asks.

"No!" Craig squeezes his arms tighter over his head so that Ronald cannot see the bruise.

"Let me see." Ronald pulls the sleeve out of the way.

He finds other marks, some of them nearly faded away and others with the blackness of newness. All of them are above the line where Craig's sleeve reaches. "Who did this?" Ronald demands. "Mark?"

"Brandon," Craig sobs. "He pinches."

"Does he do it anywhere else?"

Through his tears, Craig manages, "My tummy."

Ronald jerks up the shirt. Along Craig's ribcage are bruises. "Why does he do this to you?"

"If I don't give him the TV remote or get him a can of Pepsi."

"What does Mommy say about this?"

"She doesn't know. Brandon says he'll kill me if I tell."

Ronald half-laughs in disbelief. "Kill you? What did he say?"

Craig's fear spills into the truck. "He said he'd chop off my fingers and toes, and then stick them in my mouth so I can't yell—"

Ronald has heard enough. "I'll talk to Mommy. This shouldn't be happening to you—"

"No! No! Brandon will—"

Ronald pulls Craig against him. "No, he won't," he promises. "I'll see to it that he doesn't."

Once Craig calms down, Ronald puts the truck in gear and drives slowly through Portland's streets. He's tired of bullies, tired of standing back and letting them do what they want—and he won't allow his son to suffer for his lack of courage. At last, he pulls into the parking lot of the bank he has always used. "I have to get some money before we go home," he tells Craig. "It will only take a minute."

Inside the bank, Ronald watches Craig, who is ensconced in a plush red chair in the waiting area, out of the corner of his eye. My God, how will he protect his son? How will he save him from this? When the teller speaks to him, he jumps, as if he is planning a robbery.

"Do you still wish to maintain your security box here?" she asks. "I notice we didn't get a reply from you when we sent you this year's bill."

"I'd forgotten about it," Ronald says. "And I've moved. I need to see what's in it."

"Do you have your key?"

He fingers his keychain—where the BMW and sawmill office keys still clank—until the sharp-eyed teller identifies a likely candidate. She closes her position, then leads him to the vault. He beckons to Craig to follow.

Inside the box are photographs of his father and brother, from the early fifties. His college diploma rests in a velvety cover, and his high school diploma is folded in half. A watch his father had given him when he graduated from college rattles loose in the box. Under the title for his Beemer, he discovers Craig's original birth certificate.

Ronald balances the document in his palm, as if weighing it. Surely it should have been turned over to Becky when the divorce was final, surely it should be in her possession. He tries to remember—there was some question about where it was, he thinks. But he had been pretty lost at the time, unconcerned with Becky's problems.

"Can we go now, Daddy?" Craig whines, and suddenly Ronald is aware of the teller, waiting for him by the door.

Having the birth certificate is nearly as good as having custody.

He sweeps all the documents and junk from the drawer, then says, "I don't believe I'll keep it any longer. Tally up what I owe for it. And I want to close my savings account here. I've moved, you see, to Wyoming."

With $32,000 in his possession, he calmly straps Craig into the passenger's seat on the truck. He climbs in and pulls out into rush hour traffic on I-5. As the truck creeps through gridlock, Craig topples over, worn out by emotion, and falls asleep.

Ronald's mind races ahead.

If he does this, he will never see her again. If he does this, he will be forever on the run, forever watching over his shoulder, forever wary. But if he does this, he will have the one thing in his life that is not yet ruined, not yet tattered and rotten.

Elise's words resonate in his head. *You will always be lost, until you find the courage to honor your heart.*

His hand resting on Craig's head, he bypasses the exit that leads to Becky's apartment and heads north. He crosses the state line at four o'clock. Six o'clock comes and goes near Seattle. Ronald pulls into a K-Mart parking lot and shakes Craig awake.

"Hey, cowboy," he says gently. "Listen up, our plans have changed. We're going to spend the night together. But we need to get you some pajamas and a sleeping bag."

"Does Mommy know?" the child mumbles.

"Sure, she does. I called her."

He herds Craig inside—the boy stumbles over his untied shoelaces—and into the restroom. When they come out, Ronald grabs a cart and loads it with underwear, socks, a couple of shirts and jeans for Craig and some clothing for himself. Craig drowsily agrees to Superman pajamas and sleeping bag. Ronald lets the boy choose a Pound Puppy and a Tonka truck from the toy aisles. As Ronald is checking out, he spies a postcard display. He grabs a lurid, color-enhanced photograph of the Space Needle at sundown.

"Wait here," he says to Craig

He scribbles a message on the postcard and mails it. Carrying the packages to the car, he deflects Craig's questions: "Where are we going? Where will we sleep?"

"Don't worry about it. This will be our big adventure."

Ronald piles the clothes into the rear seat of the truck. There is a place he knows east of Bellingham . . .

Craig hums happily as Ronald speeds along the highway. The sun sets into thick blackness. The terrain grows wilder. The haloed lights of farmhouses vanish. The pavement disappears, and the roads turn to mud beneath the tires. Ronald puts the truck in four-wheel. Miles beyond the last farmhouse, he turns north.

Only a concrete slab marks the Canadian border at this spot. He glances over at Craig, cuddled in the Superman sleeping bag, clutching the Pound Puppy, and sucking his thumb. The Tonka truck rolls back and forth on the floor of the pickup.

"Tell me a story, Daddy," Craig says.

"A story?" Ronald laughs. "Oh, I have plenty of stories for you."

"About what?"

He thinks for a moment. "About a kind wolf with blue eyes and a silver coat who helped a fallen traveler. And a beautiful copper-haired princess who counted the trees and animals among her friends. And a lost boy, who searched through a place of boiling lakes for his way home."

"I like that one."

As Ronald begins to weave his tale, he silently promises: I know what I am doing. I'm doing what's best for you. You won't grow up like Jason—scared and confused and broken. You won't grow up wondering what kind of man your father is.

There are places in British Columbia so wild that they make Yellowstone look like a children's playground. Grow a beard, let his hair get shaggy, dress in denim and wool, take a job in a three-man mill somewhere up north, and he will never resemble Ronald Dailey of Portland, Oregon or Pindall, Wyoming.

Stepping on the gas, he drives deeper into Canada.

II

Jason rolls into the parking lot of the Sunny Acres Nursing Home on Saturday morning of Sawmill Days. The home is a rectangular, one-story barracks that sports enough cinder blocks to make Walt proud, although no one has thought to spruce it up with flamingo-orange paint. The building is drab, colorless, a portal to death.

Inside, the smell is that of the room above the Greenbow, only a hundred-fold. Wasted flesh, scalps that reek through thin strands of hair, clothes that haven't seen a washing machine since Reagan's Hollywood days. The blue-smocked staff of Sunny Acres is busy prodding the residents out of their rooms, rolling old people into the common room in wheelchairs, or herding the ones on walkers, who totter along in bed slippers and liver spots. An attendant turns on the television in the common room, and a blonde anchor woman's voice booms at them.

A dough-faced nurse spies Jason and snaps, "Can I help you?"

Jason can't blame her for being suspicious. His face still looks like he tied one on in every bar in town, and he walks like Frankenstein, his left arm clamped against his injured ribs. "I'm here to see Johnny Hart."

"Johnny?" The nurse calls to a fresh-faced brunette, "Hey, Bridget, where's Johnny? Is he out yet? This young man wants to see him."

Bridget comes over, clipboard in her hands. She checks down the list. "I don't think so." Eyeing Jason curiously, she says, "He's never had a visitor."

Johnny sits in his room, hands idle in his lap. He's a shrunken, little mushroom, squashed and lopsided, rooted by decay to the sagging cot. He looks up as Bridget calls his name, obviously expecting her to roust him into the T.V. room.

"Look, Johnny," she yodels. "Look who's come to see you . . .?"

She looks to Jason, and he feels the sweat on his back. "Troy," he says. "Troy Hart. I'm his son."

Bridget's eyebrows arch. Johnny would have been the age of Methuselah when he begat a boy of Jason's age. But Johnny takes the bait. "Troy," he says. "Right smart fella. Went to college—"

Jason shoots a look at Bridget, sure that he is busted, but she obviously wants to escape another of Johnny's interminable stories. Realigning the pages on her clipboard, she says, "Just bring him down to the rec room when you leave."

After she goes, Jason panics. He doesn't want to touch anything or to sit in the only chair in the room, a scarred, straight-backed affair that looks as if some oldster sat in it before his diaper was changed. He's afraid the smell will soak into his clothes or nostrils or brain. He really doesn't want to talk to Johnny, either. In fact, he really doesn't know what he is doing here. Finally, he says, "Let's get out of here."

Johnny doesn't respond, and that allows Jason to heft him up from the bed and shuttle him into the hallway. They skirt the T.V. room, where the old folks are still flocking under the impatient eye of the staff, and bustle out into the warm, summer day.

When Jason leads Johnny to the Harley, Johnny freezes. His clothes bunch around arms and legs that used to be there. His head sits, neckless, directly on his shoulders.

"Come on, Johnny," Jason coaxes. "It's just like a horse. Just climb on behind me."

Johnny stares, mute.

Jason steadies the Harley, then sort of sweeps Johnny up in one arm and lifts him onto the seat. The old man weighs almost nothing—less than a hay bale, less than the shipments of potatoes that come into the Wickiup. "See?" Jason says. "Nothing to it." Once he himself is settled on the bike, Jason swerves out onto the highway, headed toward Pindall.

Terrified, Johnny glues himself to Jason's back. His slobber drenches a spot just left of Jason's spine, and his fingers pinch Jason's ribs, making the bruises sting. "Lean with me!" Jason shouts, but Johnny leans every which way, as if he is trying to escape. It's a long, treacherous ride back to town.

The parade route has already been blocked off with traffic barrels by the time they cruise into Pindall, so Jason cuts around to Fifth Street and works his way up the hillside. When he reaches the embankment that leads to the meadow, he guns the Harley. "You okay back there, Johnny?" he yells over the roar of the bike. Receiving no reply, he advises, "Hold on tight!"

He pops up over the embankment, then bumps down the ravine into the shallow, little creek. There's a fair amount of wobbling and struggle in the bottom before Jason is able to punch the Harley up over the rise and into the meadow. Johnny reacts to it all by strangling him.

But, at last, the meadow stretches peacefully before them, the grass trotting in lazy swells. Awns dangle from the stalks in shades of purple, green and ocher, the wildflowers burst with color, and meadowlarks fly up from nests in the knee-deep grasses. The only imperfection is the sky, saturated by smoke.

"Hold on, Johnny," Jason says again. "Remember to lean with me."

He gives the Harley a couple of warm-up revs, then takes off, shooting across the meadow. The force of the rushing air bends him backward, and Johnny's hands drill into him. He swears that the old man's fingers are now firmly hooked through the bones of his aching ribs. Still, he accelerates, until they are flying through the field. Grass whips his legs, and wind squints his eyes nearly closed. His hair lifts off his scalp.

And he sees what he came for: a black oblong jets along beside the bike, then tumbles away into the field. Another rushes in and rolls off into nothingness. Jason gives a whoop and speeds up. The shapes multiply, frisking and wagging, coming at the Harley from all directions.

Behind him, Johnny comes to life. "Look! Look at that!"

"What do you see?" Jason shouts.

"Wooves!" Johnny crows. "Wooves! Look at 'em!"

The wooves are everywhere, whipping in and out of the grass, dancing in the wind. They peel off in circular patterns, rushing from the path of the Harley. Jason commands them: Run with us, ride the wind, let go and fly! He presses forward on the bike, faster and wilder. Every drop of his blood hums through his head, every nerve sears. The wooves roil and race, as if unleashed by the roar of the Harley.

Johnny keeps shouting, "Look, look! Wooves!"

Jason brakes just before the trees. The Harley slides to a stop in the loose dirt at the spot where the forest begins, and the wooves rush on, blending into the shadows of the trees. He is out of breath, panting, his arms clenched in pain against his sides, squashing Johnny's wrists against him. "You saw them, Johnny!" he yells. "You saw them!"

The two of them straddle the Harley, shaking with the vibrating engine and adrenaline and, for Johnny, the DTs. Jason laughs, a sound he hasn't heard in two years. He did it, he thinks. He ran the field without falling, without dying.

He cuts the power to the bike, and is immediately greeted by the sound of a siren. Macky Bain's cruiser bumps over the crest of the hill, at a spot where the embankment drops away. A shiny, black truck screeches to a halt behind it. Behind the truck is Erica's Honda, parked on the edge of the street, not able to navigate the field.

Judy Christensen spills out of the truck, running toward the Harley. "What in the hell is going on?" she screams. "What's Johnny doing here?"

Macky comes up behind her, and Jason says, "He's taking a day off from the Old Folks Home."

"Do something, Macky," she sputters. "He could have killed him—"

"How did you get permission to take him?" Macky asks. "Did he agree to come with you?" He addresses Johnny. "Did you want to come today, Johnny?"

Jason waits, heart wilting, but Johnny says, "There was wooves. All over the place! They was running—just black shadda, you know, that's all them wooves is." He laughs wildly, spraying spit all over Macky's shirt and Jason's arm. "There's wooves!"

Macky looks out across the field. "Wolves?"

"Wooves!" This time, Johnny's joy becomes a rackety cough. Jason grabs his elbow to keep him from toppling off the bike.

"They ain't all gone!" Johnny spews. "There's wooves here!"

Johnny spies Erica coming over through the grass. He struggles to dismount the Harley until Jason reaches over and lifts him off the motorcycle. Johnny runs—as much as an old man who hasn't moved with any purpose in decades can—toward Erica, stumbling over uneven ground. Erica opens her arms and catches him as he is about to plummet face-first into the grass.

"Marie!" Johnny shouts. "There's wooves! They ain't all dead! They ain't all killed! Did you see them? There's wooves!"

Erica glances a question at Jason, but says, "They were running with you, all of them."

"What is it that you saw?" Macky asks Jason.

"For Pete's sake, Macky, help me," Judy orders. "You could have hurt him, Jason," she scolds. "Taking an old man out on a motorcycle! Bringing him out into all this smoke! How irresponsible can you be?"

"He's spent, like, the past thirty years in the Rambler," Jason points out. "The smoke can't hurt him."

With a snarl, Judy starts toward Erica, who is gently escorting Johnny toward the Harley, her arm around his shoulders, her hand clenched in both of his. Judy grabs at Johnny, wrenching him from Erica. Macky says, "Come on, now, Johnny," and pries his hands from Erica's.

Together, they load him into the truck. As Judy closes the passenger's door, she snaps at Jason, "I'll take him back to Sunny Acres. But don't you think you can try this again. I'm telling them that he is absolutely never to leave again!"

When Judy pulls away, Johnny is still laughing and talking, still calling to Marie. Jason and Erica wave goodbye to him.

Macky returns to his cruiser, talking into the squawking radio. Below, on Main Street, the parade has started, and Jason hears the blast from the fire truck, the bass drum thump of the high school marching band, the shots of the Mountain Man muskets, people whistling and clapping.

Macky ten-fours and closes the door of the cruiser.

"What did you see, Jason?" he asks, swallowing, his Adam's apple tender and jerky.

Jason senses how badly Macky wants him to say he saw a wolf. "There was something," he admits. "I don't know what."

"Do you think it was a wolf?"

"I don't know. Like Johnny said, it was black shadow or something."

Macky mutters something that Jason doesn't catch.

"Are you going to shoot it?" he asks.

"Hell, no, I want to see it."

"Are you going to arrest me?"

"For what?"

"Then can I go?"

Macky nods. "I'm gonna look around a little, see what I come up with."

He heads for the trees on the eastern end of the field. Jason watches him go, Erica at his side.

"You really like to kidnap people, don't you?" she asks.

Jason laughs, her words rolling away from him. "Did you see those things? Did you really see them?"

"Sure. They're out in the canyons, too, at Dave's place. Rain hates them."

As soon as she says it, she whips around toward Jason, grabbing his wrist, as if she expects him to slap her or something. Yet he stands firmly, feet planted on this earth. He can do that now. He can stand here next to his sister and look at the place where his father died without wanting to run or scream or kill someone.

"I always knew he didn't do anything wrong," he says quietly. "I always knew that."

She doesn't answer, and he knows she is thinking of her own life. He doesn't say anything, though. He doesn't need to. She knows that whatever was broken in him has broken—as stupid as it sounds—and washed away. It's gone, it's over.

"So what are those things?" he asks.

"Wooves," Erica says simply.

Jason's laughter bursts from him. "Wooves?"

"Wooves!" she echoes.

Together, they fill the meadow with heart-emptying barks of merriment until Macky appears from out of the forest like a wraith and asks, "What's so funny?"

III

At Asa Pindall Park, Art Canaday and Eddie Fenton and I hold our annual practice, where we decide on our set list for the entertainment (the songs we always sing) and who will sing what (the same way we've always done it). There is a sense, though, that this is the last time, with Eddie thinking he will have to leave to find work, and my plans to go to Bozeman. Besides, what is Sawmill Days without the sawmill?

I leave the stage and hurry through the park just as the winner of the best-dressed pet contest is crowned. This year, in competition with the goats and rabbits and dogs and cats, someone has garlanded a dairy cow with flowers and a silky cape. She has vented her opinion of her victory in a stinking pile in the middle of the lawn. At the entrance of the park, I come across Robyn at The Old Ramblin' Wagon, where Walt has set up two fiery barbecue grills. She's already grumbling about slack sales.

"Nobody's spending anything," she grouses. "They brought food with them from home. And the Wickiup is offering free hot dogs. What's that all about?"

I throw up my hands. "I have never, ever pretended to know what Marguerite was up to."

She continues her diatribe, but I'm saved by Dave Phillips. He greets Robyn, then says, "Walk up to the parade with me, Shari."

Dave is dressed to the nines in his western shirt and jeans and cowboy boots and hat. His belt buckle is a silver saucer that he won at some rodeo. "You're looking pretty sharp today, Mr. Phillips," I say.

He laughs and returns the compliment. There is something different about him. He walks with purpose. He has gained weight, and the deadness has gone from his face.

"Where's Erica?" I ask as we start toward Main Street.

"I knocked on her door, but she just said something about it being too early."

I shake my head and laugh. I still haven't overcome the disbelief I felt on the morning that Marguerite called me to tell me that Erica and Jason had shown up at her house for breakfast. It was all so confusing—I couldn't figure out who had been hurt and what a Harley had to do with it—but now, Erica and Jason seem inseparable. She comes to visit almost daily, bringing odd-tasting goodies that we usually feed to the dogs The first time she saw the house, she looked at the solid log walls, the moss rock fireplace and the great cathedral window, put her hands on her hips and said, "Well, isn't this something." Just as her father might have done.

"She and I are taking a little trip," Dave says.

"Where are you going?"

"Minneapolis," he says. "Diane needs help with Renee. She's been sick, some kind of infection that the doctors just can't whip."

"Is she in the hospital?"

"No, but it don't look like she can go to school this fall. Looks like we're in for a long haul."

"Minneapolis," I say. "Big city."

"Can't be much worse than Denver." He hooks his thumbs in his jeans pockets. "Erica says she'll be my guide. She says it ain't nearly as big as Columbus."

"That's a plus."

"Anyway, she wants to look at a movie camera of some kind. She has this idea about making a movie about Pindall—a documentary, she calls it—now that the sawmill has closed. She wants to explore the sociological ramifications of it."

"Those are some mighty big words."

"That's what I told her," he says. "I said, if you ask people for that, they'll say it ain't none of your business what they ram into their sosological, and they might even tell you to do the same."

I laugh. "So we'll all be movie stars."

"If Erica has her way, I guess so."

Main Street hides behind its usual concrete barricade. We wrangle our way through a crowd of kids, dogs, lawn chairs, picnic baskets, boomboxes, and the high school cheerleaders, who are late for the parade and sprinting, pompoms in full shimmy. Finally, we come to a spot on the far side of the Wickiup with a fairly clear view of the parade route.

"Listen, Shari," he says.

I know what he is going to say. But I don't want to hear it again. I don't need to hear it. I lay a hand on his arm. "Don't, Dave," I say. "We're all right now. What about you?"

"It's been a long time coming," he says slowly. "But I think I'm okay. I got Erica to thank for it."

The America and Wyoming flags, carried by the Veterans in solemn silence, round the corner, and spectators rise from the curbs and lawn chairs where they are seated to pay respect. Dave and I both take off our hats and hold them over our hearts. After the colors pass, the parade begins in earnest with the fire truck blaring its siren. A string of convertibles follows, carrying the grand marshal and Town Council members, Marguerite among them. I wave at her, and Dave puts two fingers in his mouth and whistles.

"How's Jason?" Dave asks.

"Much better. He'll be here later."

"On his motorcycle?"

"He's not ready for that. I left my pickup for him."

The Harley strikes me yet as a strange, stray animal that showed up on my doorstep begging for a meal and a home while flashing vicious teeth and claws. So far, I haven't dared to object to it. Marguerite is a staunch protector of the Harley, and Lex has been nobly vague when I question him about his part in helping Jason to purchase it. Even Erica has weighed in, buying a book about motorcycles and Zen for him. I've been stumbling along with them, trying to form some sort of coherent quarrel. Somehow, I sense the battle is already lost.

Still, I can't rest easy. Lex and Vern fixed the chrome on the Harley that was dented when Jason was attacked, but I can't help but feel that Terry's tire iron and Russ's boot struck me, too. Jerry Whistledorn isn't a bad man. Yet when he and Jan visited me, I wondered how they had raised a son willing to attack a defenseless woman and beat a boy who has been a friend since they were both in diapers. What will they do when they all come face to face with each other again? How will they live out their lives?

The whole thing is a mess, now, with the sheriff involved, and everybody in town taking sides, and both Elise and Jason on tenterhooks until everything is settled.

The parade entries trail by: Boy Scouts in neckerchiefs; the ill-mannered mutts of the 4-H Dog Obedience Team; FFA members; and Miss Rodeo Wyoming in spangled blouse and leather pants riding a buckskin whose coat gleams with oil. A host of other rodeo royalty follows her.

From the direction of Vern's garage, Elise strolls down the sidewalk, followed by a man I've never seen before. Handsome and graying, he walks with a decided air of authority. Elise waves at me.

She, too, has been a frequent visitor at our house since the night Russ and Terry beat up Jason. Her own injuries are healing, but there's something about the way her right eye has reshaped itself that makes her look lonely.

Glimpsing her, Dave says, "I better be moving on. I'll talk to you later."

"Call me before you leave for Minneapolis."

He kisses my cheek, then slips away into the crowd.

Elise and I hug in greeting.

"I want you to meet someone," she says. "This is Aaron Malcolm, my ex-husband. Aaron, this is Shari Brock. Aaron's come from Maine to interview the men who lost their jobs at the mill. He's looking at a possible book project."

He shakes my hand. "Elise called me and suggested I come. If I weren't a diehard Mainer at heart, I'd make plans to stay. It's nearly as pretty here as in Maine." He winks at Elise.

"Have you met with any of the men yet?" I ask.

"We're still scaring up funding. I plan to compensate them."

"How would you suggest we approach them, Shari?" Elise asks.

"The best time to catch them would be early Friday night at the Rambler, before they're snockered enough to pick a fight."

"Will you help us?" Elise asks. "You know so many of them."

"Sure," I say. "As much as I can. But I'm leaving town in a couple of weeks."

"Until then, anyway," she says.

What she doesn't mention is that the two of us are harboring a secret. It's all over town that Ronald is wanted for taking his son, and I've even been teased that Ronald picked up a couple of pointers about kidnapping from Jason. Yet it's no laughing matter—at least not for Macky, who has questioned me and just about everybody in the Rambler about it. What I haven't yet divulged is that Ronald sent me a postcard from Seattle, asking me to clear out his house, take what I wanted, sell what I didn't want, and use the money for whatever I need. It was written so hastily that it took me a few readings to decipher the message. At the end, Ronald wrote, "Tell Elise there's logging in the Big Bear."

When I showed the postcard to her, she studied it for a long time.

"What's the Big Bear?" I asked.

"The Big Bear is an old growth forest in British Columbia," she said. "It would be horrible if it were logged."

We both knew that wasn't the point, but I didn't press it. She flipped the postcard back and forth, and I knew she was weighing, wondering, maybe even planning. It was obvious that Ronald had meant it as an invitation for her to join him.

The 4-H Fiddlers' float passes. Children of all ages and all abilities saw out "Oh, My Darling Clementine" under the direction of Mrs. Allen, the local violin teacher. The parade stalls behind Glenn Wexler's Wells Fargo wagon, pulled by a team of Belgians. It seems that the crowd has pressed too far forward, and Glenn can't make the turn onto Third Street. The bullhorn at the reviewers' stand squeals into action. "Move back, folks," Stuart Mace calls. "Let these fine animals through. They make wide turns—"

Lex's flame-colored Camaro rounds the corner, with Juliana riding in the passenger's seat. He's waxed and polished the car until it gleams in the warm sunshine. I wave and cheer, and he revs the motor a couple of times.

He rolls down his window to talk, but the noise from the fiddles is so loud that I have to step out in the street.

"Hi, Shari!" Juliana gleams. "When you didn't come, I decided to ride with Lex. I hope you don't mind."

"Sorry, our rehearsal went a little long—"

"Hop in," Lex says. "We'll shoot straight past the barricades and become scofflaws—"

And that's all he has time to say. The Fiddlers's float jerks forward, the kids scrambling to aright themselves. The float inches around the corner, keeping a healthy distance behind the troublesome Wells Fargo wagon.

"Here!" Juliana tosses Tootsie Rolls into the street, and kids scrimmage on the pavement, grabbing as many as they can. Lex waves goodbye to me, and the Camaro rolls forward.

The parade entries keep flowing down the street: the elementary school choir; the high school marching band in woolen uniforms and plumes; a mounted posse of rangers from Yellowstone; the Shoshone in headdresses and beads astride bareback horses; a half dozen vintage cars with horns that toot out the first lines of "Beer Barrel Polka" or "The Battle Hymn of the Republic."

Suddenly it's all drowned out by a pulsing growl. Jason segues into the parade on his Harley. His face is drawn, ashen, and I imagine the pain he's enduring to ride his bike. His ribs are heavily taped, but nowhere near healed, and his back is still a mass of bruises. He wears dark black glasses that cover half his face and a heavy jean jacket that used to be Brad's.

Erica rides on the back of the Harley. She climbs off, but Jason stays on the bike, revving it to keep it idling.

"Are you okay?" I ask. "I thought you were bringing the pickup."

"It wouldn't start."

"Again? I wonder what it is now."

He starts to answer, but spies Elise. In a flash, he cuts the power to the bike and hops off.

Their greeting is of friends who have no secrets or inhibitions between them. Elise gathers Jason in her arms, and he holds her with tender grace, his face buried in her hair. They speak, words that I can't hear, and then she lifts up on her tiptoes and kisses him on the mouth.

The sight melts me. Jason is no longer a child, no longer a boy. I watch Lex's Camaro, now a block away, and wish that he were here, so I could touch his arm or take his hand in mine or fold into him, my face against his chest, solid and warm.

Jason steps back from Elise, and she introduces Erica to Aaron Malcolm. While the three of them talk, Jason turns to me. "Listen, Mom," he says. "I want to get out of town for a while. Go visit Uncle Lance in Cheyenne and Aunt Amy, and, maybe, Grandpa Bill and Grandma Jackie."

"Now?"

The Mormon handcart brigade rounds the corner, singing a hymn. Jason glances over his shoulder at them, then says, "I have to tell Grandma goodbye first, but, yeah, why not?"

I can think of reasons—his healing bones; his job at the Wickiup; the newly forged motorcycle payments to Vern; Terry's and Russ's hearings; the onslaught of winter in a mere six weeks, if we're lucky to avoid it that long; the dangers of traveling to Cheyenne or Fort Collins or as far as Phoenix on a Harley-Davidson.

"But . . . I'm leaving in a couple of weeks," I say. "Who will take care of the animals and the house?"

He nods toward Erica, who is talking with Elise and Aaron. "Get Erica to do it."

"She's going away, too."

"Not for that long." He leans forward a little. "Hey, Erica."

She turns toward him. "Yeah?"

"Mom wants to know if you'll move into our house and take care of our animals while I'm gone and she's in Bozeman."

"Really?" Erica beams at me. "I'd love to, and I bet Dave would like having his trailer back. It's pretty crowded for both of us. You really want me to live there?"

I'm caught—to protest would seem unreasonable at this juncture, but I'm not entirely sure I'm on board. Yet what more fitting arrangement than to have Brad's daughter living in his house? Surrendering to the momentum, I say, "I'll be back now and then just to check on things. And if something goes wrong, I'm only a couple of hours away."

"Sure, yes—that's great," she says. "Thank you, Shari. It will be the perfect place to plan the documentary."

"What's this?" Aaron asks. "Are you making a documentary?"

Erica flashes her brilliant smile. "I'm going to attempt it, at least. I want to tell the story of this town, of what happens to the people here now that . . ."

"We need to talk," he says.

As Erica explains her project, I turn back to Jason. He gives a little shrug, as if to say, That wasn't so hard, was it?

"You'll call me tonight, from wherever you are?" I ask.

"I will—"

"Either at home or at Lex's—"

"I know, Mom."

But there's no irritation in his voice. Instead, I hear Brad, and when I look at him, I see Brad. Not in Jason's physical looks—he will always resemble me more than his father—but in his stance, and his demeanor, his face so set and determined. I remember how Brad looked before he left Pindall for the winter, with his conflicting expressions of excitement and hopefulness and remorse and guilt. Today, Jason wears that same que-sera-sera gutsiness.

This time, I'm smart enough to let go.

"All right," I say, pushing out the words. "That's fine."

I open my arms and put them around him, gingerly, carefully, afraid he might break into pieces. But when his arms come up around me, firm and capable, I think: When did I become the smaller one? When did he become the stronger one?

He steps back, swallowing as if he wants to say something. But he addresses Erica. "Are you coming? I need to tell Grandma goodbye."

She promises Aaron and Elise to be in touch and takes her place on the back of the bike. Jason kicks the bike to a roar and swerves into the street again. People whistle and cheer, welcoming the Harley as part of the parade.

"Hey, look, it's the Brock kids," someone says, and I think: The Brock kids, Brad's kids. My kids, now.

In acknowledgment, Erica waves like a queen.

I take the stage at Asa Pindall Park a little over an hour later. The spectators from the parade are now sprawled in the shade of the cottonwood trees that Asa Pindall planted himself. They stretch out on blankets and at picnic tables, eating free hot dogs from the Wickiup, and drinking Robyn's begrudged libations. Members of the Clown Posse wander through the crowd, handing out balloons with "D.A.R.E. to Be You" printed on them, and dogs bark when the balloons sail off into the smoky sky.

Art and Eddie plan to kick off the entertainment with a John Denver medley—"Thank God I'm a Country Boy," "Country Roads," and "Grandma's Feather Bed." We've come up with a bit of shtick around my entrance that we hope will lift the spirits of the crowd.

Art starts to strum the guitar and sing, his voice good at one time, but ruined now by too many cigarettes. I wait backstage—which is actually just behind a plywood partition tacked to the wooden frame of the stage—until I hear the line about trading it all plus the gal down the road for Grandma's feather bed. That's my cue to walk on stage, sassy and swinging, blow Art a kiss, and beckon him with a come-hither curl of my index finger.

He and Eddie stop playing and stare. Art lets out a "Whoo-ey!" and drawls, "Well, now, I'd have to think twice about tradin' the gal down the road."

"Art," Eddie says, but Art ignores him. "Hey, Art," he says again.

Art peels his eyes from me and snaps, "What?"

"I got an old mattress at home that I'd trade you."

The audience laughs and yeehaws. Eddie blows a wolf whistle on the harmonica, and Art starts strumming again. "Ladies and gents," he calls. "Welcome our own gal from down the road, Miss Shari Brock."

I wave, and the three of us join in one exuberant final chorus of the song, ending with a close harmony that sounds pretty good, considering that we have practiced it once. As we wait for the applause to wane, I spot Lex and Erica standing side by side in the crowd. Lex whispers something in Erica's ear—probably a comment about how hokey all this is—and they both laugh. She lifts her camera and takes a photo of me.

And we're off, our rough-edged trio, singing our way through the songs we've known all our lives—"Yellow Rose of Texas," "Cool Water," "Don't Fence Me In." After about five tunes, we come to "Red River Valley," which I'm to sing alone. Art plays a delicate introduction on the guitar, and I start, my voice low and rich:

From this valley they say you are going,
I will miss your bright eyes and sweet smile . . .

I look out at the faces in the crowd, faces I've known all my life. They're enjoying our show—I can see that—but I can also see the shadows, as heavy as the smoke from the Park, and I remember Lex telling me that nothing can stop change. The wolf howls, a geyser—or a stepdaughter—appears where none has been before, the mill closes, the Park burns.

And we have to change with it.

And, somehow, we do.

For they say you are taking the sunshine,
That did brighten our lives for a while . . .

Erica raises her camera to take another photo. Before she focuses, though, she turns her head, distracted by something behind her on Main Street.

And I hear the sound I've been both anticipating and dreading. A Harley cranks up and starts a slow progression through town. I can almost guess its whereabouts—leaving the parking lot at the Wickiup, waiting at the traffic light, creeping at 25 miles per hours down Main Street, past the boutiques and the Rambler. After that, the reverberation moves toward the south, toward the shuttered mill and the canyon and the highway through the Badlands to Riverton.

Come and sit by my side if you love me,
Do not hasten to bid me adieu . . .

For an instant, the timbre of the Harley's engine hangs on the same pitch as my voice, in perfect harmony, as if I'm humming along to its accompaniment. Then the engine modulates into another key as Jason accelerates at the mouth of the canyon, then into another, and another, until the echo fades away, and he is gone.

AUTHOR'S NOTE

Pindall, Wyoming is an entirely fictional town, created in honor of the disappearing small towns and livelihoods of the American West. To write *Clean Cut,* I relied on events, memories, and stories from the communities which I have lived in or visited throughout my life, and which I would like to acknowledge here: Moose Pass, Alaska; Palmer, Alaska; Sitka, Alaska; Oakhurst, California; Calhan, Colorado; Castle Rock, Colorado; Elbert, Colorado; Elizabeth, Colorado; Franktown, Colorado; Grand Lake, Colorado; Kersey, Colorado; Kiowa, Colorado; Larkspur, Colorado; Sedalia, Colorado; American Falls, Idaho; Kimberly, Idaho; Flathead County, Montana; Astoria, Oregon; Custer, South Dakota; Hill City, South Dakota; Wall, South Dakota; Buffalo, Wyoming; Dubois, Wyoming; Guernsey, Wyoming; Hulett, Wyoming; Kemmerer, Wyoming; Laramie, Wyoming; Lusk, Wyoming, Denali National Park; Yosemite National Park, and, of course, Yellowstone National Park.

The writing of *Clean Cut* has spanned many years, and countless readers have given me support and advice. I wish to thank all of them for their encouragement. I am also grateful as well to the Rocky Mountain Women's Institute, which offered me a year-long grant to work on the novel, and to Greg Michalson of Unbridled Books, who believed in the manuscript. I would also like to thank the following: C.J. Prince, Barbara Miller, Mark Putch, Sonya Craig, Tom Reeves, and the late Lana Hayward. I'm also obliged to Thomas McNeil for his ability to think in ways that I don't, and to my daughter, Julie Newlin, for sharing stories of her Wyoming adventures with me, and to her coworkers for clarifying certain Wyoming customs. My sincerest appreciation goes to Karen Steinberg, who read an early draft of the full manuscript for me. My mother, Wilma Marr, and sister, Carol Bryant, spent a weekend reading the manuscript and listening to me talk about it—an indulgence that I treasure.

Of course, I offer my deepest indebtedness to my husband, Bill, who has not only supported me and my writing throughout our years together, but who used his artistic talent to bring my vision of Pindall to life in the maps that are found in the novel. Thank you, my love.

www.ingramcontent.com/pod-product-compliance
Lightning Source LLC
Chambersburg PA
CBHW061509020726
47502CB00006B/1994